ALEX KAVA

DAMAGED

Also by Alex Kava

Maggie O'Dell series

Black Friday

Exposed

A Necessary Evil

At the Stroke of Madness

The Soul Catcher

Split Second

A Perfect Evil

Other fiction

Whitewash

One False Move

ALEX

KAVA

DAMAGED

SPHERE

Published in the United States in 2010 by Doubleday,
a division of Random House, Inc., New York
First published in Great Britain in 2010 by Sphere

Maps designed by Jeffrey L. Ward

A CIP catalogue record for this book
is available from the British Library.

ISBN 978-1-84744-338-0

Printed and bound in Great Britain by
Clays Ltd, St Ives plc

Papers used by Sphere are natural, renewable and recyclable products sourced from well-managed forests and certified in accordance with the rules of the Forest Stewardship Council.

Sphere
An imprint of
Little, Brown Book Group
100 Victoria Embankment
London EC4Y 0DY

An Hachette UK Company
www.hachette.co.uk

www.littlebrown.co.uk

TO PHYLLIS GRANN,

for your patience, your perseverance, and your wisdom.

Here's to new beginnings.

SATURDAY, AUGUST 22

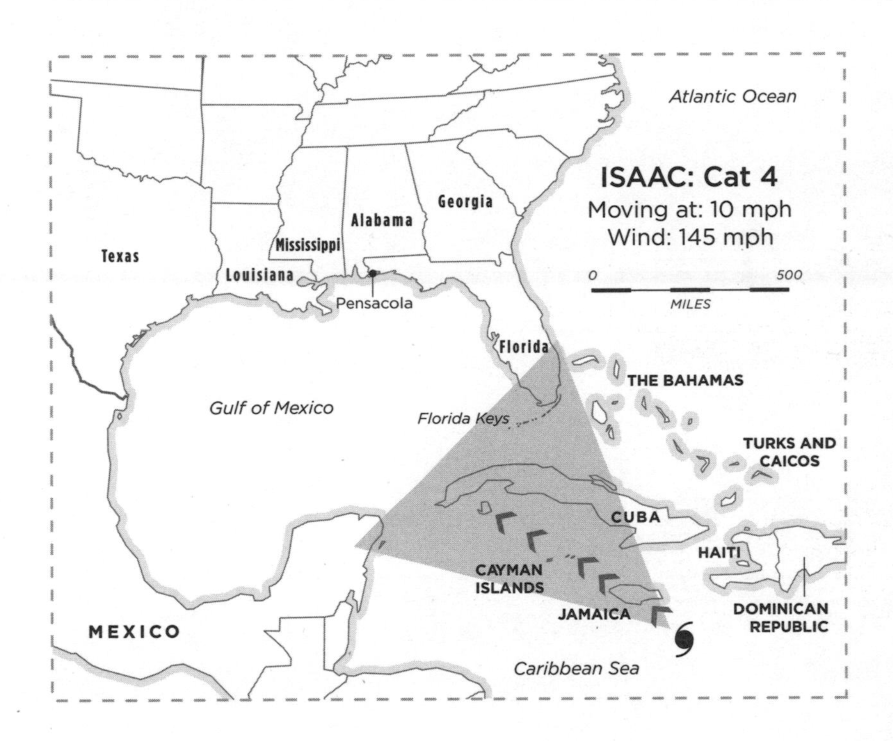

ONE

PENSACOLA BAY
PENSACOLA, FLORIDA

Elizabeth Bailey didn't like what she saw. Even now, after their H-65 helicopter came down into a hover less than two hundred feet above the rolling Gulf, the object in the water still looked like a container and certainly not a capsized boat. There were no thrashing arms or legs. No bobbing heads. No one needing to be rescued, as far as she could see. Yet Lieutenant Commander Wilson, their aircrew pilot, insisted they check it out. What he really meant was that Liz would check it out.

A Coast Guard veteran at only twenty-seven years old, AST3 Liz Bailey knew she had chalked up more rescues in two days over New Orleans after Hurricane Katrina than Wilson had in his entire two-year career. Liz had dropped onto rickety apartment balconies, scraped her knees on wind-battered roofs, and waded through debris-filled water that smelled of raw sewage.

She dared not mention any of this. It didn't matter how

many search and rescues she'd performed, because at the moment she was the newbie at Air Station Mobile, and she'd need to prove herself all over again. To add insult to injury, within her first week someone had decorated the women's locker room by plastering downloaded photos of her from a 2005 issue of *People* magazine. Her superiors insisted that the feature article would be good PR for the Coast Guard, especially when other military and government agencies were taking a beating over their response to Katrina. But in an organization where attention to individual and ego could jeopardize team missions, her unwanted notoriety threatened to be the kiss of death for her career. Four years later, it still followed her around like a curse.

By comparison, what Wilson was asking probably seemed tame. So what if the floating container might be a fisherman's cooler washed overboard? What was the harm in checking it out? Except that rescue swimmers were trained to risk their lives in order to save other lives, not to retrieve inanimate objects. In fact, there was an unwritten rule about it. After several swimmers who were asked to haul up bales of drugs tested positive for drug use, apparently from their intimate contact in the water, it was decided the risk to the rescue team was too great. Wilson must have missed that memo.

Besides, rescue swimmers could also elect not to deploy. In other words, she could tell Lieutenant Commander less-than-a-thousand-flight-hours Wilson that "hell no," she wasn't jumping into the rough waters for some fisherman's discarded catch of the day.

Wilson turned in his seat to look at her. From the tilt of his square chin he reminded her of a boxer daring a punch. The glint in his eyes pinned her down, his helmet's visor slid up for greater impact. He didn't need to say out loud what his body language said for him: "So, Bailey, are you a prima donna or are you a team player?"

Liz wasn't stupid. She knew that as one of less than a dozen women rescue swimmers, she was a rare breed. She was used to having to constantly prove herself. She recognized the stakes in the water as well as those in the helicopter. These were the men she'd have to trust to pull her back up when she dangled by a cable seventy feet below, out in the open, over angry seas, sometimes spinning in the wind.

Liz had learned early on that she was expected to perform a number of complicated balancing acts. While it was necessary to be fiercely independent and capable of working alone, she also understood what the vulnerabilities were. Her life was ultimately in the hands of the crew above. Today and next week and the week after next, it would be these guys. And until they felt like she had truly proven herself, she would continue to be "*the* rescue swimmer" instead of "*our* rescue swimmer."

Liz kept her hesitation to herself, avoided Wilson's eyes, and pretended to be more interested in checking out the water below. She simply listened. Inside her helmet, via the ICS (internal communication system), Wilson started relaying their strategy, telling his co-pilot, Lieutenant Junior Grade Tommy Ellis, and their flight mechanic, AST3 Pete Kesnick, to prepare for a direct deployment using the RS (rescue swimmer) and the basket. He was already reducing their position from two hundred feet to eighty feet.

"Might just be an empty fishing cooler," Kesnick said.

Liz watched him out of the corner of her eyes. Kesnick didn't like this, either. The senior member of the aircrew, Kesnick had a tanned weathered face with crinkle lines at his eyes and mouth that never changed, never telegraphed whether he was angry or pleased.

"Or it might be cocaine," Ellis countered. "They found fifty kilos washed ashore someplace in Texas."

"McFaddin Beach," Wilson filled in. "Sealed and wrapped in thick plastic. Someone missed a drop-off or panicked and tossed it. Could be what we have here."

"Then shouldn't we radio it in and leave it for a cutter to pick up?" Kesnick said as he glanced at Liz. She could tell he was trying to let her know that he'd back her if she elected not to deploy.

Wilson noticed the glance. "It's up to you, Bailey. What do you want to do?"

She still didn't meet his eyes, didn't want to give him the satisfaction of seeing even a hint of her reluctance.

"We should use the medevac board instead of the basket," she said. "It'll be easier to slide it under the container and strap it down."

Knowing he was surprised by her response, she simply removed her flight helmet, cutting off communication. If Ellis or Kesnick had something to say about her, she dared them to say it after her attempt at nonchalance.

She fingered strands of her hair back under her surf cap and strapped on her lightweight Seda helmet. She attached the gunner's belt to her harness, positioned the quick strop over her shoulders, made sure to keep the friction slide close to the hoist hook. Finished, she moved to the door of the helicopter, squatted in position, and waited for Kesnick's signal.

She couldn't avoid looking at him. They had done this routine at least half a dozen times since she started at the air station. She suspected that Pete Kesnick treated her no differently than he had been treating rescue swimmers for the last fifteen years of his career as a Coastie flight mechanic and hoist operator. Even now, he didn't second-guess her, though his steel-blue eyes studied her a second longer than usual before he flipped down his visor.

He tapped her on the chest, the signal for "ready"—two gloved fingers practically at her collarbone. Probably not the same tap he used with male rescue swimmers. Liz didn't mind. It was a small thing, done out of respect more than anything else.

She released the gunner's belt, gave Kesnick a thumbs-up to tell him she was ready. She maintained control over the quick strop as he hoisted her clear of the deck. Then he stopped. Liz readjusted herself as the cable pulled tight. She turned and gave Kesnick another thumbs-up and descended into the rolling waters.

Without a survivor in the water Liz quickly assessed the situation. The container was huge. By Liz's estimates, at least forty inches long and twenty inches wide and deep. She recognized the battered white stainless steel as a commercial-grade marine cooler. A frayed tie-down floated from its handle bracket. Frayed, not cut. So maybe its owner hadn't intended to ditch it, after all. She grabbed the tie-down, which was made of bright yellow-and-blue strands twisted into a half-inch-thick rope, and looped it through her harness to keep the cooler from bobbing away in the rotor wash of the helicopter.

She signaled Kesnick: her left arm raised, her right arm crossing over her head and touching her left elbow. She was ready for them to deploy the medevac board.

The bobbing container fought against her, pushing and pulling with each wave, not able to go any farther than the rope attached to her belt allowed. It took two attempts but within fifteen minutes Liz had the fishing cooler attached to the medevac board. She cinched the restraints tight, hooked it to the cable, and raised her arm again, giving a thumbs-up.

No records broken, but by the time Kesnick hoisted her back into the helicopter, she could tell her crew was pleased. Not impressed, but pleased. It was a small step.

Lieutenant Commander Wilson still looked impatient. Liz barely caught her breath, but yanked off her Seda helmet, exchanging it for her flight helmet with the communications gear inside. She caught Wilson in the middle of instructing Kesnick to open the latch.

"Shouldn't we wait?" Kesnick tried being the diplomat.

"It's not locked. Just take a peek."

Liz slid out of the way and to the side of the cabin, unbuckling the rest of her gear. She didn't want any part of this. As far as she was concerned, her job was finished.

Kesnick paused and at first she thought he would refuse. He moved to her side and pushed back his visor, avoiding her eyes. The child-safety latch slid back without effort but he had to use the palm of his hand to shove the snap lock free. Liz saw him draw in a deep breath before he flung open the lid.

The first thing Liz noticed was the fish-measuring ruler molded into the lid. It seemed an odd thing to notice but later it would stick in her mind. A fetid smell escaped but it wasn't rotten fish. More like opening a Dumpster.

Inside she could see what looked like thick plastic wrap encasing several oblong objects, one large and four smaller. Not the square bundles that might be cocaine.

"Well?" Wilson asked, trying to glance over his shoulder.

Kesnick poked at one of the smaller bundles with a gloved finger. It flipped over. The plastic was more transparent on this side and suddenly the content was unmistakable.

His eyes met Liz's and now the ever calm, poker-faced Kesnick looked panicked.

"I think it's a foot," he said.

"What?"

"I think it's a goddamn human foot."

TWO

NEWBURGH HEIGHTS, VIRGINIA

Maggie O'Dell peeled off her blouse without undoing the buttons, popping one before it came off. Didn't matter. The blouse was a goner. Even the best cleaners couldn't take out this much blood.

She folded the shirt into a wad and dropped it into her bathroom sink. Something wet was stuck to her neck. She grabbed at it, threw it in the sink.

Pink. Like clotted cheese.

She'd been so close. Too close when the fatal shot came. Impossible to get out of the way.

She swatted at her neck and yanked at her hair, expecting more pieces. Her fingers got stuck in sweaty tangles, damp, sticky. But, thank God, no more chunks.

They hadn't expected the killer to still be there. The warehouse appeared empty, only remnants of his torture chamber remained, just as Maggie had predicted. Why the hell had he stayed? Or had he come back? To watch.

Maggie's boss, Assistant Director Raymond Kunze, had

made the fatal shot. And afterward he was already taking it out on Maggie, as if it were her fault, as if she had forced his hand. But there was no way she could have known that the killer was there, hiding in the shadows. No profiler could have predicted that. Kunze couldn't possibly hold her accountable, and yet she knew he would do exactly *that*.

Harvey, her white Lab, grabbed one of her discarded, muddy shoes. Rather than taking it to play he dropped to his belly and started whining, a low guttural moan that tugged at Maggie's heart.

"Come on and drop it, Harvey," she ordered, but instead of scolding, she said it quietly, gently.

He could smell the blood on her, was already concerned. But the shoe plopped out of his mouth.

"Sorry, big guy."

Maggie swiped the shoe up and placed it in the sink with her soiled blouse. Then she knelt down beside Harvey, petting him. She wanted to hug him but there was still too much blood on her.

"Wait for me outside, buddy," she said, leading him out of the huge master bathroom and into her bedroom, telling him to sit where he could see her through the doorway. She scratched behind his ears until he relaxed, waiting for his sigh and his collapse into lay-down position.

The smell of blood still panicked him. She hated the reminder. With it came the memory of that day she found him, bleeding and cowering under his first owner's bed, right in the middle of his own bloody ordeal. The dog had fought hard and still had been unsuccessful in protecting his mistress, who had been taken from her house and later murdered.

"I'm okay," she reassured him, as she dared to take a good look at herself in the mirror to see if what she said was true.

It wasn't so bad. She'd been through worse. And at least this time it wasn't her own blood.

Her tangled, dark-auburn hair almost reached her shoulders. She needed to get it trimmed. What a thing to think about. Her eyes were bloodshot but it had nothing to do with this incident. She hadn't been able to sleep through the night for months now, waking every hour on the hour as if some alarm in her head triggered it. The sleep deprivation was bound to catch up with her.

She had tried all the recommended remedies. An evening run to exhaust her body. No exercise at all after seven. Soaking in a warm bath. Drinking a glass of wine. When wine didn't work, warm milk. She tried reciting meditation chants. Cutting out caffeine. Reading. Listening to CDs of nature sounds. Using new therapeutic pillows. Lighting candles with soothing aromas. Even a little Scotch in the warm milk.

Nothing worked.

She hadn't resorted to sleep meds . . . yet. As an FBI special agent and profiler she received phone calls in the middle of the night or the early morning hours that sometimes made it necessary for her to rush to a crime scene. Most of the meds—the good ones—required eight hours of uninterrupted sleep time. Who had that? Certainly not an agent.

She took a long, hot shower, gently washing. No scrubbing, though that was her first inclination. She avoided watching the drain and what went down. She left her hair damp. Put on a clean, loose-fitting pair of athletic shorts and her University of Virginia T-shirt. After bagging up her clothes—at least those that couldn't be salvaged—and tossing them in the garbage, Maggie retreated to the main room. Harvey followed close behind.

She turned on the big-screen TV, pocketing the remote and continuing on to the kitchen. The fifty-six-inch plasma had been a splurge for someone who watched little television, but she justified it by having college-football parties on Saturdays in the fall. And then there were the evenings of pizza, beer, and classic movies with Ben. Colonel Benjamin Platt had become a close . . . friend.

That was all for now, or so they had decided. Okay, so they hadn't really even talked about it. Things were at a comfortable level. She liked talking to him as much as she liked the silence of being with him. Sometimes when they sat in her backyard watching Harvey and Ben's dog, Digger, play, Maggie caught herself thinking, "This could be a family." The four of them seemed to fill voids in each other's lives.

Yes, comfortable. She liked that. Except that lately she felt an annoying tingle every time he touched her. That's when she reminded herself that both their lives were already complicated and their personal baggage sometimes untenable. Their schedules constantly conflicted. Especially the last three to four months.

So "friends" was a comfortable place to be for now, though decided by default rather than consensus. Still, she caught herself checking her cell phone: waiting, expecting, hoping for a message from him. She hadn't seen him since he'd spent two weeks in Afghanistan. Only short phone conversations or text messages.

Now he was gone again. Somewhere in Florida. She wasn't used to them not being able to share. That was one of the things that had brought them closer, talking about their various cases: hers usually profiling a killer; his identifying or controlling some infectious disease. A couple of times they had worked on a case together when the FBI and USAMRIID (United States Army Medical Research Institute of Infectious Diseases—pronounced U-SAM-RID) were both involved. But Afghanistan and this trip were, in Ben's words, "classified missions" in "undisclosed locations." In Maggie's mind, she added "dangerous."

She fed Harvey while tossing a salad for herself and listening to "breaking news" at the top of the hour:

"Gas prices are up and will continue to soar because of the tropical storms and hurricanes that have ravaged the Gulf this summer. And another one, Hurricane Isaac is predicted to sweep across Jamaica tonight. The category-4 storm with sustained winds of 145 miles per hour is expected to pick up steam when it enters the Gulf in the next couple of days."

Her cell phone rang and she jumped, startled enough to spill salad dressing on the counter. Okay, so having a killer's blood and brains splattered all over her had unnerved her more than she was willing to admit.

She grabbed for the phone. Checked the number, disappointed that she didn't recognize it.

"This is Maggie O'Dell."

"Hey, *cherie*," a smooth, baritone voice said.

There was only one person who got away with using that New Orleans charm on her.

"Hello, Charlie. And to what do I owe this pleasure?"

Maggie and Charlie Wurth had spent last Thanksgiving weekend sorting through a bombing at Mall of America and trying to prevent another before the weekend was over. In a case where she couldn't even trust her new boss, AD Raymond Kunze, Charlie Wurth had been a godsend. For six months now the deputy director of the Department of Homeland Security (DHS) had been trying to woo her over to his side of the fence at the Justice Department.

"I'm headed on a road trip," Charlie continued. "And I know you won't be able to say no to joining me. Think sunny Florida. Emerald-green waters. Sugar-white sands."

Every once in a while Charlie Wurth called just to dangle another of his outrageous proposals. It had become a game with them. She couldn't remember why she hadn't entertained the idea of leaving the FBI and working for DHS. She swiped her fingers through her hair, thinking about the blood and brain matter from earlier. Maybe she should consider a switch.

"Sounds wonderful." Maggie played along. "What's the catch?"

"Just a small one. It appears we most likely will be in the projected path of Hurricane Isaac."

"Tell me again why I'd be interested in going along?"

"Actually, you'd be doing me a big favor." Charlie's voice turned serious. "I was already on my way down because of the hurricane. Got a bit of a distraction, though. Coast Guard found a fishing cooler in the Gulf."

He left a pause inviting her to finish.

"Let me guess. It wasn't filled with fish."

"Exactly. Local law enforcement has its hands full with hurricane preps. Coast Guard makes it DHS, but I'm thinking the assortment of body parts throws it over to FBI. I just checked with AD Kunze to see if I can borrow you."

"You talked to Kunze? Today?"

"Yep. Just a few minutes ago. He seemed to think it'd be a good idea."

She wasn't surprised that her boss wanted to send her into the eye of a hurricane.

THREE

NAVAL AIR STATION (NAS)

PENSACOLA, FLORIDA

Colonel Benjamin Platt didn't recognize this part of the base, though he'd been here once before. Usually he was in and out of these places too quickly to become familiar with any of them.

"It's gorgeous," he said, looking out at Pensacola Bay.

His escort, Captain Carl Ganz, seemed caught off guard by the comment, turning around to see just what Platt was pointing out. Their driver slowed as if to assist his captain's view.

"Oh yes, definitely. Guess we take it for granted," Captain Ganz said. "Pensacola is one of the prettiest places I've been stationed. Just getting back from Kabul, I'm sure this looks especially gorgeous."

"You're right about that."

"How was it?"

"The trip?"

"Afghanistan."

"The dust never lets up. Still feel like my lungs haven't cleared."

"I remember. I was part of a medevac team in 2005," Captain Ganz told Platt.

"I didn't realize that."

"Summer 2005. We lost one of our SEALs. A four-member reconnaissance contingent came under attack. Then a helicopter carrying sixteen soldiers flew in as a reinforcement but was shot down." Ganz kept his eyes on the water in the bay. "All aboard died. As did the ground crew."

Platt let out a breath and shook his head. "That's not a good day."

"You were there back then, too, weren't you?"

"Earlier. Actually, the first months of the war," Platt said. "I was part of the team trying to protect our guys from biological or chemical weapons. Ended up cutting and suturing more than anything else."

"So has it changed?"

"The war?"

"Afghanistan."

Platt paused and studied Captain Ganz. He was a little older than Platt, maybe forty, with a boyish face, although his hair had prematurely turned gray. This was the first time the two men had met in person. Past correspondences had been via e-mail and phone calls. Platt was a medical doctor and director of infectious diseases at Fort Detrick's USAMRIID and charged with preventing, inoculating, and containing some of the deadliest diseases ever known. Ganz, also a physician, ran a medical program for the navy that oversaw the surgical needs of wounded soldiers.

"Sadly, no," Platt finally answered, deciding he could be honest with Ganz. "Reminded me too much of those early days. Seems like we're chasing our tails. Only now we're doing it with our hands tied behind our backs."

Platt rubbed a thumb and forefinger over his eyes, trying to wipe out the fatigue. He still felt jet-lagged from his flight. He hadn't been back home even forty-eight hours when he got the call from Captain Ganz.

"Tell me about this mystery virus." Platt decided he'd just as well cut to the chase.

"We've isolated and quarantined every soldier we think may have come in contact with the first cases, the ones that are now breaking. Until we know what it is, I figured it's better to be safe than sorry."

"Absolutely. What are the symptoms?"

"That's just it. There are very few. At least, in the beginning. Initially there's excruciating pain at the surgical site, which is not unusual with most of these surgeries. We're talking multiple fractures, deep-tissue wounds with bone exposed." He paused as several planes took off overhead, drowning out all sound. "We're starting to move aircraft out of the path of this next hurricane."

"I thought it's predicted to hit farther west, maybe New Orleans."

"Media is always looking at New Orleans," Ganz shrugged. "Better story I guess. But some of the best in the weather business are telling us it's coming here. Just hope we're on the left side of it and not the right. That's why the admiral's nervous. That's why I told him I needed to call you in. I told him, if Platt can't figure this out, no one can."

"Not sure I can live up to that."

"Yes, you can. You will. You have to."

"Pain at the site," Platt prodded him to continue, wanting to keep focused before the fatigue derailed him. "What about the med packs left at the site?"

"That's what we thought with the first cases. We removed the packs and that seemed to alleviate the pain, but only temporarily."

"Infection?"

"Surgical sites show no swelling. Patients have no fever. Although they report feeling very hot and sometimes sweat profusely. They complain about upset stomachs. Some vomiting. Headaches. And yet all vital signs are good. Blood pressure, heart rate . . . all normal. Here we are." Captain Ganz stopped as his driver pulled up to a side entrance of a brick two-story building.

The steel door was reinforced. A security keypad blinked red, its digital message flashed C CLASS I.

Ganz punched in a number then pressed his thumb on the screen. Locks clicked open: one, two, three of them. Inside was a small lobby, but Ganz took Platt down the first hallway to the right. The corridor was narrow and the two men walked shoulder to shoulder.

"The admiral wants me to evacuate these soldiers. Move them inland to the Naval Hospital instead of keeping them here right on the bay. But, as you know, moving them presents all kinds of problems."

Finally they arrived at another door, another security

keypad. Ganz went through the same process again, but when the locks clicked this time he pulled the door open just a few inches and stopped, turning back to look Platt in the eyes.

"Within a week, four, five days, the blood pressure plunges. The heart starts racing. It's like the body is struggling to get oxygen. They slip into a coma. Organs rapidly begin to shut down. There's been nothing we can do. I've lost two so far. Just yesterday. I don't want the rest of these soldiers to see the same end."

"I understand. Let's see what we can do."

Ganz nodded, opened the door, and walked into a small glass-encased room that overlooked an area as big as a gymnasium, only it was sectioned and partitioned off, each section encased in a plastic tent with sterile walls that sprouted tubes and cords, monitors and computer screens.

Platt sucked in his breath to prevent a gasp. There had to be more than a hundred hospital beds filling the space. More than a hundred beds with more than a hundred soldiers.

FOUR

PENSACOLA BEACH

Liz Bailey would have rather stayed out in the Gulf and be battered by the waves and the wind. But they were grounded for the rest of their shift and for the last five hours had been battered by the sheriff of Escambia County, the director of the Santa Rosa Island Authority, the commander of Air Station Pensacola, a federal investigator from the Department of Homeland Security, and the deputy director of DHS via speakerphone.

It was crazy and Liz couldn't help wondering if they might have gotten off easier if they had never looked inside the cooler. If only they'd just handed it over and headed back out. Too many of the questions seemed more about containment of information rather than gathering the facts.

"Who else have you told?" the sheriff wanted to know.

"We followed proper procedure for finding human remains at sea." Lieutenant Commander Wilson no longer bothered to hide his impatience. Keeping a cool head was a skill Wilson hadn't learned yet.

Liz wondered if he was sorry that he'd asked Kesnick to open the cooler. Seeing him defensive and irritated by the consequences of his actions was almost worth the detainment. Almost.

Earlier, the look on Wilson's face had convinced Liz that their pilot had never seen a severed body part before. At first she thought Wilson didn't believe Kesnick. But she saw his eyes and glimpsed what looked like fear—maybe even shock. With his visor pushed back to get a better look at the contents inside that cooler, there was no hiding his expression. At least not from Liz, who had been in a position in the helicopter to see it, to catch it straight on. Normally it may have garnered sympathy. Instead it simply reinforced her lack of respect for the guy.

Finally dismissed for the day, the four of them wandered out into the sunlight.

"Beer's on me," Wilson announced. "It's early. We can get a good seat on the Tiki Bar's deck. Watch some bikini babes."

Someone cleared his throat. Liz didn't look to see who.

"Oh, come on," Wilson said. "Bailey doesn't mind. Not if she's one of us."

Always the edge, the challenge, putting it back onto Liz.

"Actually, it sounds like a good idea," she said, putting on her sunglasses, still without looking at any of them and not slowing her pace.

"Only if we can get a couple of hot dogs." Tommy Ellis was always hungry.

"Geez, Ellis. Can you stop thinking about your stomach? We'll get them later," Wilson insisted.

"What if the hot-dog man isn't there later?"

"He'll be there," Liz told them, now leading the way to the Tiki Bar. "And he'll probably talk us into going out again for another beer with him."

"Yeah, how can you be so sure?" Ellis demanded.

"Because the hot-dog man is my dad."

FIVE

NEWBURGH HEIGHTS, VIRGINIA

Maggie O'Dell downloaded and printed the copies Wurth had forwarded to her. The photos and initial documents from the Escambia County Sheriff's Department reminded her that she'd want to take her own photos. She'd be able to decipher only the basics from these shots.

One photo showed an assortment of odd-shaped packages wrapped in plastic and stuffed inside an oversize cooler. The close-ups displayed the individual packages lined up on a concrete floor used for staging. What she could see beyond the plastic wrap looked more like cuts of meat from a butcher shop than parts of a human body.

She asked Wurth if they could wait until her arrival before unwrapping the packages. He told her it was probably too late.

"Doubtful. You know how that goes, O'Dell. Curiosity gets the best of even law enforcement." But then he added, "I'll see what I can do."

Now Maggie sat cross-legged in the middle of her living-room floor, scattered photos on one side, Harvey on the other.

His sleeping head filled her lap. She kept the TV on the Weather Channel. Initially the TV just provided background noise, but she found the weather coverage drawing her attention. She was learning about hurricanes, something that might come in handy in the following week.

Maggie found it interesting that the Saffir-Simpson Hurricane Wind Scale, though measured by sustained winds, was also based on the level of damage those winds were capable of causing. A category-3 storm produced sustained winds of 111 to 130 miles per hour and could cause "extensive" damage; a category 4, 131 to 155 mile per hour winds and "devastating" damage; a category 5, 156 miles per hour and greater winds with "catastrophic" damage.

One hundred and forty mile per hour winds were not something Maggie could relate to. Damage, however, was something she could.

Hurricane Isaac had already killed sixty people across the Caribbean. Within several hours it had gone from 145 mile per hour winds to 150. The storm was expected to hit Grand Cayman in a few hours. One million Cubans were said to have evacuated in anticipation of the monster hitting there on Sunday. Moving at only ten miles per hour, the hurricane was expected to enter the Gulf by Monday.

On every projected path Maggie had seen in the last several hours, Pensacola, Florida, was smack-dab in the middle. Charlie Wurth hadn't been kidding when he told her they would be driving down into the eye of a hurricane. Consequently, there were no available flights to Pensacola. Tomorrow morning she was booked to fly to Atlanta, where

Charlie would pick her up and they would drive five hours to the Florida Panhandle. When she asked him what he was doing in Atlanta—his home was in New Orleans and his office in Washington, D.C.—he simply said, "Don't ask."

Wurth still had difficulty acting like a federal government employee. He came to the position of assistant deputy director of Homeland Security after impressing the right people with his tough but fair investigation of federal waste and corruption in the wake of Hurricane Katrina. But Wurth, like Maggie, probably would never get used to the bureaucracy that came with the job.

Maggie knew she should be packing. She kept a bag with the essentials. She just needed to add to it. What did one pack for hurricane weather? Sensible shoes, no doubt. Her friend Gwen Patterson was always telling Maggie that she didn't have the appropriate respect for shoes.

She glanced at the time. She'd need to call Gwen. She'd do that later. The foray with today's killer was still too fresh in her mind and on her skin. Her friend the psychiatrist had a knack for reading between the lines, weighing pauses, and detecting even the slightest of cracks in Maggie's composure. An occupational hazard, Gwen always said, and Maggie understood all too well.

The two women had met when Maggie was a forensic fellow at Quantico and Gwen a private consultant to the Behavioral Science Unit. Seventeen years Maggie's senior, Dr. Gwen Patterson had the tendency to overlap maternal instincts into their friendship. Maggie didn't mind. Gwen was her one constant. It was Gwen who was always there by

Maggie's side. It was Gwen propping her up during her long, drawn-out divorce; setting up vigil alongside Maggie's hospital bed after a killer had trapped her in a freezer to die; sitting outside an isolation ward at Fort Detrick when Maggie'd been exposed to Ebola; and most recently Gwen was again by her side at Arlington National Cemetery when Maggie paid her last respects at her mentor's gravesite.

Yet there were days like today when Maggie didn't want to confront her own vulnerabilities. Nor did she want her friend worrying. Maggie knew her insomnia was not just the inability to fall asleep. It was the nightmares that jolted her awake. Visions of her brother Patrick handcuffed to a suitcase bomb. The image of her mentor and boss lying in a hospital bed, his skeletal body invaded with tubes and needles. Herself trapped inside an ice coffin. A takeout container left on the counter of a truck stop, seeping blood. Rows and rows of Mason jars filled with floating body parts.

The problem was that those nightmare images were not the creation of an overactive or fatigued imagination but, rather, were memories, snapshots of very real experiences. The compartments Maggie had spent years carefully constructing in her mind—the places where she locked away the horrific snapshots—had started to leak. Just like Gwen had predicted.

"One of these days," her wise friend had warned, "you're going to need to deal with the things you've seen and done, what's been done to you. You can't tuck them away forever."

The cell phone startled both Maggie and Harvey this time. She patted him as she reached across his body to retrieve the phone. She wouldn't have been surprised to hear Gwen's voice.

"Maggie O'Dell."

"Hey."

Close. It was Gwen's boyfriend, R. J. Tully, who happened to be Maggie's partner. That was before the FBI buckled down on costs. Now they found themselves working singularly and assigned to very few of the same cases. However, Tully had been one of the contingency there today at the warehouse, one of half a dozen agents who witnessed Kunze's kill shot.

"Thought I'd check to see if you're okay."

"I'm fine." Too quick. She bit down on her lower lip. Would Tully call her on it? Gwen would. Before he had a chance to respond, she tried to change the subject. "I was just about to call Emma."

"Emma?" Tully sounded like he didn't recognize his daughter's name.

"To stay with Harvey. I need to leave tomorrow morning. Early. Charlie Wurth has a case in Florida he wants me to check out. Is Emma home?"

Too long of a pause. He knew what she was up to. He was a profiler, too. But would he let her get away with it? Gwen wouldn't.

"She hasn't left for college yet, has she?" Maggie asked the question only to fill the silence. She knew the girl was dragging her feet about going.

"No. Not until late next week. She's not here right now, but I'm sure she'll be okay about staying with Harvey. Text her instead of calling. You'll get an immediate response." Another pause. "Does AD Kunze know about this trip?"

"Of course, he does." She hated that it came out with an

edge. "Wurth checked it out with him." She didn't add that Kunze thought it was a good idea. Tully would add it on his own. He had faced the wrath of Kunze last fall when their new boss put Tully on suspension. "It's probably not a big deal," Maggie jumped in again. "Some body parts found in a cooler off the coast."

"More body parts." She could hear Tully laugh. "Sounds like you're becoming an expert on killers who chop up their victims."

She would have laughed, too, if it wasn't so close to being true. Then, without regard to all the work she had done to change the subject, Maggie heard herself say, "Do me a favor, don't tell Gwen about today, okay?"

"Not a problem." This time there had been no pause, no hesitation. A partner backing up another partner. "Let me know if I can help. With the case," he added, allowing her cover.

SIX

HILTON PENSACOLA BEACH GULF FRONT

Scott Larsen sipped his draft beer and waited for the man he'd secretly nicknamed "the Death Salesman." It was sort of a term of endearment, one colleague to another. After all, Scott didn't mind that some people—including his own wife—sometimes called him a death merchant. Sounded sexier than funeral director or even mortician.

He watched the back door to the hotel from the deck bar. This was the first time they were meeting outside of Scott's office. Scott was good at his job, good at being the professional. He didn't do casual or social very well, and in his line of work you never mixed business with pleasure so it worked just fine.

The cute, blond bartender had already given him a refill and his head was beginning to feel a bit fuzzy. He'd never been good at holding his liquor, even beer, though he was pretty good at pretending. As soon as the buzz began, he slowed down his speech and carefully measured his words.

His wife, Trish, claimed he was too good at pretending. But

then he'd had a lot of practice. That was, after all, what the funeral business was all about, wasn't it? Pretend the deceased is at peace. Pretend he's gone on to a better place. Pretend that you care.

Scott glanced at his wristwatch and turned to look back at the water. He tried not to stare at any of the young bikinied bodies though the beach was filled with them this early on a Saturday evening. He was a married man now, or at least he could use that as an excuse. He stunk at flirting, too. He could be so charming when it came to widows, holding their hands and letting them sob on his shoulder. But put him in a room full of beautiful, sexy women and he choked. Had no clue what to do or what to talk about. His palms got sweaty, his tongue swelled in his mouth. Couldn't even fake his way around. It was a wonder he ever snagged Trish. He was lucky and grateful and he tried never to forget that.

He started to turn back around to watch the hotel door when he noticed a guy walking up the beach with a confident, relaxed stride, deck shoes in one hand and the other casually slipped into the pocket of his long khaki shorts. The hem of his pink button-down shirt flapped in the breeze. He wasn't stunningly handsome and yet that confident stride turned some heads. The guy looked like he had stepped off the cover of *GQ* and nothing like a death salesman. In fact, it took a minute or two before Scott recognized him. He certainly hadn't expected him to come walking up the beach.

Scott waved at him then felt ridiculous when he didn't receive an acknowledgment. Instead, the guy simply strolled through the crowd of bikinis and made his way to the barstool next to Scott without even a nod or glance. He was always so cool.

"What do you have for Scotch, single malt?" he asked the cute bartender, who was already in front of him by the time he settled in his seat.

"Sorry, no single malts and the best blend I've got is Johnnie Walker."

"Blue Label?"

Scott watched the bartender smile with what looked like admiration.

"No, again, sorry. Black Label's best I can do."

"That's perfect," he told her, as if that was exactly what he wanted all along. Then he turned to Scott. "Join me?"

The attention caught Scott off guard, like a spectator suddenly pulled onto the playing field. The bartender, probably thinking Scott was some total stranger, now seemed even more impressed and she was waiting for Scott's response.

"Sure. Thanks," he managed as casually as he could.

"On the rocks for both of you?" she asked.

"Yeah, that'd be great," Scott told her, pretending it was his preference when he couldn't remember if he'd ever had Scotch before.

"Neat, for me."

Another smile from the bartender that almost made Scott want to change his order.

"This place was a great choice, Scott," the Death Salesman said, and Scott immediately relaxed and felt a rush of . . . what? It was silly but there really was something about this guy that made you want to please him.

That's when Scott realized he needed to calm his buzz down a notch so that he didn't slip and call him by the nickname in his head. Scott had wondered if Joe Black was his real name from the first time he introduced himself. That was, after all, the name of a movie character. This guy didn't look at all like Brad Pitt, but he certainly had that same charm and confidence. And the irony, if it was not his real name, only garnered more admiration from Scott. Joe Black, the character in the movie, was actually death masquerading as an ordinary Joe. It was probably what triggered Scott into secretly referring to him as the Death Salesman. His new friend—no, that wasn't right, they weren't friends, though Scott would like them to be—his new colleague was far from an ordinary Joe.

"Yeah, it's absolutely beautiful out here, isn't it?" Scott said. "You'd never guess there's a hurricane on its way."

The bartender delivered their drinks and this time she brought a complimentary bowl of nuts and pretzels. Perks seemed to gravitate to Joe Black, and Scott was happy to be along for the ride.

"Are you set up if it hits?"

"Absolutely."

"Have extra room if I need some space for a couple of days?"

"Oh sure," Scott told him and he sipped the Scotch, trying not to wince as it burned a path down his throat. "One of the first things I did when I bought the place was replace the walk-in. This new one has plenty of space, extra shelves. It's top-of-the-line."

In fact, he hadn't given a second thought to the hurricane.

There had already been three this summer and none had ventured this far north into the Gulf. Scott had grown up in Michigan. Had no clue about hurricanes. Pensacola was Trish's hometown. In the two years he'd lived here he hadn't had to deal with the threat. When he bought the funeral home, he assumed it was set up for such things. He did know that there was an emergency generator, and if and when the time came he'd figure out how it worked or hire someone to do it for him.

Holmes and Meyers Funeral Home wasn't the first business Scott had run. Up in Michigan he had managed three funeral homes. Though this was the first one he'd owned, it wasn't any different. He was good at business, knew how to turn a profit, cut costs, and try innovative approaches to solving problems. He did what it took, like keeping the name even though no descendants of Holmes or Meyers worked at the place anymore. You couldn't put a dollar amount on the value of reputation, especially in the funeral business. Yeah, he was still a little nervous now that he was responsible for the place as well as for the huge banknote in his name. But his success was why Joe Black had chosen him and his funeral home in the first place.

"You're sticking around through the week?" Scott asked.

"I've got another conference in Destin on Monday. That's if they don't cancel because of the weather. I could use some storage space."

"Oh sure. Bring whatever you have with you tomorrow. I'm sure I can make room. We're still on for tomorrow, right?"

"Absolutely." He swirled the Scotch in his glass and turned to face Scott, giving him his attention. "So, this is exciting. Your first indie."

"Indie?"

"Indigent donor."

"Oh, yeah." Scott laughed, trying to hide his embarrassment. He needed to figure out the lingo or he'd never be cool. "Who knew it would be so easy."

"Already delivered?"

"And waiting."

"Good."

But now Joe's eyes were tracking someone or something just over Scott's shoulder. He glanced in the direction and sighed before he could catch himself.

"What?" Joe said. "You know her?"

The object of Joe's distraction was the only woman at a table with four men. She seemed to be the center of attention, making them laugh.

"My sister-in-law."

"Really?"

"Forget about her, though. I don't think she plays for our team."

Joe looked at him and raised an eyebrow but before Scott could explain, Joe's cell phone started ringing. He slipped it out of his shirt pocket, a razor-thin rectangle of silver and red that glowed pink when he opened it.

"This is Joe Black."

Silence as Joe listened and ran an index finger over the rim of his glass. Scott caught himself watching out of the corner of his eye but he didn't want to look like he was eavesdropping. He turned his barstool around, swinging it in the direction of Liz's table. She'd never notice him anyway. No one ever did. Besides, her table was at the restaurant next door.

Another glance and Scott saw that his father-in-law was one of the four men.

Now he almost wished they did see him, drinking expensive Scotch with a classy buddy. It would certainly give both of them a new image of him. And he wouldn't mind having an excuse for introducing Joe. Maybe even having them report back to Trish about his business dealings loosening him up. Isn't that what Trish was always telling him? That he needed to get out more? Instead he kept his back to Liz and his father-in-law. He pretended to be admiring the view.

"That's pretty short notice," Joe said into the phone. "No, I can do it. I'm just concerned how expensive it'll be for you."

Scott wiped off a smile before Joe could catch it. What a salesman. He was telling some customer that he was going to charge him a ton of money and made it sound like he was only concerned about the client.

"Let me see what I can do and I'll get back to you tomorrow."

No "goodbye." No "thanks" or "talk to you later." Just a click and a flip.

"Always working," Scott said.

"You know it," Joe Black said. "How about another one of these?"

He held up the glass and drained it in one gulp, not at all how Scott thought this expensive stuff should be drunk. But even as Joe called over the bartender, Scott could see him glance back over Scott's shoulder.

SEVEN

NAVAL AIR STATION
PENSACOLA, FLORIDA

Benjamin Platt insisted on seeing some of the worst cases. Yes, he was exhausted. Still a bit jet-lagged from the Afghanistan flight followed too soon by the one from D.C. to Florida, but he knew that if Captain Ganz took him to his hotel he wouldn't sleep. He'd be thinking about all these plastic tents with wounded soldiers waiting to find out what they'd been exposed to.

After examining just five soldiers, he grew more confused. Their injuries were all different. Their surgeries were different as well, but all were to repair limbs that had been severed, crushed, or otherwise damaged. Some were now amputees waiting to heal and be fitted with prosthetics. Many of the injuries—though it was always disheartening to see a soldier lose an arm or leg—were not necessarily life-threatening.

"Could it be something here at the hospital?" Platt asked Captain Ganz as they escaped to a lounge where they could be free of their masks and goggles and gloves.

"We haven't done anything differently. Nothing I can find that would suddenly be a problem."

"You're thinking it might be something they were exposed to in Afghanistan? That perhaps they brought back with them?"

"Is that possible? Could a strain lie dormant?"

"And what? Come alive when you cut into them?"

Ganz wouldn't meet Platt's eyes, and Platt knew that must be exactly what the captain was most afraid of.

"There's nothing like that. Not that I'm aware of," Platt told him.

"But it's not entirely impossible?"

Platt didn't have an answer. Two things his years at USAMRIID had taught him were to never say never and that anything was possible.

"How many cases do you have isolated here?"

Ganz didn't have to stop to calculate. He knew off the top of his head. "Seventy-six."

"And for how long?"

"We started isolating eight days ago. But some of these soldiers had their surgical procedures up to eighteen days ago."

"All of them were operated on here?"

"Yes, though some had temporary procedures done at Bagram before being flown here."

"Any similarities there?"

"None that we've been able to isolate. Those who remain at Bagram haven't come down with the same symptoms. In fact, they haven't lost anyone in the same manner. You'd think that's where the problem should be." Ganz attempted a laugh, but there was no humor, just frustration.

"You still have blood samples from the soldiers you lost. I'd like to take look at them."

"Our lab has already examined them extensively—" But Ganz stopped and shook his head like a sleepwalker suddenly waking himself. He waved his hand as if to erase what he had said. "Of course. I'll have someone set them up for you. What will you be looking for?"

Platt shrugged. "Sometimes when we're focused on specifics, maybe particular pathogens like MRSA, we can miss other things that might not be so obvious." He rubbed at his eyes, suddenly feeling the exhaustion again. *Methicillin resistant Staphylococcus aureus*, which surpassed HIV as the most deadly pathogen in the United States, was resistant to most antibiotics. It had become all too prevalent after surgical procedures, so it was one of the first things to look for when an infection resulted. "I'll start by looking to see if there's any cell degradation."

"You could probably use some sleep first. A few hours could help. I did pull you down here before you had a chance to catch your breath."

"I'll be fine. Maybe some good strong coffee."

The door to the lounge opened and a doctor in blue scrubs leaned inside, eyes urgent, not taking the time to enter.

"Captain, we're losing another one."

SUNDAY, AUGUST 23

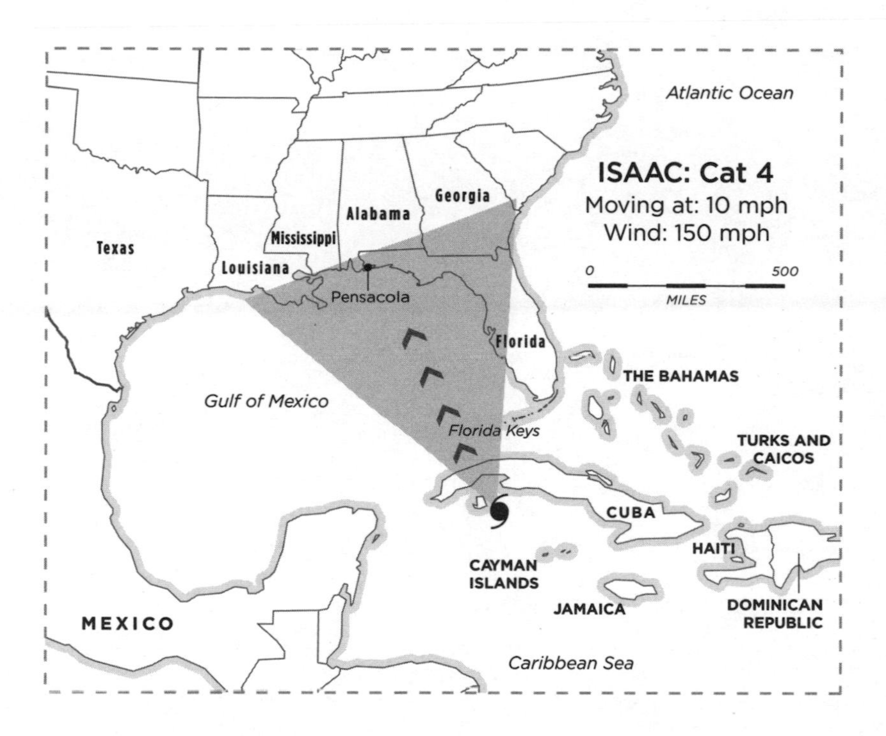

EIGHT

HARTSFIELD-JACKSON INTERNATIONAL AIRPORT
ATLANTA, GEORGIA

Maggie's 6:00 am flight put her in Atlanta just before eight. Under two hours and it was still enough to rattle her composure. She hated flying—not the crowds, not the inconvenience, not even a fear of heights, but rather being trapped at thirty-eight thousand feet without any control. Even the upgrade to first class that Wurth managed to snag for her had done little to help.

He was waiting in baggage claim. For a small man he could deliver a body-crushing hug.

"Easy," Maggie told him. "What will people think?"

"Oh, it's okay here in Atlanta," Wurth countered. "But don't touch me once we leave the city and head into the South. You may even have to sit in the backseat so I can pretend I'm driving you."

She rolled her eyes. She knew he was joking, but at the same time she knew there were still pockets in the South where a black man and a white woman in a vehicle together might draw some looks. But it couldn't be anything close to what they had already been through.

Maggie and Wurth had shared a terror-filled weekend last November. On the Friday following Thanksgiving, three young college students carrying backpacks loaded with explosives had blown up a section of Mall of America. Maggie and Wurth were dispatched to sort through the rubble and had tried to stop a second attack. In the end they had bonded against an unexpected and powerful enemy. It had been the beginning of Maggie's tumultuous relationship with her new boss, Assistant Director Raymond Kunze, and Charlie Wurth ended up becoming her ally, stepping in to defend her when Kunze would not.

"That's it?" Wurth said when she showed him her small Pullman. Dragging it behind her, she started leading him to the claims office to retrieve her firearm. "O'Dell, for most women I know, that teeny thing would be their handbag."

"Guess I'm not most women."

"You're what we men call low maintenance. I've heard stories about low-maintenance women but I've never known one until now."

With her gun safely holstered, Maggie followed Wurth outside to a black Escalade parked at the curb. An airport security officer had been watching over it and now opened the back while Wurth took Maggie's Pullman and lifted it in.

"Thanks, man." Wurth reached up to pat the officer on his shoulder. He was at least a head taller than Wurth.

"You be safe," the officer said as he opened the passenger door for Maggie.

Inside, the vehicle was spotless except for a pile of CD covers scattered in the console between them.

"I didn't realize rental places had these luxury SUVs anymore."

"Oh, they probably don't." Wurth turned the engine and blasted the AC. "This one's not a rental. It's mine."

"You're driving your personal vehicle down into a hurricane?"

"It's not about that." He smiled and shook his head. "We goin' down South, *cherie*. Into the middle of hurricane frenzy. A scrawny black man with a beautiful white woman—I'm packing all my necessary documents: registration, license, and proof of insurance, along with my badge."

She laughed but Wurth wasn't laughing.

"You're serious."

"As a heart attack." He punched a couple of buttons on the dashboard and the sound of soft jazz filled the interior. "We've got about five hours of interstate. How 'bout we hit Mickey D's drive-through for a couple of sausage biscuits?"

"In an Escalade with soft jazz? Sounds perfect."

"Low, low maintenance," he said. "I'm liking this."

She let him maneuver his way out of Hartfield-Jackson before she started prodding him.

"Have you learned anything since last night?"

"They have already unwrapped everything." He glanced at her over his sunglasses. "Sorry. I should have thought of it sooner. I'm not accustomed to dealing in body parts."

"Don't worry about it. I'm sure they followed protocol."

Maggie remembered what Tully had said about her becoming

an expert. It wasn't the kind of thing she wished to add to her résumé.

"Turns out there were five packages: one male torso, one foot, and three hands."

"Left or right?"

"Excuse me?"

"The hands and the foot. Were they left or right?"

This time he flashed an embarrassed grin. "Again, sorry O'Dell. I didn't think to ask." He shook his head. "I thought my job had some interesting variables, but you got me beat."

"Three hands? It's more than one victim."

"So did we stumble on his trophies or his disposables?"

Maggie shrugged and leaned back in the leather captain seat. The car's AC was noiseless, chilling the interior as smoothly as the jazz filled it.

"A cooler this size could act as sort of a floating coffin, taking it farther out to sea. If the lid isn't locked, predators would take care of the remains, get rid of all the evidence. But the plastic wrapping suggests this guy didn't intend for the cooler to get away from him. I should be able to tell more once I see everything firsthand. Will I be able to visit the crime scene?"

"I was told that wouldn't be a problem."

"And the cooler?"

"Waiting for you. The packages, however, are already with the ME. He'll take a look at them tomorrow morning. And yes, he's expecting your presence. You won't find much resistance. If anything, you might find a lack of interest. With this hurricane coming, the local law enforcement has more important things to worry about."

"A storm is more important than a killer on the loose?"

Wurth glanced over at her as he turned into the parking lot of a McDonald's. "You've never been in a hurricane before, huh?"

"That obvious?"

"Your killers carve up, what? Six bodies? A dozen over several months? Maybe several years? Isaac has already killed sixty-seven in forty-eight hours. This time, O'Dell, I think my killer trumps your killer."

NINE

PENSACOLA, FLORIDA

Liz Bailey fumbled around the kitchen trying to fix breakfast, silently vowing that she would take time to buy the things she couldn't find. She hadn't lived in her father's house since high school. Her sister had lived here until she married Scott. That was two years ago—just enough time for her father to arrange things so that only he could find them.

She'd moved back in temporarily only because the housing she was promised with her transfer wouldn't be available for two months. Now searching for the toaster she wondered if she'd last that long.

She turned up the radio for the local weather report.

"Hurricane Isaac is expected to slam into the western side of Cuba today. Last night it bulldozed over Grand Cayman, flooding homes, ripping off roofs, and toppling trees. More than half the homes on Grand Cayman are said to be damaged. And yet, Isaac hasn't lost any of its steam. It's now a cat 4 and traveling about ten miles an hour with sustained winds of 150 miles an hour. And guess what, folks, it's still expected

to take that slight turn to the north/northeast, which means, you guessed it, we're smack-dab in the middle of its path. Landfall may be sometime Wednesday. Time to start boarding up, stocking up, and moving out, folks."

"They're always wrong," her dad said as he shuffled in, still in his pajamas though he had been up for an hour reading the newspaper and drinking coffee.

Finally, the toaster! Liz found it in the bottom cabinet under the sink. Of course, the last place she'd think to look. She pulled it out without any comment. Trish would have commented, scolded, and instructed where the toaster should be stored.

"Not this time, Dad. The CG and the NHC has the Florida Panhandle in the crosshairs."

"Well, that's not where the media says it's gonna hit. They're all in New Orleans again, ready and waiting. This morning's *Journal* has the projected path drawn from Galveston to Tampa, and they all act like New Orleans is the only place they give a damn about."

"You should get gas today. And batteries and bottled water. Won't Trish and Scott need to come stay with you? They can't stay on the bay."

"I've got a whole container of batteries and plenty of bottled water in the garage. Enough food in the refrigerators to feed us for a week."

"You'll need a generator just to keep your three refrigerators running."

"I've got three generators."

"Then you better get gas today, Dad. Will you do that? Will you promise me you'll get the gas cans filled today?"

"Sure, sure."

"You won't put it off?"

"I'll go out before lunch. But you're not gonna be here anyway. Where will they send you?"

"Probably Jacksonville. Someplace out of the path but close enough we can fly in immediately after. Remember, I told you. We came in right behind Katrina, so close I could see the swell of the backstorm. I imagine we'll try to do the same this time."

"Those boys sure have taken a liking to you." He filled his coffee cup, standing beside her as she waited for the toaster to spit out her bagel.

"Yeah, we're all a bunch of buddies." She wanted to add that it was easy to be buddies after a few beers, but she'd never let her dad know that it was anything different.

"They have a small article in the *Journal* about that cooler you brought up yesterday."

"Really?"

"Front page. Bottom right-hand corner. I set it aside for you."

"Tell me what they said." She slathered cream cheese on her toasted bagel and took a bite. Her dad read every inch of the daily *Pensacola News Journal* and could usually repeat almost verbatim the articles he took an interest in.

"Suspicious fishing cooler retrieved by the Coast Guard," he told her, while tipping little splashes of cream into his coffee like he was rationing it. "It didn't mention anything about the contents or even suggest foul play or that it had body parts inside."

Liz almost choked on her bagel.

"Why do you think there were body parts?"

"It's okay. I won't say anything to anybody. The little guy, the one who had all the hot dogs and couldn't hold his liquor—Tommy? He let it slip about the foot. He said there was other stuff, too, so I'm just assuming there might be the rest of a body."

So much for all their training. Liz knew Wilson and Ellis were green, but this was ridiculous. The entire aircrew could get suspended for something like this.

"You know there was an article in last week's *Journal*. Someplace up near Washington, D.C. A possible serial killer. One of those sick bastards who kept pieces of his victim. Maybe this is related."

"Dad, I can't talk about it. You know I can't discuss this."

"I'm just talking about the news."

He struggled with a bagel for himself, trying to cut it in half with a bread knife. Liz gently took it from him, twisted it apart, and dropped both halves in the toaster.

"Okay, so tell me what you read about the serial killer."

TEN

NORTH SEVENTEENTH AVENUE UNDERPASS
PENSACOLA, FLORIDA

Billy Redding hit the jackpot. His battered shopping cart rattled with stacked aluminum cans. He crushed as many as he could until his hands were sore. The curse of small hands. In fact, Billy had convinced himself years ago that it had always been his worthless little hands that had prevented him from being successful in life. But maybe his luck was turning. Now with most of the cans crushed and almost flat, he could fit another two dozen into the cart.

Saturday nights always left a jackpot in the Wayside Park trash barrels. The trick, Billy had discovered, was to get here early enough on Sunday to beat the city's cleanup crew. Cashing in this pile would take care of him for a week.

He headed back to the underpass to hide his stash. The short distance exhausted him. He was out of breath when he heard a car coming from behind him. Billy pushed back onto the curb to get out of the way. The car slowed. Billy kept moving uphill, panting in the morning humidity. His T-shirt stuck to his back like a second skin. He hated that and wore a long-sleeve button-down shirt over it, thinking it would act as a layer of insulation or at least soak up the extra moisture. He didn't mind being hot. He hated being wet. Bugs would get tangled in his beard whenever it got wet. That's why he learned to stick close to the underpass. It provided shelter from the rain.

"Hey, Billy," someone called out to him.

He wanted to pretend he didn't hear them. He needed to keep going. But sometimes people stopped and gave him a couple of bucks. He glanced over his shoulder.

A police cruiser. Damn!

He stopped immediately. Secured the shopping cart with a rock under one of the back wheels. A big rock he carried strictly for that purpose.

As he got closer to the car Billy recognized the orange-haired cop. Sometimes they told him their names but he never remembered. He was always polite. As long as he was polite, they were polite back. So Billy just kept his head down and answered their questions, said "yes" a lot and called them "sir." Once he even called a female cop "sir." He was so embarrassed that he couldn't stutter out an apology. She ended up giving him five bucks and said not to worry about it.

"There's a hurricane coming this way, Billy," the cop told him through the rolled-down window of the cruiser.

"Yes, sir."

"When the time comes I'll send someone here to pick you up. You're going to need to go to a hurricane shelter. Do you understand, Billy? You won't be able to stay out here."

"Yes, sir. Will I be able to bring my shopping cart?"

"They'll have food and everything else you'll need at the shelter."

Billy kept his head down and kicked at the curb. "It's hard to find these."

The cop was quiet and out of the corner of his eyes Billy could see him shaking his head.

"Sure, Billy. We'll figure something out. I'll tell them you can bring your cart."

Billy bagged some of the cans and put them in his safe spot, a deserted grassy hideaway several yards from the underpass. If he hurried back to the park, he might be able to grab more cans before the cleanup crew arrived. He couldn't go to the recycling kiosk until tomorrow. It'd take a whole day.

His cart rattled even more now with only half the crushed cans to jump around. Billy liked the jingle-jangle. It reminded him of the sound of loose change in his daddy's trouser pocket. "Ice-cream money," he'd call it and the two of them would laugh at their secret code so Billy's mama wouldn't know they were really going out to buy and share a cheap bottle of vodka.

Billy had just gotten to the park when he heard another vehicle pull in behind him. He moved out of the way but the van stopped alongside him.

"Hey," a man called out.

Billy kept going, glancing back at the van. The man wore dark sunglasses and rested his arm out the window. Billy noticed a patch on the shoulder. A uniform. Like a cop. Had they sent someone to get him already? He stopped and looked up into the clear-blue sky then turned toward the water of the bay. The waves churned over the ledge but it didn't look like a hurricane was coming.

"You need to come with me," the man said to him. "I know it looks like a nice day, but there's a hurricane on the way."

"Yes, sir. I know that." Billy stayed on the curb. "They told me I could bring my shopping cart."

The man stared at him. Billy decided he wouldn't go if they didn't let him take the shopping cart.

"Sure, I've got room." The man climbed out of the van and slid open the side door, ready to help Billy. "You probably should climb in beside it and keep it from tipping."

As Billy started to crawl inside, stepping over all the bags of ice, he tried to remember if any of the other cops wore khaki shorts and really nice deck shoes. That was his last thought as the rock cracked the back of his skull.

ELEVEN

NAVAL AIR STATION
PENSACOLA, FLORIDA

Benjamin Platt cut himself again as the tiny bathroom fixtures shook and clattered from the vibration. Overhead, the steady buzz of airplanes and helicopters taking off continued. There would be no break anytime soon, and Platt's attempt at shaving was leaving him with enough nicks and scars that he considered growing a beard.

The latest weather reports had the eye of Hurricane Isaac heading straight for the Florida Panhandle, even though the storm hadn't entered the Gulf of Mexico yet. The base wasn't taking any chances. The naval flight school had called in pilots, flight instructors, and even students to fly aircraft to safer ground. And this morning the admiral was adamant about moving the quarantined soldiers to safer ground as well.

Platt had escaped late last night to get a couple hours' rest, though sleep didn't come easily. He couldn't get the image of the young soldier out of his mind. By the time Platt found Captain Ganz, the admiral had already called. Platt only witnessed the aftermath. Ganz had been unnerved about losing yet another patient, but the admiral's insistence on an evacuation of the makeshift isolation ward left the captain angry and frustrated. He was depending on Platt to find some answers and find them quickly.

Now as Platt headed over to the lab to participate in the autopsy, he felt a new weight on his shoulders. He hadn't even had a chance to look at the blood samples. Ganz was in a hurry, not just to come up with answers before another soldier collapsed but also to beat the storm. Platt wanted to tell him to slow down. He wanted to tell him that sometimes these things took weeks, months to figure out. But he knew that was exactly why Ganz had requested his presence. The captain was placing all his bets on Platt discovering some hidden virus, some new deadly strain of bacteria. He expected a miracle. And from what Platt had seen in the short amount of time since his arrival, he knew—barring a miracle—there would be no immediate answers.

He kept thinking about the young soldier who died last night. They said he had vomited green liquid just before falling into a coma. By the time Platt saw him, he looked remarkably peaceful. A single groan escaped his lips while his body struggled to get enough oxygen. There had been no swelling around his incision. No fever, though it was apparent from the wet bedsheets that he had perspired immensely in the preceding hours. The pupils of his eyes were not dilated nor had the blood vessels burst. Only in the last hour had his heart rate slowed and his blood pressure plummeted. He never regained consciousness. Whatever had infected these young soldiers was deceitful, clever, and lethal.

TWELVE

MONTGOMERY, ALABAMA

Gasoline exploded over the top of the can and splattered on Maggie's shoes before she snapped the pump off.

"Damn it, Wurth. Tell me again why the deputy director of Homeland Security is filling gas cans to haul in his SUV. Aren't you supposed to be arranging for trucks and caravans of trucks to deliver things to the hurricane victims?"

"What victims? This is my personal stash. Just put that last can next to the stack of bottled water."

Maggie slipped off her shoes and threw them in the back with the supplies. The asphalt burned her feet before she got back to the passenger side of the SUV. She opened her window despite the scorching heat. The fumes were already giving her a headache, and by her own calculations they had another three hours on the road.

Wurth slid into the driver's seat and handed her an ice-cold can of Diet Pepsi, his idea of a peace offering. She accepted.

"You'll be thanking me that I got a whole six-pack on ice back there for you. By the time we get down to Pensacola most of the shelves will be picked clean. Gas stations will either have long lines or be sold out. And there is absolutely nothing worse than being stuck in a hurricane area just because you can't get enough gasoline to drive away."

"I thought you weren't supposed to drive away. I thought you were supposed to be the cavalry."

Charlie Wurth laughed and shook his head.

"Where do you come up with these ideas, O'Dell?"

"You never did tell me why you're being dispatched to the Florida Panhandle when your home is New Orleans. Isn't New Orleans in this storm's path, too?"

"New Orleans is where all the media is." He pulled the SUV back into interstate traffic.

When Maggie realized that was the end of his explanation, she prodded. "Yes, so that's where all the media is and . . . ?"

"You know how this works better than I do. You've been a part of this federal bureaucracy longer than me. Media's all set up in the Big Easy then that's where the director is. Not the deputy director."

Of course. She couldn't believe she hadn't guessed.

"Which reminds me"—Wurth threw her a glance—"maybe now's a good time for you to tell me how you managed to get yourself smack-dab in the line of fire yesterday."

"Is that what you heard?"

"That's what I was told."

She shouldn't have been surprised that Kunze would characterize the incident as her fault.

"What exactly did my boss tell you?"

"I won't tell you his exact words because I don't use that

kind of language in front of a lady, but I believe the gist of what he said was that you screwed up. Didn't see it coming."

"I didn't see it coming?"

Maggie couldn't believe it. How dare Kunze blame her for a killer's unpredictable behavior. And to suggest it publicly to someone outside the bureau. What would be next? Saying that it was her negligence that made him fire his own gun three times into the killer? The first shot had been enough to stop him. Maggie wondered if the head shot that splattered her with the killer's brains had simply been overkill to do just that—splatter her.

"Did he even tell you what happened?"

"Maybe you should tell me what happened."

"Or my version. Isn't that what you're really saying?"

"Hey, I'm on your side, O'Dell." He held his hands up in surrender then dropped them back to the steering wheel. "If I believed anything Kunze said, you wouldn't be on this road trip with me."

"You're right. I'm sorry."

"You know what, it doesn't even matter what happened. You found the son of a bitch, right? And now he's out of commission. From what I read in last week's newspapers there were a few body parts involved in that case, too."

She waited for him to make the same inference Tully had—that somehow she'd become an expert in murders that included body parts. Wurth glanced at her.

"As far as I'm concerned," he said, "you did us all a favor."

Maggie settled into the oversize captain seat, tucking a bare foot underneath her, looking out the window, but her mind returned to yesterday's bizarre shooting. They had tracked down and found . . . no, that wasn't right. *She* had tracked down and found the killer's torture chamber—a deserted warehouse near the Potomac.

For Maggie it brought back memories of another killer she had caught many years ago. Sometimes she worried that all the killers she had come in contact with were morphing together. That Assistant Director Kunze had shot and killed this one didn't even bother her. She agreed with Wurth. It meant another monster wouldn't be hurting another innocent victim. That she didn't predict he would be there, who cared?

She had dug deep enough into his psyche to figure out where he hid, where he kept his dirty little secret life. Shouldn't that have been enough? Why had Kunze expected her to read his mind? Didn't Kunze realize that to dig deeper meant inching her way too close to the edge? Or maybe that was exactly what Kunze wanted. To shove her and see if she'd fall.

THIRTEEN

PENSACOLA BEACH

Liz Bailey downed her second Red Bull. She checked and rechecked the flight equipment then packed it back where it belonged. She had already gone over medical equipment piece by piece, even though they hadn't used anything yesterday. She was bored, only it was worse, waiting and knowing, the calm before the storm. Staying alert while staying put and waiting.

In their briefing this morning they were told to prepare to be on emergency standby for the rest of the week. She could see the waves from her post, churning and bucking against the seawall. Surfers were out before she arrived. She knew they'd be here until authorities made them leave and closed the beach. And they'd grumble about leaving, their eyes glazed over with adrenaline. You just didn't get waves like the ones that came right before a hurricane.

Several of the hotels had started encouraging guests to check out, but the beach was still packed with tourists. Other than the waves there was no indication of a storm, the sky still cloudless and blue, the sun baking the white sand. The last

August days before vacations ended for another year. Why would anyone believe they needed to leave this paradise and go home early?

The rest of Liz's aircrew were down the beach a mile at the heliport, crawling over their helicopter, doing their own pre-flight assessments, checks, and rechecks. She usually enjoyed the alone time. Today it added to her restlessness. They had been instructed to sit tight and wait. All they were told was that the deputy director of Homeland Security and an FBI investigator were on their way. It sounded like they would be taking over the case. Liz thought it a waste of time for them to be grilled all over again. What new questions could they ask? What more information could their aircrew provide?

She remembered what her dad had said about body parts and felt a bit sick to her stomach. How stupid could Tommy Ellis be? But then how stupid had all four of them been? Sure, Wilson prodded them to open the cooler, but Kesnick should never have gone any further once they realized what they had found. It was Kesnick who pulled out each piece. Except the large one, the one they agreed looked like a torso. The plastic had been wrapped tight but it yielded enough that they could see the parts had been sliced clean. No rips or tears. Whoever had done this knew exactly where to cut and had the tools to do an efficient job.

Now Liz wondered if Kesnick confessed to the authorities yesterday how much he had handled the wrapped pieces. Liz certainly hadn't said a word. She didn't lie. But for all the questions, no one thought about asking, "Did you handle the contents? Do you know what you found?"

Instead, the authorities were more concerned with where the cooler had been discovered and whether or not they had talked to anyone on the ground about it. Anyone outside their aircrew. Even later, when the four of them went out for drinks and hot dogs, they stayed away from the topic. Or at least, Liz thought they had. When was it that Tommy Ellis had slipped and told her dad? Had Ellis told anyone else?

She suspected that the deputy director of Homeland Security and the FBI agent would ask more pointed questions. Ones that couldn't be evaded as easily. Would they dare suspend them all with a hurricane coming?

Liz saw a sleek, black SUV loop around the parking lot, an Escalade with Louisiana license plates. It didn't park, though there were plenty of empty spaces in front of the building. Instead, it headed back onto Via De Luna Drive. She watched until it turned off into the Hilton Hotel.

They were here.

Her nerves tensed, and she wished she hadn't had that second Red Bull.

FOURTEEN

Scott Larsen hadn't taken time to change out of his suit from Sunday-morning service at First United Christ. Trish was used to him dropping her off at home before he headed over to the funeral home, but this morning she had been on edge about the hurricane.

"We need to start thinking about what we're going to do," she nagged at him all the way home. "We probably need some plywood to board up the patio doors."

"The thing hasn't even gotten into the Gulf yet," Scott had countered.

He was impatient with all this worry over something that might not even come their way. Besides, he hated leaving Joe Black the run of his embalming room. The guy insisted Scott give him a key and security code so he could start work. Other than accepting delivery and providing temporary cold storage of a few specimens for Black to pick up en route to one of his doctors' conferences, *this* was their first real business dealing.

After months of listening to Joe Black talk—actually there

was more insinuation than talk—about the impressive network, the major connections to doctors and medical equipment companies, and all the "big money" there was waiting to be made, Scott had jumped at the chance when Black finally invited him to be a major player. And Scott had already been paid handsomely for the storage fees. It was Joe who told him how to contract with the county to handle indigents. That little tip would bring in five hundred dollars a shot, just for accepting and processing the bodies. Plus, Joe Black was going to pay him another five hundred each. Scott didn't have to lift a finger.

It was a win-win situation. He couldn't believe his good fortune. And it came at just the right time. Trish had long ago overspent their budget on the house they were building. He hadn't told her that he decided to forgo buying hurricane insurance for it. How was he supposed to afford it when they were still paying renter's insurance on their condo plus the insurance on the funeral home? Now it was too late. He couldn't buy insurance after the first of June, when hurricane season started. This one sure as hell better take a turn and stay far away. Then he reminded himself that it wasn't even in the Gulf.

Some days he truly felt like a transplant down here in Florida. Just last week someone at one of his memorial services called him "a Yankee" and jokingly told him, "But maybe you won't become a 'damn Yankee.'"

"What's a damn Yankee?" Scott wanted to know.

"One that stays."

Days like this, Scott wondered why he hadn't insisted they

live in Michigan. He'd been lured by those emerald-green waters and sandy beaches. And Trish in a bikini, though she hardly ever wore one now that they were married, even though they lived right on the bay.

Scott drove around the one-story funeral home that looked remarkably like an oversize ranch house. Every time he pulled into the parking lot he felt a swell of pride. It was all his . . . his and the bank's: three viewing rooms, chapel, visitors' lounge, and corner office. The embalming room and storage facility were in a separate building that connected to the back of the funeral home via an air-conditioned walkway.

He'd added the twenty-five-foot walkway. It was crazy going even that short distance in a suit and tie and getting sweaty from the humidity or drenched from a downpour. He insisted on presenting a clean, crisply pressed appearance. Likewise, his entire place was kept meticulously.

The public areas—the viewing rooms and visitors' lounge—were vacuumed daily, stocked with fresh flowers, furniture aligned at straight angles with ample room for foot traffic as well as coffin traffic. Even the back area that included the embalming room and walk-in refrigerator was spotless. The stainless-steel tables and shelves gleamed. The white linoleum floors and porcelain basins always had a glossy finish. The state inspectors constantly praised Scott and told him they wished all the places they had to inspect looked this good.

Now as he pulled up to the back door his eyes darted around, looking for a vehicle. Joe Black had been driving something different every time they'd met. Scott figured he must use various leased cars or perhaps rentals. Last night Joe had walked up the beach so Scott hadn't even seen what he was driving. But there wasn't a vehicle anywhere in sight. Could he have finished already? Or maybe he hadn't started yet.

Scott disarmed the alarm system and had his key in the door when he heard something rattling against the back of the building. He stopped and leaned around the corner. A rusted old shopping cart had been wedged between the trunk of a magnolia tree and his Dumpster.

Damn! He hated people snooping around his property, leaving trash. It cost money to empty that frickin' Dumpster.

He was shaking his head, still cursing under his breath, when he went inside. He immediately reset the alarm.

Scott understood that there were specific reasons why he had become a mortician. He didn't really like working with people. Sure, he had to advise and guide the bereaved, but it was easier to work with people when they were at their most vulnerable. They automatically looked to him as the expert. There was a built-in respect that came with the job title.

He actually didn't mind working with dead people. Trish insisted that much of what he did was creepy and gross: the makeup, hairstyling, and clothes. Sometimes he had to paint the skin or sew up leaking orifices. And there were the plastic lenses he inserted beneath the eyelids to keep the eyes from popping open in the middle of a memorial.

Even the blood didn't bother him. You drained it out and replaced it with embalming fluid. Oh sure, you couldn't avoid blood leaking out sometimes, but it never sprayed or splattered like it did from a live, pumping heart. And yet, despite all the awkward and messy jobs Scott had done, nothing had prepared him for what he saw.

He backed up and stayed in the doorway, his hand pressed against the wall, needing it to steady himself.

Pink liquid pooled on the white linoleum floor and filled the troughs alongside the stainless-steel tables. A cardboard box blocked his entry, the type Scott used for bodies transported to the crematory, only this one held wadded-up bundles of clothes. On one of the tables lay a torso—the head, arms, and legs gone. On the other lay a corpse. It looked peaceful until Scott realized its knees and feet were cut off and lying in between its legs.

Joe Black stood at the counter. When he turned around, Scott saw the front of his lab gown, his latex gloves, and his shoe covers, all soaked with blood.

"Oh hey, Scott, you're just in time. I could use some help."

FIFTEEN

Maggie stared at the helicopter and the orange flight suit being handed to her. Obviously she hadn't given it enough thought when she asked to see the crime scene. It was the Coast Guard, for God's sake. Didn't they use boats?

A helicopter. She felt her knees go a bit weak. She could barely handle being trapped on a commercial airliner. How the hell was she supposed to do a helicopter?

"Wouldn't it be easier to take a look from a boat?" she asked, still not accepting the flight suit that the young woman offered.

She hoped the question didn't sound ridiculous. Already she felt a bit sick to her stomach just from the thought of climbing into the helicopter. She pushed her sunglasses up and crossed her arms, pretending it was no big deal how they proceeded. She didn't want the aircrew to interpret her hesitancy as fear. The slip, the tell would not be a great start to the investigation, and it would certainly hamper her credibility, let alone her authority. A refusal or even hesitancy would be a mistake, especially with this macho group. All of them were young (with the exception of Pete Kesnick), lean, and muscular, even the woman, the rescue swimmer named Elizabeth Bailey.

Earlier Maggie had watched Bailey don her wet suit instead of a flight suit, slipping the formfitting one-piece over the plain white shorts and white CG tank top that showed off her tanned, long legs and broad shoulders but failed to hide her femininity—full breasts and small waist. She wore her sun-bleached hair short, easy to slip under the wet suit's hood which she kept at the back of her neck, ready instead for the flight helmet she held under her arm.

"We're the crew that found the cooler," the pilot, Lieutenant Commander Wilson, told Maggie. "We're an aircrew." He was saying it slowly as though explaining it to a child and Maggie realized she had no choice. "Is there a problem?"

During their introductions she had detected an air of annoyance from Wilson. Forever the profiler she had already decided it wasn't due to the inconvenience but rather that he believed what Maggie was asking was somehow beneath his pay grade. At first she thought his reaction might be a knee-jerk prejudice against Wurth as a black authority figure or herself as a woman. Wurth had left after the introductions to begin his own pre-hurricane duties. And since Wilson's attitude hadn't left with Wurth, Maggie realized she might be the one Wilson had a problem with. It was silly to give his prejudices any credence.

"No problem," Maggie answered. "Just hate to take you away from more important things."

Wilson nodded, satisfied. The other two men, Kesnick and

Ellis, simply returned to their preparations. But Bailey caught Maggie's eyes as she offered the flight suit again. And in that brief exchange, Maggie realized that Bailey had recognized her fear. Would the woman give her away? Put Maggie in her place?

Bailey handed Maggie the suit, holding on to it a count longer than necessary. With her back turned to the men she let Maggie see that she was slipping something into the flight suit's pocket.

"It's gonna be choppy out there today," Bailey told her. "Be sure to buckle in tight."

Then she left to pack the rest of her own gear, including a small bag with basic medical supplies. That's when Maggie remembered that rescue swimmers were also certified EMTs.

Maggie slipped off her shoes and started putting on the flight suit. The aircrew no longer took any interest in her as they completed their preparations. She fingered the plastic inside the pocket, cupping it in the palm of her hand before bringing out two pink-and-white capsules.

Dramamine? Benadryl? Neither worked for her.

It wasn't about motion sickness. It was about losing control. It was a thoughtful and gracious gesture, and on closer inspection Maggie noticed the capsules were not over-the-counter medication. Instead, the small print on the plastic package read: *Zingiber officinale.*

She looked up at Bailey but the young woman was climbing into the helicopter. Maggie's nausea started to churn as she watched the others putting on their helmets and gloves. Soon her heart would start to race, followed by the cold sweats.

What the hell, she thought. Maybe the capsules were something new they gave to rescued survivors. Or maybe it was some prank to make the FBI lady sicker than a dog. At this point, Maggie realized that she was willing to take her chances.

She tugged open the plastic, popped the capsules into her mouth, and dry-swallowed them. Then shc pulled on her helmet and headed for the helicopter, trying to ignore the wobble in her knees.

SIXTEEN

Scott worried that he might throw up. He'd never seen body pieces. Not like this, carved and lined up, set out to rinse and wrap. His face must have registered his discomfort.

"How did you think it was done, buddy?" Joe Black asked, pushing his goggles up onto his tousled hair. "Unfortunately, there's nothing dignified about disarticulating a body. It's a messy job."

"I guess I just . . . it's not what I expected."

He couldn't move. Couldn't stop his eyes from darting around the room. He didn't want to step over the cardboard coffin stretched out in front of him. He didn't want to step into the room at all.

"You'll get used to it," Joe assured him.

Joe picked up what looked like an ordinary carving knife. He glanced at Scott, caught him wincing, and put the knife back down.

"It's a bit weird at first." There was no condescending tone, more instructive like a teacher to a student. "You learn a lot by simply doing it. A bit of trial and error. Actually, it's not that different from carving a Thanksgiving turkey." He smiled at Scott.

Joe turned back to the counter, picked up one of the pieces. Scott couldn't tell what it was. He didn't want to look and yet he found himself mesmerized by Joe's hands pulling plastic wrap and folding it over and over with a slow, almost reverent touch.

"I try not to be wasteful," Joe continued, keeping his back to Scott as he started wrapping the next piece in line. "It's the least we can do when people are generous enough to donate their bodies. Right? Every week surgeons are learning some new, innovative technique. And they'd never be able to do that without me providing working models."

Scott appreciated that Joe didn't draw attention to his reaction. Instead, Joe remained calm while Scott was acting like a total jerk. He knew exactly what he had signed up for and had read plenty about the subject. He had no illusions about what were in the previous packages that Joe Black had sent to him to store. Although he had to admit that it was certainly easier when he could accept the UPS or FedEx deliveries and cart the packages into his walk-in refrigerator or put them in one of his freezers.

All along he knew the packages contained body parts that were used for educational conferences and for research. Early on Joe had bragged about the surgical conferences that were his specialty. On paper and in his mind, Scott Larsen had justified the extra income as a noble service. So he needed to get over his squeamishness.

Like embalming and cremation, this, too, was just business.

"You really have a nice facility here," Joe told him, glancing around as he started to work on the torso that was left on the other table. "And don't worry. I'll clean everything up. Get it sparkling the way you had it."

"Oh, I'm not worried about that."

Scott hated to think Joe might believe he had a problem with any of this. In an attempt to restore their camaraderie Scott tried to take interest in what Joe was doing. "So I guess you have orders for all these different . . . parts?"

"More orders than I can supply." He took out a jar of Vicks VapoRub, dipped a gob, and started smearing it on the torso. "It's hard to keep up."

"What's that you're doing?"

"A little trick of the trade. The torsos are popular with medical-device companies to showcase their new equipment, to teach a new technique. Sometimes the surgeons'll work on them for several hours and, well, I don't have to tell you. A couple of hours and you know how bad it'll start smelling."

"Oh sure."

"I rub Vicks VapoRub into the skin before I freeze it. Then when it defrosts it smells like menthol. Which is much better than what it ordinarily smells like."

"Wow. That's really . . . smart."

"You morticians have plenty of your own tricks, right? You guys are like magicians when it comes to making corpses look good. Sometimes even better than what they looked like when they were alive."

"Families have high expectations."

Before Scott realized it, Joe had him talking about his own

techniques. He even told Joe how he cheated sometimes and left off the socks and shoes because he hated dealing with feet. He couldn't even remember when he stepped over the cardboard coffin and came into the room. Soon he was gowned up, rinsing and wrapping, and telling more stories. Even made Joe laugh a couple of times. They cleaned up the room together and planned to meet for drinks later in the evening on the beach.

Scott had gotten so carried away, actually having a good time, that it wasn't until after Joe had left that he realized he'd never asked where he parked. Nor had he dared to ask him about the second body.

SEVENTEEN

Liz watched the FBI agent grip the leather restraints in her gloved fists. She was pretty good at feigning confidence, making it sound like this ride was no big deal, even asking questions about the fishing cooler in sound bites as though she was used to the abrupt shouting conversations of a helicopter. Despite all that, she hadn't fooled Liz at all. For whatever reason, the woman had panicked back there on the beach the minute she realized she'd need to climb into the copter.

So far O'Dell appeared to be doing okay. But just as Wilson turned the helicopter around after hovering over the spot where they had found the cooler yesterday, a call came in. A boat had capsized. A recreational-fishing cabin cruiser. At least one person was in the water. Initial radio contact reported injuries. Contact since had been lost.

"Sorry, Agent O'Dell," Wilson shouted over his helmet mike. "We won't have time to drop you off."

That's when Liz first noticed O'Dell's white-knuckled grip. Now she wondered if the FBI agent would last. Liz couldn't ask whether she had taken the capsules she'd slipped to her.

Though they were definitely not a miracle cure, she hoped O'Dell had trusted her. Otherwise she'd be feeling sick very soon. In the short time since they left the beach the winds had picked up over the Gulf. Away from shore, the seas were kicking high. And now, so was Liz's adrenaline.

They found the boat quickly. Liz kept her helmet on, staying connected to their ICS while they figured this one out.

The cabin cruiser had tilted but hadn't rolled yet. The waves were battering it and had already broken apart some of the cockpit and the rail. One person bobbed in the water, not more than a head in a life jacket with an arm hanging on to a torn piece of the cockpit that dangled, barely attached to the boat. A dog, what looked to Liz like a black Labrador, paced the deck, watching his owner while trying to keep his balance.

"Radio's completely out?" Kesnick asked.

"Doesn't matter. He can't reach it," Ellis said.

"Looks like only one rescue," Wilson said.

"We can't drop the basket in the water," Kesnick told them. "Current will pull them under the boat."

"Then where the hell are you dropping it?" Wilson asked.

Liz glanced at O'Dell, who was watching her prepare. Was O'Dell wondering why the men didn't ask what she thought?

Silently Liz was planning her own strategy. Stay away from that railing. Don't put any extra weight on the tip-side or it'll roll. The boat was moving with the current, and as soon as Wilson dropped into hover the rotor wash would set the boat rocking. Initial radio contact reported injuries. If they dropped the basket onto the tilted boat, Liz would have to find a way to roll him out of the water debris, back onto the boat, and into the rescue basket.

"Direct deployment's gonna be tricky," Kesnick was saying. "Don't push it or strain yourself. Let me do the dropping."

Liz realized he was talking to her. She looked up at him.

"Let me do the heavy lifting, Bailey. We may need to quick strop him just to get him into the basket. Get it under his arms and let me hoist him while you guide him into the basket. Okay? I don't wanna lose you both under that damned boat. You got that?"

She nodded. Gave him a thumbs-up. Let out a long breath. She started to remove her helmet when she heard Wilson.

"We've got one rescue, Bailey. Unless you find someone else in the water, that basket is only coming up once. We're not sending it down again for that dog. You understand, Bailey? This isn't New Orleans after Katrina. That dog is not coming up. It'll have to wait for the cutter."

She yanked off the helmet without a response. As Liz tucked her hair into her surf hood and strapped on her Seda helmet, she purposely avoided O'Dell's eyes.

She readjusted her harness and rechecked her restraints. Her adrenaline was pumping and she needed to calm it down a notch, just enough to let it work for her, not against her. They could talk all they wanted, analyze and discuss to the last detail, but once she was out on that cable it was Liz who'd be balancing on the edge of that tilted cruiser. It'd be up to Liz to maneuver the survivor before a lift could even be made. And it'd be Liz's ass if it didn't work.

She scooted into position at the door. Kesnick waited for

her glance then held her eyes a beat longer than usual. "Let me help you on this." Maybe he had read her mind.

She nodded and he tapped her chest. She gave him a thumbs-up and crawled out. She slid down just a few feet to stop and wait for the hoist cable to tighten, but instead the wind caught it. The cable looped and bucked then jerked Liz like she was hanging on to the end of a whip. The rotor wash twisted her, pushing her in one direction then the other. Another jerk wrenched her spine. That's when she started to spin. It was like getting sucked up into a wind tunnel.

All Liz could see was a blur as she hung tight to the cable. She closed her eyes and dug her heels down around the cable, managing to keep her feet crossed at the ankles. She tucked her chin into her chest so the cable didn't wind around her neck. She made her body as rigid as possible.

She did everything she was taught to do. But the spin only accelerated.

EIGHTEEN

Maggie watched the rescue swimmer jump out of the helicopter one minute and within seconds she saw the flight mechanic, Kesnick, stumble and slide, diving headfirst toward the open door as if he were being sucked out behind Bailey.

Maggie reacted on instinct. She ripped at her restraints, her gloved fingers taking too long to break herself free. She grabbed for his safety belt that remained hooked into the deck of the cabin. She hadn't even seen the hoist cable snag Kesnick's helmet. Instead, she followed the safety belt's line, using its tautness to pull herself to her feet.

She heard Wilson and Ellis trying to figure out what the hell was going on. She couldn't see them and didn't take precious time to wait until she could. Instead, she gripped Kesnick's belt and pulled with all her weight. It was enough to jerk Kesnick out of his freefall stance. But the hoist cable that had caught his helmet still whipped his head back in the direction of the open door.

Kesnick let out a scream from the pain. For a brief, sick moment, Maggie worried it might have broken his neck. Her eyes followed the cable from its snag on his helmet to a hook on the top of the open door. She couldn't reach the hoist cable but she could reach his helmet. She clawed at it, trying to remember what clicked into what.

Wilson and Ellis were yelling at each other, at Kesnick, at Maggie. Then the helicopter shifted and rocked, slinging Kesnick backward, his head in her gut. His helmet-less head. Thank God. She saw the cable snap and fling Kesnick's helmet out the door.

Maggie grabbed on to a leather strap attached to the wall just as the helicopter rocked again and her feet started to slide toward the door. Wilson grunted a string of curses before he rocked it back and held steady.

Amazingly Kesnick was already on his knees crawling back to his feet.

Ellis yelled, "Are you okay, man?"

But without his helmet, Kesnick didn't hear and couldn't respond. He hurried back to the open doorway, clutching his safety belt still tethered by the line to the floor. He leaned out to look down for Bailey. Maggie had forgotten about the rescue swimmer. Was she still even there? Kesnick reached for the hoist cable, wrestling and jerking it until the loop that had knotted on the hook broke loose. Somehow he managed to tug it free.

"What about the rescue swimmer?" Ellis yelled at Kesnick's back.

Maggie heard the howling wind roar through the helicopter. The thump-thump of the rotors and thump-thump of her heartbeat made it difficult to hear the words and she knew it was impossible for Kesnick to hear anything without the communication system inside the helmet.

She held tight to the leather strap, readjusted her weight, and shoved herself up onto her feet. Still holding on to the strap, she swiped up Bailey's flight helmet from where she had left it and tapped Kesnick on the shoulder with it. His eyes shot her a look of surprise then he nodded, yanked on the helmet, and adjusted the mike.

"Liz's caught in a crosswind," Kesnick yelled. "She's spinning."

"Son of a bitch," Wilson answered.

"I'm pulling her back," Kesnick said, planting his feet.

In seconds Kesnick had Bailey back inside the helicopter.

Maggie handed Liz her own helmet. Then Maggie sat against the wall, gripping the leather strap with gloved fingers, noticing now how badly her hands were shaking. She could no longer hear the conversation taking place. Both Kesnick and Bailey looked remarkably calm.

It seemed like less than a couple of minutes and Bailey handed the helmet back to Maggie, replacing it with her lighter-weight swim helmet. Maggie checked her eyes in that brief exchange. There was no hesitation. No fear.

Bailey scooted back to the open doorway, waited for Kesnick's tap on the chest, gave him a thumbs-up, and to Maggie's disbelief, the young rescue swimmer rolled out of the helicopter again.

NINETEEN

Platt stared at the dead boy's face. He looked so much younger than the nineteen years recorded on his chart. Stripped of everything, including his life, his gray body appeared small, his prosthetic leg emphasizing his vulnerabilities. It gnawed at Platt to think that this brave kid survived Afghanistan and his battle wounds only to come home and die from some mysterious disease.

Gowned up again, Platt stood beside the stainless-steel autopsy table going over the chart when he realized the pathologist, Dr. Anslo, was waiting for him. The man's almost nonexistent eyebrows were raised, their presence distinct only because Anslo's shaved head and smooth face left nothing else to forecast his emotions. His latex-gloved hands were held up in front of him, signaling that he was ready—ready and waiting for this guest who had been imposed on him.

Platt quickly found what he was searching for: the boy's name, Ronald (Ronnie) William Towers. It was a small thing, but he wanted to know how to address this young man, if nowhere else but in his own mind. It was the least he could do. Ronnie Towers deserved that small, last respect.

"I'm ready," said Platt.

This part of his job always challenged his sensibilities. It didn't help matters that he had just returned from Afghanistan and had witnessed the carnage that young men like Ronnie had to deal with every day of their tours. It battered his psyche as much as the exhaustion did. Each trip to Afghanistan or Iraq reminded Platt why, as an army doctor, he had chosen laboratories filled with vials, test tubes, and glass slides rather than the OR.

"I'll need a vial of his blood."

Anslo gave a terse nod as though Platt was wasting time telling him something he already knew.

"And a tissue sample."

"Fine," Anslo said, shifting his weight in an exaggerated show of impatience as he continued to hold up his hands, waiting for instructions.

"Would you mind starting at the surgical site?" Platt asked.

The man's long, drawn-out sigh told Platt exactly what Anslo thought of his request. He didn't, however, refuse.

"If you tell me what you're looking for, perhaps I could help."

"I don't know."

"You don't know?"

"No," Platt admitted and avoided Anslo's eyes.

Since he arrived, Platt had tried to sift through as many of the files as possible looking for some common thread. All of the injuries had begun as compound bone fractures with deep tissue and bone exposed to open air for an extended period.

Dr. Anslo disconnected Ronnie's prosthetic, set it aside, and began on the surgical site just below his knee.

"Everything looks quite normal," he told Platt without glancing up at him. "If you're searching for an infection, I don't believe you'll find it here."

Initially Platt had thought it might be an airborne bacterium. In Iraq he had seen a bone infection called osteomyelitis (OM), prevalent in the Middle East. It often occurred in severe fractures where the bone was left exposed. But OM wasn't fatal or life-threatening. Sometimes, though rarely, it cost a soldier his limb. And sometimes it led to or acted as a primer for *methicillin-resistant Staphylococcus aureus*, MRSA.

Captain Ganz had told Platt there was now a compound, a bone cement pumped full of antibiotics, that allowed them to apply those antibiotics directly to the fracture site, reducing such infections. In addition, Ganz had tested for MRSA. The tests were negative. Platt should have known that it was too easy of an answer.

If not MRSA, Platt wondered, then what? Was it possibly another deadly pathogen that resembled MRSA and was not only resistant to antibiotics but could also lie dormant, hidden inside the cells, waiting for something to trigger it into action? Could a bone infection like OM mutate into something fatal? Given the right ingredients—like an open-air wound, a deep-tissue, bone-exposed wound—anything was possible. Platt had seen it happen before. But not like this. Invisible with no initial symptoms.

Dr. Anslo was staring at him again. The raised eyebrows showing his discontent while he waited for instructions.

"Go ahead," Platt told him. "Proceed with your normal routine." But before Dr. Anslo began the Y incision down Ronnie Towers's chest, Platt said to him, "Do you mind if I take this for twenty-four hours." He pointed at Ronnie's prosthetic.

"You want to take his leg?" This time Anslo didn't need a facial expression to show his disgust. His voice did it for him.

Without apology, Platt said, "Yes. Would that be okay?"

"I'll have the diener help you fill out the necessary form. May I proceed?" He pointed his chin toward his hands waiting over the boy's chest.

Platt nodded. As a medical doctor, cutting into live tissue was lifesaving. Cutting into dead tissue seemed . . . such a waste. He was relieved when Anslo turned his back to him so he couldn't see Platt wince.

TWENTY

Liz felt the adrenaline kick in again. The wind continued to whip at her. It took Kesnick three attempts to deploy her within reach of the fishing cruiser. Once, the wind shoved her over it. The second time her toes brushed the rail before the waves swept the tilted deck and the boat out of reach. The whole time she kept her eye on the dog, making sure it didn't decide to protect its master by attacking her. The dog, however, just watched.

The third time a wave crested and shoved the boat up to meet her. Liz kicked her feet out, twisting and jerking her body until she touched the deck. She prayed that her flippers didn't trip her as she caught the slippery railing with her heels just as Kesnick loosened the deployment cable. She slid down between the tilted deck and the railing.

The dog had stayed put, watching his master, almost pointing his nose into the water. His eyes followed Liz. Despite the howl of the wind and the crash of the waves she thought she could hear the dog moan. That's when she noticed the second dog inside the cabin. From the helicopter, the roof had hidden his existence. He was larger than the first dog but his weight didn't cause a shift. He paced back and forth, following the natural sway of the disabled boat.

Liz kept herself from glancing up at the helicopter. No sense in telegraphing this problem too early.

Kesnick gave more slack for her to maneuver over the sinking boat. She knew her extra weight could capsize it. She crawled slowly toward the man. He wasn't moving. It wasn't until she was within five feet that she saw his eyes watching her. A good sign. Shock hadn't completely debilitated him.

His arm draped over the railing was the only thing that prevented him from floating away from the boat, but it lay at an odd angle. He wasn't hanging on. He was caught, the arm most likely broken. It must have happened when he flipped overboard, keeping him out of the water from the waist up. That is, when the waves weren't crushing his legs against the boat.

When Liz could safely reach out without further tilting the deck, she grabbed on to his life jacket. His eyes grew wider. The slight movement had reminded him of the pain. She wouldn't be able to use the quick strop on him. The harness was meant to fit under the survivor's arms. She'd need them to deploy the basket. She took a cable hooked to her belt and started to wind it around the man's waist. If nothing else, it would prevent him from getting sucked under the boat if it capsized.

Then she waved up at the helicopter, giving the signal to send down the basket. This, too, presented a challenge. The winds swept the basket in every direction but down to Liz.

They couldn't put it in the water for the same reason she had attached the cable to the man's waist. The basket could get sucked under. Kesnick would need to place it right on the deck, steadying it with the cable so it didn't add weight to the boat.

This took several tries.

"I'm not going without my dogs," the man told Liz as she wrestled him up.

"I've been told the dogs can't go. They'll need to wait for the cutter."

He shoved at her, wincing at the pain in his arm. "Then I'll wait with them."

Again, Liz avoided glancing up at the helicopter. Had they seen him push her away? They might just think she hurt him.

"Either one of them a biter?" she asked.

He was silent and she knew immediately that he didn't want to condemn one or the other.

"Sir, you're gonna have to trust me."

"He only did it once and he was defending me."

"This one," she said turning her head, avoiding any gestures the helicopter crew might interpret.

"Yeah, Benny."

"And the other one?"

"He's a big baby. Can't you tell?" he said with a smile, but it disappeared when he said, "I didn't buy them life jackets. I can't believe I thought I'd save a couple of bucks." He shook his head, biting his lip. But it wasn't pain this time. It was regret. "You can't leave them. Please."

Liz guessed the guy was in his forties, small-framed—thank

God—and an amateur fisherman. Later she'd ask if the boat was new, perhaps a splurge. His foolish attempt at recreation had almost cost him his life. And now she knew it might very well cost her own neck.

TWENTY-ONE

Maggie slid into a position close enough to the open doorway that she could watch Bailey. Whatever the woman had given her earlier seemed to be helping. She wasn't nauseated; however, her stomach dived every time Bailey plunged. It didn't matter that the rescue swimmer was attached to the helicopter by a cable. Each attempt to drop her onto the boat looked more like a circus stunt gone horribly wrong.

Kesnick relayed every move step-by-step to his other two crew members. Minutes ago he said there might be a problem.

"The guy's refusing to get into the basket."

"From what I've heard," Ellis said, "she was able to talk her way around some real crazies in New Orleans after Katrina."

"What do mean, talk her way around?" Wilson wanted to know.

"You heard about some of the situations. The crew would hover down over a flooded area where a couple of people were stranded, and as soon as the rescue swimmer got down there other people swarmed out demanding rescue. Some nasty dudes, too. I guess Bailey had to tell them women and children or injured got first priority. They didn't much like it."

"So what happened?"

"She said what she needed to, to get them to listen to her."

"Humph."

Maggie glanced over at Wilson. His grunt sounded like he wasn't impressed.

"She's getting him in the basket," Kesnick announced.

"All right." Ellis pumped a fist.

"It's about time. Pull him up," Wilson told him.

"No signal yet."

More minutes ticked by and then Maggie realized what Bailey was up to right about the same time Kesnick did. She saw him glance back at his pilot as if looking for a way to not report what was going on below.

"What's the holdup?" Wilson wanted to know.

No answer.

"Kesnick, what the hell's going on?"

"I think she's bringing the dog up with the guy."

"She's not bringing up that dog, Kesnick." Wilson's anger rocked the controls and the helicopter jerked to the right.

"She's putting the dog in on top of the guy."

"You have got to be kidding me," Ellis yelled, but Maggie thought it sounded like he was smiling.

"I told her not to bring up that dog."

Maggie saw Bailey wave the all clear and up, and Kesnick didn't hesitate. He concentrated on raising the basket, keeping it steady. Maggie watched Bailey down below. She had crawled back farther onto the deck, under the cabin roof.

Kesnick pulled and yanked, getting the basket into the helicopter's cabin, sliding and grinding it over the entry. The whole time his attention was focused on the survivor and the dog. Maggie knew Kesnick hadn't even seen the second dog that Bailey had dragged from the cabin. She had it clutched tight to her chest and managed to harness it to her safety belt.

"Son of a bitch," Kesnick said as he grasped the deployment cable.

"What now?" Wilson asked.

Maggie glanced between Wilson and Kesnick while watching the survivor settle against the cabin wall, hugging what looked like a broken arm. The dog stayed close to his owner, panting and licking the man's hand. Maggie was glad he couldn't hear the exchange between Kesnick and Wilson.

"There's a second dog," Kesnick finally admitted.

"She better not be bringing up another dog."

"She's bringing up the second dog."

"Don't raise that dog up."

"She has it in the quick strop. She's holding it."

"Son of a bitch. Don't raise her up, Kesnick. Leave her butt down there until she puts that damn dog back."

Maggie watched Kesnick's face, the half she could see below his eye shield. She thought she saw a hint of a smile. What Wilson didn't realize and couldn't see was that the flight mechanic already had Bailey halfway up. She was almost to the helicopter.

TWENTY-TWO

Walter Bailey flipped over the open sign on his Coney Island Canteen. It was later than he'd like. Sundays were big days for him, but he'd promised his daughter Liz that he'd get gasoline first. He'd gotten extra and took a couple of five-gallon canisters to his other daughter, Trish. As he'd suspected, his son-in-law, Scott, hadn't even thought about preparing for the hurricane. Trish, as always, defended her husband.

"He's from Michigan, Dad. He has no idea what a hurricane means."

"He'll learn quickly. This one is on its way."

Walter hadn't really believed that when he said it. But it made him mad that Scott chose to "run into work"—as Trish put it—instead of helping his wife prepare. It was a father's overprotective instinct kicking in, but he didn't like Scott Larsen. Sometimes that slipped out. Lately he didn't care. Trish deserved better. Though everyone believed this young man was a charming, hardworking, devoted husband, Walter saw beyond the veneer. Maybe it was just Scott's profession that annoyed Walter. In his mind, morticians were just better-dressed salesmen.

By the time Walter got to Pensacola Beach, the winds had kicked up and surfers were riding the waves. It was what Walter liked to call "beatin' down" hot, not a strip of shade or cool around.

He had a line of customers before the first set of dogs were ready, but Walter enjoyed chatting and could make his hot, hungry customers laugh and share stories. His career as a navy pilot and commander not only made for good entertainment but also had trained him well in convincing people that his mission was their mission. They weren't just buying a hot dog and Coke from the Coney Island Canteen, they were paying tribute to Walter's boyhood. Okay, so perhaps the salesman in him simply recognized the salesman in Scott.

The crowd thinned out, finally replaced by a young guy—no more than thirty. Neat, short-cropped hair. Dressed in khaki walking shorts, a purple polo shirt—though Walter's wife would have corrected him and called it lavender—and Sperry deck shoes. Walter's wife had taught him how to dress. After thirty-five years of wearing a uniform he had no idea who Ralph Lauren was. But now he did and recognized the logo on the lavender shirt. He noticed other details, too—like the gold Rolex and Ray-Bans—without showing that he noticed. The guy was probably not a tourist. Maybe a businessman. He didn't look like he knew anything about boats, though Walter had seen better-dressed amateurs step off some of the yachts in the marina. It was ridiculous what people thought they needed to wear these days, even for recreation.

"What can I get on it?" the guy asked.

"Just about anything you want."

"Green peppers?"

"Sure. Green peppers, kraut, onions."

Walter thought he recognized the guy but couldn't place him.

"All of that sounds good. Add some mustard and relish. So what's with the Coney Island getup? You from New York?"

"Nope. Pennsylvania. But my daddy took us to Coney Island a couple of times for vacation. Those were some of the best days. You been to Coney Island?"

"No. But my dad talked about it. Where in Pennsylvania?"

"Upper Darby."

"Get out. Really?"

Walter stopped with a forkful of kraut to look at the guy. "You know Upper Darby?"

"My dad grew up in Philadelphia. He talked about Upper Darby."

"Is that right?" Walter finished, wrapped the hot dog in a napkin, nestled it into a paper dish, and handed it to the guy. "Would I know him? Where'd he go to high school?"

"You know, I'm not sure. He died a few years ago. Cancer. His name was Phillip Norris. He didn't stay in Philadelphia. Joined the navy."

"Retired navy," Walter said, pointing a thumb to his chest.

"No kidding?" The guy took a careful bite of the hot dog, nodded, and smiled. "This is one good dog."

"One hundred percent beef."

"Hey, Mr. B," a scrawny kid interrupted.

"Danny, my boy. Ready for your regular?"

"Yes, sir."

"Danny here is quite the entrepreneur." Walter always tried to bring his customers together.

"Is that right?"

"Working on the beach cleanup crew and living out of his car to save money."

"And to surf," Danny added.

"His surfboard is worth more than his car."

Danny shrugged and smiled. Walter knew the boy enjoyed the attention. He wasn't sure what the kid's story was. He looked about fifteen but Walter had seen his driver's license and it listed him at eighteen and from someplace in Kansas. Maybe the kid really did just want to surf.

Danny had the routine down. Worked the cleanup crew in the evenings till about eleven, slept in his car, surfed all day, used the outdoor showers on the beach and the public restrooms on the boardwalk, ate hot dogs with mustard, onion, and kraut with a Coke. Not a bad life, Walter supposed.

He handed the kid his hot dog and poured an extra-large Coke, then accepted the boy's two bucks. Their agreement. Walter figured this was the kid's only real meal of the day, so he cut him a deal.

Another line started forming. A bunch of college kids, pushing and shoving at one another.

While handing Walter a ten-dollar bill, Norris was watching Danny get into his faded red Impala. Maybe the kid reminded him of himself.

"On the house," Walter said.

That got his attention.

"I can't let you do that." The guy looked stunned like no

one had ever said that to him before. “Besides, I can more than afford it,” he said, swinging his head and his eyes back in Danny’s direction.

“I know you can. Come back and buy one tomorrow. That one’s on me. For your daddy—one vet to another. Now go enjoy. You’re holding up my traffic.”

Norris wandered off to the side, glancing at the people behind him. The ten-dollar bill stayed in his hand like he didn’t know what to do with it. He thought he might have offended the guy. That he might stick around and try to pay him again.

Walter wished he could figure out what was so familiar about him, even though the name Phillip Norris didn’t ring any bells. He realized he should ask where his dad was stationed in the navy. But when he looked up the guy was gone.

TWENTY-THREE

Scott Larsen ignored his ringing cell phone. It was either a grieving family calling to nag or it was Trish, and he didn't want to talk to her, either. After a quick glance he continued through the hotel lobby. It was Trish. She didn't appreciate him leaving again, even if it was for business. She'd gotten herself worked up about this frickin' hurricane. He was getting so tired of everybody worrying about this storm when there wasn't a cloud in the sky.

Trish had probably remembered one more thing to harangue him about. Something else her daddy had done for her.

"Daddy brought us some gasoline," she had told him earlier.

"Wow. He spent his entire week's hot-dog money."

"That's rude. He was being gracious."

"Taking care of his little girl."

"Maybe he thought he had to because her husband wasn't doing a very good job."

"I'm off making a living. Paying the bills."

"If this hurricane hits, none of that will matter."

And by this time she had worked herself into angry tears, which automatically clicked Scott into his professional comforter role. He'd put an arm around her shoulder, instigated the combination hand pat while whispering a series of soothing words and phrases.

By the time she spoke again the hitch in her voice was gone.

"I guess we just have to hope our insurance covers everything."

That knocked Scott cold. No way he could tell her now that he hadn't taken out insurance on their new place, the dream house that had already skyrocketed over their budget and would almost be finished if his wife would quit changing and adding.

"Daddy said we can stay with him during the hurricane. We can't stay here on the bay. We'll be safe at Daddy's."

By then Scott hadn't been listening anymore except to the key words that irritated him. Words like "daddy." Southern girls sure did love their daddies. Scott would never get used to that term of endearment. Not from a grown woman. Daddy was what a five-year-old called his father.

Trish had pouted a little while he changed clothes but didn't say much more before he left. His Midwest work ethic was one characteristic she found appealing after all the deadbeats she'd dated. Besides he promised he'd help her board up the patio doors at their new house in the morning as long as they were finished by noon. He had to move up a memorial service for a stiff in his fridge. The family had originally scheduled for Wednesday but now they were all freaked about the hurricane and wanted to bury Uncle Mel before the storm hit.

Promising to help board up had seemed to satisfy Trish. So maybe she wasn't calling just to nag at him. He pulled out his cell phone as he sat down at the hotel's deck bar. He was just about to listen to Trish's voice message when the blond bartender appeared in front of him.

"Your friend's already here," she told him with a smile. "He said to tell you to meet him inside the restaurant. He's buying you dinner."

"Really?" But Scott was more impressed with the attention she was paying him than the dinner invitation.

"Why don't you guys stop out here later for a drink," she said, then hurried across the bar to wait on another customer.

Her smile made him forget why he had his cell phone out and he simply slipped it back into his shirt pocket. As he headed into the restaurant he vowed to assuage all the stress of the day. Assuage. Yes, that was a cool word, one that Joe Black would probably use. Scott decided he'd find a way to use it in their conversation.

TWENTY-FOUR

Maggie's knees felt weak. Her ears still hummed and if she looked, she knew she'd see a slight tremor in her fingers. But she was relieved to be back on the ground, away from the thumping rotors and the nerve-rattling vibration.

Escambia County sheriff Joshua Clayton was waiting for her, and everything about his tall, lanky body—from his tapping toe to his erratic gesturing—told Maggie that he wasn't happy. But he'd promised Charlie Wurth that the DHS and FBI would have full disclosure of the evidence. Clayton didn't seem to have a problem with allowing access. It was his time he had a problem sparing, and at one point he mumbled, "I don't have time for this. There's a hurricane on its way, for Christ's sake."

Maggie had barely peeled out of her flight suit. She thanked the aircrew and they agreed to meet later for drinks on her. Clayton stood at her elbow the entire time, twisting his wrist in an exaggerated show of checking the time. Now, in his cruiser, the man was tapping out his impatience on the steering wheel.

Back at the office he handed her a form to sign then led her to a small room at the end of a hallway. There was nothing on the walls. Only a table and two folding chairs sat on the worn but clean linoleum. On the table was the battered white fishing cooler.

"Contents were photographed and bagged," Clayton told her. "They're all at the ME's office. We haven't processed the cooler yet," he said as he handed her a pair of latex gloves. "We'll dust it for prints, but with it being in the water I suspect we won't find much."

His cell phone rang. Clayton frowned at it.

"I've got to take this. You mind?"

"Go ahead."

He was out the door in three strides. Maggie couldn't help but notice that despite his initial frown, he looked relieved to have a reason to escape. His voice disappeared down the hallway. It was just as well. She preferred taking a close look without him standing over her shoulder.

She began opening the lid but snapped it shut after just a whiff of the rancid smell. She prepared herself, took a deep breath, and tried again. No wonder they hadn't processed the cooler yet. About two inches of pink liquid covered the bottom, residue from melted ice and at least one leaky package.

Maggie let the lid flap open. The initial smell would be the worst. Adding some air would dilute it. She stepped away and pulled her smartphone from its holder at her waistband. She pushed a couple buttons and activated the camera.

The cooler was huge, white paint over stainless steel. A popular name brand that even Maggie recognized was stamped on the side. The inside of the lid was unusual, with an indentation of a large fish and slots of measurement alongside it. What drew her immediate attention was the tie-down, looped around the cooler's handle.

She took several pictures, close-ups to focus on the blue-and-yellow twisted strands. The rope was made of synthetic fiber, smooth, possibly coated. One end appeared to be frayed. She took more pictures. On closer inspection it looked like the frayed end had been cut, not ripped. All the fibers, though frayed, were the exact same length.

Maggie glanced back at the door. No sight or sound of Sheriff Clayton. But, just in case, she chose to text-message her partner, R. J. Tully, rather than make a phone call.

HEY TULLY. SENDING PHOTOS. CAN U CHECK DATABASE?

It took her less than a minute to e-mail close-ups of the rope. Tully would be able to scan or download the photos and run the information through the FBI's database. Maybe they'd get lucky and be able to identify the manufacturer.

She remembered another case in the 1980s. An airman named John Joubert was arrested for murdering two little boys. Authorities found an unusual rope at one of the crime scenes. It had been used to bind the hands of one of the boys. This was before DNA analysis, so the unusual rope became a key piece of evidence. During a search of Joubert's quarters, they found a length of it.

Before she sent the last photo she had a text message from Tully.

NO PROB.

Finished with the rope, she moved on and shot photos of the cooler and the measuring tool inside the lid. Not much to see. She agreed with Sheriff Clayton's speculations about fingerprints. Maybe they'd get lucky with a print inside the lid, but the salt water had probably eliminated anything on the outside.

Maggie took a final shot of the open cooler, the smell less potent now. That's when she noticed something in the liquid. She held her breath again and leaned over for a closer look. A small piece of white paper, no larger than two inches by three inches, was stuck to the side, several inches from the bottom. Part of the paper fell below the liquid's surface and the moisture had loosened a corner. Had it not been for it flapping into the liquid, Maggie would have never noticed. And that was probably why Sheriff Clayton's staff had missed it.

She glanced over her shoulder. As she holstered her smartphone she searched the room. In a lone cupboard behind the door she found a box of ziplock bags. She grabbed one and pulled on the latex gloves Clayton had given her. Then carefully and slowly she peeled the piece of paper from the cooler wall, trying to limit her touch to the flapping corner as she eased it off little by little.

Maggie held the paper between her fingertips. She needed to be patient and let it air-dry before placing it into the plastic bag. As she waited she examined the other side of the paper. Its corners were rounded, resembling a stick-on label. The side that had been facing out was blank but the one that had been stuck to the wall of the cooler was not. The ink had bled away. Only a ghost of the hand printing remained. But Maggie could still read the three lines of letters and numbers, what looked like a code:

AMET
DESTIN: 082409
#8509000029

She glanced back inside the cooler. There was nothing else. Maybe this piece of paper didn't have a thing to do with the body parts. It could have been left over from the cooler's previous usage. Perhaps dropped in accidentally.

Or, and Maggie hoped this was the case, it had once been a label attached to one of the packages.

TWENTY-FIVE

Benjamin Platt leaned his elbows on the lab countertop. He pressed his eyes against the microscope and adjusted the magnification. Once in a while he glanced up at the test tubes he had prepared, watching for the results. Ronnie Towers's blood had already tested negative for several of Platt's best guesses. He was running out of ideas.

The small laboratory suited him despite the strong smell of disinfectants. It was well equipped and quiet, much better than the conditions he was used to on the road. Platt had learned long ago to travel with a hard-shell case filled with everything he'd need to run basic lab tests whether he was in a war zone, a hot zone, or even a tent in Sierra Leone.

He sat back on the stool and stared at the test tubes. No change. A good thing, albeit frustrating as hell. The young man's prosthetic leg rested on the counter next to him. He had carefully scraped some of the bone paste applied to the prosthetic during surgery. He smeared it on a slide then prepared a second slide from the sample tissue taken from Ronnie Towers.

What he had found so far was something he identified as a strain of *Clostridia*, a family of bacteria that caused a number of infections. The most prevalent one was tetanus. Another was sepsis leading to toxic shock syndrome. Except what Platt saw under the microscope looked more complicated.

To his left, Platt had opened his laptop, accessing a database he had worked for several years to put together. Now on the screen was a close-up of the *Clostridia* family. He needed to wait for all the files to download before he could begin clicking through the photos in his database. He hoped he would find an exact match to what he saw under his microscope.

While he waited, he pulled out his cell phone. Certainly he could get some basic information without breaking his word to Captain Ganz about keeping this situation classified.

He keyed in the number, expecting to get the voice-messaging service for the Centers for Disease Control's chief of outbreak response. Platt was surprised when Roger Bix's slow, Southern drawl answered, "This is Bix."

"Roger, it's Benjamin Platt."

"Colonel, what can I do for you?"

"I didn't expect to get you on a Sunday."

"It's a 24/7 job." He laughed. "I doubt you're calling me from a golf course. What's up?"

"I'm wondering if you have any recent reports of life-threatening infections related to . . . say, any kind of donor tissue or bone transplants?"

"Illnesses, sure. Deaths? None if your definition of recent is the last forty-eight hours. I'd have to check for sure. Are you calling to report one?"

Platt had forgotten how direct and to the point Bix could be. Not a bad thing. The last time the two men had worked together they were dealing with two separate outbreaks of Ebola.

"Just need information," Platt told him. "If there was a possible contamination at a tissue bank or a hospital, you'd know, right?"

"Depends what the contamination is. Tissue banks are required to screen donors for HIV, hepatitis B and C, and other blood-borne viruses."

"What about bacteria?"

"What kind of bacteria?"

"I don't know, Roger." He felt himself shrugging as he stared at his computer screen. "Infection-causing bacterium."

"The FDA doesn't require us to culture donors for anything beyond blood-borne viruses. Many of the accredited tissue banks don't go beyond those requirements. Infections are rare. I won't say they never happen. I remember several years back three deaths in Minnesota. Routine knee surgeries using the cartilage from a cadaver. But that was a freaky case. Even our investigation couldn't determine whether the donor was already infected or whether the tissue became infected while it was processed. The tissue bank blamed the collection agency and the collection agency blamed the shipper. It's a crazy business."

"Business?"

"Sure. It's a business. Organ transplants have strict regulations. Only one organization per region. Have to be nonprofit, so plenty of federal oversight. Whole different ball game. But you get into tissue, bone, ligaments, corneas, veins—the supply can't keep up with demand. A cadaver might be worth $5,000 to $10,000, but sliced and diced—excuse my flippancy—and sold piece by piece? That same cadaver's worth anywhere from $25,000 to $40,000."

"I thought it was illegal to sell cadavers and human body parts."

"Ben, no offense, but man, you need to get out of the lab more often. Selling body parts might be illegal but it's not illegal to charge for the service of procuring, processing, and transporting. But truthfully, a lot of good comes out of this stuff. Some of the technology is amazing. They say one donor—by using his bones, tissue, ligaments, skin—can affect fifty lives."

Platt felt his stomach sink to his knees. One donor could *infect* fifty recipients?

"Ben, I hope you're not working on another fiasco that the military is trying to keep quiet."

"No, of course not."

Platt was glad Roger Bix didn't know him well, or he'd recognize what a terrible liar he was.

TWENTY-SIX

Scott downed his Johnnie Walker—neat, this time—trying to keep up with Joe Black. Maybe he'd get used to the sting. His head started to spin. It wasn't unpleasant. In fact, he sort of liked the feeling. It didn't even bother him when Joe cut into his rare steak and the red juices leaked out and streamed across his bone-white plate, soaking into his baked potato.

Joe had ordered a bottle of wine for them to share with their porterhouses and Scott noticed he was a bit behind on the wine. Joe was pouring a second glass for himself and topping off Scott's. And the whole time Scott couldn't shake out of his mind the envelope Joe had handed him when they first sat down. It would have been uncool to pull the money out, but with only a glance Scott saw the envelope contained hundred-dollar bills. And there were certainly more than the five hundred dollars they had agreed on.

"Your finder's fee for the indie," Joe smiled at him. "And a little extra for the storage space I'm going to need. Looks like the conference is being postponed. I have some frozen specimens I'll need to bring in. So are we good?"

"Oh, absolutely. Other than what we added earlier, I only have one guy in there now and the family wants the service Tuesday morning. Not even an open casket. They wanna get the old coot buried before the storm hits."

"And you're set up with generators, just in case?"

"All set," Scott told him and made a mental note in the back of his spinning head to check.

"I have a delivery coming in tomorrow morning," Joe told him. "I asked them to reroute it to the funeral home. You'll be there around ten, right?"

"Absolutely. Not a problem."

"How old of a guy?"

"Excuse me?"

"The old coot."

"Oh, him. Sixty-nine. Bachelor. Lived alone."

"Obese?"

Scott stopped mid-bite. Even with a fuzzy head, Joe's interest seemed odd.

Joe noticed Scott's hesitancy and said, "Just curious," and sipped his wine. "You know how it is. Occupational hazard." He gave Scott one of his winning grins and Scott relaxed.

"You should hear the calls I get," Joe continued. "Independent brokers, toolers, even surgeons contact me. And the worst are these conference organizers. You should hear them. 'Hey, Joe, I need six torsos, five shoulders, and a dozen knee specimens in two weeks.' "

He slung back the rest of his wine, reached for the bottle, and filled his glass, taking time to top off Scott's again.

"And you should see these conferences." Joe pushed his

plate aside and planted an elbow in its place on the table. "Five-star resorts, usually with beaches and golf courses. First-class flight, deluxe suite, dinners, cocktail parties. It's all included for the surgeons."

Scott slid his plate aside and mirrored Joe's posture, leaning in and sipping his wine. He really didn't need any more alcohol. His head was already starting to swim. But now he just nodded and listened, grateful because he wasn't sure he could trust his words to not slur.

"And for guys like us, Scott? The sky's the limit. Don't get me wrong. I respect the rules of the trade. It's not my fault there're so few. And as long as I transport within Florida I don't even have to worry about shipping regulations."

Scott was still stuck on the phrase "guys like us." He liked that Joe finally considered him a part of his network, his 'hood.

"Can I get you gentlemen some dessert?"

The waitress's sudden presence startled Scott.

"Yes," Joe answered as smoothly as if he hadn't had several Scotches and half a bottle of wine. "How 'bout the flaming cherries jubilee?" He was asking Scott, not the waitress.

"Oh, absolutely," Scott managed, surprised at sounding so coherent.

"Excellent choice." She rewarded Joe with a smile.

"Oh, and I need to get a cheeseburger to go. Medium well," he told the waitress.

"Fries?"

"That'd be perfect."

As she left, Scott raised an eyebrow at Joe. "Still hungry?"

"Don't ask. I promised someone."

But something had changed in Joe's demeanor. Scott saw it immediately, though he couldn't put his finger on what it was exactly. It made Joe sit up. He waved a hand over the table.

"This is the lifestyle, Scott. And it only promises to grow. I can't keep up with the demand. Having a few choice funeral directors like yourself has really helped. You know, you guys are the true gatekeepers of America's donor program. You have such tremendous influence over whether a family recognizes the valuable gift their loved one can give to future generations."

Scott recognized the switch and he felt disappointed. Joe had lapsed back into his "you guys" pitch. Before the waitress interrupted, it was "guys like us." He felt like Joe had started to open up, that they were more like buddies, not the Death Salesman shoring up the ranks.

Once again, Scott wondered who Joe Black really was.

TWENTY-SEVEN

When Maggie offered to buy the aircrew drinks, she honestly didn't think they would show up. It was late. Maybe she should have offered dinner. Food had been the last thing on her mind after a second landing at Baptist Hospital to deliver the injured boater and his two dogs. Now, despite having examined the rancid cooler, she found herself hungry.

While she waited, she checked her phone messages. The Escambia County medical examiner would be processing the body parts at nine tomorrow morning. He gave Maggie directions.

She text-messaged Wurth to join them for drinks, to be her backup, but his quick response was:

Prob not happenin. Catch ya at brkfst?

Maggie hated deciphering text messages. Still none from Tully and she had to remind herself that it was Sunday. Identifying the rope wasn't a matter of life and death. It was just one of those things that nagged at her. When the aircrew arrived, they sat down around her at the table as though meeting an inquisition.

"Just one question," Maggie told them. "I promise. Have any of you ever seen a tie-down like that on a fishing cooler?"

"Commercial fishermen use a stainless-steel contraption." It was Tommy Ellis who answered. "One end hooks into the cooler, the other into the floor of the boat. There's a turnbuckle in the middle to tighten it. I noticed this cooler had a pre-molded slot for it. A marine professional would use something like that, something more secure and certainly more sophisticated than a rope, even an unusual rope."

Everyone at the table was staring at Ellis by the time he finished, like he had just revealed some long-hidden secret.

"What?" Ellis shrugged. "My uncle's a shrimper."

After one drink Kesnick called it quits. He needed to get home to his wife and kids. The pilots, Wilson and Ellis, had another but then gravitated to the beach bar next door.

"We'll be right back," they said after spotting someone they knew.

From the look of things Maggie didn't expect them to return anytime soon. She didn't mind. And Liz Bailey looked much more comfortable with her crew gone. She had showered and her short hair, still damp in the humidity, was sticking up in places. She wore khaki shorts and a white sleeveless shirt. Maggie couldn't help thinking that the clothes were fitted just enough to remind Liz's crew she really wasn't one of them. Maggie remembered the discussion back in the helicopter. The men strategizing the rescue and leaving out the opinion of its chief architect—the rescue swimmer.

"This is a new aircrew for you," Maggie said to Liz.

"That obvious?"

"Not really," she said, realizing she might sound presumptuous. She wiped at the condensation on the bottle of beer she'd been nursing for the last half hour. She wanted to guzzle it. The air was stifling and it was long past sundown. "I get paid the big bucks to figure out psychological stuff like that."

She was pleased to see Liz Bailey smile for the first time since they'd met.

"What do you expect when you put four type-A personalities together in a helicopter. It's okay, though," Liz said, pausing to take a sip of her beer. "By now I'm used to having to prove myself."

"For what it's worth, they were really worried about you."

"Really?"

"Yes, really."

"When they were worried, what did they call me?"

"What do you mean?"

"Did they say, 'How's Bailey?' Or 'Is the rescue swimmer okay?'"

"Yes," Maggie told her. "They wanted to know if the rescue swimmer was okay."

"Yeah. That's what I thought." She took a long unladylike swig from her bottle while Maggie waited for some sort of explanation. Finally Liz said, "You're the psychology expert. Even after today's rescue they're still calling me *the* rescue swimmer, not *our* rescue swimmer. What does that tell you?"

Maggie detected disappointment more than anger in Liz's voice, despite her attempt at humor.

"It tells me they're men."

This time Liz laughed and tipped her bottle to Maggie as a salute of agreement. "You got that right."

"Not to change the subject"—though it was the subject of male-female camaraderie that reminded Maggie—"but what was that you gave me before the flight? The capsules?"

"Did they work?"

"Yes, and believe me, I've tried everything."

"It's powdered ginger."

"Ginger? You're kidding?"

"Works wonders for the nausea. Doesn't make a difference what's causing the nausea, this squelches it. So what is it?"

"Excuse me?"

"What caused it? Your nausea?" Her eyes found Maggie's and held them. "I mean you're an FBI agent. You carry a gun. Someone said you're like this expert profiler of murderers. I imagine you've seen some stuff that could turn plenty of cast-iron stomachs. But being up in the air. It's about something else?"

Maggie caught herself shrugging and then felt a bit silly under the scrutiny of this young woman. After all, earlier Liz had seen that there was a problem when Maggie thought for certain she had learned to hide it.

"Hey, it's none of my business. Just making conversation," Liz told her and looked away like it was no big deal.

But after what they had just gone through in the helicopter, not to mention sneaking the gift of the capsules to Maggie—who kept almost everyone she met at a safe distance—she felt Liz deserved an answer.

"I'm sure it does seem odd," Maggie finally said. "You're right, I've seen plenty of things: body parts stuffed into take-out containers, little boys carved up. Just yesterday I had to pluck a killer's brains out of my hair." She checked Liz's face and was surprised none of this fazed her. Then Maggie remembered the guys talking about Bailey and Hurricane Katrina. "You've seen plenty of stuff, too."

Another smile. This one totally unexpected.

"You really are very good at this psychology stuff," Liz said.

Maggie winced. She hadn't intentionally meant to deflect the question.

"I don't think it's that big of a mystery," Maggie said. "I can't handle not being in control."

"Are you always in control when you face off against a killer?"

"Of course. I carry a gun." Back to brevity and humor. Keep it light, she told herself. Someone gets too close, resort to wit.

"Or maybe in the air you're just vulnerable enough to realize all the risks you take every single day on the ground."

Maggie stared at her, suddenly disarmed.

"Come on, let's walk." Liz stood and pointed to the moonlit beach. "If Isaac hits, this might be the last time we enjoy Pensacola Beach for a very long time."

Just as Maggie pushed off her barstool a man stumbled over to their table, grabbing the edge and jiggling the empty beer bottles.

"Hey, E-liz-a-beth." He purposely enunciated her name, stringing it out in his inebriated attempt at song.

"Scott?"

"Oh hey." He stopped himself when he saw Maggie, as if only then noticing there was someone else at the table. "Sorry." He grinned, looking from Liz to Maggie and back. "I didn't realize you were on a date."

TWENTY-EIGHT

"Stryker's a 3.96 billion dollar a year company," Captain Ganz said.

Platt listened, though his eyes stayed on the prosthetic leg as he manipulated the joints.

"Most people know the name Stryker from autopsy scenes in crime novels or on *CSI*. You know, Stryker bone saws? But the company's been an innovator for years when it comes to medical technology. Most hospital surgical beds are even made by Stryker."

"What about these?" Platt poked at several screws on a table beside him. "I've never seen anything like them."

"The technology isn't all that new. We use a company in Jacksonville called BIOMedics. They're able to grind the screws from bone—I guess they call it precision tooling. And they don't just do screws—chips, wedges, dowels, anchors. The human body accepts bone much more readily than plastic. Same theory as heart valves and using animal tissue versus mechanical implants. BIOMedics makes the bone paste we use, too."

"Paste? You mentioned bone cement earlier."

"Right. Cement, paste—they're similar. We use the cement to anchor a prosthetic limb. The paste fills the cracks or perforations that might be in the remaining bone. For instance, gaps left by shrapnel. If you fill the holes, bacterium doesn't have as many places to infect."

"Sort of like medical caulk?"

Ganz laughed. "I suppose you could make that comparison." He sipped his third cup of coffee since the two had taken up residence in his office. "Both the cement and paste have been lifesavers. I told you about it reducing *Staph* infections. We inject antibiotics into the cement and paste. Lets us apply doses directly to the site. Keeps the patients from having to have their bodies blasted with antibiotics, reducing the immune system."

"What are the chances of it being contaminated?"

"The bone paste?"

"The cement, the paste, the screws. Perhaps the original bone they're made from?" Platt asked, picking up one of the screws and examining it.

Ganz shook his head. "No, I'd say that's next to impossible. We use our own."

"What do you mean, you use your own?"

"We have our own supply of bone and tissue."

Platt didn't bother to hide his surprise.

"The navy was the first to use frozen bone transplants," Ganz explained. "Back in the forties at the Naval Medical

Center in Maryland. An orthopedic surgeon by the name of Hyatt started freezing and storing bones that he'd surgically removed during amputation. Instead of discarding the bone he'd freeze it, store it, and use what he could to repair fractures in other patients. Sorry," Ganz interrupted himself. "Don't mean to give you a history lesson."

"I don't mind. Go on."

"Hyatt was so successful he started one of the first body-donation programs. That's how the Navy Tissue Bank started. Even back then they were able to remove more than just bone—tissue, veins, skin, corneas—though they weren't quite sure what to do with most of it. They offered surgeons free use of the bank, only asking that they share their results so Hyatt and his colleagues could maintain their database. It was all pretty much trial and error, but Hyatt figured out a way to disinfect and screen the tissue. Even developed a way to freeze-dry it for shipping. The operation we have today is much more focused and we limit it only to military surgeons."

"Where does the bone and tissue get processed?"

"In Jacksonville. I recommended Dr. McCleary, the pathologist. He came out of retirement just to run the program. Does an amazing job with the aid of only one diener."

"So you ship him your . . . bones? Your excess . . . ?"

Ganz nodded and smiled at Platt's loss of terminology. "It's part of the program I started here."

"Why not do all of it here?"

"Jacksonville had a well-equipped facility already available. Plus it's practically next door to BIOMedics, the company that does all the precision tooling."

"Who does the screening and disinfecting?"

"Dr. McCleary does it with the help of BIOMedics. I know what you're thinking, Ben. I've already considered contamination. We've checked and double-checked. We've never had a problem before."

"Have you checked any of the precision-tooled stuff from the dead soldiers?"

Ganz's hesitation gave Platt his answer.

"No," Ganz finally said. "I don't believe we removed any of it."

Platt nodded, still staring at the prosthetic leg he had set aside on the table next to the bone screws. He wrapped his hands around his coffee mug then looked up at Captain Ganz.

"After the autopsy I took a look at a tissue sample from Ronnie Towers."

"Ronnie Towers?"

"The soldier who just died," Platt said without criticism. "I checked the bone paste used on the prosthetic, too. There were traces of the bacteria *Clostridium sordellii*. Are you familiar with it?"

Ganz scratched at his jaw. "Isn't that usually found in soil?"

Platt nodded. "It can also be found in fecal matter or inside intestines."

"That doesn't make any sense."

"Your patients' symptoms are similar to sepsis or severe toxic shock, which can be a result of an infection caused by *Clostridium sordellii*. The only problem is, I have no idea where the bacteria came from. This is something that's usually seen in one particular type of patient."

"And what type is that?"

"Pregnant women."

TWENTY-NINE

Danny Delveccio tossed the last of the garbage bags into the back of the Santa Rosa Island Authority pickup. He slapped the side door to let the driver know he was finished.

"See ya tomorrow, Andy."

"Early, dude. Gonna be some killer waves."

"Seven?"

In reply he got a thumbs-up.

Danny walked to his car, his legs tight from a day of surfing followed by the routine walk up the beach to pick up garbage. Walking in the sand had been hard to get used to, especially the burn in his calves. He remembered the first week he couldn't even hold himself up on his board. Who knew picking up other people's crap could be so physically draining.

He keyed open the trunk to his Impala. Everything he owned was back here. He didn't worry about anyone stealing the car. To a thief it'd be worthless. The tires were bald, the engine had a chronic sputter, and it needed a paint job. But it was his transportation, his home, and his lifeline.

Danny grabbed a clean towel from the stash he had just

washed at the laundromat. He'd shower, stop at the vending machine, then get some sleep. Andy had heard earlier that the hurricane was already in the Gulf, and as the resident expert of such things, he assured Danny that by morning the waves would be awesome.

He closed the trunk and that's when he saw the guy standing beside him. Scared the crap out of Danny. He jumped but didn't let on.

"Sorry," the man said. "I didn't mean to startle you. Mr. B said you usually get off work about this time. I thought you might be hungry."

"Mr. B? Coney Island Canteen Mr. B?"

The man held out a container that smelled like heaven: melted cheese, onions, French fries.

"Yeah, I met you there earlier today, remember? I'm a salesman and Mr. B mentioned you do odd jobs for hire around the beach."

Danny squinted but the man's face remained partly shadowed. He supposed the guy looked familiar. How could he tell from the hundreds of faces he saw every day on the beach? But if he was a friend of Mr. B's, he had to be cool.

"I wondered if you might help me load a couple of crates into my van."

When Danny still hesitated, the guy held out the container again.

"Cheeseburger and fries plus an Andrew Jackson? Should only take about fifteen minutes."

Danny's mouth watered. He hadn't realized how hungry he was. It beat anything he'd get in the vending machines.

"Can I eat first?"

"Sure."

He accepted the container and popped it open. He hadn't had a burger and fries in weeks, let alone one like this. And twenty dollars for fifteen minutes of work? Danny couldn't believe his good fortune.

MONDAY, AUGUST 24

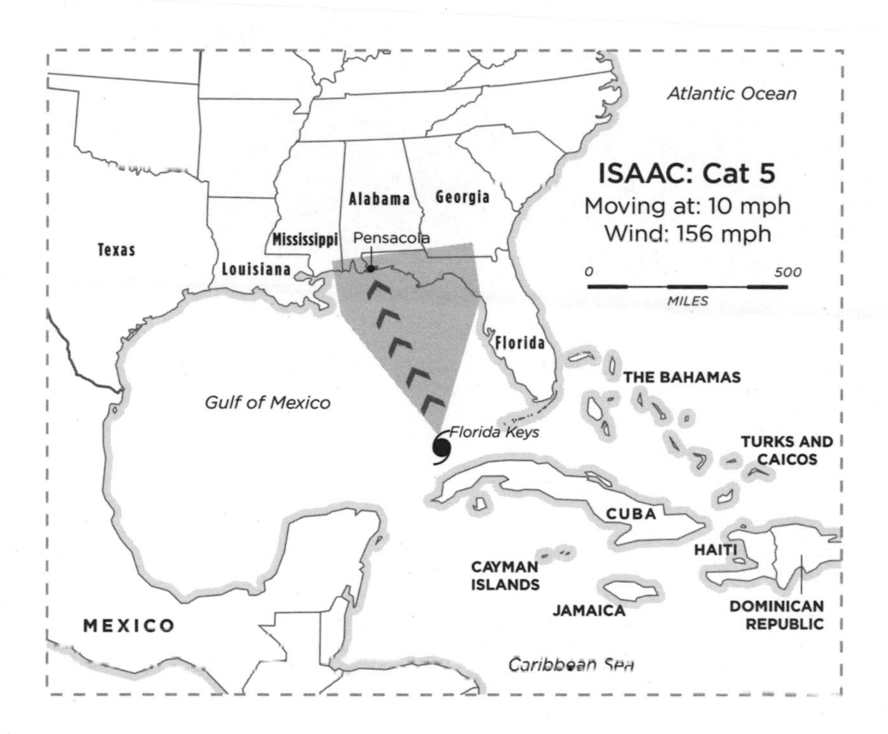

THIRTY

Platt's vision was blurred. He tried to keep focused. If the clock on the wall was correct, it was just after one o'clock in the morning.

"I'm not a scientist, Ben," Captain Ganz said as he rubbed his eyes, stood, and stretched behind his desk. "You tell me this bacteria is causing an infection but you don't know where the bacteria is coming from. I can assure you these soldiers did not contract it from pregnant women."

"No, you're missing my point." Platt slowed himself down. They were both exhausted. He leaned against the wall, but he wanted to pace. "*Clostridium sordellii* is a rare bacterium. Most of the fatal cases that I know of have been associated with gynecologic infections following a live birth or an abortion. But I've checked. There have been other fatal cases that have nothing to do with childbirth."

"Such as?"

Platt suppressed a yawn. He wouldn't tell Ganz that he had talked to Bix at the CDC, but he could share Bix's information.

"There was a case in Minnesota. A routine knee surgery using donated tissue."

Ganz shook his head. "Our donors are screened and so is the tissue."

"You screen for HIV, hepatitis B and C, and probably other blood-borne viruses. But what about bacterial diseases?"

Ganz felt behind him for his chair and dropped into it. "Even so, only a handful of these patients have received donor tissue."

"But all of them probably received some form of bone transplant."

"No, that's not true."

"The bone paste? The cement?"

"Wait a minute. Just because you found this bacteria in one patient doesn't mean it's in the others."

Platt pulled out of his shirt pocket a crumpled piece of paper where he had jotted down a few notes from his online search. "Does this sound familiar? Two to seven days after a surgical procedure or childbirth the patient complains of severe abdominal pain along with nausea and vomiting but no fever, no hypertension. When the symptoms finally show up, sepsis has already set in. The patient goes into toxic shock. About 70 to 80 percent of patients die within two to six days of developing the infection."

Ganz continued to shake his head. "Does this infection spread from person to person?"

"It's not quite known how or if it's spread from person to person or from the environment to a person. But I'll give you my best logical guess as to what might have happened in this case."

Platt waited for the captain's attention.

"Of course. Go ahead."

Platt sat down so they would be at eye level. He kept from crossing his arms or legs. He restrained from fidgeting and folded his hands together so he wouldn't be tapping his fingers on the table.

"Just suppose for a minute that a donor's body—for whatever reason—wasn't discovered and refrigerated or properly processed within twelve hours."

"Eighteen hours."

"Excuse me?"

"Eighteen hours is the time limit. Our regulations say over eighteen hours is not usable."

"Okay, eighteen. Once the blood flow stops, you know as well as I do that decomposition starts. Depending on the conditions, it can start almost immediately. My guess is that this bacterium didn't come from contaminated tools used to process the tissue or even during surgery. I believe the bacterium came from the donor's body after death when the body started decomposing. And when that donor's tissue and bone was used to make bone screws and anchors and paste, the bacteria simply got ground up and divided. As soon as it was placed back inside a warm human body, it did what bacteria loves to do—it grew and it spread by way of infection."

Silence. Ganz stared at him. Platt realized it was a lot to sort through, but he never would have predicted what the captain said next.

"I appreciate your opinion and that you came all this way on such short notice. It's obvious that you could use some rest."

Ganz stood again, and this time Platt stared up at him. Was it possible the captain was dismissing him? Dismissing his theory?

"I'll call my driver for you."

And with that, Captain Ganz walked out of the room, leaving Platt dumbfounded. He wasn't just dismissing his theory, he was sending Platt home.

THIRTY-ONE

"Don't take this the wrong way, O'Dell, but you look like something the cat dragged in."

Maggie didn't want to tell Charlie Wurth that she felt a little bit like she had been dragged. She'd been up all night with insomnia.

After her helicopter adventure she should have been exhausted enough to fall into bed and sleep. Instead, she found herself on the beach from midnight till two in the morning walking the shore and watching the full moon light up the waves. Liz had warned her that it wasn't safe to be alone on the beach at night. But Maggie figured that advice didn't apply if you carried a .38 Smith & Wesson stuffed in your waistband.

"Couldn't sleep," she told Wurth and left it at that. No sense explaining about leaky compartments in her subconscious and ghosts from past murder cases keeping her awake at night.

Wurth had promised a real breakfast. Now, as he held open the door to the café, Maggie realized that she shouldn't have been surprised to see a number of strangers waving and saying "good morning" and "hello." Less than twenty-four hours in the city and Charlie Wurth not only knew his way around but also seemed to know the hot spot for breakfast.

The Coffee Cup in downtown Pensacola was crowded, some clientele in shirts and ties with BlackBerrys and others in boots and jeans with the local newspaper scattered across the tabletop.

Despite the clatter of stoneware, the sizzle of bacon, and the shouts of waitresses to the short-order cooks, several customers immediately recognized Wurth. A businessman at a window table waved a hello and another at the counter looked up from his conversation to nod at him. A tall, skinny waitress called him "hon" like they were old friends and led them to a table that was still being bussed. As soon as they sat, she handed them menus.

"Two coffees?" she said, plopping down stoneware mugs in front of them.

"Black coffee for me, Rita. Diet Pepsi for my partner, here."

"Diet Coke okay, hon?" But she asked Wurth, not Maggie, while she retrieved the mug in front of her as quickly as she had set it down.

Wurth looked to Maggie and waited for an answer, which made Rita look to Maggie. She had to give him credit. It would have been so much easier to just say yes. But it was a big deal to Charlie Wurth that the people surrounding him were always acknowledged.

"Diet Coke's fine," Maggie said.

She waited for the waitress to leave while taking in the

café's surroundings. Then she leaned across the small table. "How do you already know all these people?"

"Had coffee here yesterday. You can meet all the movers and shakers in a community if you find their watering hole."

He paused to wave at two women who had just come in.

"And believe me," he smiled and leaned in, "with a hurricane coming, the federal guy who's promising to bring the cavalry is much more popular than Jim Cantore from the Weather Channel. You'll see there's already a couple of signs telling him to stay the hell away."

"Who's Jim Cantore?"

He tilted his head at her, trying to tell if she was serious. "I forget you're a hurricane neophyte. With the last several storms, anywhere Cantore goes so goes the hurricane. He either has an uncanny ability to predict or he's a jinx. Either way, nobody wants to see him here."

"Is he here?"

"If he isn't, he will be. It's looking like the Panhandle is Isaac's bull's-eye."

He sat back when he saw the waitress heading to their table. She brought Maggie's Diet Coke and a pot of steaming coffee to fill Wurth's mug.

"So what can I get you two?" This time she included Maggie.

"I'll have a cheese-and-mushroom omelet."

The waitress kept looking at her like she was waiting for more. Finally she said, "That's it, hon?"

"You gotta have some grits with that," Wurth told her. "Bring her some grits, Rita. I'll have two eggs scrambled, sausage links, wheat toast, hash browns, and the Nassau grits."

As soon as Rita turned to leave, Maggie raised her eyebrow at Wurth's breakfast order.

"What? There's a hurricane coming. Might be the last hot meal I get," he said.

He glanced around and leaned in again.

"This one's looking bad. Bulldozed over Cuba like it was a speed bump. Land masses usually slow them down a little. Instead, Isaac's entering the Gulf as a cat 5, sustained winds at 156 miles per hour. There's nothing between here and there to slow it down. Another day over warm waters and this monster might pick up even more steam. If it makes landfall as a cat 5, that's brutal. We're no longer talking about damage, we're talking catastrophic damage."

Maggie's eyes darted around but she stayed with elbows on the table, hands circling her condensation-drenched plastic glass. "I guess I'm surprised there doesn't seem to be much panic or anxiety."

"Oh, there's anxiety. Long lines yesterday. Hardware stores are sold out of generators and plywood. Grocery stores' shelves are picked clean. Can't find any bagged ice or bottled water. Most of the gas stations are pumped dry or just about there. But these folks"—Wurth pointed discreetly with his chin—"they look out for themselves and their neighbors. They know the drill. The Panhandle has already had a couple of tropical storms hit earlier this year, and with three hurricanes making landfall on Florida, they realize their odds.

"That's the locals. Now the transplants—and there are

plenty of them—they're the ones I have to convince to evacuate and get to a shelter. The city commissioners will be declaring a state of emergency later this morning. You watch. We start getting closer to the realization that this storm's gonna hit, that quiet anxiety will boil. Tempers will flare. Patience wears thin. We'll start getting some pushing and shoving."

Rita appeared again with half a dozen plates to set on their table. Maggie had to admit, everything smelled wonderful and it reminded her that she hadn't had dinner last night.

She sliced into the omelet with her fork and melted cheese oozed out. Wurth scooped his grits into his scrambled eggs and using a slice of toast as a wedge he proceeded to wolf down the concoction.

"I haven't exactly figured out what to do with you," he said in between bites.

"You'll drop me at the morgue. I can probably find my way back to the hotel."

He shook his head, smothering his hash browns with salt and pepper. "No, no, I can pick you up and get you back to the hotel. I mean during the hurricane. We won't be able to stay on the beach. Actually, most of the hotel guests were checking out this morning. The manager's doing us a favor letting us stay until he's ordered to leave. Which will probably be tomorrow, depending on how soon the outer bands hit."

"Ordered to leave?"

"Mandatory evacuation on the beach and in low-lying areas. Sheriff's department goes door to door. Anyone wants to stay they have to sign off that they're doing so at their own risk and are relieving the authorities of any further obligation."

"Where will you be during the storm?"

"Probably working one of the shelters."

"Then I'll work one of the shelters."

"I can't ask you to do that, Maggie."

"You're not asking. I'm volunteering."

He put his fork down and sat back to look at her. "I don't know what I was thinking when I asked you to ride down here with me. All three hurricanes this season I've been the anti-Jim Cantore. Wherever I was sent, the storm turned and headed in the opposite direction. But I should have known my luck would change. Now I've brought you smack-dab in the middle and this one looks like it'll be a monster."

"Charlie, I can take care of myself. It's one storm. How bad can it be?"

The look he gave her said she had no idea.

THIRTY-TWO

Scott Larsen had left before Trish woke up. He felt like he hadn't slept at all. His eyelids were heavy. His head throbbed. His mouth insisted he had swallowed a wad of cotton. Even his hair hurt when he combed it. Never again would he drink so much. In fact, he didn't care if he had an ounce of alcohol ever again.

To make matters worse, he saw Joe had been back to the funeral home. One tap of a button and the alarm system revealed that someone using Scott's key and code had entered at 3:10 in the morning and left at 4:00. What the hell was Joe doing?

Scott hoped he wouldn't be sorry he had given Joe the code. As he came in the back door of the funeral home he caught himself wincing, the throbbing in his head bouncing off the backs of his eyeballs. He dreaded finding another mess in the embalming room. He could already smell the pungent odor of cleaners mixed with . . . what was that? Oh, yeah. Menthol.

He stopped before he got to the doorway. Clean. Thank God, it was clean. So the odors were from their afternoon work. Maybe Joe had added some specimens to the walk-in fridge. Scott was on his way to check when the buzzer at the back door went off. He glanced at his watch. The power guy he had called earlier was right on time. Damn well should be for what they were charging just to show Scott where to flip a switch for the generator.

"Mr. Larsen?" The guy towered over Scott. Or maybe the massive tool belt and size-twelve work boots made the man seem huge. An embroidered patch on his breast pocket said his name was Ted.

"That's right, I'm Larsen," Scott told him while he straightened his tie. It was a nervous habit and he stopped himself. Stupid to think he needed to show some authority with this guy. "I think all the electrical stuff is outside, around back."

Scott led the way. He could feel sweat sliding down his back and sticking to his crisply pressed shirt. Luckily he kept spares in the office. Nobody trusted a sweaty funeral director.

The sky was murky, but it didn't seem to block out the heat. If anything it heightened the humidity. Scott noticed the wind had picked up. Son of a bitch, that storm might actually hit.

"Here it is." He pointed to the rectangular metal boxes with electrical wires weaving their way out of the top and bottom.

Ted flipped open the box's door.

"Yeah, you're all set up."

Scott held back a sigh of relief. Of course, he was set up. He just needed to know how to turn the damn generator on.

"You push this button." Ted pointed. "Followed by this one. That sequence, okay?" He was talking to him as if Scott were a third-grader.

"Yeah, sure. No problem." Scott answered, wanting to add "bastard."

"Then you pull this lever."

"Got it. Guess I'm good to go." He turned, ready to walk the guy back.

"Wait a minute. What's this one?" Ted had opened the other box.

"Oh that's some stuff I added when I bought the place. A walkway to connect the buildings. Brand-new walk-in cooler. Couple of freezers. The old ones were too small. Pretty outdated."

"You know that everything on this circuit board isn't connected?"

"What are you talking about?"

"You won't have generator power for anything you added on these circuits."

"No, that can't be right."

"It's not connected." Ted pointed down below both boxes.

"Will it take long for you to connect it?"

Ted laughed. Then he must have seen the panic on Scott's face. "Sorry, man. Even if I could connect it, your current generator wouldn't have enough juice for everything on the second panel."

"What the hell am I supposed to do?"

"If you have a separate generator, you can hook it up directly. Make sure you use the double-insulated power cord. You say you've got a walk-in cooler. That's probably going to need 5500 all to itself."

"So I just go out and buy a 5500 generator. No problem."

“Go out and buy one? You mean you don’t already have another generator?”

“No.”

“Maybe you could use your home one.”

“I don’t have a home one. So I need to go to Home Depot or Lowe’s and get one?”

Now the guy laughed again. “I don’t think you’ll find one. Not around Pensacola anyway. My guess is they’re sold out.”

THIRTY-THREE

Liz brought in the *Pensacola News Journal* and handed it to her dad on the way back to the kitchen.

"Thank you, darling."

"Dad, you'll never guess who I ran into on the beach last night."

"Who's that?"

"Scott."

"Scott?"

"Scott Larsen, your son-in-law."

"Scott? At the beach? Scott never goes to the beach."

"Well, he was there last night and he was drunk."

"Drunk? Scott? Scott doesn't drink."

"Very drunk."

"Maybe a beer now and then. That's about all I've ever seen him drink. What are you doing there?" He had followed her into the kitchen and was standing beside her, more interested in the stove top than in anything she was saying.

"I'm fixing us breakfast."

"Eggs and bacon?"

"Dippy eggs." That's what he called them because he liked to dip his toast into the yolk. When he didn't answer she added, "Sunny-side up, right? Or have you changed your preference."

"No, no, that's perfect." He stayed watching. "You can cook?"

"Dad, I've lived on my own for eight years now. What do you think I do? Eat out all the time?"

"Trish always said you didn't cook."

"Yeah, I bet she did."

"So what did Trish say?"

"About what?"

"About Scott being drunk."

"I didn't tell her."

"She wasn't with him?"

"Uh, noooo. You think he would be drunk if Trish was with him?"

"He's an odd duck. Won't even have a beer with me."

Walter shook his head. Now at the refrigerator he poured orange juice for both of them. Then he did something that almost made Liz drop her spatula. He started setting the table: plates, coffee cups, sugar bowl, cream, silverware, even napkins and place mats. She stopped herself from commenting. Trish would have to correct him, make sure he switched the fork to the other side of the plate or that he folded the napkin. Liz just dropped bread in the toaster.

"I'm off until noon today," she told him. "Anything I can do to help you?"

"In the canteen?"

"No, Dad. Here at the house. For the hurricane. Did you get everything you need? I'm sure store shelves are picked over by today."

"Apple Market had all their refrigerated items discounted. Ground beef, twenty-five cents a pound."

"Aren't your own refrigerators full enough?"

"Maybe I'll take the grill and do up a few burgers alongside the hot dogs."

"Are you really taking the canteen out on the beach today?"

"Thought I would for a few hours around lunch."

"People are going to be packing up. Everything will be closing down."

"Exactly, and folks are still gonna need to get a bite to eat."

She prepared their plates and, again, stopped herself from commenting. The canteen had saved him. Liz was willing to recognize that even if Trish wasn't. It had given him something to do after their mom was gone. He didn't need the money. The house was paid for and his pension as a retired navy commander seemed to be more than enough for him. But he did need the routine the Coney Island Canteen had brought into his life. More important, it surrounded him with people. Everybody on the beach knew the hot-dog man, or if they knew him well, it was "Mr. B."

"So what will they have you doing today?" He asked as he dipped the corner of his toast into his egg yolk.

"Little bit of everything, I imagine. Patrolling the waters, warning boaters, at least until the winds get out of hand. Then we'll probably be helping evacuate."

"You know Danny? Works on the beach cleanup crew? Little guy. Loves to surf."

She watched her dad out of the corner of her eye. He was devouring her breakfast and she wanted to smile. That was probably the biggest compliment Walter Bailey could pay her.

"I've seen him around."

"Lives in his car. An old red Chevy Impala."

"Yeah, he lives in that car?"

"Make sure he evacuates, would you? He's from Kansas where they try to outrun tornadoes. I just want to make sure he doesn't think he can do the same with a hurricane."

"Sure. I'll look for him."

"Say, whatever happened to that fishing cooler?"

Before Liz could answer there was a knock at the front door, a twist of a key followed by, "Hello, hello."

Trish stomped into the kitchen. She didn't seem to notice that she was interrupting a meal. She led off with: "I'm going to kill that husband of mine."

THIRTY-FOUR

Maggie stared down at the male torso on the stainless-steel table and couldn't help thinking how much it looked like a slab of meat.

"Body was refrigerated, possibly frozen," Dr. Tomich, the medical examiner, said into the wireless microphone clipped to the top of his scrubs. His comments were meant for his recorded notes, not necessarily for his audience. "Cuts are precise. Efficient, but not surgical."

"What does that mean?" the Escambia County sheriff asked from the corner. This morning he paced out his impatience along the wall of the autopsy suite. "I don't want to be in the way," he'd said earlier. But he didn't want to miss anything, either.

Technically the contents of the fishing cooler were under Sheriff Clayton's jurisdiction. When pieces of a body are found, the county with the heart—in this case, the whole torso—usually holds jurisdiction. Maggie had watched law enforcement agencies argue over who got to be in charge. This sheriff had put up a good fight to *not* be in charge. In his defense, Maggie understood that he was preoccupied with hurricane preparations. Making sure people were safe and ready for the storm certainly held more urgency than a body that had been missing and frozen for who knew how long.

"It means the person who did this knew how to dismember a body. But he or she is not necessarily a doctor or surgeon."

"How can you be so sure?"

Tomich straightened from his hunched-over examination. He reminded Maggie of Spencer Tracy: silver-gray hair, black square glasses framing sparkling blue eyes that could pierce as well as charm. The Eastern European accent—Russian, maybe Polish—threw the image off a bit. When he turned to look at Clayton again, he reminded her more of her high-school history teacher, who also had been able to quiet his students with that piercing glare.

"I'm just saying"—the sheriff would not be deterred—"where do you learn to do this to a body if not medical school?"

"Perhaps practice?" Maggie interrupted and both men furrowed their brows, almost in unison. "Serial killers oftentimes perfect their craft simply by trial and error."

"You're presuming who did this has done it before?" Tomich admonished.

"Can you tell me with any certainty that he has not done it before?"

This time he looked perplexed rather than irritated. "Let me rephrase. You are presuming foul play. As of this moment I don't know the cause of death. And I do not see any evidence of murder."

"Come on, Doc," Clayton said. "How do pieces of a person end up in a fishing cooler in the Gulf if it's not foul play?"

Maggie was interested in the answer but the sheriff interrupted himself.

"What's that smell?" He sniffed the air but still didn't venture any closer to the autopsy table.

"Menthol?"

"Vicks VapoRub," Maggie said with certainty.

"That's weird." The sheriff was still sniffing.

"Not necessarily," Maggie assured him. "Not if you want to cover up the smell of decomposition."

"Still, it indicates no evidence of foul play," the medical examiner insisted.

A man in blue scrubs came through a side door, wheeling a stainless-steel cart. At first Maggie thought he was another doctor or pathologist until he said to Tomich, "Here are the other contents, sir."

"Thank you, Matthew."

"The X-rays are on the shelf below. I'll be next door if you need me."

"Next door? Boiling my bones?"

"Yes, sir."

Tomich looked from Maggie to Clayton, enjoying their wide-eyed reaction.

"Someone found a set of buried bones. I doubt they're human but we shall see. Matthew is my faithful diener. He gets to have all the fun."

"Right. All the fun." The young man smiled as if it was a

joke they shared. He certainly didn't seem to mind what sounded like a grunt assignment of boiling bones when, in fact, most dieners Maggie had met in the past were as proficient at dissection as their bosses.

Matthew left and Tomich pulled down his plastic goggles. He picked up the electric bone saw, ready to cut. Maggie watched the sheriff's face lose all color.

"Oh hey, I have to make a few phone calls," he said, pointing a thumb at the door and doing a remarkable job of keeping the panic out of his voice.

Tomich watched him leave, waited for the door to latch shut behind him. He turned back to the task at hand. Without looking at Maggie he shook his head and said, "Politicians. I should ban them from my autopsies." Suddenly he glanced up at her. "You don't mind if I proceed?"

"Not at all. Please do."

He clicked on the saw and in seconds severed the rib cage. He set the saw down. With long gloved fingers inserted in each side he opened the front of the chest, spreading the ribs and exposing the heart and lungs. Almost immediately he noticed something and started poking around inside.

"What is it?" Maggie wanted to know.

"I believe we are in luck. I shall be able to tell you exactly who our victim is." He grabbed a forceps and a scalpel and began cutting.

THIRTY-FIVE

Scott worked his way through the Yellow Pages. How could there not be a single generator left in this city? He'd even called Mobile and Tallahassee. The last Home Depot manager he talked to had just laughed at him. Couldn't stop laughing. Scott finally hung up on the asshole.

He didn't have any employees coming in until after lunch today. He hadn't even started preparing for the memorial service. He'd make his people earn their keep today. Thank God he didn't have to embalm the body. The family had opted for a closed casket. They'd never know that dear Uncle Mel wasn't even inside. It was the storm's fault, not his. If the electricity went out and he didn't have a generator for the walk-in refrigerator, he couldn't just take all those body parts home with him.

"Oh, by the way, Trish," he imagined saying, "I've got a few things to stuff into our fridge." Not like he had room there, either. He wasn't like his father-in-law with two extra refrigerators in the garage.

His father-in-law also had more than one generator. He was

sure of it. He put the phone down. In fact, during the last hurricane threat Walter had bragged about having two or three generators. Why hadn't Scott thought about it sooner? He could just borrow one. No, Walter would never lend him something that substantial. Would he? No. He was fussy about his possessions. That included his daughter.

The only other alternative was to move everything from the walk-in cooler to the stand-alone freezers.

The buzzer for the back door startled him. This time it was FedEx.

The guy had already unloaded two boxes and dropped a third on top as he handed Scott the electronic signature pad.

"The tag doesn't say anything about liquids," the guy told Scott. "Whatever that is"—he pointed at the last box and the pink fluid oozing through the seam and running down the side—"it's probably against regulations."

"I'm not the one who sent it." Scott put up his hands in defense.

The guy didn't say anything, just gave him an accusing look and headed back to his truck. Scott scooped up the boxes and moved them inside the door, out of sight and out of the heat. These had to be the deliveries Joe had mentioned. But he had gotten sloppy and not wrapped them properly. What was Joe thinking?

Scott picked up the leaking package, grabbed a towel, and wrapped it around the busted seam. He hauled the box to the walk-in cooler and decided to leave the packages for Joe to deal with. Once inside the cooler Scott stopped, almost dropping the box. On a gurney in the middle of the floor was the naked corpse of a boy. On closer inspection he realized it was a small young man.

Joe hadn't mentioned a body, only parts. Did he intend to disarticulate this one, too, before the storm hit? And exactly how and from where had he transported a corpse in the middle of a Sunday night?

Scott guessed it was possible that Joe simply picked it up from another one of his networks. He had told Scott when they first met that he obtained corpses from university donor programs, county morgues, and crematories. That's probably what happened. Some other place was unloading inventory before the storm.

Oh that was just—

This time Scott did drop the box. Either he was going nuts or that corpse just moved.

THIRTY-SIX

Maggie didn't recognize the contraption Dr. Tomich had extracted from the torso, but she had a good idea what it meant. Sheriff Clayton had returned and now he stood at the sink, his lanky frame towering over Dr. Tomich's hunched right shoulder.

"It's a defibrillator," Dr. Tomich said as he flushed it with water, keeping the device pinched between his forceps. He reached to the side, practically elbowing Sheriff Clayton out of his way, and punched the intercom button.

"Matthew, come here. I need you to look up a serial number."

"It seems too easy," Clayton said. "You're telling us there's a number on this apparatus and you'll be able to match it to a name?"

"Yes. That is exactly what I am telling you."

"Sir." Matthew was there in the room before anyone heard him enter.

Maggie found herself checking out his footwear, except he wore paper shoe covers like the rest of them.

Dr. Tomich placed the defibrillator onto a stainless-steel tray and handed it to Matthew.

"Look this up, please. Bring me the patient's name and the physician's."

"Yes, sir."

As the medical examiner returned to the torso, he caught Maggie eyeing the cart with the severed foot and hands.

"You're intrigued with the parts."

It was an odd thing to say.

"Occupational hazard," she answered, without further explanation.

Tomich nodded, bowed his head as if paying homage, then he did something Maggie didn't expect. He picked up the severed foot and placed it on a separate stainless-steel table.

"We'll take a look," he said. He poked his glasses up the bridge of his nose with one gloved hand and waved his other at the torso. "This gentleman won't mind if we wait for Matthew to tell us his name."

It was an unexpected and rare courtesy. Maggie knew her surprise registered on her face, but Dr. Tomich didn't notice. He was already pulling open a new tray of instruments and resetting his wireless recording. Sheriff Clayton, who had been squeamish about watching the torso, didn't have a problem with getting a closer look at the severed foot.

"Are you trying to match any of these to one of your cases?"

It took Maggie a second to realize that Tomich was talking to her and not his wireless.

"Not this time. How many different victims do you think are here?"

"At least two." Tomich slouched over the table as he began his examination. "Or it could be five. I may be able to tell you that quickly with a simple blood test. Process of elimination. If all the parts are the same blood type, we'll need to wait for DNA tests."

"If the hands don't belong to the torso," Sheriff Clayton asked, "we might not figure out whose they are. Fingerprints don't make much difference if we can't match them to somebody already in the system."

"This is interesting." Dr. Tomich poked at the ankle. "Something beneath the skin."

He picked up the scalpel and moved the severed foot onto its side, the inside of the ankle facing up. At first glimpse the object Dr. Tomich began to remove looked like a piece of metal. Another medical device? A pin or clip jabbing its way up to the surface?

Tomich cut, then held the small object up to the light, clasped in his forceps.

"Is it a bullet fragment?" Sheriff Clayton asked.

The medical examiner gave it only a cursory look before dropping it into a stainless-steel basin.

"There's more," Tomich said.

One after another he plucked and dropped into the basin four more pieces of metal that had been embedded deep into the foot.

"Shotgun?" asked the sheriff.

Before the medical examiner had a chance to decide, Matthew appeared alongside of them. This time the sheriff jumped, but cleared his throat and shifted his weight as if he had been just readjusting his stance.

"Sir, I have the information you requested."

"The patient who belongs to the defibrillator? This soon?"

"Yes, sir. The number is registered to Vince Coffland of Port St. Lucie, Florida."

"Port St. Lucie?" Sheriff Clayton interrupted. "That's over six hundred miles away. And it's on the Atlantic side. How the hell did he end up in a cooler floating in the Gulf?"

"Any information on what happened to Mr. Coffland?" Tomich asked his diener.

"He's been missing since July tenth. He disappeared after Hurricane Gaston."

"Missing?"

"Disappeared."

THIRTY-SEVEN

Sometimes a corpse moved. Scott knew it was a fact that no one liked to talk about except at conferences after a few drinks. It'd never happened to Scott, but he'd heard stories of others who had experienced what they called "spontaneous movement." A leg or a foot twitched. He couldn't remember exactly what caused it. Some kind of biochemical reaction. But it usually occurred in the first ten to twelve hours after death. Maybe that's all this was, but when Scott called Joe he opted for the extreme. After the morning he'd experienced, he couldn't hide the stress.

"That stiff you left in my cooler is still alive."

"What are you talking about?"

"He moved."

Silence. Long enough that Scott second-guessed his approach. Would Joe think his partner prone to hysterics? That he couldn't handle the extra business?

"Look, man," Joe finally said in his usual calm and cool manner, "it's just your imagination playing tricks on you." Then he added like a buddy, a friend, "Dude, you did have a lot to drink last night."

There was something about Joe's voice—his calling him "dude"—that made Scott relax . . . a little.

By the time Joe arrived half an hour later, Scott had almost convinced himself that it probably was just his imagination. His head still throbbed. Earlier his vision seemed blurred. He hadn't gone back into the cooler and now he felt a bit ridiculous.

Scott tried to concentrate while he kept his employees busy in the funeral home preparing the memorial service for Uncle Mel, the reclusive bachelor whose family wanted him buried before the hurricane rolled in. Scott told the employees they couldn't go to the back offices because he was fumigating the walkway. It seemed like an absurd excuse even to him. Why fumigate anything before a hurricane? But no one questioned him, which further validated his salesmanship. Damn, he was good. Even in a crisis with all the stress he could make up stuff to believable levels.

He had left Joe for twenty minutes, tops. As soon as Scott could, he sneaked back, going outside and avoiding the walkway. Joe was closing and latching the walk-in refrigerator.

"Hey Scott," Joe said. "I have to tell you, man, I wish you could have heard your voice. 'The stiff moved.'" He laughed as he slapped Scott between the shoulder blades.

"Yeah, probably too much Scotch."

"Or not enough," Joe said as he pulled out his money clip and started peeling off hundred-dollar bills. "I'll have a few more specimens to add before the storm, if that's okay," he said as he placed the bills on the corner desk.

Scott couldn't count and listen at the same time.

"I'll come back tonight. Try and cut and package up as much as possible. Take less room that way."

"Sure, no problem." Scott found himself saying the words while he struggled to keep his eyes away from the pile of hundred-dollar bills.

"I'd offer to take you to dinner again, but I think you might need to rest," Joe said with a grin, the kind that went along with terms like "dude." "I'll see you later."

Scott offered a smile and a nod, feeling better as he reminded himself that this was a good business arrangement and that he really liked Joe Black. He let out a sigh. But as he watched Joe leave, Scott noticed something on the side of Joe's khaki pants. He started to point it out then stopped himself. It looked like blood. Bright red, not pink. Splattered red blood. Corpses didn't splatter blood.

THIRTY-EIGHT

This would have been a day off for Liz Bailey if it wasn't for Isaac churning a path directly at the Florida Panhandle. New projections had the storm making landfall sooner than what was earlier predicted. The wind and waves suggested the new projections were accurate.

Liz was accustomed to being out in winds like this. She wondered just how used to it Lieutenant Commander Wilson was. He tight-fisted the controls and fought against each gust. It felt like being in a car with the driver constantly accelerating, braking, and accelerating again, combined with an occasional roller-coaster plunge.

Kesnick looked at her. With his back safely to Wilson and Ellis, he rolled his eyes. She held back a smile.

From above they watched boaters coming in early, heeding the weather advisories. All the marinas were full, with lines of crafts waiting to tie up. There was no surefire protection outside of pulling your boat out of the water and hauling it as far north as possible. Some people were trying to do that by motoring up rivers and paying to dock their boats in places out of the storm's path.

They were seeing an early surge. Waves already pounded seawalls and crashed up the beach, reaching the sand dunes. Surfers dotted in between the waves, bright spots of color bobbing up and down, disappearing and springing back into sight.

In the helicopter, Liz kept reminding herself to take it all in and remember how everything looked before Isaac hit. In 2004 Hurricane Ivan had decimated the area, ripping apart and chewing up everything in its path. The Florida Panhandle was where pine trees met palm trees, and the national forests that covered acres of land became shredded sticks, many snapped in two. Four-lane highways looked like a monster had taken a bite out of the asphalt, chewed it up, and spit it out. The massive live oaks, hundreds of years old, that lined Santa Rosa Sound were blown over, their tangled roots two stories high.

Pensacola Beach is about eight miles long and only a quarter mile at its widest, a peninsula with Santa Rosa Sound on one side and the Gulf of Mexico on the other. During Ivan the two bodies of water looked like one, meeting in the middle.

Liz remembered that it had taken years to sift and separate the debris from the sand. Huge machines had occupied the coastline. Cranes became a part of the skyline. Blue-tarped rooftops were seen in every neighborhood. Hurricanes never discriminated.

The three-mile I-10 bridge between Escambia County and Santa Rosa County had taken three years to repair. It had been crippling for a community connected by bridges to have all four major ones compromised in some way by the storm's massive surge.

Liz hadn't been here for Ivan, only for the aftermath. She had just finished training in Elizabeth City, North Carolina. For some reason she always regretted missing the actual storm. Silly. Not like she could have made a difference. It was probably some form of survivor's guilt. Perhaps she would be able to make a difference this time.

THIRTY-NINE

Walter Bailey decided to close up for the day despite the steady stream of customers. He didn't like the way the wind had started to rock the canteen back and forth. He'd bought the mobile unit at the navy commissary three years ago, not looking for a business but rather for something to do. He and his wife, Emilie, had looked forward to his early retirement. After all those years of six-month cruises and being apart, the two of them had a long list of plans, things they'd never been able to do between assignments. Emilie died before they'd even gotten started.

Within the first year of her absence, Walter realized that all his new hobbies seemed to be things other people called addictions. He had to come to terms with the simple fact that nothing would stop the ache. There were certain losses, certain voids that could never be filled with anything other than that which left the void in the first place.

These days he just wanted to stay busy. That's where the Coney Island Canteen came in. The mobile canteen had been in sad shape when Walter bought it, weathered and rusted but still in good working condition. He'd scraped and cleaned and polished the stainless-steel inside, painted the outside red, white, and blue, hung curtains with stars and stripes, and named it after one of his favorite boyhood places. It had never been about making money. Instead, it was something to occupy his time and keep him company so he wouldn't think about the void, about that empty hole that was left in his heart.

"You packing up, Walter?"

He poked his head out the side door to find Charlotte Mills in her signature floppy hat and cat-eye sunglasses, the hat too big and the glasses too bright for her small, meek features. Her pants legs were rolled up and she wore a long-tailed white cotton shirt over a formfitting tank top. Yellow flip-flops accentuated bright-red toenails. Her pockets bulged with seashells. Before he had gotten to know her, he'd called her the beachcombing widow—but only in his mind.

"I have a couple of dogs still warm if you're interested."

"Only if you have time. Everyone seems in a hurry today."

"Aren't you packing up?"

"Humph." She waved a birdlike hand at him. "I've gone through worse than what's coming. Last time I left, they wouldn't let us back on the beach for weeks."

"If I remember correctly, the bridge was out."

"Or so they said."

Years ago Charlotte's husband was killed in a plane crash, just days before he was to testify in a federal investigation against a state senator. There was never any evidence that the crash had been anything more than an unfortunate accident, but Charlotte believed otherwise. Walter wondered if she had always been prone to conspiracy theories because she saw them everywhere now.

"This storm's gonna be bad." Walter had slid the window back open and started pulling out condiments to prepare her hot dog. He decided to fix himself one and join her. "If you need a place to stay, you're welcome to come to my house. I'm well above the floodplain and about a quarter mile from Escambia Bay. It'll just be me, my daughter, and maybe my son-in-law."

"That's so sweet, Walter. But no, I'm staying. Already got the plywood up. Plenty of batteries and the generator's ready to go in the garage."

"Now, Charlotte, remember how Ivan shoved water and sand right through most of these beach houses?"

"Mine's cinder block. It made it through Ivan, I'm sure it'll make it through this."

"Hey, Mr. B."

"Well, if it isn't Phillip Norris's son."

Walter almost regretted remembering the name of the young man's father. The look on Norris's face was a combination of shock and embarrassment. It was obvious he hadn't wanted Walter to remember.

He introduced Charlotte, giving the young man the opportunity to introduce himself only if he chose to. Walter was pleased, but surprised, when Norris held out his hand and told her, "I'm Joe Black."

"I was just trying to convince Charlotte that she needed to leave the beach during the storm."

"I have a nice, solid, two-story cinder-block house, one lot back from the water. I'll be fine."

"People disappear during hurricanes," Joe said, and both Walter and Charlotte stared at him, startled at his bluntness. "There were more than three hundred people who went missing after Hurricane Ike hit Galveston, Texas. I'm just saying it happens. You really might want to reconsider."

FORTY

Maggie spent the rest of the afternoon back in her hotel room. Outside, the parking lots were filled with people packing up their belongings and getting ready to evacuate the beach. Most of the businesses were closed, the owners starting to board up windows and doors. However, surfers were still riding the waves. Some of the restaurants remained open. The Tiki Bar had a huge sign out front offering free drinks till they ran out.

The hotel manager had told Maggie he'd stay until the authorities closed the bridge. Maggie and Wurth were welcome to stay until then. Almost all of the other guests had checked out. Maggie suspected, from the absolute quiet, that she was the only one on her entire floor.

Sheriff Clayton had been gracious enough to drive her back to Pensacola Beach after the autopsy.

"Sorry, I can't be of much help," the sheriff had told her. "I'll contact Vince Coffland's next of kin. But anything else will have to wait until after the storm."

Maggie asked him to give her cell-phone number to Coffland's widow. If she wanted to talk about the details of her husband's disappearance, Maggie would be interested in listening. Clayton agreed.

Now, as she sipped a Diet Pepsi and waited for her laptop to boot up, she kept glancing at her cell phone. No calls. No messages . . . from anyone. She had the TV turned on to the Weather Channel but muted. Every once in a while she glanced at the on-screen graphics of Isaac's progression. She noticed one of the weather reporters, handsome, shaved head, nice legs, standing in front of the Gulf with its emerald-green rolling waves. She read the crawl: JIM CANTORE REPORTING FROM PENSACOLA.

"Oh Charlie, he's here." She smiled as she started jotting down things she wanted to remember.

Clayton had been correct about the severed hands and the fingerprints. None on file. They would need to wait for DNA to see if any of the hands belonged to Vince Coffland. A simple blood test had already found the foot to be someone else's. Vince Coffland was type B. The foot's blood was type O.

On the hotel notepad she wrote:

Coffland disappeared July 10
Port St. Lucie over 600 miles (land miles) away
Foot: metal debris; belonged to a 2nd victim
Plastic: heavy ply (commercial use?)
Fishing cooler: Why?
Tie-down: man-made synthetic rope, blue and yellow fibers

Had the foot belonged to Vince Coffland, Maggie was ready with an explanation. She'd heard of storm victims—victims exposed out in the open—sometimes ending up with an odd assortment of items like pieces of insulation, asbestos, vinyl siding, and glass embedded in their skin.

She'd asked Dr. Tomich if she could borrow one of the pieces of metal. Now she fingered it, still encased inside its plastic bag. She set it on the desktop in front of her. It was definitely metal, bent and distorted. But where did it come from?

Perhaps the metal was something that had gotten ripped apart during the hurricane-force winds. If the foot didn't belong to Coffland, was it possible it belonged to another person who had gone missing during Hurricane Gaston?

She added to her list:

Check other victims missing after HG

Maggie had handed over to Sheriff Clayton the label—or what she suspected was a label—that she found inside the cooler. However, she had memorized the faded printing and written it down exactly as it had appeared. She pulled out her copy and laid it on the desk beside the metal fragment.

AMET
DESTIN: 082409
#8509000029

She believed the second line was "destination" and a date, 082409, which translated to August 24, 2009. She had no idea what AMET was. Probably an acronym but for what?

The last line might be a serial number. It didn't, however, match the defibrillator.

Maggie glanced at the television and the map that Jim Cantore was showing of the Florida Panhandle. Then she did a double take. Off to the right side of Pensacola was Destin, Florida. Was it possible the second line of the label wasn't meant to be an abbreviation for destination, but rather Destin, Florida?

She twisted the hotel phone so she could see the instructions on its face as well as the hotel's phone number. Sure enough, 850 was the area code. The third line wasn't a serial number but a phone number.

What would it hurt to try? She tapped the number into her smartphone, pressed Call, and waited. It was ringing on the other end. Her mind kicked over to interrogation mode. She slowed her breathing, wiped her sweaty palm, and transferred the phone to her other hand. Three rings. Was the person on the other end expecting one of the packages from the cooler?

A woman's voice answered. "Advanced Medical Educational Technology, how may I direct your call?"

Maggie's eyes darted to the piece of paper. AMET.

"Yes, I'd like to speak with someone about a delivery."

"You have a delivery for us? Is it for one of our conferences?"

"Yes, I believe so."

"That would be Lawrence Piper. He's off-site today. Can I have him return your call?"

Maggie gave the woman her name and phone number. Before she could hang up, her phone was already beeping with an incoming call.

"This is Maggie O'Dell."

"Hey, it's Tully. I think I finally found your rope."

"What is it?"

"High-tenacity rope, UV resistant, anti-chemical erosion, modified resin coating."

"Wait a minute. You're able to tell all that from my photos?"

"The weave is unique. I scanned in a couple of your close-ups and got a hit."

Maggie had hoped the rope would lead them to the killer. "So you found the manufacturer?"

"Ningbosa Material Company. They specialize in bullet-proof plate, cut-resistant fabric, all kinds of good stuff."

"Are they somewhere close by?"

"Zhejiang, China."

"You're kidding."

"I'm not sure I pronounced that correctly. My Chinese needs work."

"I guess I shouldn't be surprised. Everything's made in China these days, right?"

"There's more. This color combination is a special order."

"Excellent. So who's the customer?"

"The United States Navy."

Before Maggie could respond, her phone was beeping again. Could it be Lawrence Piper already returning her call?

"I've got another call coming in," she told Tully.

"Let me know if you need anything else."

"Thanks." She clicked over. "Maggie O'Dell."

"Now that's music to my ears."

"Colonel Benjamin Platt." She tried to keep the smile from her voice. She hadn't talked to him for several days and whether she wanted to admit it to him or to herself, she missed him. "How goes your secret mission?"

"I'm being sent home. Can I buy you dinner tomorrow night?"

"I'm not home and I won't be for several days."

"Oh." He sounded disappointed. Disappointed and tired.

"Long story. I ended up on a road trip to Pensacola, Florida, with Charlie Wurth. Now I'm stuck here because of the hurricane."

"You're kidding? Where are you right now?"

"The Hilton on the beach. I'm looking out at the emerald-green waters of the Gulf as we speak. It's absolutely beautiful. Hard to imagine a hurricane is on its way."

"Go out on your balcony."

"Excuse me?"

"What floor are you on?"

"Platt, I swear if you ask me what I'm wearing, I'm hanging up."

"Just go out on your balcony."

Maggie hesitated. The balcony door was open. She had wanted to listen to the sound of the waves. She walked out onto the small balcony.

"Now look down on the beach," Platt told her.

There he was waving up at her.

"Buy you a drink at the Tiki Bar," he said.

FORTY-ONE

"Did I tell you how good it is to see you?" Platt asked Maggie.

"Three times."

But she smiled when she said it, so he figured he must not sound as high-school annoying as he thought he did. She wore a yellow knit top that brought out the gold flecks in her brown eyes. And she was wearing shorts—real shorts, not the baggy athletic ones she wore on game day. And flip-flops. She never wore open-toed shoes. The whole package was distracting as hell.

They'd snagged a table looking out at the Gulf. Platt had been told that most of the tourists had left Pensacola Beach, but the restaurants and bars—the ones that were still open—were crowded with residents, tired from packing all day.

The Tiki Bar offered free drinks. Their waitress told them they could still order appetizers if they didn't mind an assortment chosen by the cook. In other words, whatever was left. When she delivered the platter, Maggie and Platt looked at each other like they had hit the jackpot: wild-mushroom spring rolls, grilled prawns with salsa, pineapple-glazed pork ribs. His mouth started watering from the aromas alone.

"You still can't tell me about your secret mission, can you?" Maggie asked him after devouring a spring roll.

"Probably not. It doesn't matter." He wiped the glaze from his chin, sat back, and sipped a mai tai. It was his second and the rum had begun to relax him, except that he couldn't shake Ganz's abrupt shift in attitude. His finger tapped at the yellow paper umbrella and bobbed the slice of lime poked at the end. "I gave them my opinion. They didn't like it and they sent me home."

"Hmmm." Maggie picked up one of the prawns. "Sounds like a government assignment. Was it one of the military bases here?"

"How do you do that?" he said before he realized that he had just admitted she was correct.

"Look, you really don't need to tell me. I'm okay with that."

"What about your case?"

"Coast Guard found a fishing cooler in the Gulf."

"With a body inside?"

She nodded with a mouthful. They were across the table from each other but close enough that Platt reached over and dabbed at the corner of her mouth with a napkin.

"Sorry," she said, grabbing her own napkin and wiping both corners now. He immediately regretted what had been an instinctive gesture. "Pieces of at least one victim. A man who disappeared after Hurricane Gaston."

"Gaston? I thought that one hit on the Atlantic side."

"It did."

"You think you might have a killer who preys on hurricane victims?"

"I don't know. It's possible. People go missing."

"There is a lot of chaos and now you're stuck here to experience it."

She shrugged. "You must know by now that you are, too."

"I was offered a ride to Jacksonville on a C-130."

"A military cargo plane? Wow. How generous of them."

Platt's turn to shrug. He still felt the sting of Ganz's dismissal.

"So just out of curiosity, what were the pieces?" he asked.

"A torso, one foot, three hands. Aren't you hungry? Because I'm about to consume all of this."

He smiled and plucked up a spring roll. He was hungry but almost too exhausted to eat. He couldn't remember when he slept last.

"Three hands? So at least two victims."

"It could be two people or as many as five. Blood typing has already ruled out the foot belonging to the torso."

"So the killer's either messy or very smart. Do you think he was disposing bodies at sea?"

He could tell she was considering it then shook her head.

"The body parts were wrapped individually in thick plastic wrap, almost as if he was preserving instead of disposing." She drained her second Diet Pepsi. "What's worse is that the foot has pieces of metal embedded under the skin, deep into the tissue."

"Why did Kunze send you on this wild-goose chase? And into the eye of a hurricane?"

"Long story." She waved at the passing waitress and politely pointed to her glass for a refill. "Where are you staying?"

"My duffel bag is at the Santa Rosa Island Authority office. They told me there were no check-ins on the beach. No rooms available anywhere else."

"I have a suite at the Hilton. At least until tomorrow."

"Hmmm." He couldn't tell whether it was an invitation. They joked with each other so often that sometimes he wasn't sure where he really stood with Maggie O'Dell.

"Two queen-size beds."

Ah, okay. An offer from his friend. Was that relief he was feeling in his gut? Or was it disappointment?

"Minibar?" he sparred back.

"Yep."

"Big-screen TV?"

"It's a hotel room, Platt, not a sports bar."

"You sure you don't mind sharing? I think I snore when I'm overtired."

"Not a problem. I haven't been sleeping anyway."

"What do you mean you haven't been sleeping? Like at all?"

She looked as though she had revealed too much. "Bad case of insomnia," she said.

"For how long?" The doctor in him couldn't help it. Maybe that was the reason for their inability to move past friendship. They had begun as doctor and patient when Maggie was quarantined under his directive at USAMRIID.

"I sleep a few hours now and then." She hesitated then admitted, "It's probably been a few months."

"Well, I have just what you need."

"Look, Ben, I'm not sure I want to get used to taking any meds."

"I'm not talking about meds." He raised his hands as if to show her. "My massages can work wonders."

FORTY-TWO

Scott drove past his father-in-law's house twice. Not an easy task because he lived on the edge of a cul-de-sac. He hadn't been able to get him on the phone. Walter Bailey was the only person Scott knew who didn't own a cell phone and was proud of the fact.

The front windows remained dark, not even a reflection from the TV. Walter's car was in the driveway but not his mobile canteen. Was it possible he was still out on the beach?

Scott slapped his hands against the steering wheel. That was great, just great. He needed a generator and the old man was out partying on the beach.

He had driven to five different hardware stores with a roll of cash, thinking he could surely buy a backroom generator from someone. After all, everyone had a price, didn't they?

He ignored the homemade signs in the parking lots: NO MORE PLYWOOD, GENERATORS, OR BATTERIES. At each store, he asked for the manager. Two of them just shook their heads at him. Two others laughed. One eyed the roll of cash and considered selling Scott his personal home generator, then finally said, "Hell, I better not. My wife would kick the royal crap out of me. Sorry, mister."

"Can you at least tell me," he asked that manager, while peeling a hundred-dollar bill off his roll, "how far I have to drive to go get one?"

The guy started checking his computer, anxious to help if it meant a finder's fee. He poked at the keys, winced, then poked some more. He did this several times before he finally said, "Here we go. There's one I can hold for you at the Athens, Georgia, store."

"Athens? Okay. Is that just over the Florida/Georgia border?"

"No, it's on the north side of Atlanta."

"Atlanta? Isn't that like five or six hours away?"

"You could be there when the store opens at seven tomorrow. You want me to put a hold on it or not?"

He told him to go ahead. It was a backup plan that only cost him a hundred bucks if he didn't need it. The more he thought about driving twelve hours, the more angry he got with his in-laws.

The Baileys had never embraced him like they should have. And he took good care of Trish. By the holidays, she'd be living in a brand-new custom-built home overlooking Pensacola Bay. He had her driving a BMW—a fucking 525i. He made it so she didn't have to work a single day after they got married. Even the place they were renting was plush and loaded with luxury. He was acknowledged around town as a successful businessman, invited to join the Rotary. And yet all that wasn't good enough. The Baileys still didn't treat him like he was family. What was worse, Scott felt like Walter Bailey treated him as if he wasn't worthy of Trish. Walter certainly wouldn't think he was worthy of borrowing one of his fucking generators.

Scott shut off the headlights and pulled his Lexus GX to a stop along the curb half a block from Walter's house, where he could see anyone turning into the driveway. It was late. Where the hell was the old man? He drank the lukewarm remains of his latte. He had added a splash of vodka—from the previous funeral home owner's stash that he had taken along for the ride—thinking he'd need the extra jolt to convince Walter. But even that was wearing off.

He knew there was a fifty-fifty chance the side door to the garage would be unlocked—habit more than anything else. Walter couldn't park a single vehicle in the garage since it was packed with his discounts, bargains, and supplies for the canteen.

Scott scrubbed the exhaustion from his face. It had been a hell of a day. He just wanted to go home and fall into bed. But even that promised to be a challenge. Trish had left several angry voice and text messages for him.

Scott looked at his wristwatch and let out a sigh of frustration. He sure as hell was not driving to Atlanta tonight. He turned the key but left the headlights off. As quietly as the vehicle allowed, he pulled up and backed into Walter's driveway. The garage was attached to the back of the house. Even with the sliding door open no one could see into the garage from the street. If the neighbors recognized his vehicle, that would actually be a good thing. They wouldn't call the cops on Trish's husband.

The side door was unlocked. Scott used a flashlight to hunt down the generators, not really sure what they looked like. A big engine on wheels was his best guess. Two refrigerators hummed, side by side. Loaded shelves lined three of the walls. The only path amounted to a maze winding its way through boxes and cartons, toolboxes and garden equipment, spare tires, bags of mulch, large red gas containers, two push mowers—and that was just one side of the double garage.

In the corner he found a generator covered with a gray tarp. He rocked it out of a tight squeeze between two shelves. Once he pulled it free, he was ready to open the garage door. He hit the electronic button and the whine startled him as did the bright light that flashed on as the door went up. He lunged for the light switch and flipped it off. The noise was bad enough. He didn't need a spotlight on what he was doing. He dragged over the metal railings Walter had stored with the generator, figuring out that if he positioned them against the rear bumper of his Lexus he could simply roll the contraption up into the vehicle. He had it almost in when he saw the shadow walk out from behind the bushes.

"What the hell are you doing, Scott?"

FORTY-THREE

Liz couldn't believe her dad would loan Scott a generator. He was fussy about his possessions and he didn't seem to like Scott much. But what did she know about her father? She'd been surprised to find him downing free martinis, one after another, at the Tiki Bar on the beach. Liz reminded herself that a lot had changed since her mom had died, and she hadn't been here for most of that time. If her dad had learned to set the table and drink martinis, perhaps he'd changed in other ways, too.

"Hey, Liz." Scott was out of breath but didn't seem embarrassed, and he didn't stop what he was doing. "Do you have any idea where your dad is?"

"I just brought him and the canteen home. Free drinks on the beach."

"Is he okay?"

"Sleeping like a baby. I have half a mind to leave him in the canteen for the night. So what are you doing?"

"Just picking up one of Walter's generators." He slammed shut the rear door of the SUV. "I've been waiting for him the past couple of hours."

"He probably forgot."

In the shadows Liz couldn't see Scott's face. After last night's run-in on the beach, she realized that she didn't know her brother-in-law very well, either, despite the fact that he thought he knew her. It looked like Trish had finally gotten him to prepare for the storm.

"You know how to hook up and start one of those?" she asked him.

Scott shrugged. "Not really. I was hoping Walter would show me."

Instinctively Liz looked over her shoulder. She couldn't see the canteen where she'd parked it on the street.

"Tell you what," she told Scott, "you help me get my dad into bed, I'll help you with the generator."

"Really? You'd do that?" He sounded like a little boy, suspicious that he might be tricked.

"Sure. If you throw in a ride back to the beach to get my car."

Walter proved more cooperative than Liz expected. He seemed to think Scott was an old navy friend of his. He kept mumbling something about Phillip Norris's kid. But once they got him inside his bedroom, he clicked into his routine. He mumbled and shuffled as he took off his shoes and put them where they belonged in the closet. Then he emptied his pockets into the valet tray on his dresser. Liz kissed him goodbye on the cheek and he waved her out of his bedroom.

At the funeral home Scott rolled the generator out the back of the SUV like a pro. Liz helped him fill it with gasoline. He talked too much, either because he was tired or because he was uncomfortable being alone with her. Or—and she hated that she jumped to this conclusion—because he'd been drinking. It didn't matter. She just wanted to finish here, get her car, and catch some sleep. The storm's outer bands were predicted to kick up winds and the downpour would start sometime tomorrow afternoon.

She showed Scott all the basics—how to choke the generator and how to calculate the wattage of each appliance he connected. All the while he rambled on about the new air-conditioned walkway he'd installed between the two buildings and his huge walk-in refrigerator.

"I added all this stuff only to find out none of it is connected to a backup generator. Can you imagine not having a backup for the cooler? In a funeral home?"

Finished with the instructions, she helped him pull the machine into an outdoor supply shed. It was only ten feet away from the building, hidden behind some trees.

She waited in the doorway as he spread a tarp over the generator and used bungee cords to fasten it. That's when she noticed the battered white stainless-steel cooler. It was huge. The lid had been left open, leaning up against the wall, and Liz noticed the fish-measuring ruler molded into the lid. A tie-down hung from the cooler's handle, a rope made of yellow-and-blue strands.

Liz felt a little sick to her stomach. This cooler looked exactly like the one she had pulled out of the Gulf.

FORTY-FOUR

"Oh my God, that feels good," Maggie told Platt as he settled beside her on the edge of the bed.

"You're going to have to stop talking about this case so you can relax and enjoy this."

What Maggie couldn't tell Platt was that she had to keep talking because as soon as she thought about his hands on her bare back she felt herself getting aroused.

"There's an area right around here," he said as his hands slid to her lower back. "This should put you to sleep."

She closed her eyes. He didn't have a clue. Or if he did, he was better at hiding it than she was.

"You didn't answer my question," she said and wondered if she sounded just as breathless as she felt. He was right. It was starting to be difficult to concentrate but not because she was falling asleep.

"Why wrap the body parts?" Platt's hands continued without interruption. "Maybe he's adding to a collection."

"This fishing cooler is huge." His fingers kneaded her skin, a combination of pressure and caress. "Where do you buy something like that?"

"Sporting goods store? Or a place that sells boats?"

"A boat. I didn't even think of that. He must own a boat."

"This is probably why you can't sleep," Platt said. "You won't let your mind shut off. You're still trying to figure things out."

"The subconscious does continue to work through problems and then find—" His thumbs pressed into the middle of her back and took her breath away.

"That's better," Platt said.

"So you're purposely . . . trying . . . to shut me up."

"Exactly. Just for a few minutes, okay?"

"You talk then."

"Really? You don't like silence?"

She nodded or tried to.

"Okay. If it's going to help relax you."

He started telling her about a place where his family spent vacations when he was a boy. A cottage on the North Carolina shore. The kitchen overlooked the beach. Bright-yellow curtains and a tablecloth to match. He'd stay inside on the afternoons that his mother baked. She'd tell him to go play in the sand but he wanted to be there when the cinnamon rolls or peanut-butter cookies drizzled with sugar came out of the oven. So she'd let him help. He measured and stirred while they talked about the books he'd brought to read during vacation. They'd discuss the powers of wizards, the discovery of the *Titanic*, and whether sea dragons really existed.

At some point Maggie heard the sound of waves. She

smelled the salt water, and for a second she thought she could even smell cinnamon. She had a light-headed sensation of floating on water. In her mind she saw the waves rolling, capped by white foam. Felt the spray on her face. There was nothing but water all around her. No land in sight. Just the gentle rocking of the water.

FORTY-FIVE

Liz sat in her car on the beach. Scott had dropped her off almost half an hour ago. She needed to drive home, take a shower, get some sleep. Tomorrow would be a long, hard day. And yet here she sat, staring out at the waves, her mind still reeling. Before leaving Scott, she had asked about the marine cooler, keeping her voice light and casual.

"A friend left it here. Just for a day or two," he told her.

"A friend in the business?"

"Yeah, why?"

"No reason. I just . . . " She had found herself stumbling because she could still see the plastic-wrapped body parts. "I've never seen one with a measure molded inside the lid like that."

"Oh yeah. I didn't notice that." He had walked around to the front of the cooler to get a better look. "I bet Joe didn't notice it, either. He doesn't exactly use it for fishing."

"Really? What does he use it for?"

That was where she crossed the line. She saw him shut down, a hint of suspicion replacing his need to charm and inform. In the end he shrugged like it was no big deal.

"I don't know. Whatever you use a cooler like that for."

Then he walked her out of the shed.

Liz had already called Sheriff Joshua Clayton only to have one of his deputies call her back, saying this wasn't of an urgent nature.

"We've got a hurricane on its way," the deputy told her. "Sheriff Clayton has already determined this case is on hold until after the storm."

He was right. Finding a fishing cooler that looked like the one filled with body parts didn't seem urgent. But something about finding it in the back of a funeral home kept Liz from dismissing it.

She could see the top floor of the Hilton. She pulled out her cell phone again. Punched 411 and asked for the phone number.

"Hilton Pensacola Beach Gulf Front. This is the front desk."

"Yes, I'd like to talk to one of your guests. Maggie O'Dell."

"All of our guests have checked out. Oh, wait. O'Dell. The FBI agent with Mr. Wurth?"

"Yes, that's right."

"She is here until noon tomorrow." Then he hesitated. "Is this urgent?"

Liz sighed, ran fingers through her hair as she checked the time on her dashboard. It was almost midnight.

"It's just that I usually don't ring my guests' rooms after ten o'clock," he said when she took too long to answer. "I can send you to voice mail and the red light will come on her phone."

"That's fine."

While she waited for the connection, she tried to formulate what to say. Was she simply being paranoid? Overly observant? Obsessive?

At the beep she gave her name and cell-phone number, then simply said she had some information. Lame, she knew, but safe. And maybe in the morning when the outer bands of Hurricane Isaac started battering the area, Liz would think the identical fishing cooler was nothing but a mere coincidence.

There were only a few cars left in the lot and as Liz pulled onto Pensacola Beach Boulevard she recognized the faded red Impala. She had promised her dad she'd check on the surfer kid, Danny. She'd talk to him tomorrow. It was late. No sense in tapping on his car window tonight and scaring the poor kid to death.

TUESDAY, AUGUST 25

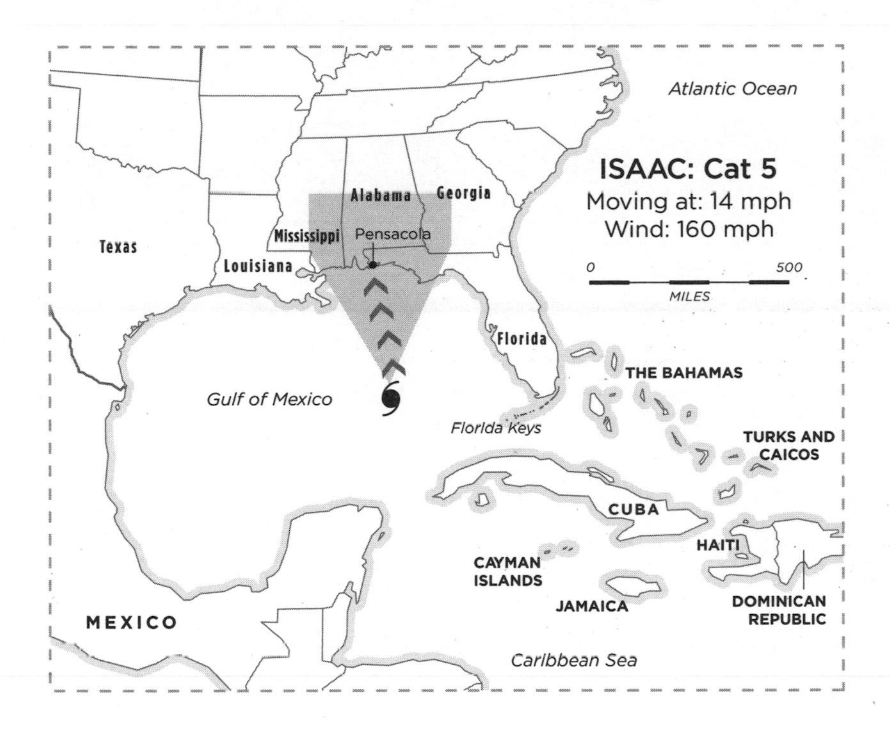

FORTY-SIX

The pounding came from someplace other than inside Platt's head. Of that he was certain, though the back of his head throbbed. He opened his eyes and took a few seconds to remember where he was.

Hotel room. The Hilton. Too many free mai tais. Rum gave him a killer headache every time.

He pushed himself off the sofa and that's when he remembered Maggie. The thought spun him around to look back at the bedroom. Awake, he realized the pounding came from the front door of the suite, not the bedroom.

Platt grabbed his shirt from a nearby chair but didn't bother with his shoes. It was probably just hotel staff. He noticed the telephone's flashing red button. He didn't remember the phone ringing but he could have missed it.

By the time he opened the door he had his shirt on but not buttoned. The black man in a green polo shirt looked puzzled.

"Yes?" Platt asked.

The man stared at him, backed up and checked the number beside the doorframe, then looked over Platt's shoulder to get a glimpse inside. Not much success. He was shorter than Platt.

"I'm looking for Maggie O'Dell."

"Are you from the hotel?"

"Ah, no. Homeland Security."

"Door-to-door check?"

"Excuse me?"

"Do we need to leave?"

"Is Maggie here?"

"Charlie?" Maggie called from behind Platt.

With a glance over his shoulder, Platt saw her come out of the bathroom. Her hair was wet and she wore one of the hotel's white robes. The fresh scent of soap wafted through the entry and as distracting as it was, Platt couldn't take his eyes off Charlie, whose eyes had widened. His jaw hung open. It was classic.

"I'm sorry," Platt said. "You're Charlie Wurth. When you said Homeland Security, I thought you were here to tell us that we had to leave. I'm Benjamin Platt."

He held his hand out and waited while Wurth processed the information, still trying to figure out what he was seeing. Platt spotted the paper bag in Wurth's right hand. He could smell the pastry as Wurth moved it to his left hand in order to shake.

"Come on in, Charlie. Keep Ben company while I put on some clothes," Maggie told him. "I overslept." Then to Platt and with a smile, she said, "I actually slept."

"I'll bet," Platt heard Wurth say, but under his breath.

Maggie was already headed through the bedroom door and Platt swore he saw a bit of a skip in her step.

FORTY-SEVEN

The sky looked as dark and murky as Scott felt. He'd taken a long shower because for some reason he could smell decomposing flesh almost as if the scent had been smeared on his skin. He put on crisply pressed trousers and shirt. No tie today. He ate breakfast with Trish. She'd prepared blueberry pancakes and sausage. She was in a good mood. Go figure.

As soon as he got in his Lexus he could smell it again. There was no mistaking the scent of decomposing flesh.

At the first intersection he pulled to the side of the road, got out, and started searching the vehicle. A splash of gasoline and a smudge of oil dirtied the plastic he'd laid in back before transporting the generator, but there was nothing else. He kept his vehicles as spotless as the funeral home.

He tried to ignore the smell. Get his mind off it. He turned up the local radio station.

"Isaac's coming, folks. The Weather Channel's Jim Cantore was reporting from our own Pensacola Beach this morning. The eye of the storm is about a hundred miles away. Winds at 160 miles per hour. That's a cat 5, and this thing is in warm

open water with nothing to slow it down. In fact, it's picked up speed and is moving at fourteen miles per hour instead of ten. That means it'll be sooner than later. We'll be seeing the outer bands about noon and this monster will be making landfall sometime tonight.

"City commissioners for Escambia and Santa Rosa counties have declared a state of emergency and shelters across both counties will start opening this morning. I'll be giving you their locations in just a minute. Folks, we're getting a big piece of this storm, and it's looking more and more like we'll be in the northeast quadrant. That means it'll be bad. Really bad."

Scott shut it off. Hell, at least he'd be ready. He was exhausted but he was back in control.

Earlier he'd received yet another phone call from Uncle Mel's family. Now they wanted to wait until after the storm.

"Is that okay? Will he be okay?" they had asked, but Scott could tell Uncle Mel was no longer their priority. There was a storm to survive. Funny, he thought, how the dead are forgotten when the business of living distracts us.

At least they weren't forgotten by Joe Black. Again, there were no signs of a vehicle but Scott could tell from the alarm system that Joe was still inside. Where the hell did he park? There was an apartment parking lot on the other side of the trees, but he'd have to walk through the brush and tall grass that separated the two properties. And when did he start dumping his coolers in Scott's shed? Liz seemed just a little too interested. Is that where he had first started smelling decomposing flesh? Had Liz smelled it last night?

Scott walked through the back door and the scent was even

stronger. He caught himself cringing. What had Joe left for him today?

"Hey, buddy." Joe came down the hall from the walk-in refrigerator.

Scott noticed empty hands and no splatters. He restrained a sigh of relief. Instead, he glanced into the embalming room. Clean. So what was he smelling?

"I probably won't see you until after the storm," Joe told him, slinging a backpack over his shoulder.

"Making a run for it?"

Joe laughed. "You might say that. I have one more pickup and then I want to get my boat out of harm's way."

"You have a boat?"

"I told you that."

But Scott knew he hadn't. He would have remembered.

"Makes it a lot easier," Joe explained, "to get around afterward when the roads and bridges are out. But I need to move and dock it at least a hundred miles west of here."

"Biloxi? New Orleans?"

"In that vicinity."

"I just heard it's moving in a lot faster than they predicted."

"Gotta go, then. I'll see you in a couple of days."

Scott watched him leave and found himself wishing Joe had invited him along. Then he started hunting for the source of the smell. At one point he even sniffed himself, pulling his shirt open and taking an inside whiff. He checked the walk-in refrigerator but the scent didn't grow stronger. Maybe once he got to work he would be able to ignore it.

He rolled out a stainless-steel table with the cardboard box containing Uncle Mel. He still needed to embalm the guy. Just as well do it before the storm. He'd sold the family an expensive casket even though they didn't want it open for the memorial. Actually, the expensive sell was always easier with families that didn't want a traditional viewing. It was their way of compensating for their guilt of not wanting to take one last look.

Scott arranged everything he needed in the embalming room. He gowned up and opened the cardboard box, ready to begin.

"That son of a bitch."

Uncle Mel's knees were cut away and both of his hands were missing.

FORTY-EIGHT

From the bedroom balcony Maggie could see that things had changed drastically overnight. The waves churned higher, crashing farther up the shore. The sky had turned into a thick gray ceiling, several layers of clouds, low and moving, each layer at its own speed. Not even noon and the heat was stifling, the humidity oppressive. She had just dried her hair and it was already damp. Her shirt stuck to her skin.

She found Platt and Wurth in the suite's living room, eating doughnuts. One of them had made coffee and the scent filled the room. Before she had a chance to sit, Platt was up getting her a Diet Pepsi from the minibar while Wurth unwrapped a chocolate doughnut to set in front of her. She held back a smile as well as any comments about the men waiting on her.

"Outer bands may start hitting the area as soon as one this afternoon," Wurth updated her. "Landfall is definitely gonna be tonight. Probably after dark."

"Isn't that sooner than predicted?" Maggie asked.

"Yep. Storm's picked up a little speed. No more islands to slow it down."

Platt had stayed drinking his coffee near the desk and now something distracted him. Maggie saw him pick up the plastic bag she'd left on top of her file folders. He was fingering the scrap of metal inside.

"That's what the coroner plucked out of the severed foot," she told him, looking at the doughnut in front of her.

She loved chocolate doughnuts but she hadn't eaten one since that day at Quantico, less than a year ago, when a box of doughnuts had been delivered with a terrorist's note at the bottom. Charlie Wurth couldn't possibly have known when he brought over breakfast that his gesture would threaten to crack the seal on one of her leaky compartments. She broke the doughnut in half and took a bite.

"Oh, I almost forgot," Platt said, pointing at the hotel phone. "There's a message for you."

She looked at Wurth.

"Not me. I have your cell phone. Though I understand you probably weren't answering that last night, either."

She wanted to laugh at his insinuation but he wasn't joking. No raised eyebrow. No typical grin. Was it possible Charlie Wurth was jealous? She shook the thought out of her mind, took another bite of the doughnut, pleased that it actually tasted good to her. Then she went to check the message.

"It's Liz Bailey," she told the men. "I'm going to call her back on my cell." She left them to retrieve the phone in the bedroom. She hadn't heard a ring last night. She really must have slept hard.

Before she could dial, her cell phone rang.

"This is Maggie O'Dell."

Hesitation, then a woman's voice. "FBI Agent O'Dell?"

"Yes."

"I was given your number by the Escambia County sheriff." A pause. "About my husband. I'm sorry I didn't even tell you my name. I'm Irene Coffland."

The torso's wife, Maggie thought before she could stop herself. But after a while it was hard to not think in those terms.

"Mrs. Coffland, thank you for calling me."

"I don't know what I can tell you that would be of help."

Maggie wasn't sure what Sheriff Clayton had told Mrs. Coffland. She had to know, however, that they had only a piece of him. Tough news for anyone to receive. Maggie proceeded gently.

"Can you tell me what you remember about the last few minutes before your husband disappeared?"

"I've already told the local authorities as well as your sheriff."

"I'm sorry. Look, you really don't have to talk to me. I know this isn't easy." Maggie knew that if Mrs. Coffland called her, she wanted to talk. Sometimes when you told people they don't have to, they suddenly wanted to tell you. A cheap bit of reverse psychology.

"We had driven back to our home. After the hurricane. Things were a mess. We were worried about looters." The woman sighed. "What a thing to worry about. Things. They're just things. We were cleaning up. Vince had just started the generator. It was getting dark. Our neighbors had returned and we were all in our backyard when we heard a boat in the bay."

"A boat?"

"Yes. The men thought it must be looters. Vince told us to stay put. He got his rifle and headed down to the water."

"Alone?"

"My husband was a retired police chief. Forced retirement after his heart attack. There was no question he could handle himself. And he wanted Henry to stay with Katherine and me. Everything had been so quiet but the generator made an awful lot of noise. We heard some shouts but they sounded like greetings. Definitely not a ruckus. We relaxed a bit. Thought it might just be another neighbor. Maybe the authorities. He was gone ten, fifteen minutes. Then we heard the boat start up again. We waited for Vince."

Another pause; this time Maggie could hear her clearing her throat. "He never came back. We looked all night. Called the local authorities. After the storm they had too many other important things to do. So many people were unaccounted for. My husband simply became just one of dozens."

"Did you ever find out if the authorities had a boat in your area?"

"No, they said they didn't. But I will tell you this, Vince would have fought hard if he thought whoever was on that boat was a threat to any of us."

"I'm not sure I understand what you're saying, Mrs. Coffland."

"We heard what sounded like greetings. An amicable exchange. Vince either recognized the person on that boat or he didn't feel threatened by him."

As Maggie ended the call she considered what she'd learned. Vince Coffland's killer had access to or owned a boat.

Probably one small enough to trailer. That would explain how Vince Coffland disappeared off the Atlantic coast and ended up in the Gulf of Mexico. She could check the Pensacola Beach marina, though without a name or even a description of the boat she knew she wouldn't have much luck.

She punched in the number for Liz Bailey as she heard a phone ring in the other room. Platt answered his phone as Liz Bailey answered Maggie.

"Hello."

"Liz, it's Maggie O'Dell. Sorry for not getting back to you sooner."

"Actually, I'm not sure if this means anything but I saw an exact replica of that fishing cooler we found in the Gulf."

"Wasn't it pretty standard? Especially down here."

"It wasn't just the cooler. It had the exact same tie-down."

"Are you sure?"

"Looked like it. Same blue-and-yellow strands. Same thickness."

Maggie hesitated. Could it be a coincidence? Her old boss, Assistant Director Cunningham, used to tell her there was no such thing as a coincidence. There was a very good chance that the person who owned this cooler also owned the one found in the Gulf.

Before Maggie responded, Liz continued. "What sort of got my attention was where I saw it. You know, considering what we found inside the first one."

"Where exactly *did* you see it?"

"In a shed back behind a funeral home."

FORTY-NINE

Platt answered his phone, still focused on the bit of metal inside the plastic bag.

"Colonel Platt, this is Captain Ganz."

Platt stopped. "Captain Ganz." He couldn't think of anything else to say to the man. Fortunately he didn't have to reply.

"I owe you an apology, Colonel."

Silence. Perhaps he wanted it to sink in.

"You found something?"

"The other two soldiers who died last week also show traces of *Clostridium sordellii.* We've started testing the other patients. So far, nine out of ten have the bacterium. We're still not quite sure where or how it got into their bodies, but you must be right. It has to be through the bone grafts or bone paste. Right now I need to save these soldiers."

More silence. Platt waited it out.

"Ben, I've been a jackass in the way I treated you. If you haven't left Pensacola yet, would you consider coming back and giving me a hand?"

Platt didn't hesitate. "Of course."

"This hurricane won't be a party. We have generators but not for everything."

"I understand."

"And we don't have the antibiotics we need."

"This isn't your ordinary bacterium."

"Tell me where you are and I'll have my driver pick you up."

"He can pick me up at the Hilton. Have him ring me twice when he gets here and I'll meet him in the lobby."

Platt got off the phone just as Maggie returned.

"You're leaving. Going back." She said it with no hint of surprise.

"Yes. Sometimes there's no pleasure in being right."

"You got that right," Wurth said, getting up, ready to leave.

"I'm going to stay on the beach this morning," Maggie told Wurth.

"That's not a good idea." He looked at Platt. "Tell her that's not a good idea."

Platt shrugged. "What makes you think she'll listen to me?"

"They'll be closing Bob Sykes Bridge," Wurth told her, "and the Navarre Bridge at one o'clock. There's no other way off Pensacola Beach."

"It's okay. Liz Bailey promised I'd have a way off."

"And what, might I ask, is it you hope to accomplish by staying?"

"Come on, Charlie, you brought me down here for a case. You can't blame me for wanting to do some footwork."

"Speaking of foot"—Platt held out the plastic bag with the metal bit—"I think I know what this is. It's shrapnel."

Maggie took the bag and looked at it again. "As in shrapnel from an explosive?"

He nodded. "I've removed my share of this stuff from soldiers in Afghanistan. I've been staring at this piece for the last hour trying to figure out how it ended up in a severed foot found in the Gulf of Mexico."

FIFTY

Liz came down the steps from her bedroom and dropped her duffel bag in the foyer. She was about to tap on the master-bedroom door to say goodbye to her dad when she heard him in the kitchen. She found him down on his knees, rummaging through one of the lower cabinets. He had food packages scattered on the floor around him. And more surprising, he was dressed in his navy jumpsuit, his canteen uniform.

"Dad, what are you doing?"

"Oh, hello, darlin'. I didn't wake you, did I?"

"No, I'm on my way out. I thought you'd be still sleeping."

"Here they are," he said as he pulled out a box. He stood and wiped at his knees while he handed her the box of power bars. "These are supposed to be really good. Lots of protein. They aren't the cheap ones. Throw a few in your bag. Take the box if you have room."

She took the box and watched him stuff the other packages back into the cabinet.

"You dug through the cabinet just for these?"

"I know they'll probably have MREs for you but they get old fast. I bought these last week thinking you'd like them."

Liz wondered if he was simply avoiding the subject of last night. Maybe he didn't remember. She wouldn't embarrass him.

"When did you get your car?"

So he did remember.

"Last night. Scott took me back to the beach."

"Scott?"

"He was here picking up the generator you loaned him."

Walter stared at her. "I know I had a bit to drink yesterday, but I haven't talked to Scott in over a week."

"Are you sure? Maybe he talked to you while you were at the Tiki Bar."

"Nope. Had a few drinks with a friend of his from out of town." He closed the cabinet and started pulling items from the refrigerator. "Nice enough but a strange young fellow. Told me his daddy's name is Phillip Norris but he calls himself Joe Black. Now why would a boy not use his daddy's name?"

"Maybe his mom and dad weren't married. He told you he's a friend of Scott's?"

"No, not exactly." He started searching through another cabinet, this time pulling out a small blender. "He said it was nice to be drinking with someone he liked. Said that he'd spent the last two evenings on the beach with a business associate who was a—okay, now this is his word, not mine—he said he was a dickhead funeral director. Doesn't that sound like Scott?

You saw Scott drunk the other night on the beach. It has to be Scott."

Liz wondered if Joe Black was the friend of Scott's who owned the fishing cooler. Didn't he say it belonged to his friend Joe?

Her dad was gathering and arranging an array of items on the countertop: a banana, a bottle of honey, a jug of orange juice, and a carton of milk.

"What are you making here, Dad?"

"Oh, just something. I've got a little bit of a headache."

"Like a hangover?"

He frowned and she let it go.

"You're not taking the canteen to the beach today, are you?"

"Just for an hour or two."

"Dad, they're closing the Bob Sykes Bridge at one."

"I'll be gone by then. Right now there'll be some hungry people on the beach. And I need to check on some friends."

"Promise me you'll be back here by noon."

He nodded. "So I won't see you until after the storm?"

"I'll call and let you know when we get to Jacksonville. We'll be doing search and rescue until they tell us to get to safety. I'm thinking that'll be sometime this afternoon."

"You be careful. No hotdogging."

"You be careful, too, hot-dog man."

He smiled and shrugged.

"I'll talk to you later." Liz kissed him on the cheek as he splashed milk and orange juice together into the blender. She thought the concoction actually looked too good to cure a hangover.

"I can't believe Scott helped himself to one of my generators without asking."

"Sorry, Dad. He made it sound like he'd talked to you."

She grabbed the box of power bars, and as she headed out the door she heard her dad say, "He really is a dickhead."

FIFTY-ONE

Maggie thought Charlie Wurth was being a bit overprotective. She knew he felt responsible for bringing her to Florida in the middle of the storm, so she wasn't surprised that all the way out her hotel door and down the hall he ranted about her staying on the beach. In fact, she could hear him still mumbling as he got on the elevator.

What she wasn't prepared for was Platt's reaction.

"You really can't stay on the beach," he told her almost as soon as she closed the door.

"I'll be with the United States Coast Guard."

He didn't smile.

"Really, I'll be okay," she said.

"When the outer bands start, there'll be torrential downpours, thunderstorms, possibly tornadoes. Have you ever been in a hurricane before?"

"No, but I've been in a tunnel dug under a graveyard with a serial killer."

"This isn't funny."

"I wasn't being funny." She stood back and looked at him.

She'd seen his serious side, the concerned doctor watching over his patient. This was something different. "I can take care of myself."

"I know you can."

He let out a deep breath and rubbed at his jaw, an exhausted mannerism Maggie recognized. It only occurred to her now that he may not have gotten as much sleep as she did last night. She'd been surprised, maybe disappointed, to wake up and not find him beside her.

"I worry about you," he said.

She started to smile until she saw the look on his face. This wasn't an easy admission for him. They teased each other a lot, but this was serious.

"I really can take care of myself," she tried again.

"But somehow you manage to get in the way of suitcase bombs and the Ebola virus. Not to mention serial killers."

"You're the one going off on secret missions to undisclosed locations." Maggie's sudden switch in tone surprised her as much as it did Platt.

This time, however, he smiled and said, "So you worry about me, too?"

She shrugged then nodded.

"It's annoying, isn't it?" He was back to teasing. A more comfortable place for both of them.

His phone rang twice and stopped. He glanced down at the number.

"My ride's here." But he didn't move. "Call me. Or text me. Let me know you're safe."

"Absolutely. You do the same."

He picked up his duffel bag and slung it over his shoulder. He started for the door, then without warning he turned back.

"What the hell," he mumbled and in three steps he was kissing her, one hand cupping the back of her neck, the other keeping his duffel bag from banging her shoulder. "Make sure you take care of yourself, Maggie O'Dell."

She was glad he sounded a little out of breath. As he headed for the door another damned phone started ringing. It was Maggie's. She wanted to ignore it.

Platt smiled at her as he closed the door. "You better get that."

She was shaking her head then realized she was smiling, too.

"Maggie O'Dell," she answered.

"Yes, Ms. O'Dell, this is Lawrence Piper returning your call."

Platt had made her forget her case. It took her a second to remember who Lawrence Piper was and why she had called him.

"You wanted to know about a delivery," he prompted.

How could she play this? She couldn't very well tell him she'd found his phone number on a label stuck to a cooler full of body parts. Or could she?

"Concerning Destin on August twenty-fourth," she said, just as she realized the twenty-fourth was yesterday.

"I don't understand. I told Joe we had to cancel Destin because of the hurricane."

He sounded like a businessman. She hadn't had the chance to research Advanced Medical Educational Technology. But there was nothing clandestine or sinister in his tone. The best interrogators Maggie had worked with had taught her that the less the interrogator said, the more the interrogated filled in. She waited.

"Are you working with Joe?" Piper asked.

"I'm trying to." She kept her remarks innocuous.

Piper laughed and added, "I told him he needed an assistant. Look, Maggie—you don't mind if I call you Maggie."

A businessman but also a salesman, Maggie decided.

"Not at all."

"I already told Joe I'd make this cancellation up to him. I've got a couple dozen surgeons coming to a conference in Tampa over Labor Day. I'm going to need at least twenty-two cervical spines. I'd prefer brain with skull base intact, if that's possible."

Maggie thought about the body parts found in the cooler, individually wrapped in plastic. Could it be that simple? A body broker making a delivery? From what little she knew, there was nothing illegal about it. Most federal regulations applied only to organs. Few states regulated anything beyond that.

"I don't want to lose Joe," he said when she didn't respond. Evidently Maggie's silence was disconcerting to Piper. "Can you tell him that? He hasn't called and the number I have for him has already been changed. That's an annoying habit your new boss has."

"Yes, I know. He likes to be the one calling." She wasn't surprised.

"It's tough to find someone with his skill and consistency.

Especially someone who delivers and sets up. Can you tell him that?"

"Yes," Maggie said.

As she pressed End, she noticed she had missed a call: Dr. Tomich.

Brokered body parts. It made sense. And it probably explained the identical cooler Liz Bailey saw outside a funeral home. It didn't, however, explain Vince Coffland's disappearance.

Maggie pressed Return Call.

"Tomich," he snapped. His clipped manner made his name sound as if it were a swear word.

"Dr. Tomich, it's Maggie O'Dell returning your call."

"Ah yes. Agent O'Dell."

Before she could tell him that the parts might be brokered, Tomich surprised her by saying, "It appears you were correct."

"Excuse me?"

"After examining the X-rays I discovered a bullet in Mr. Vince Coffland."

"Are you certain it wasn't shrapnel? I think that's what the metal is in the severed foot."

"No, no, no. This is a bullet. I went back and extracted it. Looks like a .22 caliber handgun. The trajectory path would suggest that it entered somewhere below the occipital bone and above the cervical vertebrae."

"In other words he was shot in the back of the head."

"That would be within the broad range, yes. You understand I am speculating. Without the head and neck I do not have the entrance wound. But from where the bullet was lodged and from the downward path it left in the tissue, I would estimate that the victim may have been bending over when shot."

Execution style? Maggie kept the thought to herself as she thanked Dr. Tomich and ended the call.

The body parts might have actually been meant for one of AMET's surgical conferences. However, it looked like Piper's connection, Joe the body broker, might also be a killer.

FIFTY-TWO

Charlotte Mills packed up the last plastic container and hauled it upstairs. She had secured all her important documents, jewelry, and memorabilia, including photo albums, scrapbooks, and her collection of autographed novels. One container alone held all the newspaper and magazine articles about her husband's "untimely death," or as Charlotte called it, his Mafia-style murder.

The federal government had ruled the plane crash an accident, an unfortunate engine failure on the Lear jet that was supposed to deliver him to Tallahassee so he could testify in front of a grand jury. She had warned George months before that turning state's evidence could mean his death. But he insisted it was the right thing to do, his penance for helping "the son-of-a-bitch" corrupt politician get elected. As a result, the son of a bitch kept his job.

That was fifteen years ago and Charlotte Mills had gotten nowhere in her diligent pursuit of the truth. Five years ago she gave up—or at least, that's what it felt like, when, in fact, she had depleted all of her options. She didn't want also to deplete her financial resources. George would have been furious with her if she had done that. So finally she accepted the life-insurance money, the policy that George had invested in just months before the grand jury convened.

She had already quit her job to work full-time investigating George's murder. It turned out to be way too many wasted hours. When she finally stopped, she bought this place on the beach, and now she spent her days walking along the shore collecting shells. And she spent her nights reading all the wonderful novels she hadn't had time for. It wasn't a bad life and she wasn't going to let some hurricane dismantle it.

Charlotte took a long, hot shower, knowing it might be her last for a week. She put on comfy clothes, tied her short gray hair into a stubby ponytail. She checked her list as she placed new batteries in a variety of flashlights. She filled the bathtub, all the sinks, and the washing machine with water. She stuffed extra bottled water into the freezer. The latter was a small trick she'd learned during the last hurricane threat. It meant having ice to keep things cool and water to drink later.

With the windows and patio door boarded up the house was dark, reminding her that she'd need to put the candles and matches in a plastic bag and have them somewhere she could grab when the electricity went off. Same for the extra batteries.

Her master bathroom was the only true inside room and she had set it up as her refuge. The counter was arranged with the necessities: a battery-operated radio, several flashlights, a telephone already plugged into a landline, a cooler filled with sandwiches, her prescription meds, and even a pickax almost too large for her small frame to lift. Everything she would need for a ten- to twelve-hour stay.

She was on her way back upstairs when a knock at the front door stopped her. The sheriff's department had come by earlier. Her neighbors had already left. She checked the peephole. Saw the patch on the man's sleeve and she let out a groan. Was this the county or the federal government's last-ditch effort?

"I already told the sheriff's deputy that I was staying," she insisted as she opened the door only to the security chain's length.

"Hi, Mrs. Mills," the young man said with a smile. "I met you at Mr. B's yesterday. Joe. Joe Black."

FIFTY-THREE

Walter parked the canteen as close to the marina as possible. That's where all the action was this morning. They warned him at the tollbooth that the bridge would be closing at one o'clock. Traffic was bumper-to-bumper in the opposite direction. He realized he probably should have stayed home, found something to occupy his time, but he had everything ready and there was only so much you could prepare. He didn't want to sit at home and wait. There'd be enough waiting while the storm raged on for hours.

The marina was crowded with last-minute boaters trying to tether their boats—big and small—as best as possible. Some were loading their crafts onto trailers. A few brave souls—or stupid, Walter decided—were venturing out into the swell in an attempt to get their boats out of the storm's path.

Tension filled the air along with diesel fumes. Arguments edged close to fistfights. The waiting and watching of the last several days ended with the inevitable realization that Isaac was, indeed, heading directly for them. There was no more predicting. No more hope for a last-minute turn. There was no more escaping. Now it was only a matter of battening down the hatches as best as possible.

Walter parked in a corner of the marina lot where the boaters could see him and he could chat with them. Howard Johnson, the owner of the marina and a deep-sea fishing shop, had invited Walter to set up here anytime he wanted. In exchange Walter kept a special bottle of cognac so at the end of a hard day he and Howard could sip and share stories.

Walter decided that today he'd only stay an hour. He'd serve up whatever he had on board for free until the food or the hour ran out.

At first he didn't pay attention to the panel van that pulled up next to the sidewalk leading to the docks. He noticed the owner struggling with a huge bag, yanking it out of the van then dragging it. Not an unusual scene down here. Walter had seen this type of bag before. Someone had pointed one out, calling it a "tuna bag." Fishermen used them for the big catches that didn't fit in a cooler. The bags were tough, huge, waterproof, and insulated. About six feet by three feet it looked like a giant-size tote bag with a washable lining that could be removed.

Walter thought it was a bit odd that someone would be hauling a fish to his boat. Usually it was the other way around. The guy wore a blue baseball cap, shorts, deck shoes, and a khaki button-down shirt with the tails untucked. Walter caught a glimpse of the chevron patch on the shirt sleeve. What the hell was some navy petty officer doing here in his service uniform, dragging a tuna bag? Then Walter recognized the guy.

"Hey, Joe."

Too much noise. Joe didn't hear him.

That bag looked awful heavy.

Walter glanced around inside the canteen. He hadn't turned on any appliances yet. He left a tray with hot dogs and condiments out. He'd be right back. Then he locked all the doors and headed over to the sidewalk to help.

"Hey, Norris."

This time Joe looked over his shoulder and did a double take. His face was red and dripping sweat. His eyes darted around the marina like he hadn't expected to be recognized.

"Let me give you a hand with that," Walter said, grabbing one end of the bag.

"No, that's okay, Mr. B. I've got it."

Joe tried to pull away but Walter didn't surrender his end. Instead, he asked, "You got a boat out here?" He really wanted to ask why Joe was wearing what was probably one of his father's old shirts. Even his ball cap had the U.S. Navy insignia embroidered on the front. Walter waited till Joe gave up and let him help.

"Cabin cruiser." Joe nodded at the boat in the second slip to their right.

Walter whistled. "She's a beauty." He smiled at the name, bold and black, written across the stern: *Restless Sole*.

"My dad left it to me. Thought I'd take it over to Biloxi."

"Now? You're kidding, right?"

"The eye of the storm's probably going to come over Pensacola. Maybe swing a bit to the east of here. Hurricane-force winds stretch about a hundred miles out from the eye."

He wasn't out of breath. Walter was. He found himself thinking that this kid's in good shape.

"There's already nine-, ten-foot swells," Walter told him, trying not to gasp like an old man.

"I've been out in worse. Northeast quadrant gets the worst part of the storm. Traveling west I'll be driving away from it. Got a little delayed. I'm getting a later start than I wanted."

Walter helped Joe lift the bag onto the boat deck. By now, Walter's jumpsuit was soaked at his back and chest. Sweat poured down his forehead and dripped off his nose, but he needed both hands to lift his end of the tuna bag down the steps into the cabin.

Joe dropped his end of the bag. Something inside moved and groaned. Walter's eyes shot up to meet Joe's. He was still holding his end of the bag when Joe shoved the snub nose of a revolver into Walter's gut and said, "Guess you're coming along for the ride, Mr. B."

FIFTY-FOUR

Maggie knew if she waited until after the hurricane to ask questions no one would remember a white stainless-steel cooler with a bright yellow-and-blue tie-down or its owner, a guy named Joe, who might have a boat docked at the marina. Memories of before the hurricane would be eclipsed by the chaos of the storm. Besides, she had promised Liz Bailey that she would meet her on the marina. While she waited, she might just as well ask some questions.

The condition of the body parts suggested they hadn't been in the cooler for long. Decomposition had only begun. From past experience—an unfortunate piece of trivia to have in one's repertoire—Maggie knew it took about four to five hours to thaw an average-size frozen torso. There had been no ice left in the cooler when it was found. Considering the warm water of the Gulf and the hot sun, she estimated the packages had been inside the cooler two days. Three at the most.

Even if the body parts had been destined for one of Lawrence Piper's surgical conferences, it still didn't explain how Vince Coffland ended up as an unwilling body donor.

Before Maggie had left the comfort of her hotel room she had done a quick search of Advanced Medical Educational Technology on her laptop. The company advertised educational seminars at a variety of Florida resorts, providing a venue for medical-device makers to showcase their latest technologies to surgeons from across the country. They promised hands-on experience while upholding donor confidentiality by not disclosing their procurement procedure.

After viewing competitors' websites, Maggie realized AMET was only one of several legitimate companies buying "precut and frozen body parts" from brokers like Joe. From her quick analysis, Maggie understood that demand was high and supply limited. She couldn't help wondering if Platt had been right when he asked if this killer might be taking advantage of hurricanes in order to find victims. Now Maggie realized that might be exactly what this killer was doing, using the storms as a cover to fill his growing orders. Was Vince Coffland murdered out of cold-blooded greed?

The marina was crowded and the shops were busy, trying to accommodate the desperate boat owners. In between sales Maggie struck up a conversation with the owner of Howard's Deep Sea Fishing Shop. A huge, barrel-chested man, Howard Johnson towered over Maggie. His thick white hair was the only indication of his age. Somewhere in his sixties, Maggie guessed. However, his neatly trimmed goatee had streaks of blond, hinting at the golden-haired surfer that appeared in the photos along the walls. He wore a bright orange-and-blue button-down shirt with a fish pattern, the hem hanging over his khaki cargo shorts.

His shop was kept neat, with unusual and colorful gear. A railed shelf ran along the upper quarter of the four walls, filled with models of various boats and ships. Maggie found herself mesmerized by all the paraphernalia.

Her eyes were still darting about as she absently flipped open her FBI badge to show Howard. His entire demeanor changed. He nodded politely but his eyes flashed with suspicion. One large hand ducked into his pocket, the other dropped palm-flat onto the counter as if bracing himself for what was coming. Okay, so he didn't trust FBI agents. He wouldn't be the first. Maggie showed him photos of the cooler. The last one was a close-up of the yellow-and-blue rope tie-down.

He shrugged. "Looks like a dozen other coolers I see every day. In fact, I have this same make, only the larger version, on my deep-sea fishing rig."

"What about the tie-down?"

"I use a metal one."

"Ever see one like this?"

Another shrug but he looked at the photo again. She could see he was still suspicious. He crossed his arms over his barrel chest. Guarded. An impatient frown.

"People use all sorts of things to personalize their equipment," he said. "Makes it easier to pick it out when everybody's unloading their stuff on the dock at the same time. Kind of like baggage claim. You know what I mean? People tag their bags with ribbons or bright straps so they can see them coming down the conveyor belt."

Maggie hadn't thought of that. Using the rope to track down the killer started looking like a million-to-one shot.

"Any ideas how a cooler this size would end up overboard?"

"You mean by accident?"

She nodded.

Howard's frown screwed up his face and he scratched his head like he was giving it considerable thought.

"Sometimes guys will pull them behind the boat when they're a bit crowded on board. They float no matter what they have in them. You tether them real good to the back of the boat. I suppose one could break loose. Might not notice until you've gone a ways."

"Maggie."

It was Liz Bailey. They'd planned to meet on the marina, but Liz came into the shop in a rush.

"Howard, have you seen my dad?"

FIFTY-FIVE

Benjamin Platt held the young man by the shoulders as he vomited green liquid into a stainless-steel basin. The patient was too weak to hold himself up. That was obvious from the stains already on his bedsheets.

"We're going to give you an injection," he told the soldier as he eased him back down. The man's eyes were glazed. He no longer tried to respond. Platt knew he probably couldn't hear him, but he talked to him anyway.

He nodded for the nurse beside him to go ahead with the injection while he explained. "We'll probably be poking you a couple more times." Platt grabbed a towel from the side stand and wiped vomit from the corner of the young man's mouth.

"Thanks."

The one word seemed an effort so Platt was surprised when he continued.

"This is almost worse"—he slurred his syllables—"than losing my foot."

"It's going to get better," Platt told him. "I promise you."

The nurse looked skeptical. He could see her out of the corner of his eye but Platt didn't break eye contact with the young man. He would not let him see that even his doctor wasn't sure what would work.

Platt stopped at the prep room to change gloves before he went on to the next patient.

"Controlled chaos," Ganz said coming up behind him.

"Controlled being the key word."

"I have someone bringing in more beta-lactam antibiotics. You think this will work?"

"Think of *Clostridium sordellii* as tiny egg-like spores. They have to chew away enzymes for their bacterial cell wall to synthesize. This group of antibiotics binds to those enzymes and makes them inactivate, or at least not available to the bacteria."

"So it won't be able to grow."

"Or spread."

"What about those patients where it's already spread?"

Platt took in a deep breath. "I don't know. I honestly don't know. There is no established treatment. We're shooting from the hip here." He turned to look Ganz in the eyes. "Are you having second thoughts?"

"No, absolutely not." He shook his head. "At this point we don't have anything to lose."

"This will slow the bacteria down even in those advanced cases. It'll really depend on what damage has already been done." Platt's mind looped back to what the young man had said about this being worse than losing his foot. "What do you do with the amputated limbs?"

"Excuse me?"

"The young man I just took care of—what happened to his foot once it was amputated?"

"Some families request the limbs. Others go to the tissue bank."

"In Jacksonville?"

"Right."

"What if the limb has shrapnel in it?"

"That's not my area of expertise."

"But would you send it on to the tissue bank?" Platt insisted.

"Sure. That's where the assessment would be made. But shrapnel still embedded in the tissue? I think the foot would probably be considered damaged and discarded."

Platt wondered about Maggie's case. Was it possible the severed foot that had been discovered in the fishing cooler was actually one that had been amputated from a soldier?

FIFTY-SIX

Liz's first reaction at seeing the deserted canteen had been anger. She was already frustrated with her dad for driving to the beach that morning out of boredom, curiosity. He didn't want to miss out on the action. Sometimes she wondered if she was the same way. She had his drive, that same eagerness to get out there, no matter how dangerous. Once the adrenaline kicked in, it was difficult to slow her down.

Her anger changed to concern when she glanced inside the canteen and saw the tray of hot dogs and condiments on the counter. The vehicle was locked up but it was obvious her father had intended to be away only a short time. Howard only stoked her concern.

"I saw him, maybe an hour ago. He was helping some guy drag a tuna bag onto his boat."

"Is the boat still here?" She hated that she sounded so anxious. Even Maggie stood alongside Liz, looking out the window, appearing anxious. It was getting darker by the minute. The lights in the parking lot had started to turn on. And it wasn't even noon.

Howard glanced over the two of them.

"Nope. It was in slip number two."

"It's pretty late to be moving a boat, isn't it?" Maggie asked.

"And dangerous," Liz added.

"Actually, it's stupid, but he's not the only one," Howard said. "Can't tell them anything. You know the type. They'll get in trouble and expect you and your aircrew to go out and risk your lives to save their sorry asses."

"Is that one of your slips?"

"Yep, sure is." He was already at his computer, bringing up his accounts.

Liz had heard a lot of rumors about Howard Johnson. Word was that he had been a drug trafficker for years and that he only gave it up when he knew the feds were moving in to bust him. There were also rumors that several million dollars of drug money had never been recovered and that Howard had it hidden somewhere. But her dad always said that Howard was "one of the good guys."

"Boat's named *Restless Sole*, that's s-o-l-e. Owner is listed as Joe Black. He came in Friday. Has the slip through this week."

"Maybe he took it out to get gas?" Maggie asked.

"Every place I know of is already out of gas," Howard said. "But maybe he knows something I don't."

"Wait a minute," Liz said. "Joe Black?" She turned to Maggie. "My dad had drinks with him last night. Dad said he was a friend of my brother-in-law's." Panic started to twist knots in her stomach. "Scott said he owned the fishing cooler. The one I saw behind the funeral home."

Maggie stared at her a moment. Liz knew she could see her concern.

"Any idea where Black's from? Or where he might be headed?" Maggie asked Howard.

He glanced from Maggie to Liz and back to Maggie. Howard could see it, too. "That might be an issue of privacy. Without a warrant I don't think I can give you his address in Jacksonville." Then he waved at an impatient customer. "Excuse me, ladies."

Liz leaned closer to Maggie, keeping her back to the crowded shop. "Dad said he didn't think Joe Black was his real name."

"No," Maggie said, much too calmly. "I don't think it's his real name, either."

"Do you think he's the owner of the cooler we found in the Gulf?"

"Yes," she said with certainty.

"Is my dad in danger?"

"He may have just helped Black load his boat. He could be helping someone else right now."

Liz glanced out the shop window. Her dad was in great physical shape for his age. He could handle himself. She shouldn't jump to conclusions. He probably was off helping someone else. He had been in the navy for more than thirty-five years. He knew a thing or two about securing boats.

The wind came in a sudden blast, bending palm trees and upending anything that wasn't weighted down. Buckets and empty gas cans skidded across the pier. The glass in the windows rattled. The entire shop went silent so when the rain started it sounded like stones pelting the outside walls.

The door banged open. Kesnick, wearing a bright-yellow poncho, found Liz.

"Hey Bailey, we gotta go."

He handed the women identical ponchos still folded up in neat squares. Liz reminded herself that Maggie hadn't experienced anything like this.

"We're going up in this?" The calm was gone, replaced by anxiety.

"It's just the outer bands," Liz told her. "It'll calm down again in a few minutes. We'll have about six to ten hours of this, on and off. It'll quit as suddenly as it started. The intensity and length of time will increase with each round."

She thought Maggie looked a shade paler and Liz added, "I've got more of the ground-ginger capsules in my medic pack."

Liz searched for Howard on their way out. Hated to take him away from a paying customer but he sensed her tension, and he didn't even wait for her question. Instead, he said, "I'll take care of him if I find him. And don't worry about the canteen."

FIFTY-SEVEN

The boat rolled from side to side, throwing Walter against the inside walls of the cabin. Joe Black had hog-tied Walter's hands and feet with a braided rope and left him to slide and knock against the wood panels. The tuna bag lay between him and the steps going up to the cockpit.

He tried to watch the bag, though he had to twist and look over his shoulder to see it. He couldn't turn himself around with the boat heaving him every time he made an attempt. But Walter was sure something, or rather someone, was in the bag. There had been what sounded like groans early on. Not anymore.

"How you doing, Walter?" Joe had to yell to be heard over the engine.

He poked his head down to take a peek. Walter could see only a corner of his forehead. He knew the kid didn't dare leave the cockpit. He'd have to stay put and keep his hands on the controls. From the increased tilt and raise of the boat, Walter could tell the waves were cresting even more violently. Soon it wouldn't matter how Joe steered.

He heard a crackle of static and then Joe's voice boomed through a box on the wall, just over Walter's head.

"Hey, Walter. I know you can't hit the response button but I just wanted to explain some stuff to you. It's nothing personal. It's just business."

Walter jerked onto his side to take a better look at the box on the wall about three feet above him. Was it an intercom or a radio? Light came in only through the portholes, which were being pummeled by waves. It was too dark for him to tell. He scooted against the wall, trying to gain leverage just as the boat lurched and threw him to the other side of the boat, knocking his head against the wall. It was enough for him to see shooting stars.

"Everything I told you, Walter, was true." Joe's voice came through the wall. "You know, about my dad. He was in the navy. Loved it. Even though they weren't so good to him. He didn't get this boat until he found out he was sick. Waited too long to enjoy life. Always said he couldn't afford it."

Another wave almost capsized the boat. The tuna bag slammed into Walter. He pressed his heels into one wall and his shoulders against the other, wedging himself tight. When the boat rocked back down, the tuna bag slid toward the steps but Walter stayed put.

Something told him it was all a big roller-coaster ride to this kid. He knew guys like Joe Black in the navy. They loved the adventure, the more dangerous the better. They craved it. He recognized a bit of that in himself. He saw it in his daughter Liz, and he worried it could end up getting her hurt. There always came a time when the rush wasn't enough or when you thought you were invincible because you had survived. What was it Liz had told him they said these days? You looked the beast in the face and won? So you upped the ante, took bigger and bigger risks.

No, Walter wasn't surprised that the hurricane didn't deter Joe. A moment later he was saying, "Hey, Walter, I wish you didn't have to be tied up, 'cause I think you'd be enjoying this. You should see it from up here. Bet you spent rougher times out on the seas, huh?" There was more static then a click-click and he thought the connection had failed.

Then Joe added, "Might have lost you there. These radios need updating."

Walter waited out another crest—up, up, up, and finally back down. The tuna bag rolled to one side and crashed into the other, but he stayed put.

"I learned from my dad, Walter. You can't put off living the good life. You've got to take what you can whenever you can. And after all those years when my dad got sick and the navy didn't do right by him . . . well, let's just say I'm evening the score."

Another surge.

"And you know what else, Walter? I've learned to love hurricanes. You just have to work them to your favor."

Walter thought Joe was referring to the roller-coaster ride. It didn't occur to him what Joe really meant until he saw the tuna bag moving, the zipper working its way down.

"Yup, these hurricanes have been a cash cow for me this summer. Because you know what? People disappear all the time after a hurricane. A missing person suddenly becomes a donor. You know how much one body's worth these days?"

Walter's head pounded and he blinked his eyes hard, thinking maybe he was hallucinating. He twisted and jerked around to see better, holding his breath while he watched a bruised and battered Charlotte Mills crawl out of the tuna bag.

FIFTY-EIGHT

Maggie knew she'd need more than a couple of capsules of powdered ginger to get her through this. Why had she ever thought Liz Bailey's offer of "a ride" off Pensacola Beach would be simple? Why? Because she had no idea what to expect. What was it that she had said to Charlie Wurth yesterday? "It's one storm. How bad can it be?"

Everyone kept calling these the "outer bands," but the air was already too thick to breathe. Maggie felt like the world had been tipped on its side. Trees bent sideways. The rain poured in horizontal streams. The few people outside teetered from side to side, leaning into the wind to avoid being blown over. She struggled to keep her own balance while sand pelted her skin like a million tiny pinpricks.

Then as suddenly as it began, it stopped. Maggie swore she could even see a swirl of blue sky through the layers of gray overhead. Liz had finished gearing up and was watching her.

"You gonna be okay?"

"Sure. Absolutely," Maggie said, zipping open her flight suit just enough to show Liz her shoulder holster and Smith &

Wesson tucked inside. "I've got all the control I need," she joked.

Liz smiled but was unsuccessful in covering her concern. It wasn't quite the same look Maggie had seen in Liz's eyes when she thought her father might be in danger. Earlier, there had been just a hint of panic and Maggie's immediate reaction was to squelch it. Truth was, Liz's father might be in danger if he was still with Joe Black, but there wasn't anything they could do about it right now.

She could tell Liz had switched into rescue mode.

"How can you be so brave?" Maggie asked her.

Liz smiled at her again until she realized Maggie wasn't joking.

"My first instinct is simply to survive."

Maggie raised an eyebrow. She wanted to understand.

"Just because I go up in a helicopter or plunge down into the ocean doesn't make me brave. It just makes me a bit crazy." She gave a short laugh. "Look, I know there are things you do instinctively, too. Things that I wouldn't dare. Rescuing someone and coming face to face with a killer, in the end both those situations come down to our instinct to survive." She shrugged. "I don't have time to think about being brave. I bet you don't, either."

Maggie wanted to ask her how she had gotten so wise. She realized Liz was waiting for some response, some sign of agreement or understanding. But Maggie simply nodded.

"Anyway, don't worry too much about this trip," Liz added. "We probably won't get any distress calls before we have to head to Jacksonville. They won't let us stay up for very long. As soon as the wind hits forty knots, we're out of here."

But Maggie wasn't really listening anymore. She was watching out the window as Lieutenant Commander Wilson and his co-pilot, Ellis, boarded the helicopter. Pete Kesnick was waiting for Liz and Maggie. And all Maggie could think about was how quickly the sky had turned an impossibly darker shade of gray.

FIFTY-NINE

"My God, Charlotte. Are you okay?" Walter could hardly believe his eyes.

The right side of her small face was one purple bruise. Her gray hair stuck out from her ponytail. Her lower lip was split and her eyes were wild, a combination of shock and panic. She stared at Walter as if she didn't recognize him. She crawled out of the bag, dragging her right leg. The ankle was so swollen it reminded Walter of rising bread, puffing out of her sneaker.

"Charlotte," he whispered again.

His eyes darted to the open stairwell. Joe had gone silent on the radio. Walter wanted to believe Joe wouldn't leave the cockpit. Now he prayed he wouldn't leave the cockpit.

"Do you know where we are?" Walter asked her.

She kicked the bag away and grabbed on to a leather strap in the floor just as the boat pitched sideways.

Other than the bruises and the swollen ankle, Walter couldn't see any broken bones or bleeding.

"Can you hear me, Charlotte?" He kept his voice low and quiet. He knew what it could do to a person to be stuck in a hold. A bag probably had the same effect. He worried that she might be too far gone to be of any help. "Charlotte?"

"I've heard every word that bastard said from the time he dropped me on my head."

Walter wanted to laugh with relief. "Good ole Charlotte."

She crawled up beside him and started to work on his ropes but Walter stopped her.

He pointed above him with his chin. "I can wait. Do you know how to use a two-way radio?"

SIXTY

They had only been in the air a few minutes when the distress call came in. Liz heard Wilson talking to their command post, getting the details. She glanced over at Maggie. The FBI agent had looked okay until another outer band swept in. Now she clenched the leather hold-down and tightened her seat belt.

Liz realized that being in the air, the sensation of wind and rain was different. Wilson couldn't just fly above the clouds like a jetliner and get out of it. And his tight-fisted handling of the controls made the craft rock and plunge more than necessary.

She started preparing to be deployed. From the brief description it sounded like a medical emergency. The craft, a thirty-two-foot cabin cruiser, was intact, not taking on water and not disabled. That should make things easier but not much.

The water was choppy, waves cresting nine to twelve feet. It was crazy even for a professional to be out in this.

"Let's keep the swimmer out of the water," Wilson said.

She was still "the swimmer," Liz thought and immediately

knew she needed to keep her focus on the boat below. The adrenaline had already started pumping. She didn't care about Wilson.

They could see the boat, the waves tossing it, almost perpendicular to the sky. Then the waves would crest and the boat would crash down. It looked like the boat was swallowed up whole then spit out, to begin the process all over.

"Let the boat deck rise up to meet you," Pete Kesnick was telling Liz through her helmet. "But get on before the wave crests. You want to hang on to something before it breaks."

She nodded but his eyes held hers as if he needed to see for himself that she was, indeed, up to the task.

Choppy seas always made it dangerous. The wind gusts and the moving boat contributed to the challenge.

"We'll never get a basket down with these winds," Wilson said.

"Did they say what the medical condition was?" Kesnick asked.

"No. They lost contact before giving any details."

"We try no more than three times," Kesnick said. He was talking to Liz. "If I think it's not working, I'm hauling you back up. Understand?"

"No heroics, Bailey," Wilson told her. "We don't want to lose our rescue swimmer before the hurricane even hits."

SIXTY-ONE

As soon as they heard the helicopter overhead Joe Black came pounding down the steps.

"What the hell did you do, Walter?"

They hadn't been able to untie the rope yet from Walter's feet. He couldn't stand up without immediately losing his balance but he swung a fist at his surprised captor, hitting Joe in the face. Charlotte scrambled to her feet, her swollen ankle making her hop as she tried to land a blow. Then the boat heaved and sent them all crashing to the deck.

When the boat steadied, Joe had Charlotte by the back of her collar and his snub-nose revolver pointed at Walter's chest.

"I knew I should have killed you both. I just didn't want you stinking up my boat by the time I got to Biloxi."

He pushed Charlotte down onto the floor next to Walter. Then he stood over them, glancing at the steps. Walter could see he was anxious to get back up.

If the helicopter didn't see any signs of distress, would they risk sending someone down? And dear God, Walter silently prayed, please don't let it be Liz. He hoped she was already on her way to Jacksonville and this was another crew left behind for a last-minute search.

"I haven't ruled out shooting you both," Joe was telling them. He set his feet apart and braced one hand on the wall to steady himself while the boat rocked and climbed again. "I just hate using a gun or a knife. Damages too much tissue. There's nothing worse than a cooler full of damaged goods."

He was ranting, and Walter wondered if his internal check-and-balance system had cracked under the stress. Madmen were dangerous. Was it too late or could he get through to the kid?

Walter pressed a hand against the wall, and tried lifting himself up to his feet.

"Just stay put, Walter, or I'll shoot you in the hand. I've got plenty hands. Once they figured out how to repair carpel tunnel, hands as a commodity went bust."

"It's over, Phillip Norris's son," Walter said, deliberately using his father's name.

Walter watched Joe's eyes. He wanted to bring back the boy who enjoyed Coney Island hot dogs. He was certain that if he could do that, they would be safe. He wasn't prepared for Joe's response.

Joe aimed the gun, pulled back the trigger, and Walter's left hand exploded.

SIXTY-TWO

Scott ignored Trish's phone calls. He turned the cell phone off and threw it on the embalming table.

She wanted him to get to her father's house. She couldn't find her dad. Couldn't get in touch with her sister. She was panicked again. Earlier he had told her that he needed to stay at the funeral home to make sure everything was okay. If a window blew out, he wanted to be here to board it up so there wasn't any water damage. She didn't understand. After all, he hadn't lifted a finger to protect their brand-new home.

"This is different," he tried to explain. This was their livelihood. They could stay in a hotel if their home was destroyed. But if the funeral home was damaged, they would have no money coming in. How could she not understand the difference?

He'd just finished washing his hands. He couldn't get rid of the smell of decomposing flesh. He checked cupboards. Washed down the embalming room. Sprayed disinfectants. Still the smell persisted. He'd heard about olfactory hallucinations at one of the funeral-director conferences. At the time he thought it sounded ridiculous. Now he wondered if, in fact, that's what was happening to him.

Outside the world grew dark. Power lines danced in the wind. The sporadic downpours left water flooding the streets. Pine trees had already snapped in half. With every wave, the storm grew more intense. From the radio Scott learned that once the hurricane made landfall there would be no break for six to ten hours. Twelve to fifteen if the backstorm was just as intense.

He had to admit, now that he'd seen a piece of the pre-storm, he was frightened. As a kid he had fought claustrophobia after being locked inside the trunk of a neighbor's car—his punishment for mouthing off to the older, stronger kids. This storm renewed his claustrophobia.

A crash brought him to the window.

"Son of a bitch."

A branch from the huge live oak outside the back door had been ripped off. The heavy part tumbled to the ground but power lines held up the other end. Sparks flashed. The lights in the funeral home blinked a couple of times but stayed on.

He realized the tree could end up coming through the roof. If windows exploded and branches flew in, he might not be safe inside. Trish had said that earlier, but he hadn't listened.

He grabbed a flashlight and started looking for cover. The utility closet? On the radio they had said an interior room with no windows was best. He paced the hallway. Then suddenly he stopped and turned around.

Why hadn't he thought of it sooner? The walk-in refrigerator was stainless steel. Nothing could rip that apart.

He turned on the light and pulled a chair inside. He shoved the table with Uncle Mel to one side. Joe Black had left two shelves filled with body parts. The other table was still occupied by the young man that Scott had imagined moved.

He closed the walk-in refrigerator's door and made himself sit down. This was perfect. No way this hurricane would touch him.

The lights blinked again. He heard a click, followed by two more. The electronic locks on the walk-in refrigerator's door had just engaged. He raced to the door just as the lights went out. His stomach sank. He wouldn't be able to open the door until the electricity came back on.

SIXTY-THREE

Liz wiped at her goggles. It didn't help. Just as she could see, the spray clouded her sight, again.

The wind yanked her up and down, whipping her from side to side. Once she almost made contact and Kesnick pulled too far up. Finally, her feet hit the deck. Kesnick slackened the cable. She dropped and rolled as a wave swallowed the boat. It almost pushed her overboard. She felt the cable go taut just as she grabbed on to a railing. Before Kesnick could change his mind, Liz waved that she was okay.

Communication would be tough. Almost impossible. Her hand gestures might become invisible as the rain intensified. But if the boat swirled out of control, she was still connected to the helicopter. And at the first sign of trouble Kesnick would pull her up.

She crawled along the deck, grabbing on to hooks and cables attached to the boat. She couldn't see anyone at the helm. She focused on her task. She was in control. There was no room for panic.

Liz pulled at the cabin door. The wind fought her. She hung

on and ducked just as another wave came crashing over the top. The hoist cable tugged at her waist. Kesnick was impatient, nervous. She took the time to wave up at him. Could he see her thumbs-up?

The time between crests grew shorter. She had maybe a dozen seconds. She yanked at the cabin door again, using all her strength. It popped open.

No one was at the wheel. The engines were turned off. The owner must have realized there was no fighting the waves.

"Hello," she yelled and stood still, listening for a response.

Nothing. Static behind her. The radio.

"Anyone down there?"

She pulled off her goggles. Let them dangle around her neck. She waited to catch her breath then she started down the steps.

The gun was pressed against her left temple before she even saw it.

SIXTY-FOUR

"She's in," Pete Kesnick said, but Maggie didn't hear any relief in his words. If anything, he sounded more on edge. Their swimmer was out of sight and they still didn't have any idea what the situation was down below.

"If the medical condition or injury is serious, she may not be able to use the quick strop." Kesnick practically hung out the open doorway. He leaned against his own cable, fighting the rain and wind, trying to watch for Liz.

He had double-checked the cable. A good thing, because Maggie was certain she wouldn't be able to help this time. Not with the wind violently shoving the helicopter around. The roar made it difficult to hear even the voices inside her helmet.

"She's gonna need to hurry." Wilson sounded as tightly wound as the cable. "We gotta go. Command center is telling me ten minutes. Tops."

"We can't do this in ten minutes," Kesnick told him. "She might be stabilizing someone on board."

"I'm watching the clock. That's all I'm saying."

"Can someone go down and help her?" Maggie asked.

Silence. It was as if they didn't want to acknowledge her presence. Wilson had already put up a fuss about her being on his craft. He had complained to Liz as they geared up. Didn't care that Maggie was standing right there.

"No one else is authorized to deploy except the rescue swimmer," Wilson finally told her. "We can send down anything she needs. Anything that might help her. But we stay in the helicopter. Or we have to leave and send a cutter back."

"You'd leave her down there?"

More silence.

"Sometimes you don't have a choice. You follow the rules. I have a responsibility to the entire crew."

"But the hurricane—"

"Exactly," was his one-word answer. A pause, then, "Seven minutes, Kesnick."

"You can't just leave her."

"Agent O'Dell, you do not have any authority in this craft. I do. Understand?"

"I don't see her," Kesnick yelled.

"Give her a tug."

"Nothing."

They waited.

Maggie's heart pounded against her rib cage, the rhythm the same as the thump-thump of the rotors. Sweat rolled down her back and yet she felt chilled. She watched Wilson's profile. Jaw clamped tight. His visor prevented her from seeing his eyes, but his hands were steady, fists clenched on the control. Beside him, Ellis was an exact contrast—head bobbing and twisting around, trying to see below.

"This is the Coast Guard," Ellis yelled into the radio. "*Restless Sole*, can you hear me?"

"Five minutes," Wilson said. "Where the hell is she?"

"*Restless Sole*, can you hear me?" Ellis shouted but only got static in response.

That's when it hit Maggie. *Restless Sole*. Wasn't that the name of Joe Black's boat?

"No one's answering," Ellis said.

"Kesnick?"

"I don't see her."

"We have got to get the hell out of here. Pull her up, Kesnick. PULL HER UP NOW."

Kesnick obeyed. The cable whined and spun. Maggie waited to see Liz come over the doorway. Instead, she saw Kesnick grab the cable and spin around to his pilots. He didn't say a word as he held up the cable. It had been cut.

SIXTY-FIVE

Liz couldn't do a thing as the cable whipped away from her and flew out of the cabin. Her lifeline was gone.

But she wouldn't have left now anyway. Not without her dad.

She asked if she could bandage his hand. He held it up and against his chest, the front of his jumpsuit already drenched in blood.

"I'm okay, darling," Walter insisted.

She recognized the woman from the beach. She had never seen the man who casually introduced himself as Joe Black, never letting the revolver slip from her temple.

"We'll just all stay put for a while and the helicopter will go away." Joe didn't sound fazed.

"They won't leave their rescue swimmer," Walter said.

Liz couldn't tell her dad that wasn't the way it always worked. It had happened once after Katrina. The helicopter had been dangerously low on fuel and packed with injured survivors. Liz had told them to go ahead while she waited on an apartment rooftop with a dozen others, angry and impatient for their turn. It was nightfall before her aircrew was able to return.

"I'll end up with three healthy specimens," Joe continued to rant. "I don't have enough ice but I suppose I could tether a couple of you to the back of the boat. Put life jackets on."

"Specimens." The woman spit it out like she was disgusted and certainly not afraid. "You're gonna nickel-and-dime my body parts? Is that what you have in mind, young man?" She was holding her ankle but it didn't stop her. "I'll have you know that my husband was murdered for millions of dollars. Millions."

Joe Black ignored the woman. He stood, braced inside the stairwell, blocking their way but also able to keep an eye on all of them. He'd tethered himself to the railing and was able to ride out the boat's pitching back and forth. When Liz almost fell, the revolver swung down with her.

The boat rocked more violently, climbing and falling with the cresting waves. The noise was deafening. There was a crash somewhere up above them. Something had come down hard on the deck. Their eyes lifted to the ceiling. That's when they heard the helicopter rotors moving away. Within seconds the sound grew faint. They were leaving.

Liz's eyes met her dad's across the cabin. She knew her crew couldn't stay. A cutter would take forever to find them in these conditions. It probably wasn't even safe to try. This wouldn't be like her Katrina rooftop experience. This time her aircrew wouldn't return.

Joe Black was grinning.

"So who wants to go first?" he asked.

If Liz rushed him, he'd shoot her before she could get the gun away from him. What had she told Maggie O'Dell? It wasn't about being brave; it was about surviving. Fighting against crushing waves or dangling from a cable didn't scare her. Even when survivors challenged her, she'd count on her training, redirect her adrenaline. Maybe she could talk this guy off his ledge.

Joe Black pointed the gun at Liz as though he could hear her thoughts.

"A cutter's on its way," she lied. "The helicopter probably had it in sight. That's why they left."

She saw him consider it. Something crashed above again, and his eyes shot up but only briefly. Another wave slammed the boat. There was a high-pitched screech of something skidding across the deck.

"The boat's being ripped apart," the old woman yelled.

"Shut the hell up," Black screamed at her, repositioning himself in the stairway and taking aim.

"NO." She heard her dad yell, followed by the blast of a gunshot.

Liz closed her eyes against the pain, but there was no pain. When her eyes flew open she saw Joe Black fall forward, grabbing at his leg with one hand, the gun still in his other.

There was a shout from the top of the stairs. "FBI. Drop it. Now."

He hesitated.

Another shot chewed up the carpet next to him.

He threw the gun aside.

Liz stood paralyzed as Maggie climbed down the steps, her gun still pointed at Black.

"Liz, grab his weapon."

She obeyed.

"Is he the only one?" Her eyes darted around the cabin and quickly returned to Black. When she glanced up for an answer, all Liz could manage was a nod.

"Everybody okay?" Maggie finally asked.

Liz heard the helicopter returning. All eyes lifted to the ceiling again.

"How did you—"

But Maggie interrupted her. "We have to do this quickly." Then to Liz she said, "Wilson's in a pissy mood."

THURSDAY, AUGUST 27

SIXTY-SIX

PENSACOLA, FLORIDA

Liz woke up as the last stream of sunset lit the room. She had slept hard. Her mouth was dry, her eyelids still heavy. It took a few seconds to remember where she was. Second floor. Her dad's house. Her old room had been made into a guest bedroom but there were still remnants of her childhood—a porcelain doll on the dresser, the embroidered pillow shams—and reminders of her mother.

She could hear chain saws down below despite the hum of the window air conditioner. Her dad had set up the unit especially for her, dropping a bright-orange electrical cord out her window, stringing it down the side of the house and along the backyard to the garage where he had it plugged into one of his generators. A definite luxury, since the window air conditioner took almost as many watts as one of his refrigerators.

"You deserve to sleep," he had told her when she came home for the first time around noon. It was already in her bedroom window. She hadn't asked how he'd managed to put it there with only one hand, his left one wrapped in a soft cast that made it look like he was wearing an oven mitt.

In the last two days Liz had napped for only a few hours at a time, rotating in barracks set up for them at NAS. The hurricane had lost some of its steam, winds dropping to 135 miles per hour as it made landfall. Its path had slipped to the east, sparing Pensacola the brunt of the storm. By the Saffir-Simpson Hurricane Wind Scale, a cat 4 meant "devastating damage" but not "catastrophic damage" like a cat 5.

Liz and her aircrew had rescued dozens of people from their flooded homes. Some still refused to leave, insisting they needed to stay and protect what belongings remained from looters. One man argued with Liz, refusing to leave his roof unless she allowed him to take four suitcases he had stuffed with valuables. By the end of the first day, Wilson no longer complained about sharing cabin space with an assortment of cats and dogs that accompanied their injured owners. And after having a madman almost shoot her, everything else seemed tame. But she'd bagged too many hours and now she was grounded.

Liz got up, pulled on a pair of shorts and a T-shirt. She glanced out the window, looking down over the street. Electrical wires still dangled from branches. Debris piles lined one side of the cul-de-sac where neighbors continued to drag and toss pieces of huge live oak trees, several of them uprooted. And in the middle of the street was the Coney Island Canteen. Lawn chairs were gathered around the mobile unit while her dad and Trish cooked dinner for their neighbors. He'd mentioned to Liz earlier that they were grilling steaks, burgers, hot dogs—even lamb chops—salvaging what they could from everyone's freezers. County officials were estimating the power being out for at least a week.

Liz could see him wiping the sweat from his forehead as he stood over the grill. She still couldn't shake that image of him holding his bloodied hand, the front of his jumpsuit soaked with blood. His face so pale. He'd spent the hurricane in the hospital, calling Trish to pick him up as soon as the main roads were cleared. From what Liz understood, Trish hadn't left his side.

Trish had refused to talk about Scott. All Liz knew was that he had spent the hurricane locked inside the funeral home's walk-in refrigerator. Liz had heard that Joe Black had left several corpses with Scott, and now he and the funeral home were under investigation.

As soon as Liz left her bedroom, the warm air hit her. She was damp with sweat by the time she joined her dad in the street.

"You didn't sleep very long, darling."

"I'm hungry."

"Well, sit yourself down. You came to the right place."

The aroma of grilled meat and the spices her dad used overpowered the gasoline fumes from generators and chain saws. The sun was almost down. It would be pitch-dark in a couple of hours. Several neighbors were bringing out lanterns and setting them up for their evening meal in the street. The one advantage after a hurricane was that there were no mosquitoes, no bugs of any kind. But also no birds.

"Liz, you're just in time," Trish said. "Why don't you set up some plates and cups."

"She needs to rest," her dad said, surprising both of his daughters. Usually he let Trish boss Liz around. It was easier than getting in the middle. "Ask Wendy to help."

Trish stared at him for a minute before finally taking his advice.

"Have you heard anything from your FBI friend?" her dad asked.

"Just for a few minutes this morning when I was still at NAS. Otherwise, cell-phone towers are down."

"She's one brave girl." He pulled an ice-cold bottle of beer from the cooler at his feet and handed it to Liz. "And so are you."

SIXTY-SEVEN

JACKSONVILLE, FLORIDA

Maggie stopped her rental car at the security booth. She handed over her badge and waited while the guard picked up the phone. She lifted her arm to adjust the rearview mirror and a pain shot through her elbow. Actually, her entire body hurt. Who knew jumping from a helicopter could be so physically strenuous?

The guard passed back her badge.

"First building to your right. The others are waiting."

Maggie had gotten up early to catch footage of the storm damage. Charlie Wurth had told her earlier that Pensacola was lucky. At the last minute the storm had suddenly weakened and veered to the right. It made landfall as a category 4, but that was better than they expected. Watching the news reports, Maggie certainly didn't think Pensacola was lucky. The storm had still ripped apart roofs, blown out windows, and flooded homes. Electricity was out for more than a hundred thousand customers and not expected to be up and running for at least a week.

She had talked to Liz Bailey earlier, too, relieved to hear that Walter and Charlotte were okay. She was especially glad to hear that Walter would retain full use of his left hand, but it would take months of rehab. And despite sounding totally exhausted, Liz seemed to be handling the aftermath of the storm.

A military cargo plane flew low over Maggie's car, preparing to land. As she parked in front of the building she could feel the vibration. She eased out of the car and was grateful there was only a set of five steps. Ridiculous. She thought she was in good shape. She didn't like being reminded of dangling from that cable. Without effort she could conjure up the terror. She could hear the wind swirling around her and feel the rain pelting her face.

She needed some sleep, that's all. Last night she had dreamed of severed hands coming up out of the water and clinging to her. Okay, she needed dreamless sleep. Maybe another of Platt's massages. That brought a smile.

Inside, she had to show her badge again. A small woman in uniform led her down a hallway and into a conference room. Benjamin Platt was in uniform. She didn't recognize the other two men.

Platt did the introductions.

"Agent Maggie O'Dell, this is Captain Carl Ganz and Dr. Samuel McCleary."

Dr. McCleary decided to open defensively. "Joseph Norris has been a respected part of this program for almost ten years."

Maggie could see Platt bristle.

"Then you understand, Dr. McCleary," she began, "that means you may have contaminated tissue and bone from as long ago as ten years."

"All of our tissue is tested."

"But only for certain diseases," Platt said.

"No one could have predicted what happened at NAS in Pensacola," McCleary insisted, shaking his head. "That was one mistake. One out of thousands. And we've traced the grafts and bone paste Captain Ganz used. We think it all came from one donor." He pointed to a document already set among a pile on the table. "One donor who may have been dead longer than twelve hours."

"Actually, it was more like twenty-one hours," Platt said.

"We don't know that for certain."

"He was dead long enough for his bowels to burst and *Clostridium sordellii* to start spreading to his tissue."

"You have no proof of that," McCleary said.

"What about the donors Joe Black obtained without certification?" Maggie asked.

"Joseph Norris," McCleary corrected her, "followed procedure as far as I am able to judge."

"There's a funeral home in Pensacola," Maggie told him, "that has two bodies. The Escambia County sheriff says both are homeless men who disappeared just days before the hurricane. The funeral director insists Joe Black brought them there and cut one of them up to be sold and used for educational conferences."

This time McCleary was speechless.

"Joe Black was making a nice living on the side," she

continued. "Diener by day, body broker during the weekends and on his days off. He admits to using soldiers' amputated parts when he came up short on an order. He already confessed that he used a few of your donors' bodies. The surgical conferences paid big bucks and he couldn't keep up with the demand."

"You'll need to check our entire supply," Ganz said to McCleary. "Norris also admits to making substitutions, replacing healthy tissue with damaged tissue."

Dr. McCleary nodded, an exaggerated bobbing of his head that told Maggie he would allow the possibility but didn't agree.

"Come," he said, and he led them out of the room and down a long hallway. "You want to do this, fine. I'll show you what you're in for."

He slid a key card and waited for the security pad to blink green. He waved the three of them into a huge room that reminded Maggie of a police evidence room, only the shelves were replaced with drawers, one on top of another. Refrigerated and freezer drawers. Rows and rows.

"Would you like to start with the feet?" McCleary said, pointing at one end. "Or perhaps the eyes?"

AUTHOR'S NOTE

I've spent most of my life in tornado country so I have a healthy respect for the forces of nature. In 2004 I bought what I believed would be a writing retreat just outside of Pensacola, Florida. Six months later, Hurricane Ivan roared ashore.

It's difficult to describe the damage and even more difficult to explain how deep the damage cuts beyond that to physical property. There's a transformation that takes place within the community. You spend long, hot days without running water and electricity. Gasoline and groceries are limited to what you've stocked before the storm. The clean up is physically and emotionally draining but you find yourself grateful to be working alongside neighbors, in my case, people I had only recently met. They taught me what true strength and perseverance looks like.

Nine months after Ivan, Hurricane Dennis made a direct hit. And the Pensacola community simply rolled up their collective sleeves and started cleaning up all over again.

To the community of Pensacola, please know that it was out of respect and admiration that I decided to use your piece of paradise as the backdrop of *Damaged*.

As in all my novels I blend fact with fiction. For the record, here are some of the facts and some of the fiction.

The premise of infecting an entire tissue bank is based solely on my speculation. There have been, however, fatal deaths caused by using infected donor tissue. One such case in 2001 found that a twenty-three-year-old man who died after routine knee surgery was killed by a rare bacterium—*Clostridium sordellii*—and that he contracted the infection from cadaver cartilage that was used to repair his knee.

Unlike organ donor banks, the standards for tissue, bone and other donated body parts are more loosely regulated. Even though the FDA established the HTTF (Human Tissue Task Force) in 2006, by their own admission, they continue to lack the resources to inspect and regulate this vast and growing industry.

The Uniform Anatomical Gift Act does prohibit the buying and selling of dead bodies, but the law does allow for companies to recover their costs for expenses such as labor, transportation, processing and storage. Demand is high, supply low, which sometimes gives way to fraudulent brokers such as the case of a New York funeral home where PVC pipe was swamped out for bones.

Yet, because of this industry, amazing technological advances have resulted. BIOmedics is fictitious, but similar companies have been creating and manufacturing innovative products like bone screws and bone paste, which have helped save the limbs of many soldiers returning from Afghanistan and Iraq.

It's true that the Naval Tissue Bank at the Naval Medical

Center in Maryland was the first to use frozen bone transplants and to set up the first body donation program. However, to my knowledge you will not find a similar tissue bank in Jacksonville, Florida. Nor will you find Captain Ganz's surgical program at the Naval Air Station in Pensacola.

Likewise, I must offer my apologies to the Coast Guard's Air Station Mobile and Air Station Pensacola. I've taken a few liberties with take-offs and landings, many of which would not include Pensacola Beach.

While it is true that before Hurricane Dennis there were homemade signs asking the Weather Channel's Jim Cantore to "stay away" or to "go home," I'm sure Mr. Cantore has witnessed many similar signs in other communities. Hopefully he views these with the good nature they're intended as well as a tribute to his expertise.

And last, Charlie Wurth would have found the Coffee Cup closed on Sundays, but if you're in Penascola any other day of the week, be sure to stop and try their award-winning Nassau grits.

ACKNOWLEDGEMENTS

Thank you to the men and women of the United States armed forces, especially the Coast Guard, for what you do every single day to keep us safe. And special thanks to those few women rescue swimmers for quietly and bravely shattering glass ceilings that most of us wouldn't dare attempt.

Thanks also to:

The incredible team at Doubleday—Jackeline Montalvo, Judy Jacoby, Alison Rich, Suzanne Herz, Lauren Lavelle, and John Pitts—for your warm welcome, your enthusiasm, dedication, and expertise.

Same goes to David Shelley, Catherine Burke and the crew at Little, Brown UK.

Amy Moore-Benson, my agent, for refusing to use the words 'never' or 'impossible'.

Lee Child, Steve Berry and Tess Gerritsen, three of the most generous authors in the business.

Ray Kunze, for lending his name to Maggie's boss. Just for the record, the real Ray Kunze is a gentleman and all-around nice guy who would never send Maggie into the eye of a hurricane.

Lee Dixon, for giving me the idea of identifying a torso by its defibrillator implant.

Darcy Lindner, funeral director, for sharing your expertise.

My friends—Sharon Car, Marlene Haney, Sandy Rockwood, Leigh Ann Retelsdorf, Patti and Martin Bremmer, and Patricia Sierra—for keeping me sane and grounded.

My family: Patricia Kava, Bob and Tracy Kava, Nancy and Jim Tworek, Kenny and Connie Kava, and Patti Carlin.

My Florida neighbors: Lee and Betty Dixon, Terry and Bea Hummel, Sharon and Steve Kator, Elaine and Kelly McDaniels, Lee and Carol McKinstry, Mike and Jana Nicholson, Steve and Anna Ratliff, Bill and Barb Schroeder, and Larry and Diane Wilbanks.

The booksellers, book buyers and librarians across the country, for mentioning and recommending my novels.

All you faithful readers—there's plenty of competition for your time, your entertainment, and your dollars. I thank you for continuing to choose my novels.

And, as always, special thanks to Deb Carlin, for everything. You are my Rock of Gibraltar.

Last, to Walter and Emilie Carlin. Walter passed away September 2008, and Emilie November 2005, but their enduring personalities, life stories, and spirit continue to inspire. Walter would have loved seeing his bright red, white, and blue Coney Island canteen come back to life, even if briefly and only in the pages of a novel.

A BREATH OF HOT AIR

An exclusive short story by

Alex Kava & Patricia A. Bremmer

Alex Kava is the *New York Times* bestselling author of the critically acclaimed Maggie O'Dell series. Her standalone novel, *One False Move*, was chosen for the 2006 One Book One Nebraska and her political thriller, *Whitewash*, made *January Magazine*'s best thriller of the year list for 2007. Published in twenty-four countries, Kava's novels have made the bestseller lists in the UK, Australia, Germany, Italy and Poland. She is also one of the featured authors in the anthology *Thriller: Stories to Keep You Up All Night*, edited by James Patterson and the upcoming anthology, *First Thrills*, edited by Lee Child. In 2007 she was the recipient of the Mari Sandoz Award presented by the Nebraska Library Association. Kava divides her time between Omaha, Nebraska and Pensacola, Florida. She is a member of the Mystery Writers of America and the International Thriller Writers.
www.alexkava.com

Patricia A. Bremmer is the author of eight titles in the Elusive Clue Series. Her series is being considered for movies with Red Feather Productions. A standalone book, *Guided Destiny*, has already been optioned for a major motion picture. Patricia has also penned the Westie Whispers Collection of picture books for children and is currently writing mysteries for middle grade. Patricia has traveled the nation with a stable of thoroughbred racehorses, including Miami, Florida, where she lived for a short time. She currently resides in Western, Nebraska. To add to the excitement of her author appearances, she frequently includes the real life detective who has become the sleuth in her novels. Together they charm and entertain the crowds. She is a member of Sisters in Crime and the International Thriller Writers.
www.patriciabremmer.com

Detective Karst, the sleuth in Patricia A. Bremmer's mystery novels, is best summed up as, "the guy next door who's 50% Bond and 50% Walker." His charm and charismatic intelligence balance perfectly with his rugged denim appearance while on the back of a horse. His looks, personality, and talent offset his vice . . . er, love for top-shelf bourbon and gourmet cheesecake!

Alex Kava and Patricia Bremmer met at a library book talk. Their passion for writing, love of dogs and Nebraska roots made them instant friends. They've shared the spotlight on mystery panels and have spent hours discussing the business of publishing. Put them in a room together and eventually they'll end up talking about murder.

While spending Thanksgiving together at Alex's Pensacola home, they discussed the possibility of co-authoring a short story. As authors they've both grown to know their sleuths as personal friends and for Patricia it is especially true since her sleuth is a real live person. Alex and Patricia tossed around the idea of Alex's sleuth, FBI profiler Maggie O'Dell, meeting Patricia's sleuth, Detective Glen Karst. That conversation spawned the short story, *A Breath of Hot Air*, as well as plans for future writing collaborations.

THE POUNDING CAME from somewhere outside her nightmare. Maggie O'Dell fought her way to consciousness. Her breathing came in gulps as if she had been running. In her nightmare she had been. But now she sat up in bed and strained to hear over the drumming of her heartbeat as she tried to recognize the moonlit room that surrounded her.

It was the breeze coming through the patio door that jump-started her memory. Hot, moist air tickled free the damp hair on her forehead. She could practically taste the salt of the Gulf waters just outside her room. The Hilton Hotel on Pensacola Beach, she remembered.

A digital clock beside her, with glow-in-the-dark numbers, clicked and flipped to 12:47. She was here on assignment, despite a category-5 hurricane barreling toward the Florida Panhandle. But forty minutes earlier all had been calm. Not a cloud in sight to block the full moon. Only the waves predicted the coming storm, already rising higher, with white caps breaking and crashing against the shore. Maggie liked the sound and had left the patio door open—but only a sliver—keeping the security bar engaged. She had hoped the sound would lull her to sleep. It must have worked, at least for forty minutes. That's if you considered nightmares with fishing coolers stuffed full of body parts anything close to sleep.

She hadn't been able to shut off the adrenaline from her afternoon adventure, hovering two hundred feet above the Gulf of Mexico in a Coast Guard helicopter. It hadn't been the strangest crime scene Maggie had ever visited in her ten years with the FBI. The aircrew had recovered a marine cooler floating in the waters just off Pensacola Beach. But instead of finding some fisherman's discarded catch of the day, the crew was shocked to discover human body parts—a torso, three hands and a foot—all carefully wrapped in thick plastic.

However, it hadn't been the body parts that had tripped Maggie into what she called her "nightmare cycle," a vicious loop of snapshots from her memory's scrapbook. Some people slipped into REM cycle, Maggie had her nightmare cycle. No, it wasn't the severed body parts. She had seen and dealt with her share of those. It was the helicopter flight and dangling two hundred feet above control. That's really why she had opened the patio doors earlier. She wanted to replace the thundering sound of the rotors.

The pounding started again and she jerked up, only now remembering what had wakened her. Someone on the other side of the door.

"Ms. O'Dell." A man's voice. High pitched. No one she recognized.

Maggie stumbled out of bed, pulled on khaki shorts and a T-shirt over damp, sticky skin. She had shut off the room's air-conditioning when she opened the patio door and the air inside was now as hot and humid as it was outside. Florida in August. What was she thinking, shutting off the A/C?

She picked up her holstered revolver on the way to the door. Her fingers slid around the handle, her index finger settling on the trigger, but she kept the gun in its holster.

"Yes, who is it?" She asked, standing back and to the side of the door as she waved her other hand in front of the peephole. An old habit, borne of paranoia and self-preservation. If there was a shooter on the other side, he'd be waiting for his target to be pressed against the peephole.

"The night manager. Evans. I mean, Robert Evans." The voice sounded young and panicked. "We have a situation. My boss said you're with the FBI. I'm sorry to wake you. It's sort of an emergency."

This time Maggie glanced out the peephole. The fisheye version made Robert Evans look geekier than he probably was—tall and lanky with nervous energy that kept him rocking from one foot to the other. He tugged at his shirt collar, one finger planted inside as though it was the only thing keeping his company-issued tie from strangling him.

"What kind of an emergency?"

She watched his bobble-size head jerk left then right, making sure no one else was in the hallway. Then he leaned closer to the door and tried to keep his voice low but the panic kicked it into a whispered screech.

"I think I got a dead guy in Room 347."

GLEN KARST SIPPED his bourbon from a corner stool at the outdoor tiki bar. To his left he had a perfect view of the hotel's back door and to his right was a sight off a postcard—silver-topped waves shimmering in the moonlight, lapping at sugar-white sands. If he ever decided to afford himself a vacation, this would be a great place; that is, if he didn't mind sweating. After midnight and it felt like he had a hot, damp towel draped around his neck that he couldn't knock off.

Didn't help that he was exhausted. It had taken him most of the day to get here. All flights to Pensacola had been canceled because of Hurricane Isaac, which meant the closest Glen could get from Denver was Atlanta. He'd spent the last six hours in a rent-a-car, a compact, the only thing left on such short notice. Not quite his style, nor his body's. But he couldn't blame the Ford Escort for all the tension in the small of his back. A good deal of it had been there before he began this journey, one that he hoped wouldn't be a wild goose chase. As a veteran detective, Glen Karst had come to rely on his hunches, his gut instinct, as much as he did his expertise. But coming this far on such short notice and with a hurricane coming, he figured he had maybe twenty-four hours.

A flash of light came from behind him and Glen glanced over his shoulder. A group of college kids mugged for a camera, all holding up bright red drinks in a toast. Hurricane glasses, Glen noticed, shook his head and smiled. Sure didn't look like a hurricane was anywhere near. The beach's restaurants and bars were full of tourists and residents, some spilling out onto the shore and into the parking lots. But he'd also noticed quite a few pickups and moving vans packed and stacked full of belongings, ready to roll. It was Florida. Glen figured the residents knew the drill. But if they were still out eating and drinking, then he knew he still had time.

He pulled a brochure from his shirt pocket, laid it on the bar next to his glass and smoothed out the crease. The man in the photo had added a good thirty pounds to his hefty frame. His blond hair had been cut short, dyed dark brown and peppered with gray at the temples. The goatee was new and attempted to hide the beginning of a double chin. At a glimpse, the man looked nothing like Dr. Thomas Gruber, but Glen recognized the eyes, deep-set and ice blue. In his arrogance the good doctor had failed to disguise the one trait that betrayed him most.

"They've canceled," said a young man three bar stools over, pointing at Glen's brochure.

"What's that?"

"The conference. It's been canceled because of the hurricane."

"Damn, are you sure?"

"Don't take this the wrong way, but you don't look like a doctor."

"That's good, 'cause I don't like doctors."

The guy stood up, his drink in one hand, and nodded at the stool next to Glen. "You mind?"

"I'm not expecting anyone."

Glen sipped his bourbon, not giving the guy much attention. But in the time it took for the man to sidle up next to him, Glen had noted the guy's short cropped hair—military style would have been Glen's first guess except for the Rolex, Sperry deck shoes and Ralph Lauren polo that he left untucked over khaki cargo shorts. Expensive wares for a guy who, according to Glen's estimate, was probably thirty at the most.

"Name's Joe Black," he tipped his glass at Glen instead of offering his hand. The glass was a rocks glass like his own, Scotch or bourbon, neat.

"Glen." From the corner of his eyes he could see Joe Black assessing him, too. He was cool, calm, and took only a casual glimpse at the brochure on the bar between them. "So you go to these conferences?"

"You might say I'm a regular."

Glen gave him a sidelong look. "Hell, you don't look like a doctor either."

Joe laughed, but he didn't bother to answer, nor did he look like he was going to. However, his eyes darted to the brochure again before he shifted on the bar stool and reached for his glass.

"You know this doctor?" Glen tapped the photo, looking down at it as if he needed to remember the name, "This Dr. Eric Foster?" But in fact, he had memorized every detail about Dr. Foster, alias Dr. Gruber. The only thing he couldn't figure out is why Gruber would risk coming back to the states.

Just over a year ago Gruber had fled Colorado after being the main suspect in a triple homicide. Gruber had abandoned his surgical practice, skipped out on a million-dollar mortgage, and left his wife penniless. He had escaped to South America, somewhere in Brazil, according to Glen's last effort in tracking him. Rumor was that the good doctor might be trafficking body parts, even going as far as buying kidneys from poor struggling schmucks who had nothing else to sell.

Ironically, the conference that had Gruber scheduled as a featured speaker bragged about having human specimens for surgeons to perfect their skills. Nothing illegal. Glen had checked it out. These conferences took place all over the country, though usually at some beachfront resort as an added incentive. Medical device companies planned and arranged them, offering surgeons all-expense-paid trips in exchange for them to come try out the company's newest gadgets and hopefully put in several orders before they returned home.

The fact was the triple homicide in Colorado remained open. No other suspects. All evidence pointed to Gruber and the bastard had slipped away during the investigation. Glen was more than anxious to finally nail the guy.

"Yeah, I know Foster. You might say he's my competition," Joe Black finally said without offering anything more. He waved down the bartender and pointed to his glass. "Another Johnnie Walker Black Label." Then to Glen he said, "How bout you? Another Buffalo Trace?"

Glen hid his surprise then he simply nodded at the bartender. Joe Black knew what he was drinking. Why the hell had this guy been watching him?

"So what do you want with Dr. Foster?" Joe asked.

"Just want to have a friendly chat."

"You a cop?"

"I don't look like a doctor, but I do look like a cop, huh?"

Joe shrugged and went quiet while the bartender placed fresh drinks in front of them.

"If not a cop, maybe a jealous husband?" This time he looked at Glen, waiting to see his reaction.

Glen fidgeted with his glass but didn't say a word. Sometimes people filled in the silence if you waited long enough. It seemed to work.

Satisfied with Glen's response—or rather his non-response—Joe continued, "I told him it'd catch up with him one of these days. So the blond with all the expensive jewelry? She must be yours?"

This was easier than Glen expected. "Is she with him?"

Joe nodded and tipped back the rest of his Scotch. "Finish your drink," he told Glen. "I'll take you up to his room."

Glen could hardly believe it. He looked the guy over, this time allowing his suspicions to show. "Why would you do me any favors?"

"Maybe because I don't much like the bastard myself."

AS SOON AS MAGGIE walked into the room she knew that the big man sprawled on his back in the king-size bed had not died of natural causes. His bloodshot eyes stared at the ceiling. His mouth was twisted into a sardonic grin. Trousers lay crumpled in a pile on the floor, a belt half pulled from the loops. Shoes peeked out from under.

"Who found him?" Maggie glanced back at Evans. The night manager had grown pale before they reached the room. Now he stayed in the open doorway, unwilling to move any farther into the room.

"Someone from housekeeping. There was a request for more towels."

Evans couldn't see the body from his post inside the door-well and Maggie realized he couldn't see her either. Without stepping on or touching anything, she ventured closer. The dead man wore bright blue boxers and a button-down shirt, half unbuttoned. His skin looked like it was on fire—bright red, but not from sunburn.

"He probably had a heart attack, right?" Evans sounded hopeful.

"Was he alone?" Maggie asked, noticing an empty wine bottle with one glass on the nightstand.

"No one else is listed under his registration."

"But he wasn't alone," another voice said from outside in the hallway.

Maggie came around the bed, back into the entrance just in time to see two men standing over the night manager's bony shoulder.

"Are you from the sheriff's department?" she asked.

"I didn't call the sheriff's department," Evans said, bracing his hand on the doorway and making a barrier with his skinny arm.

"911?" Maggie tried again.

"I didn't call anyone," Evans said. Then with wide eyes and an attempted whisper, he leaned toward her and added, "My boss said to get you."

"I'm Detective Glen Karst," the man in the hallway poked his arm over Evans, offering a badge and ID.

Maggie reached out and took the ID but instead of turning on the light in the entrance, she leaned into the bathroom, using its light.

"You're a long way from home, Detective Karst." She handed him back his ID and stood with hands on her hips, waiting for his explanation while Evans kept up his pathetic barrier.

"I have reason to believe the man inside is a suspect in a triple homicide. I just want to ask him a few questions. Mr. Black told me—" Karst stopped, turned then looked around the hallway as though he'd lost something or someone. The man who had accompanied him was gone.

Maggie glanced at her watch. It was late and she was exhausted. She'd been on the road for half the day and dangling over the Gulf in a helicopter for the other half. Her forty-minute nap had been invaded by nightmares. This dead guy wasn't even her jurisdiction.

"Mr. Evans, I think you should go call the sheriff's department." She put a gentle hand on his shoulder, waiting for him to drop his arm from the doorjamb.

"The sheriff's department?" He said it like it still hadn't even occurred to him to do so.

"Yes." She kept eye contact, hoping to transfer her calm and cool composure over to him. "Detective Karst and I will secure the room until someone from the sheriff's department gets here."

Both Maggie and Karst watched Evans leave, his lanky frame wobbled like a drunk attempting to walk on tiptoes. He missed the turn for the elevators, stopped and backtracked, giving them an embarrassed wave, then straightened up like a sleepwalker suddenly coming awake. Maggie waited until she heard the ping of the elevator before she turned back to the room.

"Don't touch anything," she told Detective Karst as she gestured for him to follow her inside.

"Don't worry about me. I didn't catch your name."

"Maggie O'Dell."

"You're not local law enforcement."

It wasn't a question. He said it with such certainty Maggie stopped in the entrance and looked back at him. She wanted to ask how he knew then decided it wasn't important.

"FBI. I'm down here on another assignment. The night manager thought it would be more convenient to wake me up rather than call the sheriff."

"Son of a bitch, don't tell me Foster's dead?" Karst asked as he came into view of the bed.

"Do you recognize him?"

He didn't need to come any closer. "Yeah, I do. He goes by Eric Foster, but his real name is Thomas Gruber. What's your guess? Suicide?"

"No."

"You sound pretty sure of yourself."

This time she smiled at him. "I do this for a living, Detective Karst."

"I'm not questioning your qualifications, just asking how you reached that conclusion."

Maggie pointed at the dead man's eyes. "Petechial hemorrhages."

Karst leaned closer. "His neck doesn't show any signs of strangulation."

"The ruptures probably occurred during convulsions, maybe seizures. He strangled but from the inside out."

He raised an eyebrow at her, waiting for more.

"I recognize that twist of the mouth and the bright red skin, almost cherry red. I've only seen this sort of skin discoloration once before but it's something I'll never forget. The tissue can't get any oxygen. It happens quickly. Ten to fifteen minutes."

"You think he was poisoned?"

Maggie nodded, impressed. The detective from Colorado was sharp.

Karst noticed her look and it was his turn to smile. "I do this for a living, too."

Then he started looking at the bedding, careful not to touch but bending over and searching the pillows.

"Usually there's vomit," he said and started sniffing the linens, now leaning even closer over the dead man. Then Karst's body stiffened and he stood up straight. "Cyanide."

"Excuse me?"

"I can smell it," he said. "Like bitter almonds."

Maggie came up beside Karst and he stepped back while she bent over the dead man's face. Only forty to fifty percent of people could smell the aftereffects of cyanide. It was a genetic ability. The scent was faint but she could smell it, too.

"I thought it might be something like that," she said. "Cyanide stops cells from using oxygen. He would have felt like he was suffocating—a shortness of breath followed by dizziness. Then comes the confusion and possible seizures, bursting the capillaries in the eyes. Last would be cardiac arrest. All in a matter of minutes."

"Potassium cyanide is a crystal compound." Karst looked around the room and pointed to the wine bottle. "May have slipped it into the wine. Where does someone get cyanide these days?"

Maggie had to stop and think, retrieve the information from her memory bank. The case she had worked on had happened too many years ago—six young men in a cabin in the woods had chosen to obey their leader and take cyanide capsules rather than be taken into custody. She'd lost a friend that day—a fellow FBI agent—so the memory didn't come easily.

"Potassium cyanide is still used in several industries. Certain kinds of photography," she finally said. "Some processing of plastics, electroplating, and gold plating in jewelry making. If a person buys it on a regular basis for their business, it usually doesn't draw any attention."

Now she wanted to dismantle the memory and started looking over the room again. She plucked a tissue from its container on the nightstand and gently pressed her covered fingertip against the dead man's jaw then his neck. "No rigor."

"So he's been dead less than twelve hours."

"Maybe less than six. Rigor sets in more quickly with cyanide poisoning. You said he wasn't alone?" She turned to see Karst had moved to the desk and was lifting open a folded wallet using the tip of a pen.

"Guy I met at the bar downstairs told me he saw Gruber leave with a blond."

"The guy who took off as soon as he saw your badge?"

He glanced up at Maggie. "Coincidence?"

"I don't believe in coincidences."

"Me either. I'll bet he gave me a bogus name. Hell, he probably lied about the blond, too."

Maggie used the tissue again as she tipped a wastebasket out from under the nightstand. The only thing inside was another tissue, this one crumpled with a blotted stain of bright pink lipstick. She gently lifted it by a corner, pulling it up high enough to show Karst.

"Unless there's something a little freaky about Dr. Foster, I think your friend might have been telling the truth about the blond."

"I'll be damned."

Maggie took a good look at the stain under the light, then gently placed it back where she had found it. Later she'd point it out to the sheriff's investigator.

"What did he do?" she asked.

Karst folded his arms and stared at the dead man. "His nurse was two-timing him with a rich ex-patient. He murdered her plus the patient and his wife. Then Gruber set the nurse's house on fire, hoping to hide all the evidence. He hightailed it to South America before we could even question him."

"So there were a few others beside you, looking for him."

"Not to mention some new enemies. The guy from the bar mentioned something about Gruber being his competition."

Maggie watched Karst's face. He was still grinding out the case in his mind. She checked her watch again.

"I'd say you no longer have a case, Detective Karst."

There was knock at the door followed by, "Sheriff's department."

GLEN KARST FOUND himself back down at the hotel's tiki bar. This time he and Maggie shared one of the high-top tables. He'd asked to buy her a drink and was surprised when the tough, no nonsense FBI agent ordered a Diet Pepsi. He ordered another Buffalo Trace, glancing around to see if Joe Black was somewhere close by, watching again.

The waves had kicked up and the moon had slid over a bit. A breeze almost made the hot, humid air feel good. The beach restaurants and bars were still full but not quite as crowded and noisy as earlier.

"I can't believe I came all the way down here and the son of a bitch cheated me out of dragging his ass back to Denver. It's hard to let it go."

"Sheriff Clayton will do a good job," Maggie told him. "Anything you can tell him about Gruber will help his investigation."

Glen rubbed at his eyes, only now remembering how exhausted he was. "I suppose the bastard got what was coming to him."

"A wise medical examiner once told me, we die as we live."

"Is that the equivalent of what goes around comes around?"

She smiled and tipped her glass at him, "Touché."

He raised his glass and was about to take a sip when he saw a woman sidle up to the bar. She looked familiar but he couldn't place her. Then he realized. Her hair was shorter. She looked much thinner than when he'd met her over a year ago. But he recognized her walk, the way she handled herself.

"Someone you know," Maggie asked. "Or someone you'd like to know?"

"What? Oh, sorry. No, I think I know her." He sipped his bourbon and continued to watch out of the corner of his eyes.

She was at the bar, ordering drinks and laughing with her friends, three women at a table near the bar.

"Not a blond," Maggie said as if reading his mind. She sat back and took another look. "Even from this distance I'd say the lipstick's a match."

His eyes met Maggie's. She was thinking exactly what he was thinking.

"No such thing as coincidences, right?" he said.

"It's no longer your case," Maggie reminded him. "She wore a wig, probably stole her wineglass and the bottle was wiped down. I checked. They'll never pull DNA off that tissue."

"The least I can do is say hello."

The woman's back was to Glen when he walked up and leaned on the bar. He ordered another round of drinks and watched, waiting for her to notice him. The glance was subtle at first, almost flirtatious. Then he saw the realization.

"Hello, Mrs. Gruber."

"Detective." She kept her body turned away from him and looked for the bartender. "I'm sorry, I don't remember your name."

But he knew she did remember. He told her anyway, "Glen. Glen Karst. Are you here on vacation?"

"We are. Yes, actually, we were until the hurricane."

"No other reason you chose Pensacola?" His eyes waited for hers. She met his stare and didn't flinch. Didn't look away. In a split second he thought he could see her confirmation, her admission that she knew exactly what he was talking about, that she knew he was there and what he had found.

Without a blink, she said, "Just having some fun and my friends can vouch for that."

The bartender interrupted with a tray of colorful drinks ready and hovering. Before Mrs. Gruber took them she pulled out a business card from her pocket, hesitated, then handed it to Glen.

"I have my own business now," she told him, taking the tray and handing the bartender a fifty-dollar bill. "Keep the change, sweetie," she told the young man and without giving Glen another look, she returned to her table and friends.

Glen returned to the high-top with fresh drinks and scooted his chair closer. He placed the business card on the table without looking at it or at Maggie.

"You got lucky. She gave you her number?"

"No, I already have it. What she gave me was a cold shoulder." Glen said. "That's Gruber's ex-wife."

"I think she may have given you more than that," Maggie told him and he looked up to see her reading the business card. She handed it to him and immediately Glen knew.

Elaine Gruber had her own business all right. Making fine jewelry and specializing in gold plating.

How to Find Love in a BOOK SHOP

Also by Veronica Henry

Wild Oats
An Eligible Bachelor
Love on the Rocks
Marriage and Other Games
The Beach Hut
The Birthday Party
The Long Weekend
A Night on the Orient Express
The Beach Hut Next Door
High Tide

THE HONEYCOTE NOVELS
Honeycote
Making Hay
Just a Family Affair

How to Find Love in a BOOK SHOP

Veronica Henry

First published in Great Britain in 2016 by Orion Books,
an imprint of The Orion Publishing Group Ltd
Carmelite House, 50 Victoria Embankment
London EC4Y 0DZ

An Hachette UK Company

1 3 5 7 9 10 8 6 4 2

All the characters in this book, except for those already
in the public domain, are fictitious, and any resemblance to
actual persons, living or dead, is purely coincidental.

A CIP catalogue record for this book is
available from the British Library.

ISBN (Hardback) 978 1 4091 4688 9
ISBN (Export Trade Paperback) 978 1 4091 6568 2
ISBN (Ebook) 978 1 4091 4687 2

Typeset at The Spartan Press Ltd,
Lymington, Hants

Printed in Great Britain by Clays Ltd,
St Ives plc

www.orionbooks.co.uk

This book is dedicated to my beloved father,
William Miles Henry
1935–2016

'Reading is everything'

NORA EPHRON

Prologue

February 1983

He would never have believed it if you'd told him a year ago. That he'd be standing in an empty shop with a baby in a pram, seriously considering putting in an offer.

The pram had been a stroke of luck. He'd seen an advert for a garden sale in a posh part of North Oxford, and the bargain hunter in him couldn't stay away. The couple had two very young children but were moving to Paris. The pram was pristine, of the kind the queen might have pushed – or rather, her nanny. The woman had only wanted five pounds for it. Julius was sure it was worth far more, and she was only being kind. But if recent events had taught him one thing it was to accept kindness. With alacrity, before people changed their minds. So he bought it, and scrubbed it out carefully with Milton even though it had seemed very clean already, and bought a fresh mattress and blankets and there he had it: the perfect nest for his precious cargo, until she could walk.

When did babies start to walk? There was no point in asking Debra – his vague, away-with-the-fairies mother, ensconced in her patchouli-soaked basement flat in Westbourne Grove, whose memory of his own childhood was blurry. According to Debra, Julius was reading by the age of two, a legend he didn't quite believe. Although maybe it was true, because he couldn't remember a time he couldn't read. It was like breathing to him. Nevertheless, he couldn't and didn't rely on his mother for child-rearing advice. He often thought it was a miracle he had made it through childhood unscathed. She used to leave him alone, in his cot, while she went to the wine bar on the corner in the evenings. 'What could go wrong?' she asked him. 'I only left you for an hour.' Perhaps that explained his protectiveness towards his own daughter. He found it hard to turn his back on her for even a moment.

He looked around the bare walls again. The smell of damp was inescapable, and damp would be a disaster. The staircase rising to the mezzanine was rotten; so rotten he wasn't allowed up it. The two bay windows either side of the front door flooded the shop with a pearlescent light, highlighting the golden oak of the floorboards and the ornate plasterwork on the ceiling. The dust made it feel other-worldly: a ghost shop, waiting, waiting for something to happen, a transformation, a renovation, a renaissance.

'It was a pharmacy, originally,' said the agent. 'And then an antique shop. Well, I say antique – you've never seen so much rubbish in your life.'

He should get some professional advice, really. A structural survey, a quote from someone for a damp course – yet Julius felt light-headed and his heart was pounding. It was right. He knew it was. The two floors above were ideal for him and the baby to live in. Over the shop.

The book shop.

His search had begun three weeks earlier, when he had decided that he needed to take positive action if he and his daughter were going to have any semblance of normal life together. He had looked at his experience, his potential, his assets, and the practicalities of being a single father, and decided there was really only one option open to him.

He'd gone to the library, put a copy of the Yellow Pages on the table, and next to it a detailed map of the county. He drew a circle around Oxford with a fifteen-mile radius, wondering what it would be like to live in Christmas Common, or Ducklington, or Goosey. Then he worked through all the book shops listed and put a cross through the towns they were in.

He looked at the remaining towns, the ones without a book shop at all. There were half a dozen. He made a list, and then over the next few days visited each one, travelling by a complicated rota of buses. The first three towns had been soulless and dreary, and he had been so discouraged he'd almost given up on his idea, but something about the name Peasebrook pleased him, so he decided to have one last look before relinquishing his fantasy.

Peasebrook was in the middle of the Cotswolds, on the outer perimeter of the circle he had drawn: as far out as he wanted to go. He got off the bus and looked up the high street. It was wide and tree-lined, its pavements flanked with higgledy-piggledy golden buildings. There were antique shops, a traditional butcher with rabbit and pheasant hanging outside and fat sausages in the window, a sprawling coaching inn and a couple of nice cafés and a cheese shop. The Women's Institute were having a sale outside the town hall: there were trestle tables bearing big cakes oozing jam and trugs of mud-covered vegetables and pots of herbaceous flowers drooping dark purple and yellow blooms.

Peasebrook was buzzing, in a quiet way but with purpose, like bees on a summer afternoon. People stopped in the street and talked to each other. The cafés looked pleasingly full. The tills seemed to jangle: people were shopping with gusto and enthusiasm. There was a very smart restaurant with a bay tree outside the door and an impressive menu in a glass case boasting nouvelle cuisine. There was even a tiny theatre showing The Importance of Being Earnest. *Somehow that boded well. Julius loved Oscar Wilde. He'd done one of his dissertations on him: The Influence of Oscar Wilde on W.B. Yeats.*

He took the play as an omen, but he carried on scouring the streets, in case his research hadn't been thorough. He feared turning a corner and finding what he hoped wasn't there. Now he was here, in Peasebrook, he wanted it to be his home – their *home. It was a mystery, though, why there was no book shop in such an appealing place.*

After all, a town without a book shop was a town without a heart.

A book shop could only make things better – for everyone in Peasebrook. Julius imagined each person he passed as a potential customer. He could picture them all, crowding in, asking his advice, him sliding their purchases into a bag, getting to know their likes and dislikes, putting a book aside for a particular customer; knowing it would be just up their street. Watching them browse, watching the joy of them discovering a new author; a new world.

'Would the vendor take a cheeky offer?' he asked the estate agent, who shrugged.

'You can but ask.'

'It needs a lot of work.'

'That has *been taken into consideration.'*

Julius named his price. 'It's my best and only offer. I can't afford any more.'

When Julius signed the contract four weeks later, he couldn't help but be amazed. Here he was, alone in the world (well, there was his mother, but she was as much use as a chocolate teapot) but for a baby and a book shop. And as that very baby reached out her starfish hand, he gave her his finger to hold and thought: what an extraordinary position to be in. Fate was peculiar indeed.

What if he hadn't looked up at that very moment, nearly two years ago now? What if he had kept his back to the door and carried on rearranging the travel section, leaving his colleague to serve the girl with the Rossetti hair…

And six months later, after weeks of dust and grime and sawing and sweeping and painting, and several eye-watering bills, and a few moments of sheer panic, and any number of deliveries, the sign outside the shop was rehung, painted in navy and gold, proclaiming 'Nightingale Books'. There had been no room to write 'purveyors of reading matter to the discerning', but that was what he was. A bookseller.

A bookseller of the very best kind.

One

Thirty-two years later . . .

What do you do, while you're waiting for someone to die? Literally, sitting next to them in a plastic armchair that isn't the right shape for *anyone's* bottom, waiting for them to draw their last breath because there is no more hope.

Nothing seemed appropriate. There was a room down the corridor to watch telly in, but that seemed callous, and anyway, Emilia wasn't really a television person.

She didn't knit, or do tapestry. Or sudoku.

She didn't want to listen to music, for fear of disturbing him. Even the best earphones leak a certain timpani. Irritating on a train, probably even more so on your deathbed. She didn't want to surf the Internet on her phone. That seemed the ultimate in twenty-first-century rudeness.

And there wasn't a single book on the planet that could hold her attention right now.

So she sat next to his bed and dozed. And every now and then she started awake with a bolt of fear, in case she might have missed the moment. Then she would hold his hand for a few minutes. It was dry and cool and lay motionless in her clasp. Eventually it grew heavy and made her feel sad, so she laid it back on the top of the sheet.

Then she would doze off again.

From time to time the nurses brought her hot chocolate, although that was a misnomer. It was not hot, but tepid, and Emilia was fairly certain that no cocoa beans had been harmed in the making of it. It was pale beige, faintly sweet water.

The night-time lights in the cottage hospital were dim, with a sickly yellowish tinge. The heating was on too high and the little room felt airless. She looked at the thin bedcover, with its pattern of orange and yellow flowers, and the outline of her father underneath, so still and small. She could see the few strands of hair curling over his scalp, leached of colour. His thick hair had been one of his distinguishing features. He would rake his fingers through it while he was considering a recommendation, or when he was standing in front of one of the display tables trying to decide what to put on it, or when he was on the phone to a customer. It was as much part of him as the pale blue cashmere scarf he insisted on wearing, wrapped twice round his neck, even though it bore evidence of moths. Emilia had dealt with them swiftly at the first sign. She suspected they had been brought in via the thick brown velvet coat she had bought at the charity shop last winter, and she felt guilty they'd set upon the one sartorial item her father seemed attached to.

He'd been complaining then, of discomfort. Well, not complaining, because he wasn't one to moan. Emilia had expressed concern, and he had dismissed her concern with his trademark stoicism, and she had thought nothing more of it, just got on the plane to Hong Kong. Until the phone call, last week, calling her back.

'I think you ought to come home,' the nurse had said. 'Your father will be furious with me for calling you. He doesn't want to alarm you. But...'

The 'but' said it all. Emilia was on the first flight out. And when she arrived Julius pretended to be cross, but the way he held her hand, tighter than tight, told her everything she needed to know.

'He's in denial,' said the nurse. 'He's a fighter all right. I'm so sorry. We're doing everything we can to keep him comfortable.'

Emilia nodded, finally understanding. Comfortable. Not alive. Comfortable.

He didn't seem to be in any pain or discomfort now. He had eaten some lime jelly the day before, eager for the quivering spoons of green. Emilia imagined it soothed his parched lips and dry tongue. She felt as if she was feeding a little bird as he stretched his neck to reach the spoon and opened his mouth. Afterwards he lay back, exhausted by the effort. It was all he had eaten for days. All he was living on was a complicated cocktail of painkillers and sedatives that were rotated to provide the best palliative care. Emilia had come to hate the word palliative. It was ominous, and at times she suspected ineffectual. From time to time her father had shown distress, whether from pain or the knowledge of what was to come she didn't know, but she knew at those points the medication wasn't doing its job. Adjustment, although swiftly administered, never worked quickly enough. Which in turn caused her distress. It was a never-ending cycle.

Yet not *never*-ending because it *would* end. The corner had been turned and there was no point in hoping for a recovery. Even the most optimistic believer in miracles would know that now. So there was nothing to do but pray for a swift and merciful release.

The nurse lifted the bedcover and looked at his feet, caressing them with gentle fingers. The look the nurse gave Emilia told her it wouldn't be long now. His skin was pale grey, the pale grey of a marble statue.

The nurse dropped the sheet back down and rubbed Emilia's shoulder. Then she left, for there was nothing she could say. It was a waiting game. They had done all they could. No pain, as far as anyone could surmise. A calm, quiet environment, for incipient death was treated with hushed reverence. But who was to say what the dying really wanted? Maybe he would prefer his beloved Elgar at full blast, or the shipping forecast on repeat? Or to hear the nurses gossiping and bantering, about who they'd been out with the night before and what they were cooking for tea? Maybe distraction from your imminent demise by utter trivia would be a welcome one?

Emilia sat and wondered how could she make him feel her love, as he slipped away. If she could take out her heart and give it to him, she would. This wonderful man who had given her life, and been her life, and was leaving her alone.

She'd whispered to him, memories and reminiscences. She told him stories. Recited his favourite poems.

Talked to him about the shop.

'I'm going to look after it for you,' she told him. 'I'll make sure it never closes its doors. Not in my lifetime. And I'm never going to sell out to Ian Mendip, no matter what he offers, because the shop is all that matters. All the diamonds in the world are nothing in comparison. Books are more precious than jewels.'

She truly believed this. What did a diamond bring you? A momentary flash of brilliance. A diamond scintillated for a second; a book could scintillate forever.

She doubted Ian Mendip had ever read a book in his life. It made her so angry, thinking about the stress he'd put her father under at a vulnerable time. Julius had tried to underplay it, but she could see he was upset, fearful for the shop and his staff and his customers. The staff had told her how unsettled he had been by it, and yet again she had cursed herself for being so far away. Now she was determined to reassure him, so he could slip away, safe in the knowledge that Nightingale Books was in good hands.

She shifted on the seat to find a more comfortable position.

She ended up leaning forwards and resting her head in her arms at the foot of the bed. She was unbelievably tired.

It was two forty-nine in the morning when the nurse touched her on the shoulder. Her touch said everything that needed to be said. Emilia wasn't sure if she had been asleep or awake. Even now she wasn't sure if she was asleep or awake, for she felt as if her head was somewhere else, as if everything was a bit treacly and slow.

When all the formalities were over and the undertaker had been called, she walked out into the dawn, the air morgue-chilly, the light gloomy. It was as if all the colour had gone from the world, until she saw the traffic lights by the hospital exit change from red to amber to green. Sound too felt muffled, as if she still had water in her ears from swimming.

Would the world be a different place without Julius in it? She didn't know yet. She breathed in the air he was no longer breathing, and thought about his broad shoulders, the ones she had sat on when she was tiny, drumming her heels on his chest to make him run faster, twisting her fingers in the thick hair that fell to his collar, the hair that had been salt and pepper since he was thirty. She held the plain silver watch with the alligator strap he had worn every day, but which she had taken off towards the end, as she didn't want anything chafing his paper-thin skin, leaving it on the table next to his bed in case he needed to know the time, because it told a better time than the clock over the nurse's station; a time that held far more promise. But the magic time on his watch hadn't been able to stop the inevitable.

She got into her car. There was a packet of buttermints on the passenger seat she had meant to bring him. She unpeeled one and popped it in her mouth. It was the first thing she had eaten since breakfast the day before. She sucked on it until it scraped the roof of her mouth, and the discomfort took her mind off it all for a moment.

She'd eaten half the packet by the time she turned into Peasebrook high street and her teeth were furry with the sugar. The little town was wrapped in the pearl-grey of dawn. It looked bleak: its golden stone needed sunshine for it to glow. In the half-light it looked like a dreary wallflower, but in a couple of hours it would emerge like a dazzling debutante, charming everyone who set eyes upon it. It was quintessentially quaint and English, with its oak doorways and mullions and latticed windows, cobbled pavements and red letterboxes and the row of pollarded lime trees. There were no flat-roofed monstrosities, nothing to offend the eye, only charm.

Next to the stone bridge straddling the brook that gave the town its name was Nightingale Books, three storeys high and double fronted, with two bay windows and a dark blue door. Emilia stood outside, the early morning breeze the only sign of movement in the sleeping town, and looked up at the building that was the only home she had ever known. Wherever she was in the world, whatever she was doing, her room above the shop was still here; most of her stuff was still here. Thirty-two years of clutter and clobber.

She slipped in through the side entrance and stood for a moment on the tiled floor. In front of her was the door leading up to the flat. She remembered her father holding her hand when she was tiny, and walking her down those stairs. It had taken hours, but she had been determined, and he had been patient. When she was at school, she had run down the stairs, taking them two at a time, her school bag on her back, an apple in one hand, always late. Years later, she had sneaked up the stairs in bare feet when she came in from a party. Not that Julius was strict or likely to shout: it was just what you did when you were sixteen and had drunk a little too much cider and it was two o'clock in the morning.

To her left was the door that came out behind the shop

counter. She pushed it open and stepped into the shop. The early morning light ventured in through the window, tentative. Emilia shivered a little as the air inside stirred. She felt a sense of expectation: the same feeling of stepping back in time or into another place she had whenever she entered Nightingale Books. She could be whenever and wherever she wanted. Only this time she couldn't. She would give anything to go back, to when everything was all right.

She felt as if the books were asking for news. He's gone, she wanted to tell them, but she didn't, because she didn't trust her voice. And because it was silly. Books told you things, everything you needed to know, but you didn't talk back to them.

As she stood in the middle of the shop, she gradually felt a sense of comfort settle upon her, a calmness that soothed her soul. For Julius was still here, amidst the covers and the upright spines. He claimed to know every book in his shop. He may not have read each one from cover to cover, but he understood why they were there, what the author's intent had been and who might, therefore, like to read them, from the simplest children's board book to the weightiest, most indecipherable tome.

There was a rich red carpet, faded and worn now. Rows and rows of wooden shelves lined the walls, stretching right up to the ceiling – there was a ladder to reach the more unusual books on the very top shelves. Fiction was at the front of the shop, reference at the back, and tables in the middle displayed cookery and art and travel. Upstairs, on the mezzanine, there was a collection of first editions and second-hand rarities, behind locked glass cases. And Julius had reigned over it all from his place behind the wooden counter. Behind him were stacked the books that people had ordered, wrapped in brown paper and tied with string. There was an old-fashioned ornate till that tinged when it opened, which he'd found in a junk shop and, although he didn't use it any more, he kept it, as decoration and sometimes he kept sugar mice in the drawer to hand out to small children who had been especially patient and good.

There would always be a half-full cup of coffee on the counter that he'd begun and never finished, because he would get into a conversation and forget about it and leave it to get cold. Because people dropped in to chat to Julius all the time. He was full of advice and knowledge and wisdom and above all, kindness.

As a result, the shop had become a mecca for all sections of society in and around Peasebrook. The townspeople were proud of their book shop. It was a place of comfort and familiarity. And they had come to respect its owner. Adore him, even. For over thirty years he had fed their minds and their hearts, aided and abetted in recent years by his assistants, warm and bubbly Mel, who kept the place organised, and lanky Dave the Goth who knew almost as much as Julius about books but rarely spoke – though once you got him going it was impossible to stop him.

Her father was still here, thought Emilia, in the thousands of pages. Millions – there must be so many millions – of words. All those words, and the pleasure they had provided for people over the years: escape, entertainment, education . . . He had changed minds. He had changed lives. It was up to her to carry on his work so he would live on, she swore to herself.

Julius Nightingale would live forever.

Emilia left the shop and went upstairs to the flat. She was too tired to even make a cup of tea. She needed to lie down and gather her thoughts. She wasn't feeling anything yet, neither shock nor grief, just a dull heavy-heartedness that weighed her down. The worst had happened, the worst thing possible, but it seemed the world was still turning. The gradual lightening of the sky told her that. She heard birdsong, too, and frowned at their chirpy heralding of a new dawn. Surely the sun wouldn't rise? Surely the world would be grey forever?

All the rooms seemed drained of warmth. The kitchen, with its ancient pine table and battered old units, was chilly and austere. The living room was sulking behind its half-drawn curtains. Emilia couldn't look at the sofa in case it still held the imprint of Julius: she couldn't count the number of hours the two of them had spent curled up on it with tea or cocoa or wine, leafing through their current read, while Brahms or Billie Holiday or Joni Mitchell circled on the record player. Julius had never taken to modern technology: he loved vinyl, and still treasured his Grundig Audiorama speakers. They had, however, been silent for a while now.

Emilia made her way to her bedroom on the next floor, peeled back her duvet and climbed into the high brass bed that had been hers since she could remember. She pulled a cushion from the pile and hugged it to her, for warmth as much as comfort. She drew her knees up and waited to cry. There were no tears. She waited and waited, but her eyes were dry. She thought she must be a monster, not to be able to weep.

She awoke sometime later to a gentle tapping on the flat door. She started awake, wondering why she was in bed fully clothed. The realisation hit her in the chest and she wanted nothing more than to slide back into the oblivion she had been in. But there were people to see, things to do, decisions to be made. And a door to answer. She ran downstairs in her socks and opened it gingerly.

'Sweetheart.'

June. Stalwart, redoubtable June, arguably Nightingale Books' best customer since she had retired to Peasebrook three years before. She had stepped into Julius's shoes when he went into the cottage hospital for what looked like the final time. June had run her own company for more than forty years and was only too willing to pick up the reins along with Mel and Dave. With her fine bone structure, and her thick dark hair, and her armful of silver bangles, she looked at least ten years younger than her three score years and ten. She had the energy of a twenty-year-old, the brain of a rocket scientist and the heart of a lion. Emilia had at first thought there might be a romance between June and Julius – June was twice divorced – but their friendship had been firm but purely platonic.

Emilia realised she should have phoned June as soon as it happened. But she hadn't had the strength or the words or the heart. She didn't have them now. She just stood there, and June wrapped her up in an embrace that was as soft and warm as the cashmere jumpers she draped herself in.

'You poor baby,' she crooned, and it was only then Emilia found she could cry.

'There's no need to open the shop today,' June told Emilia later, when she'd sobbed her heart out and had finally agreed to make herself some breakfast. But Emilia was adamant it should stay open.

'Everyone comes in on a Thursday. It's market day,' she said.

In the end, it turned out to be the best thing she could have done. Mel, usually loquacious, was mute with shock. Dave, usually monosyllabic, spoke for five minutes without drawing breath about how Julius had taught him everything he knew. Mel put Classic FM on the shop radio so they didn't feel the need to fill the silence. Dave, who had many mysterious skills of which calligraphy was one, wrote a sign for the window:

It is with great sadness that we have to tell you
of the death of Julius Nightingale
Peacefully, after a short illness
A beloved father, friend and bookseller

They opened a little late, but open they did. And a stream of customers trickled in throughout the day, to pay their respects and give Emilia their condolences. Some brought cards; others casseroles and a tin full of home-baked muffins; someone else left a bottle of Chassagne Montrachet, her father's favourite wine, on the counter.

Emilia had needed no convincing that her father was a wonderful man, but by the end of the day she realised that everyone else who knew him thought that too. Mel made countless cups of tea in the back office and carried them out on a tray.

'Come for supper,' said June, when they finally flipped the sign to CLOSED long after they should have shut.

'I'm not very hungry,' said Emilia, who couldn't face the thought of food.

June wouldn't take no for an answer. She scooped Emilia up and took her back to her sprawling cottage on the outskirts of Peasebrook. June was the sort of person who always had a shepherd's pie on standby to put in the Aga. Emilia had to admit that she felt much stronger after two servings, and it gave her the fortitude to discuss the things she didn't want to.

'I can't face a big funeral,' she said eventually.

'Then don't have one,' said June, scooping out some vanilla ice cream for pudding. 'Have a small private funeral, and we can have a memorial service in a few weeks' time. It's much nicer that way round. And it will give you time to organise it properly.'

A tear plopped onto Emilia's ice cream. She wiped away the next one.

'What are we going to do without him?'

June handed her a jar of salted caramel sauce.

'I don't know,' she replied. 'There are some people who leave a bigger hole than others, and your father is one of them.'

June invited her to stay the night, but Emilia wanted to go home. It was always better to be sad in your own bed.

She flicked on the lights in the living room. With its deep red walls and long tapestry curtains, there seemed to be more books here than there were in the book shop. Bookcases covered two of the walls, and there were books piled high on every surface: on the windowsills, the mantelpiece, on top of the piano. Next to that was Julius's precious cello, resting on its stand. She touched the smooth wood, realising it was covered in dust. She would play it tomorrow. She was nothing like as good a player as her father, but she hated to think of his cello unplayed, and she knew he would hate the thought too.

Emilia went over to the bookcase that was designated as hers – though she had run out of space on it long ago. She ran her finger along the spines. She wanted a comfort read; something that took her back to her childhood. Not Laura Ingalls Wilder – she couldn't bear to read of big, kind Pa at the moment. Nor Frances Hodgson Burnett – all her heroines seemed to be orphans, which Emilia realised she was too, now. She pulled out her very favourite, in its red cloth cover with the gold writing on the spine, warped with age, the pages yellowing. *Little Women.* She sat in the wing-backed chair by the fire, slinging her legs over the side and resting her cheek on a velvet cushion. Within moments, she was by the fire in Boston, with Jo March and her sisters and Marmee, hundreds of years ago and thousands of miles away...

By the end of the following week, Emilia felt hollowed out and exhausted. Everyone had been so kind and thoughtful and said such wonderful things about Julius, but it was emotionally draining.

There had been a small private funeral service for Julius at the crematorium, with just his mother Debra, who came down on the train from London, Andrea, Emilia's best friend from school, and June.

Before she left for the service, Emilia had looked at herself in the mirror. She wore a long black military coat and shining riding boots, her dark red hair loose over her shoulders. Her eyes were wide, with smudges underneath, defined by her thick brows and lashes. Her colouring, she knew from the photo kept on top of the piano, was her mother's; her fine bone structure and generous mouth her father's. She put in the earrings he had given her last Christmas with shaking fingers and opened the gifted Chassagne Montrachet, knocking back just one glass, before putting on a faux fox fur hat that exactly matched her hair. She wondered briefly if she looked too much like an extra from a costume drama, but decided it didn't matter.

The next day, when they had put Julius's mother back on the Paddington train – Debra didn't like being away from London for too long – Andrea marched her over the road to the Peasebrook Arms. It was a traditional coaching inn, all flagstone floors and wood panelling and a dining room that served chicken Kiev and steak chasseur and had an old-fashioned dessert trolley. There was something comforting in the way it hadn't been Farrow and Balled up to the rafters. It didn't pretend to be something it wasn't. It was warm and friendly, even if the coffee was awful.

Emilia and Andrea curled up on a sofa in the lounge bar and ordered hot chocolate.

'So,' said Andrea, ever practical. 'What's your plan?'

'I've had to jack in my job,' Emilia told her. 'They can't keep it open for me indefinitely and I don't know when I'm going to get away.' She'd been teaching English at an international language school in Hong Kong. 'I can't just drift from country to country for ever.'

'I don't see why not,' said Andrea.

Emilia shook her head. 'It's about time I sorted myself out. Look at us – I'm still living out of a backpack; you're a powerhouse.'

Andrea had gone from manning the phones for a financial adviser when she left school to studying for exams at night school to setting up her own business as an accountant. Now, she did the books for many of the small businesses that had sprung up in Peasebrook over the past few years. She knew how much most people hated organising their finances and so made it as painless as possible. She was hugely successful.

'Never mind comparisons. What are you going to do with the shop?' Andrea wasn't one to beat about the bush.

Emilia shrugged. 'I haven't got any choice. I promised Dad I'd keep it open. He'd turn in his grave if he thought I was going to close it down.'

Andrea didn't speak for a moment. Her voice when she spoke was gentle and kind. 'Emilia, deathbed promises don't always need to be kept. Not if they aren't practical. Of course you meant it at the time, but the shop was your *father's* life. It doesn't mean it has to be yours. He would understand. I know he would.'

'I can't bear the thought of letting it go. I always saw myself as taking it over in the end. But I guess I thought it would be when I was Dad's age. Not now. I thought he had another twenty years to go at least.' She could feel her eyes fill with tears. 'I don't know if it's even viable. I've started to look through the accounts but it's just a blur to me.'

'Well, whatever I can do to help. You know that.'

'Dad always used to say *I don't do numbers.* And I don't either, really. It all seems to be a bit disorganised. I think he let things slip towards the end. There're a couple of boxes full of receipts. And a horrible pile of unopened envelopes I haven't been able to face yet.'

'Trust me, it's nothing I haven't dealt with before.' Andrea sighed. 'I wish people wouldn't go into denial when it comes to money. It makes it all so complicated and ends up costing them much more in the end.'

'It would be great if you could have a look for me. But no mate's rates.' Emilia pointed a finger at her. 'I'm paying you properly.'

'I'm very happy to help you out. Your dad was always very kind to me when we were growing up.'

Emilia laughed. 'Remember when we tried to set him up with your mum?'

Andrea snorted into her wine glass. 'That would have been a disaster.' Andrea's mother was a bit of a hippy, all joss sticks and flowing skirts. Andrea had rebelled completely against her mother's Woodstock attitude and was the most conventional, aspirational, law-abiding person Emilia knew. She'd even changed her name from Autumn when she started up in business, on the basis that no one would take an accountant called Autumn seriously. 'They would never have got anything done.'

Julius was very easygoing and laissez-faire too. The thought of their respective parents together made the two girls helpless with laughter now, but at the age of twelve they had thought it was a brilliant idea.

As they finished laughing, Emilia sighed. 'Dad never did find anyone.'

'Oh come off it. Every woman in Peasebrook was in love with your father. He had them all running round after him.'

'Yes, I know. He was never short of female company. But it would have been nice for him to have met someone special.'

'He was a happy man, Emilia. You could tell that.'

'I always felt guilty. That perhaps he stayed single because of me.'

'I don't think so. Your dad wasn't the martyr type. I think he was really happy with his own company. Or maybe he did have someone special but we just don't know about it.'

Emilia nodded. 'I hope so . . . I really do.'

She'd never know now, she thought. For all of her life it had just been the two of them and now her father had gone, with all his stories and his secrets.

Two

1982

The book shop was in Little Clarendon Street. Away from the hurly-burly of Oxford town centre and just off St Giles, it was bedded in amongst a sprinkling of fashionable dress shops and cafés. As well as the latest fiction and coffee-table books, it sold art supplies and had an air of frivolity rather than the academic ambience of Blackwell's or one of the more cerebral book shops in town. It was the sort of book shop that stole time: people had been known to miss meetings and trains, lost amongst the shelves.

Julius Nightingale had started working there to supplement his student grant since he'd first come up to Oxford, just over four years ago. And now he'd completed his Masters, he didn't want to leave Oxford or the shop. He didn't want to leave academia either, really, but he knew he had to get on with life, that his wasn't the sort of background that could sustain a life of learning. What he was going to do he had no idea as yet.

He'd decided to spend the summer after his MA scraping some money together, working at the shop full-time. Then maybe squeeze in some travel before embarking upon the gruelling collation of a CV, job applications and interviews. Apart from a brilliant first, there was nothing much to mark him out, he thought. He'd directed a few plays, but who hadn't? He'd edited a poetry magazine, but again – hardly unique. He liked live music, wine, pretty girls – there was nothing out of the ordinary about him, except the fact that most people seemed to like him. As a West London boy with a posh but penniless single mother, he'd gone to a huge inner city comprehensive. He was streetwise but well mannered and so mixed easily with both the toffs and the grammar school types who had less confidence than their public school peers.

It was the last weekend in August, and he was thinking about going up to his mother's and heading for the Notting Hill Carnival. He'd been going since he was small and he loved the atmosphere, the pounding bass, the pervasive scent of dope, the sense that anything could happen. He was about to close up when the door open and a girl whirlwinded in. She had a tangle of hair, bright red – it couldn't be natural; it was the colour of a pillar box – and china-white skin, even whiter against the black lace of her dress. She looked, he thought, like a star, one of those singers who paraded around as if they'd been in the dressing-up box and had put everything on.

'I need a book,' she told him, and he was surprised at her accent. American. Americans, in his experience, came in clutching guidebooks and cameras, not looking as if they'd walked out of a nightclub.

'Well, you've come to the right place, then,' he replied, hoping his tone sounded teasing, not tart.

She looked at him, then held her finger and thumb apart about two inches. 'It needs to be at least this big. It has to last me the plane journey home. Ten hours. And I read very fast.'

'OK.' Julius liked a brief. 'Well, my first suggestion would be *Anna Karenina*.'

She smiled, showing perfect white teeth.

'"All happy families are alike. Each unhappy family is unhappy in its own way."'

He nodded.

'OK. What about *Ulysses*? James Joyce? That would keep you quiet.'

She struck a theatrical pose. '"Yes I said yes I will yes."'

She was quoting Molly Bloom, the hero's promiscuous wife, and for a moment Julius imagined she was just how Molly had looked, before reminding himself Molly was a work of fiction. He was impressed. He didn't know many people who could quote Joyce. He refused to be intimidated by her apparently universal knowledge of literature. He would scale his recommendation down to something more populist, but a book he had long admired.

'*The World According to Garp*?'

She beamed at him. She had an impossibly big dimple in her right cheek.

'Good answer. I love John Irving. But I prefer *The Hotel New Hampshire* to *Garp*.'

Julius grinned. It was a long time since he had met someone as widely read as this girl. He knew well-read people, of course: Oxford was brimming with them. But they tended to be intellectual snobs. This girl was a challenge, though.

'How about *Middlemarch*?'

She opened her mouth to respond, and he could see immediately he'd hit upon something she hadn't read. She had the grace to laugh.

'Perfect,' she announced. 'Do you have a copy?'

'Of course.' He led her over to the bookshelf and pulled out an orange Penguin classic.

They stood there for a moment, Julius holding the book, the girl looking at him.

'What's your favourite book?' she asked.

He was flummoxed. Both by the question and the fact she

had asked it. He turned it over in his mind. He was about to answer when she held up a finger.

'You can only have one answer.'

'But it's like asking which is your favourite child!'

'You have to answer.'

He could see she was going to stand her ground. He had his answer – *1984*, small but perfectly crafted, never failed to chill and thrill him – but he wasn't going to give in to her that easily.

'I'll tell you,' he said, not sure where his boldness had come from. 'If you come out for a drink with me.'

She crossed her arms and tilted her head to one side. 'I don't know that I'm that interested.' But her smile belied her statement.

'You should be,' he answered, and walked away from her over to the till, hoping she would follow. She was capricious. She wanted a tussle and for him not to give up. He was determined to give her a run for her money.

She did follow. He rang up the book and she handed over a pound note.

'There's a band on tonight,' he told her. 'It'll be rough cider and grubby punks, but I can't think of a better way for an American girl to spend her last night in England.'

He slid the book into its bag and handed it to her. She was gazing at him in something close to disbelief, with a hint of fascination.

Julius had always been quietly confident with girls. He respected them. He liked them for their minds rather than their looks, and somehow this made him magnetic. He was thoughtful, yet a little enigmatic. He was very different from the rather cocky public school types at Oxford. He dressed a little differently too – a romantic bohemian, in velvet jackets and scarves, his hair lightly bleached. And he was pretty – cheekbones and wide eyes, which he occasionally highlighted with eyeliner.

Growing up in London had given him the courage to do this without fear of derision from those who didn't understand the fashion of the times.

'Why the hell not?' she said finally.

'I'll be there from eight,' he told her.

It was twenty past eight by the time he got to the pub. She was nowhere to be seen. He couldn't be sure whether she was late too or had been and gone. Or simply wasn't going to turn up at all. He wasn't going to let it worry him. If it was meant to be...

He ordered a pint of murky cider from the bar, tasting its musty appleness, then made his way out to find a bench in the last of the sunshine. It was a popular but fairly rough pub he loved for its unpretentiousness. And it always had good bands on. There was a sense of festiveness and expectation in the air, a final farewell from the sun in this last week of summer. Julius felt a change coming. Whether it would be to do with the girl with the red hair, he couldn't be certain, but he had a feeling it might.

At nine, he felt a sharp tap on his shoulder. He turned, and she was there.

'I wasn't going to come,' she told him. 'Because I didn't want to fall in love with you and then have to get on a plane tomorrow.'

'Falling in love is optional.'

'Not always.' She looked serious.

'Well, let's see what we can do to avoid it.' He stood up and picked up his empty pint glass. 'Have you tried scrumpy yet?'

'No.' She looked doubtful.

He bought her half a pint, because grown men had been known to weep after just two pints of this particular brew. They watched the band, a crazy gypsy-punk outfit that sang songs of heartbreak and harvest moons. He bought her another half and watched her smile get lazier and her eyes half close. He wanted nothing more than to tangle his fingers in her pre-Raphaelite curls.

'Where are you staying tonight?' he asked, as the band started packing up and tipsy revellers began to make their way out of the pub into the warm night.

She put her arms around his neck and pushed her body hard against his. 'With you,' she whispered, and her mouth on his tasted of the last apples of summer.

Later, as they lay holding each other in the remains of the night's heat, she murmured, 'You never told me.'

'What?'

'Your favourite book.'

'*1984*.'

She considered his answer, gave a nod of approval, closed her eyes and fell asleep.

He woke the next morning, pinioned by her lily-white arm. He wondered what time her flight was, how she was getting to the airport, whether she had packed – they hadn't discussed practicalities the night before. He didn't want to wake her because he felt safe with her so close. He'd never experienced such a feeling before. A feeling of utter completeness. It made so many of the books he had read start to make perfect sense. He had thought he understood them, on an intellectual level, but now he had a deeper comprehension. He could barely breathe with the awe of it.

If he stayed very still and very quiet, perhaps she wouldn't wake. Perhaps she would miss her flight. Perhaps he could have another magical twenty-four hours with her.

But Julius was responsible at heart. He didn't have it in him to be so reckless. So he picked up a tress of her hair and tickled her cheek until she stirred.

'Hey,' he whispered. 'You have to go home today.'

'I don't want to go,' Rebecca murmured into his shoulder.

He trailed a hand across her warm, bare skin. 'You can come back.'

He touched each of her freckles, one by one. There were hundreds. Thousands. He would never have time to touch them all before she left.

'What time is your flight? How are you getting to the airport?'

She didn't reply. She picked up his arm and looked at the watch on his wrist.

'My flight's at one.'

He sat up in alarm. It was gone ten. 'Shit. You need to get up. You'll never make it. I can drive you, but I don't think you'll get there in time.'

He was grabbing for his clothes, pulling them on. She didn't move.

'I'm not going.'

He was doing up his jeans. He stared at her.

'What?'

'I made up my mind. Last night.' She sat up, and her hair tumbled everywhere. 'I want to stay here. With you.'

Julius laughed. 'You can't.' He felt slight panic.

She looked up at him from the middle of the bed, wide-eyed.

'You don't feel the same as me? As if you've met the love of your life?'

'Well, yes, but . . .' It had been an incredible night, he had to admit that. And he was smitten, if that was the right word. But Julius was sensible enough to realise you didn't make momentous decisions off the back of a one-night stand.

Rebecca, it seemed, thought differently.

'It makes perfect sense. I want to major in English. I want to do it in the best place in the world. Which is here in Oxford, right?'

'Well, yes. I suppose so. Or Cambridge.'

'I'm smart enough. I know I am. If I can get into Brown, I can get into Oxford.'

Julius laughed again. Not at her, but at her confidence. The girls he knew were never as brazen about their abilities. They were brought up to be modest and self-effacing. Rebecca wore her brilliance with pride.

She crossed her arms. 'Don't laugh at me.'

'I'm not. I just think you're being a bit rash.' That was an understatement.

'I'm not getting on that plane.'

Julius gulped. She was serious. Besides, there was no way she was going to get her plane now. And as far as he knew, she had nowhere else to go.

'What are your parents going to say?'

'How can they argue?'

'Easily, I'd have thought. Aren't you supposed to be going to college?'

'Yes. But you know what? It never felt right. I was just going because that's what I was expected to do. But this feels right. I can *feel* it here.'

She pressed a fist to her heart. Julius looked at her warily, not sure if she was serious. He knew plenty of fanciful girls but they usually had a limit to their capriciousness. He felt anxious: clever, wilful and rich was a deadly combination, and he was pretty sure Rebecca was all of those. He'd got enough insight into her life to know it was very privileged.

Which was why she felt entitled to the ultimate privilege.

'It's what I deserve.' She scrambled out of bed. 'I'm going to get a job. Right here. In Oxford. And I'm going to sit the entrance exam and get a place to study here next year.'

She looked a little crazed. He wasn't sure how to handle her.

She was alien to him. The usual arguments weren't going to work. He decided to pretend he thought she was joking.

'It's the scrumpy,' said Julius. 'It does that to you.'

'You think I'm kidding, right?'

Julius scratched his head. 'I'm not sure you've thought it through.'

'Sure I have. I mean, what's the problem? Why not? Seriously, tell me why not. It's not like I'm running off with the lead singer of a rock band. I want to go to the best university in the world. Surely that's a good thing?'

She was one of those infuriating people who made the craziest of ideas seem utterly plausible.

'Look, let me drive you to the airport. You can change your ticket, go home and talk to your parents. If they agree, you can come back.'

'Am I freaking you out?'

'Well, yes, actually. A bit.'

She came over and put her arms around his neck. He breathed her in, his heart pounding. He felt weightless from lack of sleep and too much of her. He felt electrified, but he also felt responsible, because he knew his reaction would dictate what happened next: their future. He should take control; slow things down a bit.

'This is the most amazing thing that's ever happened. You and me. Don't you feel that?' she demanded.

'Well, yes. It actually is. Amazing. I am . . . amazed.' Julius could see she was carried away. Would there come a moment when she stopped to think and realised she was fantasising? That her vision was riddled with complications? 'But I still think you should talk to your parents.'

As he said it, he thought how boring he sounded. But he wasn't going to be responsible for her screwing her life up, or incurring the wrath of her family.

'I'm going to. Right now.' By Rebecca's reaction, it didn't seem to occur to her they might not think it a good idea. 'I think they'll be really excited. My dad loves England – he did an exchange when he was just a bit older than me and spent six months here. It's why he sent me over for the summer. Where's the nearest phone?'

'There's a pay phone downstairs in the hall,' said Julius. 'But you'll have to reverse the charges. And do you think they'll appreciate being woken up? Maybe you should wait until this afternoon?'

'Maybe you're right. It's three in the morning. Let's go and get something to eat while we wait. I'm starving!'

He took her off for a traditional English fry up – the ultimate hangover cure – and prayed that after some sustenance the combined effects of the scrumpy and their torrid night might recede a little. No such luck. By three o'clock that afternoon she was as determined as ever to see her plan through. She was resolute as she phoned them – he imagined her parents in their perfect New England kitchen being shocked to discover that they weren't going to be driving to the airport that afternoon to collect her after all. He wondered if they were used to flights of fancy from Rebecca. Whether she would come upstairs in a few minutes, crushed and dissuaded.

He listened to her voice floating up the staircase.

'Oxford is me, Daddy. As soon as I got here I knew. This is where I want to be. This is where I want to study. It's in my bones and my blood and my heart and my soul . . .' Julius raised an eyebrow. She was very convincing. 'You *know* how wonderful it is. You told me yourself. You'll just have to come back here and see for yourself. If you don't agree with me, I'll come home with you. That's the deal, Daddy.'

Wow. She was a fierce negotiator all right.

She came back up the stairs and jumped into the middle of his bed.

'Daddy's coming over. He thinks it's a fabulous idea, but he wants to see everything for himself.'

Julius looked round his room. 'He's not going to be too impressed with this.'

Julius loved his bedroom, but it wasn't the sort of room that would gladden a father's heart. He'd painted the walls inky dark purple. They were smothered in postcards he'd collected over the years, of his heroes and heroines, from Hemingway to Marilyn Monroe. There was a record player in the corner – his biggest investment – and a stack of records four feet long. A mattress on the floor served as both a sofa and a bed. His clothes were hung on a makeshift rail: charity shop suits and a collection of hats. He was quite the dandy. In another corner were a kettle and a gas ring. Despite his best intentions there were more empty Pot Noodle pots in the bin than he could count. There were so many more interesting things to do than try and conjure up something nutritious in the health hazard that was the kitchen downstairs. Julius liked food, and cooking, but he didn't want tetanus.

'It's fine. I don't have to show him this. I'll tell him I'm staying in some all-girls' hostel and I'm looking for accommodation. And we need to make sure you stay out of the way.'

'Oh.' Julius was a little stung.

She put her arms around him.

'I didn't mean that like it sounded. If my dad thinks there's a guy involved, he'll drag me back home by the scruff of my neck. Give it a few weeks. Then I can casually mention you. Maybe you could come to New England for Christmas!'

Julius nodded, not a little daunted by the plan. It was all going a bit too fast for him. He had, after all, only met her the day before, and she had turned her whole life upside down on the basis of one night together. Yet he had to agree: the attraction between them was undeniable. He was enchanted by her; she was besotted with him. It was physical and mental and spiritual. All-consuming and intoxicating. He was secretly delighted by her nerve. He was fairly sure he wouldn't have the same mettle. He, after all, had nothing to lose by going along with her plan.

By the time Rebecca's father arrived the following Thursday and checked into the Randolph, Rebecca had persuaded Julius's manager to give her a part-time job in the shop. On her first day of work there, she sorted through all the miscellaneous boxes of old books in the stockroom and either returned them or put them out on the shelves, a job no one ever wanted to do.

And she had worked her way through the colleges and grilled several of the admissions tutors as to the likelihood of her getting a place to study. She came back with a sheaf of past papers to revise with. She had less than two months to get up to speed for the entrance exam.

Julius was impressed. When this girl wanted something, she went all out to get it.

'I knew my life was going to change as soon as I met you,' she told him. 'This is the most exciting thing that's ever happened to me. I can't believe I could be packing to go to the most boring college on the planet right now.'

When Julius answered the door to her after her visit to her father, he didn't recognise her. She was dressed in a pair of grey trousers ('pants') and a white blouse, her hair parted in the middle and tied back in a neat ponytail. She burst out laughing when she saw his puzzled face.

She pulled her hair out of its band and started to undo her shirt as she pushed her way past him and headed up the stairs.

'He thinks I'm a genius,' she told Julius. 'We walked around all his old haunts and he's totally fallen back in love with Oxford. And it will be such a status symbol – none of his friends will have a daughter at college in England. He's paying my rent, and my fees if I get in. I have to go home for Thanksgiving and Christmas and Easter. That's the deal. It's a small price to pay.'

The two of them fell back onto the rumpled sheets, laughing in delight, at each other and the thrill of her new adventure. Julius couldn't resist Rebecca's enthusiasm or her guile or her body. There was a tiny little voice that warned him to be careful, but as he raked his fingers through her red hair to mess it up again, and ran his mouth over her small, round breasts, it was easy to ignore it. He was older and wiser than she. He could manage her.

Couldn't he? Julius knew this was something different; attraction on another scale to anything he had experienced before. Was it infatuation, he wondered, or would it become true love? And if so, which kind? Love, he knew from books, was not always a force for good, but he would do his best to make his so.

Yet he had a feeling Rebecca would not be able to control her feelings in the same way he could. She was far more passionate and impetuous. In just a short time, he could see she was a little bit of a fly-by-night, and the last thing you did with fly-by-nights was try to pin them down. He would give her his heart, and her head.

In the meantime, he showed her more of her new world. It was wonderful, rediscovering Oxford through someone else's eyes. He'd been there over four years now, and he'd stopped seeing the beauty and the wonder in quite the same way. He'd begun to assume everyone lived in a cosy bubble of cobbles and cloisters and grassy greens and bicycles. But he was fiercely proud of it, and showing Rebecca the landmarks made him realise why he had been dragging his feet, how he hadn't wanted to make a decision about his future in case it involved leaving Oxford, and now he didn't have to.

He showed her his room in his old college, and she gasped at its antiquity and its rudimentary facilities and the fact it was straight out of *Brideshead Revisited*.

'Where is your teddy bear?' she demanded, laughing.

'I promise you: I couldn't be less like Sebastian Flyte. There's no stately home to take you back to.'

'Oh,' she said, feigning disappointment. 'And there was me imagining myself as the lady of the manor.'

'We'll get our own little manor,' he said, pulling her to him. 'It might not be *Brideshead*, but it will be ours.'

He took her to a concert he was playing in. He played the cello, and the orchestra was decidedly third rate, because Oxford was stuffed with brilliant musicians and players and he wasn't up to one of the more elite outfits, but she thought he was incredible, sitting in the front pew of the church and not taking her eyes off him once during Fauré's *Requiem*.

'Is there anything you can't do?' she asked. 'I've never met anyone who can do so many things.'

'Scrape out a tune on the cello and make a chicken casserole?' he laughed, self-deprecating to the end. She was even impressed with his cooking skills, which were self-taught and based on years of trial and error brought about by his mother's utter disinterest in anything on a plate.

They worked out they could stay together in Oxford for the next four years, while she studied. Julius was going to look for something that paid better than the book shop, so they could find a little house of their own to rent.

'You're not to worry too much,' said Rebecca. 'I only have to wire home for more cash if we get short.'

Julius looked at her, appalled. 'We will do no such thing.'

He didn't believe in sponging off your parents. It was one of the first things he taught her, the idea of standing on your own two feet. And she understood the principle, even if he knew she was still being subsidised. He couldn't expect her to break the habits of a lifetime straight away.

Summer turned to autumn, and was even more idyllic. They took long walks by the river and ate sausages and chips in the pub, wandered through all the curious exhibits in the Pitt Rivers museum – she exclaimed incessantly over the stuffed dodo – and went to more concerts. Her musical knowledge was scanty, but Julius introduced her to string quartets and garage bands; choral works that made tears course down her cheeks, and lazy Sunday afternoon jazz.

And Julius coached her for her exam, pushing her to read texts and memorise quotes and write essay after essay. Not that she needed pushing. She was more motivated than any student he'd ever met, and her memory was seemingly infallible. She could quote reams after just one reading.

'I'm a freak,' she told him. 'I could recite the whole of *What Katy Did* by the time I was seven.'

'You *are* a freak,' he teased her, but in fact he was more than a little daunted by her brain power. He thought she could probably take over the world. Yet she wasn't wrapped up in scholarship. She wanted as much fun as the next student. He nursed her through her first hangover, let her try her first joint, gave her a driving lesson in his ancient brown Mini around a disused airfield – she had her American licence, but gears were a mystery to her, and he was secretly pleased when it took her a little while to understand clutch control.

'So you're not perfect,' he teased, and she was furious with him.

She took the entrance exam and was confident she'd passed (yet again Julius was entranced by this confidence of hers and explained to her that everyone in England always insisted they had failed every exam they sat). She told her parents she'd moved out of her digs and into a shared house, without going into too much detail about whom she was sharing it with.

'They trust me,' she told Julius.

'That's their first mistake,' he replied, and she pretended to be outraged.

Socially, they were a king and queen. Everyone wanted their company, at the most Rabelaisian of parties. They were young, and they ran on very little sleep and very little money. Wine and music were all that mattered, and good conversation, and books. They talked about books day and night. They were allowed to take books from the book shop and return them once read, as long as they didn't damage them. They read a book a day each, sometimes two. It was bliss. She fell upon Muriel Spark and Iris Murdoch and was entranced by her namesake, *Rebecca*, devouring every other Daphne du Maurier she could lay her hands on. On her recommendation he discovered John Updike and Philip Roth and Norman Mailer. He wrote her his ultimate list of cult classics; she made him read *Middlemarch* when he admitted he hadn't.

More than once, it occurred to Julius to ask Rebecca to marry him, but something stopped him. He wanted them to be financially secure, and to be able to afford a house of their own. Although he fantasised about a discreet wedding in the registry office followed by a wild party to celebrate on the banks of the Cherwell, marriage was definitely for grown-ups and they weren't grown up yet. Instead, he began to put away some of his wages into a building society account, to save for a deposit, and if it meant just one bottle of red wine instead of two to go with the spaghetti on a Friday night, she didn't notice.

'You're my princess,' he told her.

'Princess is not such a good thing where I come from. It's a pejorative term, for a woman who wants her own way all the time,' Rebecca told him.

'Like I said,' replied Julius. 'You're my princess.' And she laughed.

He knew his mother, Debra, would be tolerant of the situation, because Debra was broad-minded and he didn't think she had told him off, ever, in his life.

They drove up to London and Debra took them out for lunch at a wine bar in Kensington. The walls were covered in a mural of grape vines, and they ate chicken cacciatore and chocolate fudge cake.

Rebecca was fascinated by Debra, with her strings of amber beads and endless St Moritz cigarettes and her husky drawl. Debra had a world-weariness about her. You got the sense she had seen and done everything, even though she now lived a very tame existence. She wasn't in the least intimidated by Rebecca's fierce IQ or force of personality or brazen dress sense. They were a match for each other in their own inimitable ways.

When Rebecca went to the loo at the end of lunch, Debra lit another cigarette.

'Be careful, darling,' she said. 'The bubble won't last forever.'

Julius told himself his mother was just being protective. Which was odd, because she hadn't been when he was young. She'd left him to get on with it much of the time. He wondered what had changed.

He sighed. 'Better to have loved and all that.'

'I just don't want to see you hurt, if things go wrong.'

'What can go wrong?'

Debra blew out a plume of smoke. 'Any number of things.'

Julius was determined not to be unsettled by his mother's warning. And when Rebecca came back to the table and put her arm around him and called him her guardian angel, he smiled at Debra as if to say 'See?'

'Your mum is so cool,' said Rebecca as they trundled back down the A40.

Julius rolled his eyes.

'My mum's never had to worry about anyone except herself,' he said, trying to shake off the sense of foreboding Debra had given him. He was cross: just because she was world-weary didn't mean she had to spoil it for everyone else, did it? 'She doesn't care what anyone else thinks.'

'She's the exact opposite of mine, then,' said Rebecca. 'My mom cares what everyone thinks. Right down to the mail man.'

Debra was right, though.

Julius supposed he should have seen it coming. But then – why should he?

The thing was, all the girls he'd ever dallied with had been on the pill. It was almost a given – most girls put themselves on it when they went off to university, if they weren't already. A quick trip to their local doctor and they were covered. It had never occurred to him that Americans might be different. That Rebecca might have landed on English soil without organising contraception before she left. Of course, everyone at Oxford was pretty casual about sex. There was a fair amount of bed-hopping. Julius had been as guilty as anyone, but not once he met Rebecca. He knew the love of his life when he saw it. Yet he'd forgotten the key question.

So when she sat up one morning, looking green at the gills, then bolted to the bathroom, he was shocked into silence when she told him why.

'I think I'm pregnant.'

'Aren't you on the pill?'

She shook her head.

'Why didn't you tell me?' He was appalled – at both his

negligence and hers. 'I just assumed... Surely you realised this might happen?'

She put her face in her hands. 'I guess I just hoped.'

'Hoped?'

'For the best.'

'That's not the most reliable form of contraception.'

'No.' She looked utterly forlorn. She sat in the middle of the bed, holding her stomach.

'Well, I suppose we should go to the Family Planning Clinic.'

'What's that?'

'It's where you go for contraception. Or, um...'

She held up a hand.

'Don't say it. Don't say that word.'

He didn't want to say the word. 'They can arrange... things for you.'

She stared at him. 'It's out of the question.'

He blinked. It hadn't occurred to him that wasn't the route she would want to go down. 'Oh. Right. OK. Um...' He scratched his head. 'So what is the plan?'

'What do you mean?'

'You want to go to university. We live in one room. We don't really have any money.'

She lay back on the bed and stared at the ceiling. 'We don't have any choice. I'm not getting rid of it. I'm not getting rid of our baby.'

Julius wasn't sure what to think or feel. This was an eventuality he hadn't prepared for. He didn't really know anyone else who'd been in this situation. He knew a couple of girls who'd been caught out, but they'd sorted things quickly and quietly and learned their lesson. He certainly didn't know anyone who'd gone ahead and had a baby. But he wasn't going to force Rebecca into anything she didn't want to do.

'What are you going to tell your parents?'

She gave a heavy sigh. She didn't answer for a moment.

'I'll tell them when I go home for Thanksgiving. At the end of the month.' She sat up, and to his surprise, she was smiling. 'A baby, Julius. I knew when I saw you, you were going to be the father of my children.'

'Well, that's lovely,' said Julius, thinking that was all very well but he would have liked to wait a little longer. He didn't say that, though. 'We're going to have to find somewhere better to live. And I'll have to get a decent job.'

Bugger, he thought. It was his own stupid fault. It was his responsibility as much as hers. He should never have assumed.

Rebecca got up to be sick again. And Julius looked around the room that had been their home for the past few months and thought: I'm going to be a father.

Rebecca didn't tell her family when she flew back to New England for Thanksgiving. She was still as slim as a reed, because she wasn't even three months gone, and she had thrown up every morning and every evening like clockwork, despite devouring sugary, fatty lardy cakes Julius brought her from the bakery.

'There just wasn't a good time. I wasn't there for long enough, and there were so many visitors. I'll tell them at Christmas.'

By Christmas, she was putting on weight, but it was cold, so she was able to wrap herself in swathes of baggy clothing. She still didn't reveal her secret.

'I didn't tell them. I didn't want to ruin the holiday.'

'It's getting a bit late.' Julius was anxious. He had told his mother, who had expressed no surprise. But nothing surprised or shocked Debra, who'd been there and seen it and done it all.

'Just don't expect me to babysit,' was all she told him, and he laughed, but didn't say she was the last person he would leave a child with.

By the time Rebecca was four months pregnant, she found

out she had got a place at Oxford and finally told her family. Julius realised it was because before then she'd been afraid they might force her into something she didn't want to do. She had a will of iron, but pregnancy had made her vulnerable and pliable and she'd feared that on home territory she might be brainwashed.

'You? Brainwashed?' Julius was disbelieving.

'I'm not as tough as I make out,' she told him. 'And you don't know my family.' She made a face. 'Daddy's flying over.'

'I thought you had your dad wrapped around your little finger?'

'There's a difference,' she said, 'between wanting to study at the best university in the world, and having a baby at nineteen.'

'It'll be fine,' Julius told her. 'I'm here to back you up.'

She was frightened, Julius realised, despite her fighting talk. And he thought perhaps she feared she might capitulate, because it would be the easy option. How awful, he thought, to fear manipulation by your own family. Debra might be on her own planet, but she was never interfering or controlling. In that moment, he swore to himself that he would never try and control his own child. That he would be supportive without being manipulative.

He wondered if Thomas Quinn was going to turn up with a shotgun. He was ready for him, if so. Julius didn't much care about how Thomas Quinn felt – he was only concerned for Rebecca and his unborn child. There was a limit, in certain situations, as to how many people's sensibilities you could address.

Thomas Quinn was surprisingly measured and calm about the situation. Rebecca came back from meeting him a little subdued, but relieved that there hadn't been a scene.

'It would have been different if my mom had come over,'

she told Julius. 'Dad says she can't even speak about it. I know Mom. She'll turn it round to be her crisis. Her drama.'

'She sounds awful,' said Julius.

'She just doesn't like anything that doesn't fit into her vision of how things should be.'

'I suppose she's not alone in that.'

'No. But boy, do you know about it if it's your fault.'

'Well, it's lucky she's not here.'

'Yes,' agreed Rebecca. 'Dad wants to meet you, though.'

'No problem,' said Julius. 'I think we should meet.'

He wanted to reassure Thomas Quinn as much as he could.

Rebecca eyed him with interest. 'You're very brave.'

Julius shrugged. 'I've done nothing wrong.'

'You do know most guys would have totally freaked out.'

'There's no point in getting hysterical. Or pretending it hasn't happened. You've just got to get on with it.'

Rebecca hugged him. 'You know what? You make me feel safe. I never knew that's what I wanted . . .'

Julius met Rebecca's father Thomas the next day in the drawing room of the suite he had hired. Rebecca had decided to keep out of the way.

'I'll only get emotional if he says something I don't want to hear. Don't let him bully you.'

'Don't worry,' said Julius. He wasn't nervous, though he was apprehensive. He didn't want to make a tricky situation turn nasty.

Thomas Quinn was scrupulously polite, ushering him in and ordering coffee. It was a little bit surreal, thought Julius, sitting in opposing armchairs in this formal setting. He felt like a head of state about to discuss foreign policy.

'I want to make this situation as least disruptive as possible,'

Thomas told him. 'You know, of course, what a smart girl Rebecca is. She has a very bright future.'

'Yes,' said Julius. 'She's very clever. Far cleverer than I am.'

'And, as her father, it would be wrong of me not to want her to make the most of her potential.'

'I'm sure that's what we all want for our children.'

Julius held his gaze.

Thomas Quinn cleared his throat.

'I appreciate that you have been a gentleman and agreed to stand by her. Rebecca tells me what a tower of strength you are. How supportive. I'm very grateful.'

This wasn't quite the tack Julius had expected. He'd anticipated disapproval. Criticism.

'Thank you,' he replied, wondering what was coming next.

'However, I think you're both being idealistic. I don't think either of you really have any idea of the impact having a baby will have on your careers, your lifestyle, your economic circumstances. I mean, you don't actually have a career, as yet – do you? You're working in a book shop?'

Julius stared, intense dislike starting to boil up inside him. He'd thought it was too good to be true. He remained calm and polite.

'Yes. But I have a good degree. I'm quite confident—'

'Your confidence is charming. But you're being naïve. Take it from me. I've had three children. Good intentions are all very well in theory. Admirable. But you will find the reality a very different story.'

'Mr Quinn, people have children every day and bring them up perfectly well—'

Thomas Quinn cut him off again. 'I don't want to see my daughter's potential wasted. I want her to be the best person she can be. I don't think having a baby at nineteen is going to enable that. No matter how much support she has from you.'

'She can carry on her studies. We'll find a way.'

Quinn gave a dismissive snort.

'Look, I'm not going to pretend I think this is a good idea on any level. Rebecca is a pistol, on the surface. But underneath, she's actually very vulnerable. And not as strong as she comes across. Believe me, I'm her father. I know Rebecca. Which is why I'm so very concerned. I know you think this is about her mother and me, but it isn't. I'm very worried. And I can see she thinks the world of you, and would listen to what you have to say.'

Julius felt a growing sense of horror. 'It's too late for an abortion. If that's what you're thinking.'

He was pleased to see Thomas flinch. Julius wasn't going to mince his words to spare this man's feelings.

'I know that,' said Thomas carefully. 'But it's not too late to give the baby up for adoption.'

Julius couldn't hide his shock. He wasn't sure he'd heard right. 'What?'

He crossed his arms and stared at the man who, in theory, had things gone in the right order and more happily, might have been his father-in-law.

Thomas walked over to the latticed window of the hotel room. Julius stared at his broad back and wondered what he was actually thinking. Was he really doing the best for his daughter, or was there another agenda? Was this all about saving her reputation? Protecting the family name?

'Let me make a deal with you.' Thomas turned back, walked across the room and sat down. 'If you can persuade Rebecca to give the baby up for adoption, I will write you a cheque for fifty thousand pounds. And I will help find the very best family possible.' He held up his hand. 'Don't say anything for at least a minute. Please know that this comes from a desire to do the best for my daughter.'

Julius walked over to the window and stood where Thomas had stood. He looked out at the buildings, the colleges: the hopes and dreams of so many young people, himself included, Rebecca included, were held inside those walls. Eventually he turned.

'I suppose there aren't many problems you don't think can be solved by money.'

Thomas gave a smile.

'I am sure one day you will understand my need to protect my child,' he said. 'Especially if it's a girl.'

'I would let my daughter make her own decisions. With my guidance.'

'If you turn this offer down, I won't be giving you and Rebecca any financial support. You do understand that?'

'It hadn't even occurred to me that you might. It wasn't something I was relying on.' Julius stood up and held out his hand. 'Please – be assured that I will look after your daughter and grandchild to the best of my ability.'

'If you change your mind, the offer is there until the end of the week. Until I go back.'

'I won't be telling Rebecca about our conversation,' Julius told him. 'I don't want her upset. I'll just tell her you wished us the very best.'

Thomas Quinn didn't look shamefaced in the slightest as he shook Julius's hand.

In the end, he did tell her, because she pestered him to reveal what they had discussed.

'Did he offer you money?' she asked. 'I bet he did.'

'He wanted me to persuade you to give the baby up. For adoption.'

Rebecca was furious. 'He is *so* manipulative.'

'I think it's because he cares. I tried to put myself in his situation.'

Julius wasn't sure why he was trying to protect Thomas Quinn, but it was mostly because he didn't want Rebecca upset. He was feeling more and more protective of her, especially now the baby was showing. And so he suggested they get married. After a certain amount of laborious paperwork, they left the registry office one sunny spring afternoon.

'You know what we should do? We should open our own book shop,' Rebecca said as they walked home, hand in hand.

Julius stopped in the middle of the pavement. 'That,' he said, 'is the best idea I've heard for a long time.'

'Nightingale Books,' said Rebecca. 'We could call it Nightingale Books.'

Julius felt a burst of joy. He could see it now, the two of them with their own little shop.

In the meantime, he got a managerial position at the book shop, which gave him a slightly higher wage, and found them a house of their own to rent: the tiniest two-bedroomed terrace in Jericho. The second bedroom was only a box room, but at least they had their own space. He spent all his spare time painting it out, until it was bandbox fresh. He put up shelves and hooks so they had plenty of storage. He took Rebecca to Habitat to choose them a sofa.

'Can we afford it?' she asked.

'We'll use it every day, for the next ten years at least, so it's worth spending money on it.'

He didn't tell her Debra had given him five hundred pounds to make their lives more comfortable. He didn't want to get into comparing parents. He didn't consider taking her money to be sponging, either: Debra had offered it happily. Debra was infuriating in her own way, but she had a generous streak, and she hadn't said 'I told you so'. Just knowing she was there made him feel secure, so he understood that Rebecca must find it difficult, being semi-estranged. He wondered how her parents would react once the baby was born. He suspected they were just playing a waiting game, hoping she would crack. Hoping, no doubt, that perhaps he would abandon her when the going got tough.

Which it did.

By her third trimester, Rebecca changed in front of his eyes. She swelled up. Not just her tummy, but everything: her fingers, her ankles, her face. She was miserable. Fretful. She couldn't sleep. She couldn't get comfortable. She stopped working at the shop and lay in bed all day.

'You have to keep active,' Julius told her, worried sick. She no longer seemed enchanted by the idea of a baby, as she had been at first. She was frightened, and fearful.

'I'm sorry. I don't feel like I'm me any more. I guess I'll be better when the baby gets here,' she told him one night, and he rubbed her back until she fell asleep.

She woke one night, three weeks before the baby was due, writhing in pain. The bed sheets were soaked.

'My waters broke,' she sobbed.

Julius phoned for an ambulance, telling himself that women went into labour early all the time and that it would be fine. Giving birth was the most natural thing in the world. The staff at the hospital reassured him of the same thing. Rebecca was put in a delivery room and examined.

'You've got an impatient baby there,' said the midwife, smiling, not looking in the least perturbed. 'It'll be a little preemie, but don't worry. We have a great track record.'

'Preemie?'

'Premature.' She put a hand on his arm. 'You're in safe hands.'

For eighteen agonising hours, Rebecca rode the waves of her pain. Julius was privately horrified that anyone should have to go through this, but if the noises coming from adjoining suites were anything to go by, it was the norm. None of the staff seemed disconcerted by Rebecca's howls as the contractions peaked. Julius did his best to keep her distress at bay.

'Does she really have to go through this?' he asked the midwife at one point, who looked at him, slightly pitying, as if he knew nothing. Which was true – until now, he had never been in close contact with anyone pregnant, let alone watched them give birth.

Then suddenly, as if it couldn't get any worse, the complacency of the staff turned to urgency. Julius felt cold panic as the nurses compared notes and a consultant was ushered in. It was almost as if he and Rebecca didn't exist as the three of them conferred, and a decision was made.

'The baby's distressed. We're taking her into theatre,' the midwife told him, with a look that said 'don't ask any more'.

The system swooped in. Within minutes, Rebecca was wheeled out of the delivery room and off down the corridor. Julius ran to keep up with the orderlies as they reached the double doors of the theatre.

'Can I come in?' he asked.

'There's no time to gown you up,' someone replied, and suddenly there he was, alone in the corridor.

'Please don't let the baby die; please don't let the baby die,' Julius repeated, over and over, unable to imagine what was going on inside. He imagined carnage: blood and knives. At least, he thought, Rebecca's screams had stopped.

And then a nurse emerged, with something tiny in her arms, and handed it to him.

'A little girl,' she said.

He looked down at the baby's head, her shrimp of a mouth. She fitted into the crook of his arm perfectly: a warm bundle.

He knew her. He knew her already. And he laughed with relief. For a while there he had really thought she was in danger.

'Hello,' he said. 'Hello, little one.'

And then he looked up and the surgeon was standing in the doorway with a solemn expression and he realised that he had been praying for the wrong person all along.

They kept the baby in the special care baby unit, because she was early and because of what happened.

They left the hospital two weeks later, the smallest family in the world. The baby was in a white velour Babygro, warm and soft and pliant. Julius picked up a pale yellow cellular blanket and wrapped her in it. The nurses looked on and clucked over them, as they always did when sending a new little family out into the world.

There was still a plastic bracelet on her wrist. Baby Nightingale, it said.

He really hoped that this was as complicated as his life was ever going to get as he stepped out of the hospital doors and into the world outside.

The baby snuffled and burrowed into his chest. She'd been fed before they left the ward, but maybe she was hungry again. Should he try another bottle before getting in the taxi? Or would that overfeed her? All this and so many questions was his future now.

He put the tip of his finger to her mouth. Her tiny lips puckered round it experimentally. It seemed to placate her.

She still hadn't got a name. She needed a name more than she needed milk. He had two favourites: Emily and Amelia. He couldn't decide between the two. And so he decided to amalgamate them.

Emilia.

Emilia Rebecca.

Emilia Rebecca Nightingale.

'Hello, Emilia,' he said, and at the sound of his voice her little head turned and her eyes widened in surprise as she looked for whoever had spoken.

'It's me,' he said. 'Dad. Daddy. I'm up here, little one. Come on, let's take you home.'

'Where's the missis, then?' the taxi driver asked him. 'Still a bit poorly? Aren't they letting her out?'

'It's just me, actually,' said Julius. He couldn't face telling him the whole story. He didn't want to upset the driver. He didn't want his sympathy.

'What – she's left you holding the baby?'

The driver looked over at him in surprise. Julius would have preferred him to keep his eyes on the road.

'Yes.' In a way, she had.

'Bloody hell. I've never heard of that. Picked up plenty of new mums whose blokes have done a runner. But never the other way round.'

'Oh,' said Julius. 'Well, I suppose it is unusual. But I'm sure I'll manage.'

'You're not very old yourself, are you?'

'Twenty-three.'

'Bloody hell,' repeated the driver.

Julius sat in the back as the taxi made its way through the outskirts of Oxford and wondered why on earth he didn't feel more scared. But he didn't. He just didn't.

He had met Thomas Quinn very briefly a few days' after Rebecca's death. The Quinns were flying her body home, and Julius didn't argue with their wishes. She had been their daughter and he felt it was right for her to be buried in her homeland.

Their meeting was bleak and stiff, both men shocked by the situation. Julius was surprised that Thomas didn't blame him for his daughter's death. There was some humanity in him that made him realise anger and resentment and blame would be pointless.

Instead, he gave Julius a cheque.

'You might want to throw this back in my face, but it's for the baby. I handled everything wrongly. I should have given you both my support. Please put it to good use.'

Julius put it in his pocket. Protest and refusal would be as pointless as blame.

'Should I keep you informed of her progress . . . ? A photo on her birthday?'

Thomas Quinn shook his head. 'There's no need. Rebecca's mother would find it too distressing. We really just need to move on.'

Julius didn't protest. Though he was surprised anyone could turn their back on their own flesh and blood, it would be easier for him, too. To have no interference.

'If you change your mind, just get in touch.'

Thomas Quinn gave a half nod, half shake of his head that indicated they probably wouldn't, but that he was grateful for the offer.

Julius walked away knowing that he had made the final transition from boy to man.

He got back to the house. It was mid-afternoon. It felt like the quietest time of day. He made himself a cup of tea, then made up a fresh bottle of baby milk and left it to cool. He put Nina Simone on the record player.

Then he lay on his bed with his knees crooked up and put Emilia on his lap so her back was resting against his thighs. He held her in place carefully and smiled. He picked up his camera and took a photo.

His baby girl, only two weeks old.

He put the camera down.

As the piano played out he pretended to make Emilia dance as he sang along.

He'd never really met a baby before, he realised. Not to pick up and hold. How funny, he thought, for the first baby he'd ever met to be his own.

Three

It was a delicate balance, trying to hit the right note between a tribute and a shrine. The last thing she wanted to be was mawkish, yet she couldn't think of a nicer memorial than filling the book shop window with all of Julius's favourite books. But at the rate she was going, thought Emilia, every book in the shop would be in here.

Amis (father and son), Bellow, Bulgakov, Christie, Dickens, Fitzgerald, Hardy, Hemingway – she was going to run out of space long before she got to Wodehouse.

She had resisted the temptation for a black backdrop, instead opting for a stately burgundy. Nor had she put up a photo or his name or any kind of pronouncement. It was just something she wanted to do: capture his spirit, his memory.

And it took her mind off the fact that she missed him.

The shop had been busy over the past week, busier than usual, with people dropping by. Every time the bell tinged, she looked up expecting it to be him, walking in with a takeaway coffee and the day's newspaper. But it never was.

Her eye was caught by a large car drawing up and parking on the double yellow lines outside the shop. She raised her eyebrow: the driver was taking a risk. The traffic warden in Peasebrook was notoriously draconian. No one usually dared flout the rules. When she looked closer, however, she realised this particular driver had no regard for the rules. It was an Aston Martin, with a personal plate.

Ian Mendip. Her stomach curdled slightly as he got out of his car. He was tall, shaven-headed, tanned, in jeans and a leather jacket. She could smell his aftershave already. He stood for a moment looking up at the shop, eyes narrowed against the sunlight. She could imagine him calculating the price per square metre.

It was ironic he had chosen not to use the book shop car park, as that was what he was after. Nightingale Books fronted onto the high street next to the bridge over the brook. Behind it was a large parking area owned by the shop, with room for at least ten cars. And adjacent to the book shop, behind the high street and backing onto the brook, was the old glove factory, disused and rundown, which Ian Mendip had snapped up for his portfolio a few years ago. He wanted to turn it into luxury apartments. If he had the book shop car park, he could increase the number of units: without the extra allocated parking his hands were tied, as the council wouldn't grant him permission without it. Parking was enough of an issue in the small town without extra stress being put on it.

Emilia knew Ian had approached Julius, who had quietly shown him the door. So she wasn't surprised to see him, though it was a bit soon, even for someone as hard-bitten as Ian. She knew him of old: he'd been a few years above her at Peasebrook High. He'd never looked at her twice then. He'd been a player, a chancer; there'd been an air of mystique about him that Emilia had never bought into, because she could see how he treated women. Not well. He had a trophy wife, but there were always rumours. He turned her stomach slightly.

She clambered out of the window so as to be ready for him. The bell tinged as he came into the shop.

'Can I help?' She smiled her widest smile.

'Emilia.' He held out his hand and she really had no choice but to shake it. 'I've come to give you my condolences. I'm really sorry about your dad.'

'Thank you,' she said, wary.

'I know this might seem a bit previous,' he went on. 'But I like to strike while the iron's hot. You probably know your dad and I had conversations. And I thought it was more polite to come and see you in person to discuss it. I like to do business out in the open. I like a face-to-face chat. So I hope you're not offended.'

He gave what he thought was a charming smile.

'Mmm,' said Emilia, non-committal, not giving him an inch.

'I just want you to know the same offer I gave your dad is open to you. In case you're wondering what to do.'

'Not really,' said Emilia. 'I'm going to be running the shop from now on. And trust me – no amount of money will change my mind.'

'It's the best offer you'll get. This building's worth more to me than anyone else.'

Emilia frowned. 'I don't understand what you don't understand: I'm not selling.'

Ian gave a smug shrug, as if to say he knew she would come round in the end.

'I just want you to know the offer is still on the table. You might change your mind when things have settled down. I think it's great that you want to carry on, but if you find it's a bit tougher than you first thought . . .' He spread his hands either side of him.

'Thank you,' said Emilia. 'But don't hold your breath. As they say.'

She was proud to stand her ground. Proud that her father had taught her there was more to life than money. The air felt tainted with the scent of Mendip's wealth: the expensive aftershave he wore that was cloying and overpowering.

Seemingly unruffled, he held out his card.

'You know where to find me. Call me any time.'

She watched as he left the shop and climbed back into his car. She rolled her eyes as it glided off down the high street. Dave loped over to her.

'Was he after the shop?'

'Yep,' she replied.

'I hope you told him where to get off.'

'I did.'

Dave nodded solemnly. 'Your dad thought he was a cock.'

With his dyed black hair tied back in a ponytail, his pale skin and his myriad tattoos, Dave wasn't what you'd expect to find in a book shop. All she really knew about him was he still lived with his mum and had a bearded dragon called Bilbo. But his knowledge of literature was encyclopaedic, and the customers loved him. And Emilia felt a surge of fondness for him too – for his loyalty and his kindness.

'I just want you to know, Dave, I don't know exactly what I'm doing with the shop yet. Everything's a bit upside down. But I don't want you to worry. You're really valued here. Dad thought the world of you . . .'

'He was a legend,' said Dave. 'Don't worry. I understand. It's tough for you.'

He put a gentle paw on her shoulder. It was heavy with skull rings.

Emilia gave him a playful punch. 'Don't. You'll make me cry again.'

She walked away to the shelves, to choose another tranche of books. She hoped desperately that things could stay the same. Just as they were. But it was all a muddle of paperwork, probate and red tape. She had gone through her father's paperwork and bank statements and handed them all over to Andrea with a sinking heart. She wished she'd discussed things with him in greater depth, but when someone was on their deathbed the last thing you wanted to talk about was balance sheets. The problem was it didn't look as if they were balancing.

It couldn't be *all* bad, she thought. She had the shop itself, loyal staff, hundreds of books and lovely customers. She'd find a way to keep it all afloat. Perhaps she should have come back earlier, instead of mucking about travelling the world and trying to find herself. She didn't *need* to find herself. This was her – Nightingale Books. But Julius had insisted. He had as good as kicked her out of the nest, when she'd had a disastrous fling with a man from Oxford whose ex-wife had turned out not to be so very ex after all when he had realised how much the divorce was going to cost him. She'd been in no way responsible for his marriage break-up, and thought she was doing a good job of getting him over it, but it seemed she was not sufficient compensation. Emilia had thought herself heartbroken. Julius had refused to let her mope and had bought her a round-the-world ticket for her birthday.

'Is it one way?' she'd joked.

He was right to make her widen her horizons, of course he was, because she'd realised very quickly that her heart wasn't broken at all, but it had been good to put some distance between herself and her erstwhile lover. And she'd seen amazing things, watched the sun rise and set over a hundred different landmarks. She would never forget feeling as if she was right amongst the clouds, on the eighteenth floor of her Hong Kong apartment block, overlooking the harbour.

Yet despite all her adventures and the friends she had made, she knew she wasn't a free spirit. Peasebrook was home and always would be.

*

Once a month, Thomasina Matthews would go into Nightingale Books on a Tuesday afternoon – her one afternoon off a week – and choose a new cookery book. It was her treat to herself. The shelves of her cottage were already laden, but to her mind there was no limit to the number of cookery books you could have. Reading them was her way of relaxing and switching off from the world, curling up in bed at night and leafing through recipes, learning about the food from another culture or devouring the mouth-watering descriptions written by renowned chefs or food lovers.

Until recently, she had spent these afternoons chatting to Julius Nightingale, who had steered her in the direction of a number of writers she might not have chosen otherwise. He was fascinated by food too, and every now and then she would bring him in something she had made: a slab of game terrine with her gooseberry chutney, or a piece of apricot and frangipane tart. He was always appreciative and gave her objective feedback – she liked the fact that he wasn't afraid to criticise or make a suggestion. She respected his opinion. Without Julius, she would never have discovered Alice Waters or Claudia Roden – or not as quickly, anyway; no doubt she would have got round to them eventually.

'It's not about the pictures,' Julius had told her, quite sternly. 'It's about the words. A great cookery writer can make you see the dish, smell it, taste it, with no need for a photograph.'

But Julius wasn't here any more. She had read about his death in the *Peasebrook Advertiser* in the staffroom. She'd hidden behind the paper as the tears coursed down her cheeks. She didn't want anyone to see her crying. They all thought she was wet enough. For Thomasina was shy. She never joined in the staffroom banter or went on nights out with the others. She was painfully introverted. She wished she wasn't, but there was nothing she could do about it. She'd tried.

Julius was one of the few people in the world who didn't make her feel self-conscious. He made her feel as if it was OK just to be herself. And the shop wouldn't feel the same without him. She hadn't been in since she'd heard the news, but now, here she was, hovering on the threshold. She could see Emilia, Julius's daughter, putting the finishing touches to a window display. She plucked up the courage to go in and speak to her. She wanted to tell her just how much Julius had meant.

Thomasina had been three years below Emilia at school, and she still felt the awe of a younger pupil for an older one. Emilia had been popular at school: she'd managed to achieve the elusive status of being clever and conscientious but also quite cool. Thomasina had not been cool. Sometimes she had thought she didn't exist at all. No one ever took any notice of her. She had few friends and never quite understood why. She certainly wasn't a horrible person. But when you were shy and overweight and not very clever and terrible at sport, it turned out that no one was especially interested in you, even if you were sweet and kind and caring.

Food was Thomasina's escape. It was the only subject she had ever been any good at. She had gone on to catering college, and now she taught Food Technology at the school she had once attended. And at the weekends, she had A Deux. She thought it was probably the smallest pop-up restaurant in the country: a table for two set up in her tiny cottage where she cooked celebratory dinners for anyone who cared to book. She had been pleasantly surprised by its success. People loved the intimacy of being cooked for as a couple. And her cooking was sublime. She barely made a profit, for she used only the very best ingredients, but she did it because she loved watching people go out into the night glazed with gluttony, heady with hedonism.

And without A Deux, she would be alone at the weekends. It gave her something to do, a momentum, and after she had done the last of the clearing up on a Sunday morning she still had a whole day to herself to catch up and do her laundry and her marking.

She was used to being on her own, and rather resigned to it, for she felt she had little to offer a potential paramour. She had a round face with very pink cheeks that needed little encouragement to go even pinker and her hair was a cloud of mousy frizz: she had been to a hairdresser once who had looked at it with distaste and said with a sniff, 'There's not much I can do with this. I'll just get rid of the split ends.' She had come out looking no different, having gone in with dreams of emerging with a shining mane. She did her own split ends from then on.

To her surprise, her students loved her, and her class was one of the most popular, with girls and boys, because she opened their eyes to the joys of cooking and made even the most committed junk food junkie leave her class with something delicious they had cooked themselves. When she spoke about food she was confident and her eyes shone and her enthusiasm was catching. Outside the kitchen, whether at home or school, she was tongue-tied.

Which was why she had to wait until the shop was empty before approaching the counter and giving Emilia her condolences.

'Thomasina!' said Emilia, and Thomasina blushed with delight that she had been recognised. 'Dad talked about you a lot. When he was in hospital he said he would take me to your restaurant when he got better.'

Thomasina's eyes filled with tears. 'Oh,' she said. 'It would have been an honour to cook for him. Though it's not really a restaurant. Not a proper one. I cook for people in my cottage.'

'He was very fond of you – I know that. He said you were one of his best customers.'

'You are staying open, aren't you?' asked Thomasina anxiously. 'It's one of the things that keeps me going, coming in here.'

'Hopefully,' said Emilia.

'Well, I just wanted to tell you how – how much I'll miss him.'

'Come to his memorial service. It's next Thursday. At St Nick's. And if you want to say a few words, it's open to everyone. Just let me know what you'd like to do – a reading, or a poem. Or whatever.'

Thomasina bit her lip. She wanted more than anything to say yes, to honour Julius's memory. But the thought of standing up in front of a load of people she didn't know petrified her. Maybe Emilia would forget about the idea? Thomasina knew from experience that if she protested about things, people became fixated, whereas if she concurred in a vague manner very often their ideas faded away.

'It sounds a wonderful idea. Can I have a think and let you know?'

'Of course.' Emilia smiled, and Thomasina was struck by how like her father she was. She had his warmth, and his way of making you feel special.

She drifted back over to the cookery section, and spent a good half-hour browsing. She had narrowed it down to two books, and was holding them both, considering them, when a voice behind her made her jump.

'The Anthony Bourdain, definitely. No contest.'

She turned, and felt her cheeks turn vermilion. She recognised the speaker, but struggled to place him. Had he been to A Deux? He was as tall and thin as she was short and round. She was mortified that she couldn't recognise him, for she was certain she should.

'It's the best book about food I've ever read,' her unknown observer went on. And then she remembered. He worked in the cheesemonger. She didn't recognise him without his white hat and striped apron – he was in jeans and a jumper and she realised she had never seen his hair properly: it was curly and fair and he looked a bit like a cherub, with his cheeky baby face. She always bought her cheese from there – she always included a cheese course, with home-made oat biscuits and quince jelly and rhubarb chutney – and he had served her a couple of times, cutting little slivers of Comté or Taleggio or Gubbeen for her to try, depending on the theme of the meal she was cooking that night.

'Sorry,' he went on, and she saw his cheeks went as pink as her own. 'I didn't mean to interrupt you, but it's one of my favourite books.'

'I shall have it, then.' She smiled, and put the other one back. 'I didn't recognise you at first.'

He pulled his curls back from his face and made the shape of a hat with his hands. She laughed. For some reason, she didn't feel awkward. Yet she couldn't think of a thing to say.

'Do you like books, then?' was all she could manage. How ridiculously lame.

'Yes,' he said. 'But I couldn't eat a whole one.'

She frowned, not sure what he meant.

'It's a joke,' he said. 'A bad one. It's supposed to be *do you like children*?'

She looked at him blankly.

'I love books,' he clarified. 'But I hardly ever have time to read. You have no idea how hectic the world of cheese can be.'

'No,' she said. 'I don't. But I think it must be fascinating. Have you always been in cheese?'

He looked at her. 'Are you taking the mickey?'

'No!' she said, horrified that he might think so. 'Not at all.'

'Good,' he said. 'Only people do. They seem to find the idea of working in cheese hilarious. Whenever I go out, I just get cheese jokes.'

'Cheese jokes? Are there any?'

'What kind of cheese do you use to disguise a small horse?"

Thomasina shrugged. 'I don't know.'

'Mascarpone. What type of cheese is made backwards?'

'Um – I don't know. Again.'

'Edam.'

Thomasina couldn't help laughing. 'That's terrible.'

'I know. But I have to tell the jokes before anyone else does. Because I can't bear it.'

She looked at him. 'There must be a camembert joke in there somewhere.'

'There is.' He nodded gravely. 'But let's not go there. Anyway,' he looked around the shelves, 'I've come to get a present for my mum. She loves cookery books, but I think I've bought her just about every book in this shop. So I'm a bit stuck for ideas.'

'Does she like novels?'

'I think so . . .' He wrinkled his nose in thought. 'She's always reading. I know that.'

Thomasina nodded.

'You could get her a food-related novel. Like *Heartburn*. By Nora Ephron. It's kind of funny but sad but with recipes. Or maybe *Chocolat*? You could get her a big box of chocolates from the chocolate shop to go with it.' Thomasina was getting carried away. 'If it was me, I'd love that.'

He looked at her, impressed. '*She'd* love that. You're a genius.' He looked around the shop. 'Where do I find them?'

Thomasina led him over to the fiction shelves and found the books in question.

'These two are keepers,' she told him.

He looked puzzled.

'You know, some books you lend or lose or give to a charity

shop, but these are books for life. I've read *Heartburn* about seventeen times.' She blushed, because she always blushed if she ever talked about herself. 'Maybe I need to get out more.'

More? To misquote *Alice in Wonderland*, how could she go out *more* if she didn't go out at all?

He patted her on the shoulder and she felt all fizzy inside. Fizzy and fuzzy.

'Well, you're a star and no mistake. I'll see you in the shop?'

She smiled at him and wanted to say more, but she didn't know what to say, so she just nodded, and he sauntered off to the counter and she realised she didn't even know his name.

She watched him chatting to Emilia while he paid. He was so warm and friendly and open. And she realised something. He hadn't made her feel shy and tongue-tied. She had almost felt like a normal person when she spoke to him. It had been easy. Yes, she'd gone pink, but she always went pink. It was just what she did.

The only other person who hadn't made her feel self-conscious was Julius. Maybe it was the shop? Maybe there was something in the air that made her the person she wished she were? Someone who could actually hold a conversation.

She went to pay for her books and plucked up the courage to ask Emilia.

'You don't know what that bloke's name is? The one I was just talking to? I know he works in the cheese shop.'

'Jem?' said Emilia. 'Jem Gosling. He's a sweetheart. He always used to bring my father the last of the Brie when it was running out of the door.'

Thomasina looked down at the counter. She couldn't, she just couldn't, ask if he had a girlfriend. She knew there were women, more brazen than she, who would be bold enough. But that just wasn't the sort of person Thomasina was.

Emilia was looking at her. She looked knowing. But not in an unkind way.

'As far as I know,' she said casually, 'he's unattached. He had a girlfriend but she went off to Australia. He used to come and talk to my father about it, when she first left. But I think he's probably over it.'

Thomasina felt flustered. She didn't know what to say. She didn't want to protest that she didn't need to know any of that, because it would seem rude. But she was mortified that Emilia thought she was after Jem. She hoped Emilia wouldn't say anything to him if she saw him, even in jest. The very thought made her feel ill. She changed the subject as quickly as she could, hoping Emilia would forget she'd ever mentioned him.

'By the way, I'd love to do a reading,' she found herself saying. 'At the service.'

'That's wonderful,' Emilia smiled. 'If you can let me know what you're going to read, I can put it into the order of service.'

Thomasina nodded, hot blood pounding in her ears. What on earth had she said that for? She couldn't stand up and speak in public, in front of a full church. It was too late now, though. Emilia was writing her name down on a list. She couldn't back out, not without looking disrespectful to Julius.

Feeling slightly sick, she paid for her book as quickly as she could and left.

Four

'The Desprez à Fleur Jaune is going to have to come out. It's just not thriving. It'll break my heart. It's been there ever since I can remember. But I don't think there's any hope.'

Sarah Basildon spoke about her rose as if it were a beloved animal she was having put down. Her fingers moved gently over the space on the planting plan taken up by the sick flower, as if she were stroking it better.

'I'll take it out for you,' said Dillon. 'You won't have to know about it. And once it's actually gone, perhaps you won't notice.'

Sarah smiled a grateful smile. 'Oh, I'll know. But that's good of you. I'm just too much of a wimp.'

Of course, Sarah was far from a wimp in reality. She was redoubtable, from her gumboots to her chambray denim eyes. Dillon Greene thought the world of her.

And she him. They were as close as could be, the aristocrat and the horny-handed son of toil, thirty years apart in age. They loved nothing better than sitting in the dankness of the garden room, drinking smoky builders' tea and dunking custard creams. They could easily get through a packet in a morning as they put the world and the gardens to rights.

Sarah's planting plans for the next year were spread on a trestle table in the middle of the room, the Latin names spidered all over the paper in her tiny black italics. Dillon knew the proper names as well as she did now – he'd been working with her at Peasebrook Manor since he left school.

As stately homes went, Peasebrook was small and intimate: a pleasingly symmetrical house of Palladian perfection, built of golden stone topped with a cupola, and set in two hundred acres of rolling farmland. When Dillon joined as a junior gardener in charge of mowing the lawns, he quickly became Sarah's protégé. He wasn't sure what it was she had recognised in him: the shy seventeen-year-old who hadn't wanted to go off to university as his school had suggested, because no one else in his family ever had done. They'd all worked outdoors: their lives were rugged and ruled by the weather. Dillon felt comfortable in that environment. When he woke up, he looked at the sky, not the Internet. He never lay in bed of a morning. He was at work by half seven, come rain or shine, sleet or snow.

One teacher had tried to persuade him to go to horticultural college, at the very least, but he didn't see the point of sitting in a classroom when he could learn hands-on. And Sarah was better than any college tutor. She grilled him, tested him, taught him, demonstrated things to him, and then made him show her how it was done. She gave praise where it was due and her criticism was always constructive. She was brisk and always knew exactly what she wanted, so Dillon always knew exactly where *he* was. It suited him down to the rich, red clay on the ground.

'You really have got green fingers,' she told him with admiration and increasing frequency. He had a gut feeling for what went with what, for which plants would flourish and bloom together. To supplement his innate ability, he plundered her library and she never minded him taking the books home – Gertrude Jekyll, Vita Sackville-West, Capability Brown, Bunny Williams, Christopher Lloyd – and he didn't just look at the pictures. He pored over the words describing their inspiration, their visions, the problems they faced, the solutions they came up with.

Dillon, Sarah realised one day, knew much more than she did. More often than not these days he questioned her planting plans, suggesting some other combination when redesigning a bed or coming up with a concept for a new one. He would suggest a curve rather than a straight line; a bank of solid colour instead of a rainbow drift; a bed that was conceived for its smell rather than its look. And he used things he found around the estate as features: an old sundial, an ancient gardening implement, a bench he would spend hours restoring. It was reclamation at its best.

Her greatest fear was losing him. There was every chance he would be headhunted by some other country house because the gardens at Peasebrook Manor had become increasingly popular over the past few years. There were three formal rose gardens, a cutting garden and a walled kitchen garden, a maze and a miniature lake with an island and a ruined temple for visitors to wander around. There had been a flurry of articles in magazines, many of them featuring pictures of Dillon at work, for there was no doubt he was easy on the eye. More than once her own heart had stopped for a moment when she'd rounded a corner and seen him in his combat shorts and big boots, his muscles coiling as he dug over a bed. He'd be television gold.

She would do anything in her power to keep him. She couldn't imagine life at Peasebrook without him now. But there was a limit to how much she could afford to pay him. Times were hard. It was always a struggle to balance the books, despite all their best efforts.

But today, at least the stress took her mind off her grief. Her secret grief. She'd had to put her heart in a straitjacket and she'd hidden her heartbreak well. She didn't think anyone was any the wiser about how she was feeling or what she had been through.

Six months, if you counted it from the beginning. It had ripped through him, devoured him with an indecent speed and she could do nothing. They had snatched as much time together as they could but—

She shut off her mind. She wasn't going to remember or go back over it. Thank God for the gardens, she thought, day after day. She had no choice but to think about them. They needed constant attention. You simply couldn't take a day off. Without that momentum she would have gone under weeks ago.

'What about the folly?' asked Dillon, and Sarah looked at him sharply.

'The folly?'

'It needs something doing to it. Doing up or pulling down. It could make a great feature but—'

'We'll leave it for now.' Sarah used her '*don't bring up the subject again*' voice. 'That's a long-term project and we don't have the budget.'

He looked at her and she held his gaze, praying he wouldn't push it. Did he know? Is that why he'd brought it up? She had to be careful, because he was perspicacious. More than perspicacious. He almost had a sixth sense. It was one of the things she liked about him. Sensitive wasn't quite the right word, she thought. Intuitive, maybe? He'd once told her his grandmother had 'the gift'. That kind of thing could be hereditary. If you believed in it. Sarah didn't know if she did, but either way she wasn't going to give anything away at this point.

He was right, though. The folly did need attention. It was on the outer edge of the estate, high on a hill behind a patch of woodland. An octagon made of crumbling ginger stone, it was straight out of a fairy tale, smothered in ivy and cobwebs. It had been neglected for years. Inside, the plaster was falling off the walls, the floorboards were rotten and the glass doors were coming off their hinges. There was just an old sofa, steeped in damp and mildew. Sarah could smell it now, its comforting mustiness mixed with the scent of his skin. She'd never minded the insalubrious surroundings. To her, it could have easily been the George V or the Savoy.

She didn't want anyone else going in there.

'Let's just shut off the path to the folly for the time being,' she told Dillon.

She thought of all the times she had been along it, the tiny woodland path that led up the hill to their meeting place. He would park his car in the gateway on the back road, behind a tumbledown shed. The road was barely used except by the odd farmer, so with luck no one had ever noticed. Although sometimes drunk drivers used it as a rat run from the pub, and it only took one person to put two and two together...

She couldn't worry about it. It was almost irrelevant now, and certainly no one could prove anything. She tried to put it out of her mind and concentrate on the wedding instead. As the mother of the bride, it should be her priority. But it seemed to be organising itself. There didn't seem to be the usual hysteria that accompanied most weddings. They had plenty of experience, after all: Peasebrook Manor had had a wedding licence for some years, and it was one of the things that had filled the gaping coffers, so when it came to organising a wedding for one of their own, they were well prepared. And Alice wasn't a highly strung, demanding bride-to-be. Far from it. As far as Alice was concerned, as long as everyone she loved was there, and there was enough champagne and cake, it would be a perfect day.

'I don't want fuss and wedding favours, Mum. You know I hate all that. It's perfect to be getting married at home, with everyone here. What can go wrong? We can do this with our eyes shut.'

Alice. The apple of her eye. Alice, who treated life like one long Pony Club camp, but with cocktails. Alice, whose sparkle drew everyone to her and whose smile never seemed to fade. Sarah could not have been more proud of her daughter, and her need to protect her was primal. Though Alice was quite able to look after herself. She was charmed. She strode through life, plumply luscious, in her uniform of too-tight polo shirt, jeans and Dubarrys, her flaxen hair loose and wild, face free from make-up, always slightly pink in her rush to get from one thing to the next.

There had been a couple of years of worry (as if she'd needed more worry!), when Alice had gone off to agricultural college to do estate management – she was, after all, the heir to Peasebrook Manor, so it seemed logical, but she failed, spectacularly, two years running. She had never been academic, and the course seemed beyond her. Of course there was too much partying going on, but the other students seemed to manage.

So Alice came home, and was put to work, and it suddenly became abundantly clear that running Peasebrook Manor was what she had been put on earth to do. She had vision and energy and a gut feeling for what would work and what the public wanted. Somehow the locals felt included in Peasebrook Manor, as if it were theirs. She had been the mastermind behind converting the coach house in the middle of the stable yard into a gift shop selling beautiful things you didn't need but somehow desperately wanted, and a tea room which sold legendary fruit scones the size of your fist. And she was brilliant at orchestrating events. In the last year there'd been open-air opera, Easter Egg hunts, and a posh car boot sale. She was thinking of running children's camps the following year: Glastonbury meets Enid Blyton.

And the most exciting upcoming event, of course, was Alice's own wedding, to be held at the end of November. She couldn't have a summer wedding, because they were too busy holding them for other people.

'Anyway,' said Alice, with typical optimism. 'I'd much prefer a winter wedding. Everything all frosty and glittery. Lots of ivy and lots of candles.'

She was to marry Hugh Pettifer, a handsome hedge fund manager who set hearts a-flutter when he raced through the lanes in his white supercharged sports car, bounding from polo match to point-to-point.

If Sarah had her doubts about Hugh, she never voiced them. He was perfect on paper. And utterly charming. She supposed it was her maternal need to protect Alice that made her wary. She had no evidence that Hugh was anything other than devoted. His manners were faultless, he mucked in at family events, he was thoughtful, and if he partied hard, then all Alice's crowd did. They were young and beautiful and wealthy – why shouldn't they have fun? And Hugh worked hard. He earned good money. He wasn't a freeloader. And anyway, if he was looking for a meal ticket, he wouldn't get one from the Basildons. They were classic asset rich/cash poor. If anything, they needed him more than he needed them.

So Sarah kept any doubts about Hugh to herself. She had to learn to let go. It was time to hand Alice over. She would still be very much part of life at Peasebrook Manor – it would fall apart without her – but she was a woman in her own right. And Sarah wasn't gold-digging on Alice's behalf. It would be nice for her to have a husband who could support her when the time came for her to have children. Sarah was in no doubt of her daughter's capabilities, but she knew how deep the pressures dug. And nobody could deny that money didn't make things easier, especially when it came to motherhood.

'I'll put a gate up, shall I?'

Dillon's voice startled Sarah and dragged her back to the matter in hand.

'Yes. And put a lock on it for the time being. I don't think the folly's safe. We don't want anyone getting injured.'

Dillon nodded. But he was eyeing her with interest. Sarah started to doodle on the edge of one of the planting plans. She couldn't quite look at him. He knows, she thought. How she wished she could talk to someone about it, but she knew the importance of keeping secrets. And if you couldn't keep your own secret, how on earth could you trust someone else to keep it?

'Right.' Dillon stood up. 'I better get on. It's starting to get dark early. The days are getting shorter.'

'Yes.' Sarah couldn't decide which was worse. The days or the nights. She could fill her days with things to do but she had to pretend to everybody, from Ralph and Alice down to the postman, that nothing was wrong, and that was wearing. At night she could stop; she didn't need to pretend any more and she could sleep. But her sleep was troubled and she couldn't control her dreams. He would appear, and she would wake, her face wet with tears, trying not to sob. Trying not to wake Ralph because what could she say? How could she explain her distress?

She sighed, and took another custard cream. Her brain had no respite these days. Everything whirled around in her head, day and night; a washing machine filled with thoughts, fears, worries that seemed to have no answer.

And she missed him. God, she missed him.

She picked up their used mugs and took them back to the kitchen. On the kitchen table was a copy of the *Peasebrook Advertiser*. Ralph must have been reading it, or one of the staff. Sarah kept her kitchen open to the people who worked for her, because she felt it was important for them to feel part of the family. The kitchen was enormous and there was a back door out into the courtyard so they didn't have to traipse through the rest of the house, and there were just less than a dozen full-timers working in the estate office and the tea room and the shop, and in the grounds. They were usually all gone by five o'clock so it wasn't too much of an imposition, and she was convinced it was an advantage.

She looked down at the paper. There was a picture of him on the left-hand page. His dear face; his kind smile; that trademark sweep of salt-and-pepper hair.

Memorial service to celebrate the life of Julius Nightingale . . .

She sat down, reread all the details. Her head swam. She knew about the funeral – it was a small town, after all. It had been tiny, but this memorial was open to anyone who wanted to come. Anyone who wanted to do a reading or a eulogy was to go and see Emilia at the shop.

A eulogy? She would never be able to begin. Or stop. How could she put into words how wonderful he had been? She could feel it coming, a great wave of grief, unstoppable, merciless. She looked up at the ceiling, took deep breaths, anything to stop it engulfing her. She was so tired of being strong; so tired of having to fight it. But she couldn't afford to break down. Anyone might come in, at any moment.

She gathered herself and looked down at the page again. Should she go? Could she go? It wouldn't be odd. Everyone in Peasebrook knew Julius. Their social circles overlapped in the typical Venn diagram of a small country town. And in her role as 'lady of the manor' Sarah attended lots of funerals and memorials of people she didn't know terribly well, as a gesture. No one would think it odd if she turned up.

But they would if she broke down and howled, which is what she wanted to do.

She wished he was here, so she could ask his advice. He always knew the right thing to do. She imagined them, curled up on the sofa in the folly. She imagined poking him playfully, being kittenish. He made her feel kittenish: soft and teasingly affectionate.

'Should I go to your memorial service?'

And in her imagination, he turned to her with one of his mischievous smiles. 'Bloody hell, I should think so,' he said. 'If anyone should be there, it's you.'

Five

Jackson had been dreading his meeting with Ian Mendip. Well, meeting made it sound a bit formal. It was a 'friendly chat'. In his kitchen. Very informal. Ian had a proposition.

Jackson suspected it would mean doing something he didn't want to do yet again. Breaking all the promises he had made to himself about getting out of Ian's clutches and getting some backbone. He had no alternative though. He had no qualifications, no references, no rich dad to bail him out like so many of the kids he'd been at school with.

That was the trouble with this area, thought Jackson, as he took his seat at Ian's breakfast bar: you were either stinking rich or piss poor. And whilst he had once been filled with ambition, and optimism, now he was resigned to a life of making do and being at Ian Mendip's beck and call. Somewhere amongst it all he'd lost his ambition and his drive. The galling thing was he knew it was his own fault. He'd had the same opportunities as Mendip: none. He just hadn't played it as smart.

He looked around the kitchen: white high shine gloss units, a glass-fronted wine fridge racked up with bottles of vintage champagne, music coming as if from nowhere. There was a massive three-wick scented candle oozing an expensive smell, and expensive it seriously was – Mia had wanted one, and Jackson really couldn't get his head round anyone thinking spending hundreds of pounds on a candle was a good idea.

Ian hadn't got all this and the Aston Martin parked outside by being nice. Next to it was Jackson's ancient Suzuki Jeep, the only set of wheels he could afford now, what with the mortgage payments and the maintenance for Mia, which took up nearly all his salary. His mates told him he'd been soft, that he'd let Mia walk all over him. It wasn't as if they were even married. He didn't have to give her a penny, they told him. But it was about Finn. Jackson had responsibilities and a duty to his son, which meant he had to look after his mother. And to be fair, Mia hadn't actually asked for anything. He'd known it was his duty.

Which was why he was still running around after Ian instead of setting up on his own, which had been his original intention. But you needed cash to start up, even as a jobbing builder who just did flat roof extensions and conservatories. That's how Ian had begun. Now he did luxury apartments and housing developments. He was minted. He had proven that you could claw your way up from the bottom to the top.

Jackson was Ian's right-hand man. He kept an eye on all his projects and reported back. He scoped potential developments: it was Jackson who had given Ian the heads-up on the glove factory, which meant Ian had been able to swoop in and get it at a knock-down price before it went on the market.

Which was why Jackson knew he was capable of achieving what Ian had. He could spot the potential in a building. He had the knowledge, the experience, the energy; he knew the tradesmen who could crew it. He just didn't have the killer instinct. Or, right now, the money he needed to invest in setting up on his own. He'd missed the boat. He should have done it years ago, when he was young and had no responsibilities. Now he was trapped. Not even thirty and he'd painted himself into a dingy little corner.

He hunched down in the chrome and leather barstool opposite Ian. Ian was spinning from side to side in his, smug and self-satisfied, tapping a pencil on the shiny black granite. In front of them were his development plans for the old glove factory: line drawings of the building and its surroundings.

'So,' said Ian, in the broad burr he hadn't lost despite his millions. 'I want that book shop. That is a prestige building and I want it as my head office. It's classy. If I do that up right, it'll do more for my reputation than any advert.'

Ian was obsessed with how people perceived him. He longed for people to think he was a class act. And he was right – the book shop was one of the nicest buildings in Peasebrook, right on the bridge. Jackson could already see the sign hanging outside in his mind's eye: Peasebrook Developments, with its oak leaf logo.

'And I've gone over the drawings for the glove factory again and done a bit of jiggling. If I get the book shop car park, I can have parking for four more flats. Without it, I'm down to eight units, which doesn't make it worth my while. Twelve will see me a nice fat profit. But you know what the council are like. They want their allocated parking. And that's like gold dust in Peasebrook.'

He tapped the drawing of the car park with his pencil.

'Julius Nightingale wasn't having any of it,' Ian went on. 'One of those irritating buggers who don't think money's important. I offered him a hefty whack, but he wasn't interested. But now he's gone and it's just his daughter. She insists she's not interested either. But now the dad's gone, she's going to struggle to keep that place afloat. I reckon she could be persuaded to see sense. Only she's not going to want to hear it from me. So . . . that's where you come in, pretty boy.'

Ian grinned. Jackson was, indeed, a pretty boy, slight but muscular, with brown eyes as bright as a robin's. There was a little bit of the rakish gypsy about him. His eyes and mouth were wreathed in laughter lines, even though he hadn't had that much to laugh about over the past few years. With his slightly too long hair and his aviator sunglasses, he looked like trouble and radiated mischief but he had warmth and charm and a ready wit. He was quicksilver – though he didn't have a malicious bone in his body. He just couldn't say no – to trouble or a pretty girl. Although not the pretty girls any more. His heart wasn't in it. He wasn't even sure he had a heart these days.

Jackson listened to what Ian was saying and frowned. 'But how am I going to get to know her? I've never read a book in my life.'

'Not even *The Da Vinci Code*? I thought everyone had read that.' Ian wasn't a great reader himself, but he managed the odd thumping hardback on holiday.

Jackson shook his head. He *could* read, but he never did. Books held no thrall for him. They smelled bad and reminded him of school. He'd hated school – and school had hated him. He'd felt caged and ridiculed and they had been as glad to see the back of him as he had been to leave.

Ian shrugged.

'It's up to you to work out how to do it. But you're a good-looking boy. The way to a girl's heart is through her knickers, surely?'

Even Jackson looked mildly disgusted by this. Ian leant forward with a smile.

'You get me that shop and you can manage the glove factory development.'

Jackson raised his eyebrows. This was a step up, letting him manage an entire project. But Ian's offer was a double-edged sword. He was flattered that Ian thought him capable of the job. Which of course he was.

But Jackson wanted to be able to do what Ian was doing for himself. He needed money if he was going to do that. Proper money. Right now, Jackson couldn't even put down a deposit on a pigsty.

Ian was smart. He knew he'd got Jackson by the short and curlies. He was taking advantage of him. Or was he? He paid him well. It wasn't Ian's fault that Jackson had screwed up his relationship. Or that keeping Mia was bleeding him dry. He only had himself to blame for that. If he hadn't been such an idiot . . .

Ian opened a drawer and pulled out a wad of cash. He counted out five hundred.

'That's for expenses.'

Jackson pocketed the cash, thinking about what else it could buy him.

He'd love to be able to take Finn on holiday. He imagined a magical hotel on a beach, with four different swimming pools and palm trees and endless free cocktails. He longed for warmth on his skin, and the chance to laugh with his son.

Or he could put it towards a decent van. He'd just need one job to get him started. If he did it well, there would be word of mouth. He could move onto the next job, start saving, keep his eye open for a house that needed doing up . . . He could do it. He was certain.

In the meantime, he had to keep in with Ian. Ian was his bread and butter, and he wouldn't want to let Jackson go. He had to play it smart.

Emilia Nightingale shouldn't take him long. Once Jackson had a girl in his sights, she was a sitting target. He had to muster up some of his old charm. He used to have them queuing up. Pull yourself together, he told himself.

Jackson held out his hand and shook Ian's with a cocky wink that would have done credit to the Artful Dodger.

'Leave it with me, mate. Nightingale Books will be yours by the end of the month.'

*

After his meeting with Ian, Jackson drove to Paradise Pines, where he was living with his mum, Cilla. He wasn't going to tell her about the deal, because she wouldn't approve.

He hated the park. It was a lie. It was advertised as some sort of heavenly haven for the over fifty-fives. 'Your own little slice of paradise: peace and tranquillity in the Cotswold countryside.'

It was a dump.

Never mind the rusting skip in the car park, surrounded by untaxed cars and wheelie bins and the mangy Staffie tied up in the corner that represented the 'security' promised in the brochure ('peace of mind twenty-four hours a day, so you can sleep at night').

He slunk past the Portakabin where Garvie, the site manager, sat slurping Pot Noodles and watching porn on his laptop all day. Garvie was supposed to vet visitors, but Ted Bundy could have floated past arm in arm with the Yorkshire Ripper and Garvie wouldn't bat an eyelid. He was also supposed to take deliveries for the residents, deal with their maintenance enquiries and be a general all round ray of sunshine for them all to depend upon. Instead he was a malevolent presence who reminded each resident that he was all they deserved.

Garvie was obese, with stertorous breathing, and smelt like the boy at school no one wanted to sit near. He turned Jackson's stomach. Cilla said she was fond of him, but Cilla liked everyone. She had no judgement where people were concerned.

Jackson wondered how he could have turned out so differently from his mother. He didn't like anyone. Not at the moment, anyway.

Except Finn, of course. And Wolfie.

He ploughed on along the 'nature trail' that led to his mother's home. It was an overgrown path with a very thin layer of bark to guide you. There was no nature apparent, though more than once Jackson had seen a rat scuttle into the nearby undergrowth. He should let Wolfie loose up here one day, even though you were supposed to keep dogs on a lead on the site. He would have a field day, routing out the vermin. But there was no point. The residents left their garbage rotting. The rats would be back in nanoseconds.

The fencing that surrounded the little patch of grass belonging to each home was rotting and the grass itself was bald and patchy. There were lamp-posts lighting the paths, but hardly any of them worked, and the hanging baskets hanging from them trailed nothing but weeds.

Maybe it had been all it had proclaimed in its brochure once upon a time. Maybe the grass *had* been lush and manicured; the grounds tended immaculately. Maybe the owners had taken pride in their own homes.

Jackson had felt utter despair the day his mother told him what she had done. She had been conned. Taken into a show home and given a glass of cheap fizzy wine and bamboozled by a spotty youth in a cheap suit and white socks, who had convinced her this was the best place for her to invest her savings. She'd had a fair old nest egg, Cilla, because she'd always been a saver. And Jackson was shocked by her naiveté. Couldn't she see the park homes would lose value the minute the ink was dry on the contract? Couldn't she see the management fee was laughably high? Couldn't she see that the park owners had absolutely no incentive to keep their promises once all the homes were leased? As a scam it was genius. But it made him sick to his stomach that his mother was now going to be forced to live out her days here. No one wanted to buy on Paradise Pines. Word was that you went there to die. It was one step away from the graveyard.

And now here he was, living with her in the place he had come to hate. It had only been supposed to be temporary. When

Mia had first thrown him out, two years ago, when Finn was three, he had thought it wouldn't be long before she allowed him back. He knew now he'd been useless, but he just hadn't been ready to be a dad. It had been a shock, the realisation that a baby was there round the clock. It had been too easy for him to slide out of his share of the childcare, coming home late from work, stopping off at the pub on the way, having a few too many beers.

And to be fair to him, Mia had changed. Motherhood had made her overanxious, sharp. She fussed over Finn too much, and Jackson told her repeatedly to stop worrying. It had caused a lot of friction between them. He spent more and more time out of the house, not wanting to come back to arguments and disapproval and crying (usually Finn's, sometimes Mia's). He tried to do his best but somehow he always managed to end up displeasing her. So it seemed easier to stay out of her way.

Then she'd booted him out, the night he'd come back half cut at one in the morning, when she'd been dealing with a puking Finn for four hours and had to change the sheets twice when she'd taken him into bed with her, desperate for a moment's respite. Jackson had protested – how was he to know the baby had a tummy bug? But he knew he was in the wrong and had got everything he deserved.

He thought it was only going to be temporary, that Mia was just giving him a short sharp shock. But she didn't want him back.

'It's easier without you,' she said. 'It's easier to do everything all on my own, without being disappointed or let down. I'm sorry, Jackson.'

He didn't bother knocking on the flimsy white door, just pushed it open. There was his mum, in the gloom of the caravan. Wolfie lay at her feet but jumped up as soon as Jackson came in. At least someone was glad to see him. He'd got Wolfie once it was clear Mia wasn't going to have him back. He'd gone to the dog rescue place and looked at everything they had: Jack Russells and collies and mastiffs. At the far end was a Bedlington lurcher, far too big to be practical and ridiculously scruffy. But he'd reminded Jackson of himself. He was a good dog, deep down, but sometimes he couldn't help himself... How could he resist?

His mum was as delighted to see him as Wolfie was. Her face lit up, her eyes shone. He still couldn't get over how frail she looked. He didn't want to admit to himself that his mum wasn't getting any younger. He was going to cook her a decent dinner. He was no chef, but he'd bought some chicken pieces and some vegetables with the cash he'd been given.

She'd always taken pride in cooking them proper meals when they were young but somewhere, between husbands three and four, she'd lost interest in food.

He didn't want to look at his once beautiful mother, sitting in her chair, bird-like and frail. He didn't want to look at the hair that had once been dark and lustrous, tumbling over her shoulders. Now, the black dye she used to recreate her former glory had grown out, showing three inches of grey.

It was depression at the root of it. Obviously. Which wasn't surprising when your looks and your husband left you at the same time. Was it easier, Jackson wondered, not to have been beautiful in the first place? He knew he'd got by on his looks more than once. His looks and an easy charm.

'Shall we go out somewhere?' he asked, knowing what the answer would be. He wanted her to surprise him and say yes, and yet he didn't. He didn't want to see her out in the real world, because it made her situation even more depressing.

'No, love,' she replied, just as he'd thought. 'It's enough for me to have you here.'

He sighed and made the best he could of the food he had bought with the facilities available. He dished it up, coating it all in a glistening layer of packet gravy.

They ate it together at the tiny table. Jackson had no appetite, but he wanted to set an example. He forced more carrots on her. Gave her the rest of the Bisto. At least now he knew she'd had some vitamins, some calories.

He'd bought a ready-made apple pie and a carton of custard, but she declared herself full.

'I'll heat it up for you later.'

'You're a good boy.'

She'd always said that to him. He could remember her, lithe and vibrant, dancing in the kitchen, holding him in her arms. 'You're a good boy. The best boy.' He would touch her earrings with his tiny fingers, entranced by the glitter. He would breathe in the smell of her, like ripe peaches.

Where had she gone, his mother? Who had stolen her?

He did the washing up in the sink, which was too small to put a dinner plate in flat. He tried to suppress his despair for the millionth time. He washed all the cups and glasses that were lying around, and wiped down the surfaces.

He could imagine Mia's voice: 'You never did that for me.'

He had. Once upon a time. But nothing was ever right for Mia; she was a control freak. He couldn't even breathe right.

'I'm off to see Finn, Mum.' He bent down to kiss her, not leaning in too close. 'I'll be back in a bit.'

'Ta ta. I'm going to have a snooze now.' She settled back in her chair with a smile. He whistled for Wolfie and the dog jumped to his feet. He was like a cartoon, his eyes coal black and inquisitive, his legs and tail too long; his shaggy grey coat like a backcombed teddy bear. He loped beside Jackson, amiable and eager.

Jackson lugged the bin bag back down the path and hurled

it over the side of the skip. The stygian gloom of the caravan stayed with him.

'Oi!' shouted Garvie from his lair, but Jackson knew he was safe. Garvie wouldn't bother to chase after him, or to fish the bag out.

He left the park and broke into a run, gulping in gusts of fresh air, trying to expel the stifling staleness of the past two hours. Wolfie ran beside him, joyful, his ears streaming behind him.

There's got to be something better out there for us, he thought.

He walked back into Peasebrook with Wolfie, then along the main road that led to Oxford. Eventually he reached the small cul de sac of houses where Mia and Finn lived. And where he had once lived. It had been one of Ian's most lucrative projects, a mix of executive four-beds and the low-cost housing he was obliged to build as part of the deal. The homes that only locals were allowed to buy. It was one of the reasons Jackson remained loyal to Ian, because he'd let him have one of them cheap. Ian had flashes of generosity, though there was usually something in it for him. This had been an act of pure selflessness, as far as Jackson could make out, though he was always waiting for Ian to call the favour in. He was convinced one day he'd have to get rid of a dead body.

Of course, Jackson's plan *had* been to get his hands on something that needed doing up. A project for him and Mia. They could make some money on it, sell it on and buy something bigger. Keep doing that until they had a total palace. But then Mia had got pregnant and they'd needed a place of their own quickly, somewhere suitable for a baby. You couldn't bring a baby up in a building site.

So it had been a compromise. Nevertheless, Jackson had been

proud to get on the property ladder. He remembered Mia's face when he led her over the threshold. They were pretty little faux mews houses, built in imitation of the weaver's cottages traditional in the town. He'd chosen everything off-plan: the pale blue Shaker kitchen, the silver feature wallpaper in the lounge, the pale green glass sink in the downstairs toilet. Mia had been speechless.

'Is it ours?' she had whispered. 'Is it really ours?'

Now there was no 'ours' about it.

He knocked on the pale cream front door. He remembered choosing the colour and being so proud. Mia answered. Her dark curly hair was tied back; she was wearing a baby pink sweatshirt and grey yoga pants and eating a low-fat yoghurt.

'Can Finn come out for a bit?'

She sighed. 'Don't you ever listen? He does tae kwon do on Tuesdays. At the leisure centre.'

Jackson nodded. 'I'll walk over there and pick him up.'

'It's OK. I've got it covered. The coach is bringing him back.'

'I can tell him not to worry—'

'No. He's bringing me some protein powder for my training.'

'Training?'

'For the triathlon. I was supposed to be going for a swim, but . . .'

Mia had become a fitness freak since he'd left. She was obsessed. Jackson thought she'd lost way too much weight. Her curves had gone; she looked angular and her face had lost its softness.

He looked at her. On closer inspection, she seemed positively drawn.

'Are you OK?'

She looked startled. They never expressed concern for each other in their current relationship. They avoided the personal.

'Course,' she said. 'Just – you know – wrong time of the month.'

She'd always suffered. He used to make her tea and hot water bottles and rub her back. Before he'd become a total twat. He opened his mouth to commiserate or console her but wasn't sure what to say. Anything seemed too personal now, to this woman who had become a stranger to him.

She spooned in some more yoghurt, still on the doorstep, no intention of asking him in.

'You didn't come to Parents' Evening.'

Her voice had that horrible accusatory edge. He was glad he hadn't sympathised.

'What?' He frowned. 'When was it? You didn't tell me.'

'It was last Thursday. I shouldn't have to tell you.'

'How am I supposed to know?'

'By taking an interest?' She glared at him. 'You never have a clue what he's doing.'

'I have.'

'Really? What's his topic this term, then?'

Jackson couldn't answer.

'Vikings, Jackson. It's Vikings.'

He sighed. 'I'm a loser, Mia. We know that. You don't have to prove it.'

'It's a shame for Finn, that's all.'

'We have a laugh. Finn and me. We have a great time when he's with me.'

'It's not all about the laughs.'

He looked at her. When had she become so bitter? And why?

'Are you happy?' he asked suddenly.

She looked startled, as if he'd caught her doing something she shouldn't.

'Of course.'

'Really? Only happy people don't try and make other people feel bad.'

She looked away for a moment. Jackson couldn't tell what she was thinking. He never could. Since Finn had been born, he felt as if the real Mia was somewhere else.

When she spoke, he could hardly hear her.

'I'm just tired, that's all.'

That was what she used to say when he was with her. She was tired all the time.

'It must be the training. It's no wonder. Give yourself a break, Mi.'

He stepped towards her. He wanted to give her a hug. Tell her it was going to be all right. But she sidestepped him.

'I'm fine.' She gave him a half-smile. 'The training's what keeps me going.'

'I don't understand, Mi. You've got this house. You've got our lovely boy. You've got rid of me. What more could you want?'

She rolled her eyes. 'You can have him tomorrow after school. Don't be late.'

She put another spoonful of yoghurt in her mouth and shut the door with her foot. Jackson stood on the step for a moment, unable to believe that she had the power to make him feel worse every time he saw her. It was obvious she thought little of him. Obvious she thought he was a shit dad. Well, he wasn't a shit dad. They *did* always have a laugh, him and Finn. He took him fishing. Took him to the skate park and taught him tricks. Bought him decent food; not that rubbish she kept feeding him: lentils and quinoa. And Finn loved Wolfie with a passion.

What did he have to do to prove himself?

He turned and walked back along the drive to the main road, Wolfie trotting along by his side, looking up at him every now and again. Dusk was falling, and he mulled over the events of the day. And gradually, as he walked, an idea emerged. He could do Ian's bidding *and* prove he was a good father. And if all went according to plan, maybe he could get himself out of this mess.

Six

'It's a can of worms, Em,' Andrea told her. 'You'd better come to my office. But don't panic. We can sort it. That's what I'm here for.'

Emilia felt her heart sink. She felt grateful she had Andrea. She couldn't have asked for a better friend, even though they were so different. Andrea called her every day to see how she was. And she brought her thoughtful presents: last week she'd given her a Moroccan rose-scented candle, expensive and potent.

'Just lie on the bed and breathe it in,' Andrea instructed. 'It will make you feel better at once.'

Strangely, it had. The scent was so soothing; it had wrapped itself around her and made her feel comforted.

Emilia walked from the shop to Andrea's office in a slick modern block built from glass and reclaimed brick, and was ushered in to a room with sleek Scandinavian furniture, a Mac and a space-age coffee machine. There wasn't a scrap of paper in sight.

Andrea swept in, with her figure-hugging navy blue dress and designer spectacles that ensured she missed nothing. Emilia immediately felt as if she should have dressed more formally. She was in jeans and Converse and her favourite old grey polo neck jumper – not very businesslike.

Then Andrea hugged her, and Emilia felt her strength. They

got straight down to business, though: Andrea brooked no nonsense, took no prisoners and pulled no punches. She sat behind her desk and brought up Nightingale Books on a computer screen that was the size of a kitchen table.

'It's taken me quite a while to trawl through everything and make sense of it,' she said. 'I'm not going to pretend. It looks as if the shop's been in financial trouble for quite a while. I'm so sorry. I know that's not the sort of news you need at the moment, but I really felt you should be put in the picture as soon as possible. So you can decide what you want to do.'

She handed Emilia a neatly bound sheaf of papers.

'Here are the balance sheets for the past two years. Balance not being the operative word. There's been far more going out then coming in.' She gave a rueful smile. 'Unless your dad was operating in cash and we don't know about it.'

'Dad might have been useless with money but he was honest.'

'I know. I was joking. But look – he hadn't even been drawing much of a salary for himself for the past few years – he was only ever worried about paying his staff. If he'd been paying himself properly there'd be an even greater loss.'

Emilia didn't need a huge understanding of numbers to see that none of this was good news.

'If he hadn't owned the building outright he'd have been in even bigger trouble. He would never have been able to afford the rent or the mortgage repayments.'

'Why didn't he say anything?'

Andrea sighed. 'Maybe he wasn't bothered. It's not all about profit for some people. I think the book shop was a way of life for him, and as long as it was ticking over he was happy. It's a shame, because with a bit of professional help, he could have made it much more efficient without changing the way he did things too much.' She clicked through a few more pages of depressing numbers. 'He made a lot of classic mistakes, and missed a lot of tricks.'

Emilia sighed. 'You know what he was like. Dad always did things his own way.' She looked down at the floor. 'He was always sending me money. I didn't realise he couldn't afford it. I would never have taken it off him . . .'

She couldn't cry in Andrea's office. But the tears leaked out.

'Sorry.' She looked up and to her surprise Andrea was crying too. Well, just a bit misty-eyed.

'Oh, I'm sorry too,' Andrea said. 'How unprofessional of me. But I was really fond of your dad. I used to pretend he was mine when we were kids, you know. He was just so . . . *there*. Unlike mine.' Andrea's father was a flaky figure who appeared once in a blue moon, usually when he had run out of money and had come to beg off her mother.

She pulled open a drawer and brought out a box of tissues. 'These are for bankruptcy proceedings. Even grown men cry at those.'

'So,' said Emilia, when she'd mopped up her tears and felt a bit stronger. 'Are you saying the shop needs to close?'

Andrea had composed herself now.

'No. Not at all. It really depends on you, and what you want to do. But it will take a great deal of hard work to turn it round and make it profitable.'

Emilia nodded.

'You're sitting on a valuable piece of real estate. The building was bought in your name, which is one good thing, so there would be no capital gains. And he made you a director of the company as soon as you were eighteen, so that makes things easier too, once we get probate. You're free to do whatever you want.' Andrea paused. 'You *could* sell that building straight away and be very well off. And save yourself a lot of trouble.'

'I've already had an offer. From Ian Mendip.' Emilia hadn't

mentioned his visit to Andrea, because she'd had a sneaking feeling Andrea might think it was a good idea.

Andrea looked awkward. 'Ah.' She cleared her throat. 'I've got to admit to a slight conflict of interest here. I do Ian's accounts. I should tell you that before we go any further.'

Emilia had forgotten how everything in Peasebrook connected up in the end. Suddenly she felt unsettled and slightly paranoid.

'Did he tell you he'd made me an offer?'

'No. But I'm not at all surprised. I know he's got the glove factory and I was going to suggest you asked him what he would offer you. But he's ahead of me.' She breathed a sigh. 'I'd have thought he'd have waited a bit. It's a bit predatory even for Ian.'

Emilia shrugged. 'I think he wanted me to know the offer was there. For all he knows I might want to sell up. He'd talked to Dad about it a few times but Dad wasn't interested.'

'It was one of the lovely things about your dad, that he wasn't interested in money. Not like Ian, who's obsessed with it.' Andrea laughed, then looked a bit shamefaced. 'Sorry. I shouldn't talk about my other clients like that. It's very indiscreet. And don't worry. I'm not going to influence you either way. I just want to help you stand back and look at the options. Without being sentimental or emotional.'

Emilia leafed through the balance sheets Andrea had given her. She felt her heart sink. She didn't feel equipped to make an informed decision. She understood enough to know the figures weren't good, but not how to come up with a solution.

'So – do you think I can make the shop work?'

'Well. It would have to be a very different shop. You would have to invest quite considerably. And the problem is there's not a lot of ready cash in the coffers. Of course, you could take out a loan. You've got plenty of equity.'

Emilia chewed the side of her thumbnail while she thought.

'I don't understand why it's in such trouble. I mean, he's got masses of customers. The shop's always full of people.'

'Yes. Because it's a lovely place to come in for a chat and a browse and wander around. But those customers don't always buy. And when they do it's not much. And I know for a fact he was always giving people discount, because he used to offer it to me. I told him off about it more than once.' Andrea sat back in her chair with a sigh. 'Nightingale Books was a wonderful, warm place to be. He made people feel welcome and want to stay in there for hours. But it was a terrible business model. He'd make them cups of coffee and talk to them for hours and they'd wander out without buying anything. Then they'd go up the road and spend twenty quid on lamb chops or cheese. He was very easy to take advantage of.'

'I know,' sighed Emilia. Her lovely father, who was as kind and easy going as a man could be.

Andrea drummed her French-polished fingernails on the glass tabletop.

'But there's nothing I hate more than seeing a potentially good business go down the pan. I'm very happy to give you my advice. But it's no good just listening. You have to be proactive.'

'Well, I'm very happy to take your advice,' said Emilia. 'And I want you to be honest with me. Do you think it's salvageable?'

Andrea sat back in her chair. 'OK,' she said. 'Here's the thing. I know Peasebrook and how it works. My guess is at the moment, it's really only locals and old customers who go in the shop. People who'd built up a relationship with Julius. And they are still valuable. Of course they are. What you need to do is widen your net. Make it an attractive destination for tourists, weekenders and people who live further out. Diversify. Find different revenue streams. Monetise!'

Emilia could already feel rising panic. She forced herself to carry on listening. Andrea was smart.

'You should open on a Sunday for a start. There are lots of people who come to Peasebrook for a weekend break from London. Or who drive here for Sunday lunch. There's nothing much else for them to do but spend money. So you need to find a way to pull them in. The shop is slightly out of the way, being at the end of the high street, so if you're from out of town and you don't know it's there you might miss it. You need to make it a little more eye-catching. And do some marketing and advertising. Get a decent website and start a database – send your customers a newsletter. Put on events and launches and—'

Emilia put her hands over her ears. She couldn't take it all in.

'But all this costs money,' she wailed. 'Money I don't have!'

'I've got an idea there. The obvious thing to do would be to rent the flat out. That would bring in a regular income – at least a thousand a month if you're clever. There's a huge demand for holiday accommodation in Peasebrook. I've got an agency on my books. I can introduce you – get them to give you an estimate. You'd need to spend some money on it, though. People expect luxury.'

'I'd have to find somewhere to live myself.'

'Well, yes.'

Emilia's head was spinning with all the possibilities.

'I can't think straight.'

'I'll help you as much as I can,' said Andrea. 'There's nothing I would love more than to see Nightingale Books turn a healthy profit. But we've got to be realistic. You need to do a watertight business plan.'

'I wouldn't know where to start! I've never done a spreadsheet in my life.'

'Well, that's what I'm here for. I love spreadsheets.' Andrea grinned at her. 'But it won't be easy. It's a question of whether you want to live, breathe, sleep, and eat books for the foreseeable future.'

'It's how I was brought up.'

'Yes, but you won't be able to float around plucking novels from the shelf and curling up in a corner.' Andrea laughed. 'Every time I went in your father had his nose in a book, away with the fairies. That's not going to work. You're running a business. And that means being businesslike.'

Emilia nodded. 'I understand,' she said. 'But I need to get the memorial service out of the way first. I feel as if I can't move on until that's happened.'

'Of course,' said Andrea. 'There's no rush. The shop will tick over for a few months yet. And in the meantime, if you've got any questions, just pick up the phone. I want to help you make the right decision. But the right decision for you, not one made out of sentiment or a sense of duty.'

The two women hugged. Emilia left Andrea's office, not for the first time gratified by how kind people were, and reassured at how perceptive and caring Andrea was. She felt that whatever decision she made, she'd be in safe hands.

Later, Emilia sat in the familiarity of the kitchen.

On a shelf were rows of glass jars, with stickers on, their contents carefully stated in Julius's copperplate handwriting: basmati rice, red lentils, brown sugar, penne. Below them were smaller jars containing his spices: bright yellows and brick reds and burnt oranges. Julius had loved cooking, rustling up a huge curry or soup or stew and then freezing it in small portions so he could pull whatever he fancied out in the evening and heat it through. Next to the food was his collection of cookery books: Elizabeth David, Rose Elliot, Madhur Jaffrey, all battered and stained with splashes. Wooden chopping blocks, woks, knives, ladles.

She could imagine him in his blue and white apron, standing at the cooker, a glass of red wine to one hand, chucking in ingredients and chatting.

Never had a room felt so empty.

She had an A4 pad in front of her on the table. She picked up a pen and began to make a list of ideas.

Staff rota
Open Sunday (extra staff?)
Website - Dave (She was pretty sure Dave would be able to help).
Redecorate
Relaunch. Party? Publicity?

It all looked a bit vague and nebulous. The problem was Nightingale Books had been the way it was for so long she couldn't imagine it any other way. She completely understood Andrea's concerns, and that it couldn't carry on the way it was. But did she have the wherewithal to turn it around?

She had no idea what to do for the best. She tried to empty her mind and focus, so she could identify what she wanted, but it was impossible, because what she wanted was for everything to still be the same, for her father to be here, and for her to be able to drop in whenever she liked; have coffee with him, a meal with him, just a chat with him.

She sighed. It was only half past two, and she felt as if she could go to bed now and not wake up until tomorrow.

She couldn't though. Julius's friend Marlowe was coming over to give her a lesson on Julius's cello. She desperately wanted to play 'The Swan' by Saint-Saëns at his memorial, but she hadn't played for so long, and she'd sold her own cello when she went abroad.

Julius had been a founder member of the Peasebrook Quartet

along with the formidable Felicity Manners, who had retired from the quartet a couple of years ago when her arthritis became too bad for her to play the more intricate pieces. Marlowe, who had been second violinist, had taken over as first and now did a wonderful job of choosing and arranging pieces that pleased both the hoi polloi and the music snobs (of which there were quite a few in Peasebrook).

The quartet was affiliated to Peasebrook Manor and played a variety of concerts in the gardens every summer, and at half a dozen carefully chosen weddings, as well as a popular Christmas carol service in the chapel. That way the quartet didn't take over their diaries, and left them room to get on with other things. They were respected and enjoyed, and although they were never going to make millions, they were all passionate about the music they made.

And Marlowe fuelled that passion. Marlowe was a true renaissance man. He quietly earned a small fortune, composing music for adverts, and he was an exquisite violinist. He was one of those understated people who made you believe anything was possible. He was never still for a minute, yet he had time for everyone.

Although Marlowe was nearer Emilia's age – mid-thirties, she thought – he and Julius were as thick as thieves, sitting at the kitchen table for hours drinking bottles of New World Cabernet while they decided on the programmes for the quartet. They'd watched every series of *Breaking Bad* together, fuelled by tequila and tacos, and compiled an annual New Year's Eve quiz for the Peasebrook Arms, with fiendishly difficult questions.

Emilia had always been drawn to him, and occasionally wondered if there could be more between them, but somehow, over the years she had known him, either she or Marlowe had always been attached to someone else. He had a string of glamorous girlfriends, usually musicians, whom he treated with benign absent-mindedness, always preoccupied with his latest project.

When Emilia had phoned and asked Marlowe for help to practise the piece she wanted to play at Julius's memorial, Marlowe hadn't hesitated.

'That is quite wonderful,' he told her on the phone. 'Your father would be delighted. I can't tell you what a loss to the quartet he is. We've asked Felicity back pro tem, though it will limit what we can play. Petra's still on viola, of course. Delphine's going to take over from Julius, though cello's not her first instrument and so she won't be a patch on him. But don't tell her I said so or she'll have my balls for earrings.'

Delphine was the French mistress at a nearby prep school and Emilia was fairly sure that Marlowe and Delphine were an item. Julius had hinted at it, expressing the merest hint of disapproval, which surprised Emilia. Her father was rarely judgemental, but he found Delphine terrifying.

'She stands too close. And I never know what she's thinking.'

'She's very attractive,' Emilia had pointed out. She'd met Delphine briefly on several occasions, but knew instinctively they would never be kindred spirits. Delphine was a fashion plate, always perfectly made-up, inscrutable, with a hint of the dominatrix that Emilia knew she could never pull off in a million years.

Julius shook his head. 'She's scary. And she doesn't eat. I'm not sure what Marlowe sees in her.'

Emilia could see exactly. Delphine was the stuff of male fantasy.

'She's very demanding,' added Julius. 'Maybe Marlowe will get fed up with it in the end.'

Emilia laughed. 'Just don't criticise her,' she advised. 'Or you'll only make her more attractive to him.'

Marlowe arrived promptly. He gave Emilia a huge hug. He

felt warm and comfortingly solid in a big cashmere overcoat, his curls stuffed underneath a bobble hat.

'How've you been?' he asked.

Emilia just shrugged. 'You know. Vacillating between grief and despair.'

'It's awful for you.'

'It is.'

'I bloody miss him. I keep thinking *I'll drop in and have a drink with old Julius*. And then I remember . . . So I can't imagine how you must feel.'

Marlowe took off his coat and threw it on the sofa. Underneath he wore black skinny jeans and a grey cable-knit sweater and a pair of oxblood Chelsea boots. When he took off his hat his black curls sprang free, wild and untamed.

He looked at Julius's cello, standing in the corner of the room.

'May I?' he asked, mindful of its significance.

'No, please – go ahead.'

He strode across the room and lifted the cello off its stand. He ran his long, slender fingers over the strings, expertly listening to see if it was in tune, adjusting the pegs until the notes were just as he wanted them. Emilia felt a pang, wondering about the last time Julius had played it: what had he played? He had played every day. It was his way of switching off. He never considered it a chore.

She watched Marlowe tune up, fascinated, always intrigued by the way a true musician handled an instrument: with absolute confidence and mastery. She could never take her playing to the next level because she was always slightly afraid the instrument was in charge, rather than the other way round.

He picked up Julius's bow and ran it over a small block of resin until the fine hairs were as smooth as silk. Then he sat down and let the bow dance over each string and the notes rang out loud and true in the stillness of the living room. He began playing a tune, short sharp staccato notes, and Emilia smiled in delight as she recognised it. 'Smooth Criminal'. Not what one would expect from a cello.

Then he segued into something sweeter, something she didn't recognise. He finished with a flourish, stood up and pointed her to the seat. 'Let's see how you are.'

'I haven't played for years. I meant to practise before you got here—'

'Ah. The fatal words. *I meant to practise*. I don't want to hear you say that again.'

Emilia blushed. Now he had pointed it out, it did sound lame. Brilliant musicians were brilliant because they practised, not just because they had talent.

She warmed up, playing a few scales. It was surprising how well she could remember. It was almost instinctive as she moved her fingers up and down the strings, stretching and curling them to capture just the right note, then moving on to arpeggios to reignite the muscle memory.

'There you are, you see?' Marlowe looked delighted. 'It doesn't go away. It's like riding a bicycle. You just need to put the time in now.'

She took out the sheet music for 'The Swan' from the pile on the piano. She began to play. She had done it years ago for one of her grades. She couldn't remember which – six, she thought. She had been note perfect then, and had got a distinction. But after all this time, her playing was dreadful. She scraped and scratched her way through it, determined not to stop until she got to the end.

'It's awful,' she said. 'I can't do it. I'll do something else. I'll read a poem.'

'No,' said Marlowe. 'This is perfect for your father. And yes, it was bloody awful. But you can do it. I know you can. I'll help you. If you practise two hours a day between now and the memorial, it will be the perfect tribute.'

He started breaking the music down for her, picking out the fiddly bits and getting her to master them before putting them back in, marking up the manuscript with his pencil. After an hour and a half of painstaking analysis, he asked her to play it through again.

This time it sounded almost like the tune it was. Not perfect, far from perfect, but at least recognisable. She laughed in delight, and he joined in.

'Bravo,' he said.

'I'm exhausted,' she told him.

'You've worked hard. We better stop now. There's only so much you can take in.'

'Would you like a glass of wine before you go?' she asked, hoping he'd say yes. 'It's going to take me years to work my way through Julius's wine collection if I don't have help.'

He hesitated for a moment. 'Go on then. Just a glass. I mustn't be late.'

She couldn't help wondering if it was Delphine he mustn't be late for, but she couldn't really ask.

She flicked on the sound system in the kitchen. Some Paris jazz sessions flooded the room: cool, smooth sax and piano with an infectious beat. It took her breath suddenly. It must have been the last thing Julius listened to.

Marlowe found his way around the kitchen, pulling a bottle of red from the rack, opening the drawer to find Julius's precious *bilame*, the corkscrew favoured by French wine waiters. He opened the bottle effortlessly and poured them each a glass.

He looked at her, and she couldn't hide her tears.

'I'm sorry,' she laughed. 'You just don't know when it's going to get you. And it's always music that does it.'

'Tell me about it,' said Marlowe, handing her a glass. 'But it's OK to cry, you know.'

Emilia managed to compose herself. She wanted to relax, not grieve. As she drank her wine, Emilia managed to unwind properly for the first time since she'd come home. The kitchen felt alive again, with the music and the company, and she found herself laughing when Marlowe told her about the disastrous impromptu poker school he and Julius had set up the winter before last.

'We were rubbish,' he told her. 'Luckily the maximum stake was only a fiver, or you probably wouldn't have a roof over your head.'

Emilia didn't mention that she was slightly worried she might not anyway.

When he left, after two glasses of wine not one, the flat seemed a slightly dimmer place. He ruffled her hair as she left, an affectionate gesture, and she smiled as she turned and shut the door. People were kind; people were loving. At least, the people her father had attracted were.

When Emilia went to bed that night, her head was spinning with accidentals and spreadsheets and pizzicato and bank loans and opening hours and crescendos. And the running order for Julius's memorial – everyone in Peasebrook wanted to do something, it seemed. But despite all the things whirling around in her brain, she thought how lucky she was to have the support of such wonderful people – June and Mel and Dave, and Andrea, and Marlowe. Whatever she decided, she was going to be all right.

It was unusual for a house like Peasebrook to be passed down the distaff side, but Sarah's parents handed it over to her when she turned thirty and scarpered off to live in the Scilly Isles, and she took on the responsibility with gusto. Ralph was working in the City as a financial analyst and making plenty of money for them to maintain the house and have a good life. But when the pressure of that became too much, he took early retirement. He claimed to have done the maths, and assured her there was enough in the coffers to keep them in Hunter wellies and replace the roof tiles when necessary. He had the rent from his bachelor flat in Kensington and he still played the stock market.

'We'll never be helicopter rich,' he told her, but he knew helicopter rich wasn't Sarah's bag. And it meant a much more relaxed life, having him around instead of up in London during the week, and he was there for Alice – whom they both adored – and somehow it was as it should be. They both did their own thing, and agreed it had been the right thing to do when they met in the kitchen for coffee or were able to turn up as a couple to Alice's nativity play or when they went off to the White Horse for lunch just because they could. When Ralph had worked, they had barely seen each other, and that was no way to run a marriage.

It was the horses that did for Ralph. He couldn't help it. He was used to taking risks with money, and missed the adrenalin. Sarah knew he had a flutter every now and again, but she didn't mind. It was important for men to have an interest, and if that meant Ralph poring over the *Racing Post* at breakfast and trotting off to the races with his cronies she didn't mind – she liked the occasional trip to Cheltenham or Newbury herself if there was a decent meeting or a horse they knew running.

Until one day she came into the kitchen and saw Ralph sitting at the table. In front of him were a bottle of Laphroaig and a set of keys. With a lurch, Sarah recognised them as the keys to the gun cabinet.

'Take them away,' said Ralph, his voice thick with whisky.

'What's going on?' Her heart was hammering as she picked them up. 'You're drunk.' Ralph wasn't the type to get drunk at eleven o'clock in the morning. Eleven o'clock at night, yes.

He rubbed his face in his hands and looked up. His eyes were bloodshot.

'I'm sorry.'

'You're going to have to spell it out.' Sarah was crisp. 'What's going on?'

'I should have quit while I was ahead. I was at one point. But I couldn't resist, could I? And I should know, better than anyone. The only one that wins is the bookie.'

Sarah sat down at the table opposite him.

'You've lost money?'

He nodded.

'Well, at least you've told me. We can deal with it. Can't we?'

'I don't think you understand.'

Ralph put his hand on the neck of the bottle to pour another drink, but Sarah stopped him.

'That's not going to help. Come on. Tell me.'

'I've lost the lot,' he said.

'What lot?' Sarah felt fear.

'All my money. Everything I had.'

Sarah swallowed. All his money? She had no idea how much that was. Not that Ralph would have hidden it from her, but his assets went up and down every day. Sarah had her own bank account, with her own family money, and they had a joint account for bills and housekeeping, but they didn't really get involved in each other's financial matters.

'I don't understand.'

'It's all on my account on the computer if you want to look

at it.' There was a bleakness in his eyes Sarah found harrowing. 'I broke all my own rules, didn't I? I let emotion get in the way.'

'How much?'

He turned the laptop screen towards her. She thought she might be sick.

'What do we do?'

He could only manage a shrug.

She tried to think. Her brain couldn't take it in: the staggering sum, or how she could have missed what he was doing. She'd been too engrossed in Alice and Peasebrook to notice.

'It was going to be all right.' His voice was cracked. 'I would have stopped.'

'Ralph. You know better than anyone . . .'

'That's why I thought I was being clever.'

Sarah's mind raced. It settled on the most logical conclusion.

'You'll have to sell the flat.'

The flat was their safety net.

He looked at her. His eyes said it all.

'Oh God!'

She stood by him, of course she did. She still loved him, and she didn't want to destroy their little family, or what they had together. Her support of him was unstinting: practical and no-nonsense. She made him face up to the fact he had an addiction. She cut up his credit cards, took away his laptop, made him give her access to his online bank accounts – all with his permission; she wasn't trying to emasculate him. They needed a strategy to stop him being tempted, ever again, and if that meant she had to police him, then so be it.

And it was then she decided to make Peasebrook work for them and open it to the public. It was the best chance they had of a steady income. It would be hard work, but Sarah certainly wasn't afraid of that. After all, Peasebrook was her life already, so it might as well be her living too.

But her trust in Ralph had gone, and she didn't know if she would ever be able to get it back. He had risked everything he had because he was a fool, and she felt sure Peasebrook had only been spared because it was a step too far. It made her blood run cold to think of what might have happened. Her respect for him had gone too. He was weak. And no matter how he tried to excuse it, or explain it, he just wasn't the man she thought he was. In no way did she blame herself for what had happened. She was a good wife, and she wasn't insecure enough to start looking for imperfections or ways in which she didn't measure up. She bloody well did. It was Ralph who didn't.

She didn't share what had happened with many people. She hated gossip and speculation. She didn't want Ralph being a public spectacle, for Alice's sake as much as anything. Sarah was a very private person. It was a huge burden to shoulder all alone. Every now and then she longed for a friend to share the truth with, but she didn't trust anyone. A few glasses of wine and your private business was public knowledge. She'd heard enough intimate secrets splurged at dinner parties to know that. So she kept quiet.

The first Christmas was awful. They had to tighten their belts. They didn't send out invitations to their usual Christmas Eve party and Sarah ended up fabricating an excuse involving a tricky and unpleasant varicose vein procedure to stop people thinking they had been left off the guest list because the party had become a tradition locally. She found the pretence dispiriting and exhausting, and all the excitement of Christmas was tainted. Tainted by the stupid, awful, ridiculous debt. She still didn't understand why Ralph had felt the need, because there'd always been sufficient, or so she thought, but when he tried to explain that gambling wasn't driven by any logic, she got upset. And tried not to get angry.

But when there wasn't enough money for Christmas presents, because every last penny was going into the development fund for Peasebrook, she felt resentful. All those bloody acres, she thought, and no cash in the kitty. She was determined that Alice should have what she wanted, and not have any sense of the crisis they were in, so she bought everything on her list to Father Christmas – more than she would usually – and everyone else was going to have books.

Books, after all, were her escape from the horror she had been through. At night she could curl up with Ruth Rendell or Nancy Mitford and the stress melted away and for a couple of hours she could be somewhere else. Reading gave her comfort.

She went into Nightingale Books. Until now, she had been working her way through the books in the library at Peasebrook, but she wanted to choose specific books for everyone in the family.

Julius Nightingale was behind the counter when she walked in, wearing a distinguished pair of half-moon glasses and peering at a catalogue. She gave him a smile.

'Can I help?'

'I've come to do my Christmas shopping. I'm just going to have a wander round.'

'Shout if you need me.'

She saw a pile of Dick Francis novels on one of the tables and thought how in previous years she would have bought one for Ralph. Not this year though.

As she browsed, she found the horrors of the recent past fading away. She lost herself somewhere in amongst the shelves as she chose for her friends and family: a thick, weighty historical biography for her father, a sumptuously illustrated cookery book for her mother, the Narnia Chronicles for Alice, the latest escapist fiction for her younger sisters, jokey books for the downstairs loo for her brothers-in-law. Choosing the books was soothing her soul.

The pile was enormous. As she handed over her debit card, she hoped there'd be enough in the account to cover it. She thought she'd probably overdone Alice's stocking. She was definitely overcompensating. Sarah busied herself looking at a rack of Penguin classics while he processed the payment, her heart hammering.

'I'm so sorry,' said Julius. 'It's been declined. It happens a lot at Christmas,' he added kindly.

Sarah felt her cheeks burn. She was mortified. She was going to cry, she realised with horror. Thank goodness she was the only person in the shop at that moment. And then it struck her that, throughout all the turmoil and the trauma and the chaos and the fear and the panic, she hadn't cried once. Ralph had, great snivelling gulping sobs of self-pity, and it made her want to scream, because the whole situation could have been avoided if only he hadn't been such a fool. He had brought it on them through his own stupidity. But Sarah wasn't a shouter; she was a stiff-upper-lip-and-get-on-with-it sort of person who came up with solutions rather than wallowing.

Only now, suddenly, she felt as if she were six years old and the world had come crashing down around her because she'd smashed her piggy bank on the kitchen floor. She swallowed back the tears.

'I'm so sorry,' she stammered.

'Take them anyway. You can pay me later,' Julius said, and he grinned. 'I know where you live, as the Mafia say.'

'No, I can't possibly,' said Sarah, and this time she couldn't stop the tears.

Julius was the perfect gentleman. He made her an industrial strength cup of tea and sat her down. And he was so understanding and so unjudgemental she found herself spilling out everything that had happened.

'What a horrible time you've had,' he sympathised.

Sarah put her face in her hands. 'Please. Don't tell anyone. I shouldn't have said anything.'

'I won't breathe a word,' he promised solemnly. 'Honestly, sometimes I feel like a priest in here. People tell me all sorts of extraordinary things. I *could* write a book. But I'm too busy selling them.'

In the end, he made her laugh so much the world seemed a much better place.

'Look,' he said. 'Take the books. Pay me when you can. It's honestly no skin off my nose.'

He was so insistent that it was easier to take them than to refuse. And it gave her an excuse, a few days later when she'd managed to scrape together some cash, to go in and pay him. And she stayed nearly an hour and chatted, because the great thing was you could stay in a book shop talking about books for as long as you liked and nobody thought it strange.

The books she'd chosen made Sarah's Christmas brighter. Even the book she had chosen for Dillon, the lad she had taken on to help with the garden, went down better than she had expected. She'd given him a copy of *The Secret Garden*. It was a book she herself returned to time and again, and she never failed to find the story one of hope.

She wrapped it in white tissue with a dark green ribbon and gave it to him.

'You probably think this is a really weird and inappropriate present,' she told him. 'But this book means the world to me. And I want you to know how much I appreciate what you're doing here at Peasebrook. You make me feel as if I can achieve what I want to.'

He was so polite when he opened the book. He thanked her effusively, and assured her he didn't think it was a boring present. It was the only present he'd had that was actually wrapped. His mum and dad had got him some safety goggles and a bottle of Jägermeister.

'I wasn't expecting anything at all from you, to be honest,' he told her.

She thought he would probably take it home and shove it away somewhere, never to be seen again. But to her surprise he came to her a few days into the New Year and told her how much he'd enjoyed it.

He might have just been being polite, but the next time she went past Nightingale Books, she went in and told Julius, and he was delighted.

'It must happen to you all the time,' said Sarah. 'People telling you how much a book has meant.'

'Yes,' said Julius. 'It's why I do what I do. There's a book for everyone, even if they don't think there is. A book that reaches in and grabs your soul.'

And he looked at her, and she felt a tug deep inside, and she thought – that's *my* soul.

She looked away, flustered, and then she looked back, and he was still looking at her.

She could remember every detail of that moment as she took her navy coat off the peg in the cloakroom and then tucked a silk scarf around her neck. The last one he had given her. They had always given each other scarves at Christmas. After all, no one ever questioned a new scarf the way they might a piece of jewellery, yet they were pleasingly intimate. Sarah cherished the feel of the silk against her skin, as soft and caressing as her lover's fingers had once been.

She buttoned up her coat and walked briskly to her car.

*

Thomasina was grateful, for once, for the distraction of her unruly class. Trying to keep them in check kept her mind off the stress. They were particularly skittish today: clearly the rigours of making a béchamel sauce weren't enough to hold their attention. They liked things they could take home and share, like pizza or muffins or sausage rolls. And béchamel sauce was tricky: difficult not to burn, even harder to get rid of the lumps. It took practice and patience, neither of which came naturally to her Year Elevens.

Her star pupil, Lauren, proffered her saucepan, showing her a glossy smooth sauce, and Thomasina smiled.

'Perfect,' she said.

The result particularly pleased her because Lauren was one of the school's problem pupils. She'd been threatened with exclusion on more than one occasion for disruptive behaviour. Lauren took bubbly to a new level. She was incapable of keeping quiet or concentrating for any length of time. Thomasina had sat in on endless staff meetings to discuss Lauren's behaviour, and had heard every teacher express exasperation.

'She's either going to end up in prison or on the *Sunday Times*' Rich List,' sighed the head.

For some reason, Lauren behaved impeccably in Thomasina's class. She was the only member of staff who seemed to have any influence over her. Which was odd, because Thomasina usually found people took no notice of her whatsoever.

She'd taken a risk two months before, and with the head's permission asked Lauren if she would like a Saturday job with her at A Deux.

'Good idea,' the head agreed. 'She'll only be out shoplifting or drinking cider otherwise.'

She wasn't stereotyping. Lauren had been cautioned for both in the past. Thomasina was surprised at how pleased she was when Lauren agreed to the job.

'What do you want me to do?'

'Help me prep. Lay the table. Make sure the glasses and plates and cutlery are spotless. Run to the shops if I need anything. And wait at the table while I do the cooking.'

'Be your bitch, you mean,' grinned Lauren.

'If you like,' said Thomasina. She knew she was taking a big risk, but she had seen something in Lauren the other staff had overlooked. She'd seen her concentrate while she was cooking, her total absorption in the process. Lauren wasn't interested in the written theory, but she threw herself into the practical work with something bordering on passion, and she wanted to please Thomasina – again, something none of the other teachers had ever experienced. Thomasina wanted to capture that passion and do something with it, and giving Lauren a job out of school, where she didn't have the rest of the class to show off to, was a step in the right direction.

Thomasina was halfway out of the classroom door when Lauren stopped her.

'Do you need me this weekend, miss?'

'Yes, please. I've got an anniversary dinner booked in.' She looked at Lauren. 'But you know the drill. Short nails. No scent. Hair tied back.'

Lauren came to school with glittery fake nails, her blonde hair backcombed into a bouffant mane, drenched in noxious perfume. She rolled her eyes. 'Yeah, yeah.' She looked at her nails – silver with black lightning streaks appliquéd on. 'Do you know how long these take?'

'It's non-negotiable.' Thomasina was putting on her coat. Her stomach was churning. Why had she said yes? She was starting to hope for a natural disaster – a hurricane, perhaps? It was too early for a snowstorm. Or maybe her car wouldn't start? It wouldn't be her fault, then, if she didn't turn up.

'You all right, miss?' Lauren was looking at her.

'I'm nervous about something.'

'What?'

'I promised to do a reading at a friend's memorial.'

Thomasina couldn't even begin to think about it. If she thought about it, she wouldn't do it. She had the book in her bag – *Remembrance of Things Past*, by Proust. It had seemed obvious to her, to do the most famous literary passage about food. She had practised it over and over and over, at home. But practising at home was worse than useless, because there was only ever her there.

Lauren was staring at her, puzzled.

'What are you scared of? You'll be ace, miss. Knock 'em dead.' She made a face when she realised what she had said. 'Well, you know what I mean.'

Thomasina couldn't help laughing. And she felt a little bit cheered by her pupil's faith in her.

'Thanks, Lauren,' she said.

'That's all right,' said Lauren. 'You tell me I can do things I don't think I can do all the time. No one minds if you mess up, that's what you say. But you have to try.'

Thomasina was touched by Lauren's logic. She hadn't realised her words of encouragement went in. It gave her the courage she needed.

Sarah arrived at the church door just before the service was about to begin. She slipped inside and her eyes widened in surprise at the size of the congregation. She scanned the pews for a space, hoping that no one would turn and notice her. She reminded herself there was no reason for her not to be here, but nevertheless she didn't want to be under scrutiny. There was a space next to a pillar. She wouldn't have the greatest view, but in a way the pillar gave her protection. She sat down as the vicar stepped forward to begin his welcome.

Oh Julius, she thought, and clasped her hands in her lap tightly.

Thomasina's reading was one of the first. With terror, she read her name on the order of service and realised there was no time to back out now. On the other hand, her ordeal would be over more quickly. She was in the front row, along with the others who were doing a reading or a performance. Her heart raced, and her palms felt sweaty. She wanted to run out, but she couldn't make a spectacle. She had to go through with it.

And then suddenly, the preceding hymn – 'Fight the Good Fight' – came to an end and it was her turn. She made her way out of her pew, and walked across to the pulpit as if she was walking to her execution. She climbed up the winding steps. She felt as if she was high up, in the clouds. She put the book down on the lectern, open at the page she was going to read. She'd underlined the words in red and they swam in front of her. She couldn't look out at the congregation. The thought that every single person in the church was looking at her, waiting for her to start, made her feel hot with fear. She was trembling. Just begin, she told herself, and then it will end. Before you know it.

She started to read, but her voice was barely there. She paused, cleared her throat, ignored the little demon inside her that was telling her to run down the steps and down the aisle and out of the door, and forged on. Her voice found itself. As she read on, it became clear and true:

'She sent for one of those squat, plump little cakes called "petites madeleines," which look as though they had been moulded in the fluted valve of a scallop shell. And soon, mechanically, dispirited after a dreary day with the prospect of a depressing morrow, I raised to my lips a spoonful of the tea in which I had soaked a morsel of the cake. No sooner had the warm liquid mixed with the crumbs touched my palate than a shudder ran through me and I stopped, intent upon the extraordinary thing that was happening to me. An exquisite pleasure had invaded my senses, something isolated, detached, with no suggestion of its origin. And at once the vicissitudes of life had become indifferent to me, its disasters innocuous, its brevity illusory – this new sensation having had on me the effect which love has of filling me with a precious essence; or rather this essence was not in me it *was* me. I had ceased now to feel mediocre, contingent, mortal. Whence could it have come to me, this all-powerful joy? I sensed that it was connected with the taste of the tea and the cake, but that it infinitely transcended those savours, could not, indeed, be of the same nature.

'Whence did it come? What did it mean? How could I seize and apprehend it?'

By the time she reached the last three sentences, she had hit her stride. She lifted her eyes and looked out as she spoke the words. The congregation was rapt, and she felt a surge of joy that she had managed to do for Julius what had seemed impossible. She smiled as she finished, and closed the book, calm, composed. And confident. She felt confident.

Luckily for Sarah, there wasn't a dry eye in the church when Emilia played her piece on Julius's cello.

She stood at the front of the church and spoke before she began.

'My father gave me a love of books first and foremost, but he also gave me a deep passion for music. I was five when he first let me play his cello. He taught me to play "Twinkle, Twinkle, Little Star" one Sunday afternoon, and I was hooked. I went on to do my grades, though I was never as good as he was. We played together often, and this was one of his favourite pieces. It's "The Swan", by Saint-Saëns.'

She gave a little nod, sat in her seat, picked up her bow and began to play. The notes were achingly sad, their melancholy sound echoing round the church, sweet and lingering. Sarah could feel them make their way into her heart and break it. She fell on her knees onto the prayer stool in front of her and buried her head in her arms, trying not to sob. She breathed as deeply as she could to calm herself until the last note died away. There was a silence, punctuated only by other members of the congregation sniffing and clearing their throats and wiping away their tears, and then someone began to clap, until the entire church was united in their applause. Sarah gathered herself, sat up, and joined in. She knew how very proud Julius would have been, how much he had loved his daughter, and she wished she could tell Emilia of the way his eyes had shone when he spoke of her.

Emilia felt elated when she finished playing. She had spent the last two weeks rehearsing every night until she was note perfect, but she was still afraid that she would freeze midway through, or her fingers would betray her. But they hadn't. And then she sat and listened to the quartet play Elgar's 'Chanson de Nuit'. Somehow under Marlowe's direction they made the music not sad but uplifting. Emilia didn't think her battered little heart could take it, but as the last notes faded away she was still breathing. She was still alive.

Thomasina was making her way out of the churchyard, through the toppled gravestones. She needed to be back at school to teach the last lesson of the day. She felt a hand on her arm. She turned, and saw Jem smiling at her.

'That was a really great reading,' he told her. 'I wish I'd had the nerve. But there aren't many readings about cheese, and that's all we had in common.' He made a lugubrious face, but it was obvious he was joking.

Thomasina laughed.

'Thank you. I was really nervous.'

'You didn't look it.'

'Really?' Thomasina was surprised. She'd thought her fear would have been apparent.

'Not at all. My mum loved those books by the way. Thank you . . .'

'I'm really pleased.'

They stood for a moment, the autumn leaves scuttling around their feet.

'I've got to go,' said Thomasina. 'I've got a class.'

'Yeah, and I've got to get back to the shop.' He held up a hand. 'See you.'

He strode off down the path towards the town and Thomasina watched him go, feeling as if she should have said more – but what more could she have said?

After the service, Emilia was putting away her cello in the vestry. She was glad to have something to occupy her. It had all been so perfect, and all she could think of was how much her father would have enjoyed everyone's contributions. She reminded herself she would have to send everyone a thank you letter.

'You played beautifully.'

She jumped, and turned.

There was Marlowe, smiling. 'You see? I told you. Practice makes perfect.'

'I don't know about perfect.'

'It was at *least* a merit.'

She pretended to pout. 'I got a distinction when I did it. For Grade 6, I think.'

'Good. Because there's something I want to ask you.'

He looked a bit awkward. Emilia felt her cheeks go slightly pink. Was he going to ask her out? Surely not, just after her father's memorial service? But a little bit of her hoped he might. She could do with a drink, she liked Marlowe, and her father had thought a lot of him. He was interesting and fun and—

'I wondered if you'd take your father's place in the quartet.'

'*What?*' This wasn't what Emilia had been expecting.

'Poor old Felicity is so limited with what she can do now and I don't want to put her under pressure. If you join, Delphine can go back to second violin, which will make her happy.' He gave a rueful grin. 'Which makes my life easier, I can tell you.'

Delphine. Of course. She had been at the service today, demure in a black shift dress. How on earth had she thought Marlowe might be interested in her?

Emilia shook her head. 'No way am I good enough. Look how long it took me just to get one piece right.'

'No way would I be asking you if I thought you weren't up to it. It's my reputation at stake. I wouldn't risk it.'

'I don't know what's happening. I don't know how long I'll be around. I don't know what I'm doing with the shop.' She was gabbling excuses.

'Just join till the end of the year. It's quiet for us, except for a few carol concerts. And Alice Basildon's wedding.' He was looking at her, his brown eyes beseeching behind his glasses. 'I can give you some lessons. Get you up to speed.'

Emilia could feel herself weakening. Of course she wanted to join the quartet. But it was daunting.

'I don't want to let you down.'

'We'll just be doing carols, and the usual wedding repertoire. No Prokofiev or anything too fiddly.'

She looked at him. How would she resist that disarming smile? Being in the quartet would be the perfect distraction from the stress of the shop and all the decisions she had to make. And even if she were to close Nightingale Books tomorrow, she would be tying up the loose ends for a few months yet. Most importantly, Julius would be so proud and pleased to think she had taken his place. She remembered his patience as he had taught her to pick out her first notes; shown her how to hold the bow correctly. They had played duets together, and Emilia remembered being transported by the music, the joy of being in sync with someone else. She missed that feeling. The quartet would give that to her.

'Promise me that if I'm not up to it, you'll say.'

'I promise,' said Marlowe. 'But you'll be fine. Is that a yes?'

Emilia thought for a moment, and then nodded.

'It's a yes.'

Marlowe looked delighted. 'Your dad would be so proud. You know that, don't you?'

He hugged Emilia, and she felt a warm glow.

She told herself it was the pleasure of doing something she knew her father would have wanted.

Sarah drove back to Peasebrook Manor feeling dry-eyed and hollowed out, numb with the effort of trying not to feel. She had suppressed her emotions so ferociously she thought she might never feel anything ever again. A wave of gloom hit her as she turned into the drive. Oh God, Friday night fish pie and false smiles. That was what the evening held. Could she really live the rest of her life like this?

Eight

That evening, Dillon stopped off at the White Horse. He always dropped in on a Friday. He and a few mates met for a pint of Honeycote Ale, a bag of cheese and onion crisps and a chat about how their week had gone, before they all drifted off home for a shower and their dinner. Some of them had wives and girlfriends to go home to; some of them came back later, for a few more beers and maybe a game of darts or pool.

The White Horse was the perfect country pub. Perched on the river just outside Peasebrook, on the road to Maybury, it was rough and ready but charming. There was a small restaurant with wobbly wooden tables and benches, serving hearty rustic cuisine: game terrine with baby pickled onions and home-made Scotch eggs and thick chewy bread and pots of pale butter studded with sea salt. The bar had a stone floor, a huge inglenook fireplace, and a collection of bold paintings by a young local artist depicting stags and hares and pheasants. It was frequented by locals and weekenders alike and you could turn up in jeans or jewels: it didn't much matter.

Dillon had been coming here ever since he could remember. His dad used to bring him and his brothers in on a Sunday while his mum cooked lunch, and it had become part of his life now. There was always someone he knew at the bar. If you didn't know anyone, it wouldn't be long before you did, because the atmosphere was convivial and everyone mucked in. It was easy to strike up a conversation.

That evening Alice was in there with Hugh and a horde of their friends. Dillon immediately felt tense.

Dillon loathed Hugh Pettifer with a vengeance. He could tell how difficult Hugh found it to treat him with politeness. He knew that if Hugh had his way, Dillon would never be allowed to speak to any of the Basildons and would bow and scrape and tug his forelock all day long. But that wasn't how the Basildons worked, and whenever Alice saw Dillon she threw her arms round him and chattered away, teasing him in a manner some might consider flirtatious but that Dillon knew was just Alice.

Hugh would look at him with distaste, just about managing to acknowledge him with a nod and a smile that didn't go anywhere near his eyes, and would draw Alice away at the first opportunity. It was all Dillon could do not to put two fingers up to Hugh's retreating back.

Once, Sarah had asked him what he thought of Hugh. He wanted to say what he thought, but he would never say the c-word to Sarah.

Of course Hugh wanted to marry Alice. She had social standing, which Hugh didn't, and was due to inherit quite the prettiest manor house in the county. She would be a wonderful wife, and a wonderful mother. Dillon could imagine a clutch of sturdy blonde-haired moppets stomping around Peasebrook in their wellies, with puppies and ponies galore.

Dillon couldn't help wondering what was in it for Alice. Good genes? Hugh was pretty good-looking, if you liked that minor-royalty-polo-player sort of look: thick hair and year-round tan. Was it money? He was wealthy, certainly, but Dillon didn't think Alice was that superficial. Maybe Hugh was a demon in bed? Maybe it was a combination of all three?

He made Dillon's teeth go on edge. He told himself he

was jealous. He would never have that kind of pull. A mere underling, on a fairly paltry salary, with no power or influence.

He and Alice got on like a house on fire when they were alone at Peasebrook Manor, but he felt awkward when she was out with her gang. They were spoilt and loud and drank and drove too fast.

'They're all really lovely,' Alice would protest.

'I'm sure they are,' said Dillon. 'But when they're in a big crowd they come across as tossers.'

Alice looked wounded. Dillon knew he had to be careful. There was a limit to how horrible you could be about someone's friends without it being a reflection on them.

So he tried to slink up to the bar and get a pint without her seeing him, but she did. She leapt out of her chair and came to give him a big hug. 'Hello, Dillon! We're all a bit sloshed. We've been to the races.' She beamed and pointed over to a crowd of her friends around a big table in the window. 'Come and join us.'

Dillon declined, as politely as he could. 'Got to see a man about a ferret.'

This wasn't a lie. He had a pair of ferrets at home, and the jill had just had a litter of kittens. He wanted to get shot of them before too long. A mate of his was interested.

Alice wouldn't give up. 'Come on. Come and meet everyone. I bet they'd all love a ferret. How many are there?'

Dillon sighed. Alice just didn't understand, God bless her. Her friends were no more interested in him than he was in them. They had absolutely nothing in common except Alice. And they certainly wouldn't want a ferret.

Alice was a little sunbeam who loved everybody, saw the bad in no one and treated everyone the same. To her, life was one long party. She fizzed with fun and bonhomie and that was why she was so good at her job. She understood what her clients wanted and did her utmost to get it for them. But she was shrewd underneath it. She knew how to get the best price for everything, and how to get the effect her clients wanted without paying over the odds.

That was how Dillon had really got to know her. She had become tired of paying astronomical sums for flower arrangements. After every wedding she looked at the florists' handiwork and sighed. And she came to Dillon, and asked him to plant her a cutting garden.

'I'm going to do the flowers myself from now on,' she declared. 'Everything has to be grown at Peasebrook. That's our selling point. If they don't like it, they can go somewhere else.'

So she and Dillon had spent hours poring over florists' websites and leafing through seed catalogues. He told her what they could grow: tulips, narcissi, peonies, dahlias, roses of course, sweet Williams, sweet peas, alchemilla... She sent a couple of the girls who worked for her on a floristry course, and by the next wedding season they were doing the bouquets, buttonholes, table arrangements – everything.

'I want that freshly-plucked-from-the-garden look,' said Alice. 'Not those awful stiff formal arrangements. I want it all frondy and feathery and Thomas Hardy-ish.'

In the end, Dillon had suggested a polytunnel, to get the biggest seasonal range, and Alice had declared him an utter genius.

So they had got quite close, and sometimes they ended up in the White Horse having a drink, and Alice bobbed about the pub like the butterfly she was, chatting to everyone. And then she'd met Hugh, at a friend's party in London, and Dillon backed off. He could tell it was time for him to cut the ties, because there was absolutely no way a man like Hugh wanted the likes of Dillon cosying up to his girlfriend. And he tried to make it so that Alice didn't realise he was deliberately avoiding her, because he knew the minute she twigged she would be insistent about including him, and Dillon simply couldn't face the humiliation or the power struggle.

This was the first time he had been cornered in public, and he didn't have a watertight excuse. He felt the prickly panic of a socially awkward situation.

'You've got to meet everyone,' Alice urged him. 'They'll all be at the wedding. Come on.'

She was tugging at his arm. Across the pub, Dillon saw Brian Melksham come into the bar for his Friday pint. Relief flooded him, just as Hugh walked over and put a proprietorial arm around Alice. There was no mistaking the underlying message.

'I can't,' said Dillon. 'There's Brian. He's having my ferrets off me.'

Alice's face fell.

Hugh smirked and gave an unpleasant laugh.

'It's like the bloody *Archers* in here.'

Dillon grabbed Brian's arm and walked him over to the bar. 'Don't look over. Just pretend we're deep in conversation.'

'What's going on?'

'Alice wants me to go and sit with all her mates.'

'Is she here with that knob?'

'Yep.'

No one in the White Horse thought much of Hugh. They all thought Alice deserved better.

'I seen his white tart trap in the car park,' said Brian. 'Nothing that a squirt of slurry wouldn't put right.'

He pulled a fiver out of his pocket for his pint. That was what Dillon loved about people in the White Horse. They didn't suffer fools.

At the end of the evening, the landlord called time. Dillon had stayed on for a game of pool in the back room but he decided he'd leave now, before the traditional Friday night lock-in. You had to be in the mood and he wanted a clear head for the weekend.

He walked back through into the main bar and saw Alice and her friends getting ready to leave. Most of them were unsteady on their feet, draped all over each other, braying and swaying. He looked at Hugh, who was holding his car keys. His face was flushed red, his eyes slightly glazed. He couldn't possibly be fit to drive. Dillon looked at the empty champagne bottles littering the table. They'd had shots too. Someone had set up a Jäger train – shot glasses of Jägermeister balanced on glasses of Red Bull. There had been much hilarity as the domino effect pushed each shot glass into the next one.

But Dillon knew Hugh's type. He wouldn't let a small thing like being over the limit stop him. Dillon had only had two pints over the course of the evening. He wasn't going to risk his licence. Besides, drink driving was illegal for a good reason.

He walked over to Alice, who was just coming out of the loo. He could see she had drunk too much to have any common sense left.

'You shouldn't get in the car with Hugh. You shouldn't let him drive.'

Alice waved a hand. 'It'll be fine. It's only the lanes.'

'Please. I'll give you a lift.'

Hugh came looming up behind Alice. He was waving his keys. 'What's up, ferret boy?'

Dillon didn't falter. 'You shouldn't be driving.'

Hugh's stare was flat and hard.

'Mind your own bloody business.'

'Come on, man,' said Dillon, distressed. 'I can give you guys a lift.'

Hugh prodded him in the chest. 'Butt out. I'm fine to drive.'

Dillon bunched his fists and stepped forward. One of Alice's mates spotted what was going on and started shouting 'Fight! Fight!'

Alice looked worried. 'Honestly, Dills – he's fine.'

Dillon scowled. It went against all his instincts, to let Alice get in the car with Hugh.

'Piss off, Mellors,' said Hugh. 'Come on, Alice.'

Dillon could see her falter for a moment. As Hugh led her away she turned, then shrugged, as if to say 'What can I do?'

Dillon stared after them. His jaw was set. His heart hammered in his chest. He should grab Hugh and stop him; take away his keys. But he could see the look in Hugh's eyes. He'd try and punch his lights out. And if he got physical with Dillon, Dillon would fight back and there was no doubt who would come off the worse. Dillon worked outside all day; Hugh sat behind a desk and went out for boozy lunches. He couldn't beat up Alice's fiancé. Sarah would be horrified.

He pulled his own keys out of his pocket. He would follow them home. Make sure Alice didn't come to any harm. It was his duty. If anything happened to her, how could he ever look Sarah in the eye again? He headed out into the car park. The night air was crisp and cold; frost starting to settle on the branches.

Hugh's car was waiting in the car-park exit, the engine idling.

Dillon got into his old Fiesta. He drove up behind the Audi, waiting patiently. He wasn't going to pip his horn. He knew that was what Hugh wanted him to do. He was goading him. The seconds seemed like minutes. Dillon tapped his fingers on the steering wheel, trying not to get wound up. He wondered what Alice was thinking, if she knew what game Hugh was playing. She probably wouldn't have a clue. Dillon was pretty sure she had no idea of her fiancé's true colours.

Finally the Audi shot out of the car park and into the road, accelerating at a terrifying rate. He could imagine Hugh at the wheel, laughing his head off. There was no way his little car could keep up with his high-powered vehicle. Dillon's lips tightened as he joined the road and followed in Hugh's wake.

The lanes back to Peasebrook Manor were inky black at this time of night with trees looming on either side. Dillon dropped down a gear and put his foot down, taking the bends carefully. And then he turned the blind bend half a mile before the entrance to Peasebrook Manor and saw his worst fear in front of him. The massive oak tree that loomed over the corner was pierced by Hugh's car.

The driver's door was open. Dillon could see Hugh in the road, hands at his head. The passenger side had taken the full impact.

There was a horrible silence.

Dillon pulled out his phone. Thank God there was a signal here. He pulled into a gateway, flicked on his hazard warning lights, dialled the police and opened his door in one fluid movement, jumping out into the road.

Hugh came running up to him. There was panic on his face.

'Have you got your phone? I can't find my phone.'

Dillon pushed him out of the way and spoke into the phone. 'Ambulance, please. And police.'

He strode past Hugh who pulled at his arm. 'Not the police—'

Dillon pushed him away. 'There's been an accident at the Withyoak turn. Car's gone right into the tree. I don't know how many casualties yet but definitely one!'

Dillon hung up and ran towards the car, jumping into the driver's side.

Alice was slumped over the airbag, unconscious. Her side of the car was crushed. There was broken glass, and blood on her face and her hands and in her hair. He could see that her legs were trapped. Dillon couldn't begin to try and get her out. He might do more harm than good. He realised he was crying. He should have stopped her. Hugh poked his head through the door.

'Shit. Is she all right?'

'No she fucking isn't! There's blood everywhere.'

'Oh Jesus. Jesus Jesus Jesus.'

'Alice! Can you hear me?' Dillon put a tentative hand on her shoulder. 'You're going to be OK. The ambulance is on its way. Alice?' Dillon felt sick as he realised there was no response. He took her wrist and felt for a pulse. It was still there, and now he knew she was still alive he could see her breathing.

What should he do? Dillon was racking his brain for first aid rules, but he couldn't think of anything. Her legs were trapped. He couldn't pull her out. He didn't want to move her in case he did more damage. All he could do was reassure her. He was shaking. With shock and fear and anger.

'It's your fucking fault,' said Hugh. 'You were following us. I saw you pull out right behind me. You were harassing us.'

'Don't talk crap.'

'I'm going to make sure they have you for dangerous driving.'

'They'll think you're having a laugh. My car doesn't do over sixty.' Dillon pointed a thumb over to his ancient car in the nearby gate. 'And they'll see the tyre tracks.'

Hugh looked at the road in the moonlight. Dillon was right. There was a pair of black lines imprinted on the road where he'd lost it on the corner. They'd be able to work out his speed.

'Fuck's sake. I'll lose my licence. I'll lose my job. I won't be able to support her.' He grabbed Dillon's shoulder. 'You do realise that's all they want me for, the Basildons? My money? They think it's going to save Peasebrook. They need me.'

Dillon looked at him. What a bloody state. But now he thought about it, it explained a lot. Hugh was loaded. It would take the pressure off if Alice married him. A source of ready cash.

That was how these families worked, wasn't it? It wasn't so far from an arranged marriage. He felt ill at the thought. Was Alice having to pretend to love Hugh, in order to save Peasebrook?

'If she dies,' Dillon told Hugh, 'I'll kill you.'

'She's not going to die,' said Hugh, but he looked as pale as the moonlight as lights appeared around the bend accompanied by wailing sirens.

Next to him, Alice stirred and moaned. She reached out a hand. Dillon took it.

'It's all right,' said Dillon, squeezing her hand as hard as he could. 'It's all right, Alice. The ambulance is here. You're going to be all right.'

In no time, there were people swarming everywhere, shouting instructions, the elaborate choreography of an emergency procedure taking shape.

Dillon and Hugh were taken to one side, removed from the scene of the accident.

'I lost it on the bend,' Hugh was telling a policeman. 'I'm not used to this car, and there was some black ice. I was taking Alice home to Peasebrook. We're due to get married in three months . . .'

He was trying his best to look the modicum of respectability.

'Come and sit in the car with me a moment, sir,' said the copper to Hugh.

'No problem,' said Hugh, but he looked daggers at Dillon.

Dillon didn't know what to think as he watched Hugh follow the policeman. He didn't want trouble for Alice, but the man was an idiot. He'd got what was coming to him. Dillon hoped they locked him up and threw away the key.

It seemed to take forever for the ambulance men to get Alice out of the car. The minutes seemed like hours. Eventually they lifted her gently onto a stretcher. She looked so small, so still, as they carried her over to the ambulance.

'Who's coming with her? Is anyone coming with her?' One of the paramedics asked.

'Yeah. I'll come.' He didn't want Alice turning up to the hospital on her own. He climbed into the back.

'Are you her husband? Boyfriend?'

'No – I work for the family. Is she going to be all right?'

No one answered. Someone was taking her blood pressure. Someone else was wiping away the blood.

Then suddenly Hugh was banging on the door. Someone opened it to let him in.

'Is she all right? I'm coming with her.'

'There's only room for one.'

Hugh looked at Dillon. 'Out.'

Dillon was astonished. It looked as if Hugh was in the clear. How on earth could he be? Dillon had seen him with his mates. They were all roaring drunk. What had he done? Had he bribed the policeman? Or was he genuinely not over the limit? Dillon couldn't understand it.

'Can you blokes sort yourself out?' asked a paramedic. 'We need to get going.'

Hugh's eyes met his. There was a message in them to say his card was marked. Dillon didn't care. Hugh couldn't touch him. All he cared about was Alice.

Without another word, Dillon climbed out of the ambulance.

Another policeman walked past.

'Somebody get on to Peasebrook Manor,' Dillon heard him say into a radio. 'Best for them to meet us at the hospital.'

Dillon felt sick at the thought of Sarah being given the news. She would be distraught. He couldn't imagine there was anything worse than being told your child had been in a car accident. He wished he could be with her, to reassure and comfort her, but it wasn't appropriate. It wasn't his place. Even though Dillon spent hours with her every day, it was Ralph who would and should be with her. He didn't even feel entitled to go to the hospital. This was a family matter. He was staff. It was his duty to step away, and wait until he was needed.

The ambulance doors slammed shut and the driver turned on the siren. Dillon wondered if Hugh would hold Alice's hand and tell her it was all going to be all right. He thought probably not. All Hugh would be worried about was saving his own arse. How was he going to explain the accident to the Basildons? He looked up into the night sky. He couldn't believe the stars were there, twinkling happily. How was it possible, when Alice lay there so still and small?

The ambulance drove off and Dillon was left there, watching Hugh's car being hoisted onto the tow truck. There was the sound of hydraulics and clanking chains, the mechanics shouting instructions to each other. A remaining policeman removed the accident sign.

And suddenly, everyone was gone and it was deathly quiet. It was as if the accident had never happened, except for the scar on the old oak tree. Dillon stared at it and wondered how fast Hugh had been going. He felt sick thinking about it. He felt totally helpless. What could he do? Pray, he supposed, but he'd never been a praying man. As far as he was concerned, nature took its course, man interfered from time to time, and what happened, happened. No greater force had any influence.

He went back to his car, still parked in the gateway. He drove slowly home, seeing ghosts in the shadows as the light turned from granite to gun-smoke. If he phoned the hospital, they wouldn't give him any information: he wasn't family. Was Alice a cadaver, under a white sheet, eyes shut? Was she on an operating table, waiting for a surgeon to perform his magic? Was she sitting up in bed, pale and shaken but laughing, drinking tea and chatting to the nurses? How was he going to find out?

At Peasebrook Manor, when Sarah Basildon heard the sound of a bell drill through the house, she sat up in bed and thought, Oh God, no. Please. Not so soon after Julius. Not someone else. I can't take it.

Nine

Sarah sat upright, her hands pressed between her knees, staring at an awful painting of a wood in autumn hung on the pale green wall of the hospital waiting room. Waiting, she thought. Waiting for news. A diagnosis. A prognosis. Suddenly nothing else in life held any import or urgency. Eating, sleeping, drinking – all were irrelevant. They'd been here since two o'clock in the morning. Alice was having a brain scan, or an X-ray, or was in theatre, or something – she couldn't remember which, or in what order. The information was a jumble and Alice was the staff priority, not giving out information. And they couldn't give information until they had answers. Sarah kept telling herself everyone was doing their best, but it was agony.

Ralph came in with a mug of tea in each hand and held one out to her. He'd gone off to find the friendly Scottish nurse with the bleached blonde hair and the smiling eyes, to see if she had any idea what was going on.

Ralph, for all the blundering blustering hopelessness he usually used to dissemble, had come into his own. His mantle of fecklessness slipped away, and out came a man of integrity and grit. It must have been his army training. He'd only had a couple of years in the Blues and Royals, but it must have been lying dormant in him. Maybe that was what had been lacking in his life over the past years? A proper crisis.

Sarah stared down at her tea.

'Come on,' he said. 'Drink up, darling. We're going to need all our strength.' He fished in his pocket and brought out a brace of digestives. 'Not much of a breakfast, but they'll see you through. An army marches on its stomach.'

Sarah took the mug and one of the biscuits. A tentative sip told her the tea was too hot, so she dunked the biscuit in.

'The consultant should be here in a few minutes,' Ralph added, and their eyes met. It was the moment they had been longing for and dreading, the consultant's verdict. Ralph put a hand on her shoulder. 'We'll get through this, darling. She's a fighter, Alice. That spirit of hers . . .'

He trailed off and his voice caught on his words. Sarah put up her hand and squeezed his arm. He needed reassurance too. He looked down at her, surprised and grateful, and she realised with a start of guilt that they barely had any physical contact any more. It hadn't been a conscious decision, but a gradual withdrawal. Sarah wondered for a moment if he had noticed, or, indeed, if he minded. She felt a rush of regret, tinged with guilt.

The door opened and they both stood to attention, Sarah sliding her arm into Ralph's. Now she had touched him, she felt the need to be close. They both stood there, clutching their mugs of tea, staring at the young doctor in the maroon jersey.

He smiled. 'Mr and Mrs Basildon?'

They nodded, mute with dread. They couldn't read into his smile. Was it just a greeting, or a barometer? If it was bad news, would he bother smiling?

'Well, she's in a bit of a pickle, I'm afraid.' He grimaced. 'But the good news is we've done a brain scan and there doesn't seem to be any great injury. Obviously we need to keep her monitored. There's never any guarantee. Bleeds can occur unexpectedly after trauma. But so far, so good.'

'Oh, thank God.' Sarah leaned against Ralph, limp with relief.

'It's not all good news. Her left leg is in very bad shape. There are multiple fractures, and we're going to have to operate and pin it all back together. It's a bit of a mess. It's going to be a while before she can walk. There'll be a lot of rehab work. A lot of physio.'

'We want the best people,' said Sarah. 'We can pay, if necessary.' God knows how, but they'd find the money. Sell a painting. She'd sell her soul if necessary.

'You don't need to worry about that just yet. She's in the best hands at the moment. Although there is more.' He cleared his throat and Sarah looked at him. Somehow she knew this was going to be the bad bit. 'Her face is badly lacerated. There's a very nasty cut on her left cheek. She may well have to have some cosmetic surgery.'

'Oh God,' said Sarah. 'She's getting married in November.'

'We'll do our very best for her.' He paused. 'Look, there's a lot to take in, and we don't know yet which order we are going to be doing things. But in some ways she's been very lucky—'

'Lucky?' Sarah looked appalled. Beautiful Alice, who was the least vain person Sarah knew.

'We should tell Hugh,' said Ralph. Hugh had gone out for fresh air. He said he was feeling odd after the crash. But he'd probably gone for a cigarette.

Sarah stiffened slightly at the mention of Hugh's name. 'It's all his bloody fault.'

'Darling. It was an accident. Black ice . . .'

'Yes.' Sarah didn't sound convinced.

'It must be awful. Imagine how he feels.'

'He drives too fast. I know he does.'

More than once Sarah had had to brake in her Polo, meeting

Hugh coming the other way in the narrow lanes leading to Peasebrook.

'Boys will be boys.'

'How can you *say* that?'

'Come on. We should be celebrating the fact that she's not got a brain injury—'

'As soon as she comes back from X-ray, you'll be able to see her,' said the consultant.

'She's going to be as right as rain. I know it,' said Ralph. 'She's made of stern stuff, my daughter.' He managed a smile. 'Like her mother.'

Sarah looked up from her seat in the waiting room when Hugh walked back in, smelling of freshly smoked cigarette and Wrigley's. He gave a tentative smile. He was, quite rightly, wary of Sarah.

'The nurse just told me. She's going to be all right—'

Sarah cut him off.

'You were driving too fast,' she said flatly.

'Sarah!' Ralph stood up.

Hugh looked down at the floor, then sighed.

'I know I was,' he said, quietly. 'And I'll never forgive myself. But there'd been a bit of an incident in the pub. I was trying to get Alice home as quickly as I could.'

'What do you mean – incident?'

There were fisticuffs in the White Horse sometimes. Not often, but it was inevitable sometimes after a few too many beers.

'It was your gardener chap. He was being a bit . . . aggressive.'

'Dillon?' Sarah was incredulous.

'Yes,' said Hugh. 'I should have taken him outside, but I didn't want trouble.'

'What do you mean – aggressive? That doesn't sound like him.'

'Everyone's different after a few.' Hugh put on a pained expression. 'I think he's got a bit of a thing about Alice. It was pretty embarrassing. He was following us. In his car. I put my foot down to get away from him. It was just instinct.'

Sarah shook her head. 'I don't believe you. Dillon wouldn't put Alice in danger.'

'Well, I can assure you it happened.'

'Following you and then what, exactly? What was he going to do then?'

Sarah was staring at Hugh, her eyes hard. He shrugged.

'I don't know. Beat me up? I think he'd had a few too many. Maybe I should have reported him. Stopped him from driving. In retrospect, that would have been the responsible thing to do—'

'I don't think any of this is true.'

Ralph stepped forward. 'Darling, I don't think this is the time.'

Hugh looked distressed. 'I'm sorry. I was trying to protect Alice. And yes, I put my foot down on the gas—'

'So it *was* your fault.'

'Sarah – this isn't an inquisition.'

'I want to get to the bottom of what happened. And I'm not convinced Dillon had anything to do with it. It sounds completely out of character.'

Ralph and Hugh shared a complicit look.

'Oh, Sarah,' said Ralph. 'You always see the best in everyone.'

'Not everyone.' She looked at Hugh. 'I don't always see the best in everyone.'

Hugh attempted a disarming smile. 'Look, we're all a bit upset. We're bound to be. The great thing is Alice is going to be all right. Let's not lose sight of that.'

'All right?' said Sarah. 'She's going to be scarred for life.'

'Sarah.' Ralph's tone was sharp. 'This isn't helping.'

The door swung open and the three of them looked towards the nurse. She was smiling.

'If you want to come and see Alice, just for five minutes . . .'

'Just me,' said Sarah. 'I want to see her. Three will be too much for her.'

Neither Hugh nor Ralph dared to remonstrate.

Alice was a tiny bundle in a bed in the middle of intensive care, a mass of bandages and wires and bruised flesh. There was barely a bit of her Sarah recognised. Even her voice was just a croak.

Sarah didn't want to say much. She didn't want drama. She didn't really do drama. The confrontation in the waiting room was as high as her voice had been raised for years. She was the epitome of calm, brought up to be serene and gracious.

She held Alice's little paw, the one without the cannula, and stroked it gently.

'Poor sweetheart,' she whispered.

'How bad is it?' asked Alice. 'I can't move anything and my head hurts. I can't *think*.'

'You've bashed your poor leg up a bit,' said Sarah. 'They'll need to pin it back together.'

She swallowed. She couldn't look at Alice's face. She couldn't say anything about her face. Not yet.

'We'll have to cancel, won't we? The wedding?' Alice's voice was a quaver.

Sarah looked at the floor. Something inside her said yes. That would be the answer to everything. Cancel the wedding. She had a bad feeling about it. About Hugh. But she didn't want to upset Alice by agreeing, because it would imply that things were terribly serious. Which indeed they may well be, but Alice had been through enough already. She needed soothing.

'We don't have to worry about that at the moment. It's a long way off.'

She suddenly felt drained, and incredibly emotional. She didn't want to cry in front of Alice.

'What happened, darling?'

'I don't know. I can't remember. There were loads of us. In the pub . . .'

'Was Dillon there?'

'Dillon?' Alice was trying hard to recollect the events. 'Maybe.'

'Did he and Hugh have a row?'

'I don't think so.'

'Only Hugh seems to think they did.'

Alice shook her head. 'I can remember the Jäger train . . .'

Sarah wasn't going to push it. She didn't want Alice distressed.

'Would you like to see Daddy?'

'Yes, please. I'm sorry, Mummy.'

'Sorry? What on earth are you sorry for?'

She could see Alice struggling with a thought, a memory.

'I don't know,' answered Alice, and her eyes filled up with tears.

It was eight o'clock before Sarah and Ralph got back to Pease-brook Manor from the hospital. The nurse had insisted they go in the end; had assured them repeatedly that Alice would be comfortable, and that they would end up being a nuisance if they stayed any longer.

Hugh had gone to stay with a friend. He had sensed, quite rightly, that he was best out of Sarah's line of fire for the time being.

Sarah sank down into her chair at the kitchen table. Yesterday morning seemed a lifetime away, when she had sat here preparing for Julius's memorial. You never knew what lay ahead.

'Shall I make scramblers?' asked Ralph. She shook her head. She couldn't bear the thought of food. 'You've got to eat.'

'Not now. Honestly. I'm beyond it.'

'Tea.' He grabbed the kettle and put it on the Aga. 'That hospital tea was definitely made from scrapings off the factory floor.'

How could he be so jovial?

She stared at the dresser on the wall opposite. She could see Alice's Noddy egg cup. It had been hers when she was small: a Noddy cup with a little blue felt hat with a bell on, to keep the egg warm. She thought about all the boiled eggs she'd made her daughter.

She could feel it coming. The grief. It was gathering speed, and was going to smash into her any moment. And this time, she didn't have to brace herself to withstand it. This time, she could let it engulf her. She'd been through every emotion today. Shock. Fear. Anger. Fury. Worry. Relief. Then more worry, doubt, fear, anxiety . . . There was only so much you could take.

And being at the hospital had reminded her. Of the day she had said goodbye to Julius at the cottage hospital. It was two weeks before he had finally slipped away. She'd been in to see him; brought him the new Ian Rankin, which she was going to read to him because his eyes kept going blurry and he couldn't concentrate.

She hadn't been prepared for him telling her he didn't want her to come in to see him again.

'I feel OK today. But I know it's just a temporary respite. Tomorrow I might be out of it. Or gone altogether. I want us to quit while we are ahead. I don't want you here when I don't know you are there. I don't want you to watch me die. I want to say goodbye to you while I am still me. A pretty ropey version of me.' He managed a self-deprecating smile. He was thin; his skin had an awful pallor; his hair was wispy. 'But me.'

'You can't ask me to do that,' she had whispered, appalled. She stroked his cheek. She loved every bone in his poor failing body.

'Please,' he said. 'I don't want to argue about it. It's for the best.'

Their fingers had been entwined while they spoke. And she knew him well enough to know that he had thought this through, that what he was saying was right. Emilia was on her way home to be with her father. Sarah couldn't be seen with him any more.

She held his hands in hers and kissed them. She kissed his forehead. She leant her cheek on his and held it there for as long as she could bear. She looked deep into his eyes, those eyes she had looked into so many times and seen herself.

She couldn't see herself any more. He had shut her out. It was time for her to go, and he was preparing himself.

'You're the love of my life,' she told him.

'I'll save you a place. Wherever I'm going,' he said back. 'I'll be waiting for you.'

He gave a smile, and then he shut his eyes. It was his signal for her to go. She recognised that he couldn't take any more. If she loved him, she had to leave him.

She drove home, staring at the road ahead. She felt nothing. She had shut down. It was the only way to cope. There was nothing in her that was able to deal with the horror of that final goodbye. She had wanted to climb into his bed and hold him forever. To die with him, if that were possible. Drift off into that final never-ending sleep with him in her arms.

She went to the folly when she got back. She curled up on the sofa with a cushion in her arms, folding herself into the smallest ball. There was a copy of *Anna Karenina* she had been reading. It was the last book Julius had given her. She tried to read it but the words were too small. She shut her eyes and prayed for sleep. She couldn't bear to be awake. It was Dillon who found her, hours later, and shook her awake. She had looked up at him, wide-eyed, confused for a moment.

'Are you all right?' he asked, and she nodded, slowly. She had to be. She had no choice.

But now, here, in the kitchen, she embraced the grief when it finally hit. She put her head down and sobbed. Great big jagged sobs that threatened to choke her and take her very breath away. She could hear them, resounding round the kitchen: a primal keening, ungodly and harsh. She melted down into them until she almost became her own tears. In the midst of it all a small voice told her she was hysterical; that she needed to pull herself together.

But she'd waited a long time for this chance. The chance to purge herself of her grief. The chance to cry for the loss of her lover; her best friend. She wondered if she was wicked to hide behind Alice's accident for the chance to have this outpouring. She wondered if Alice's accident was a punishment for what she had done. Neither of these thoughts helped her regain control. On the contrary, she felt reason slipping further and further away. It was the sort of crying that would never stop.

Until she felt Ralph take hold of her arms. He took hold of her arms and shook her.

'Sarah.' His voice was firm but kind. 'Sarah. You must stop this. This isn't doing you any good at all. You or Alice.'

She juddered to a halt. He looked at her, concern in his eyes.

'Listen to me. I've never told you how magnificent I think you are. How grateful I am for the way you stood by me. I wouldn't have blamed you for walking away after everything I did. But you got us through that bloody awful time like the fighter you are. And you're going to get us through this as well. Because you're a brave and wonderful woman, Sarah.'

He trailed off, looking a bit embarrassed. Ralph wasn't one

for gushing speeches. He wasn't sure where the words had come from. But he had meant them, of that there was no doubt.

Sarah shut her eyes and breathed in deeply. Her breaths were jagged but her sobs eventually stopped.

'I'm sorry,' she said, but of course he had no idea what she was sorry for.

'Come here,' he said, and folded her into his arms. And although he wasn't who she wanted him to be, she felt safe, and knew that he was going to be there for Alice, and that they would get through it, that she would be able to live without Julius . . .

And that she wasn't going to cry again.

Ten

Bea Brockman loved Peasebrook on a Saturday. It seemed to be fuel-injected: it was faster, busier, more animated than it was during the week. The market was full of interesting stalls: people selling berry-bright liqueurs made from local fruits, tables piled high with artisan bread, handmade beeswax candles in hot pink and emerald green and cobalt blue. She was ever on the lookout for the next new thing. It was – or had been – her job for so long, she had never lost the habit.

She dressed up on a Saturday more than she did during the week – though there was no point in doing full-scale London-style dressing. Monday to Friday she wore her casual-trendy mum-uniform of Scandi chic – asymmetric jumper, black skinny jeans and black trainers. Today, though, she had on a pretty dress, red suede boots and an Alexander McQueen scarf. Her hair was tied in a messy knot, and she'd painstakingly painted her mouth a luscious dark pink. She knew people looked at her. She was a tiny bit vain, Bea, and she missed the attention she'd had as a single girl. Though she loved being a mother. She adored Maud, who was proudly showing off her new beaded moccasins to anyone who cared to look from the depths of her fashionable all-terrain pushchair.

Bea had done the market, her favourite café, The Icing on the Cake, for a blueberry friand, and the butcher for a French-trimmed rack of lamb. She decided to head up to Nightingale Books for something to read. She had lists of all the paperbacks she should be reading to keep in the know, but there was nothing like a good browse in a book shop to broaden your horizons. She rolled the pushchair along the pavement, relishing the autumn sunshine that turned the buildings in Peasebrook to golden treacle. She was looking forward to their first winter in the country. London was so drab and bitter once the chill wind got a grip, chasing litter along the streets and alleys. Here, the air would be rich with the scent of woodsmoke, and there would always be a pub to hunker down in; game from the butcher to be transformed into a warming casserole. She'd already spent the happiest of days that week making damson jam and apple chutney from the windfalls in the garden, with fashionably minimalist labels she'd designed herself.

She was quite the country mouse.

Nightingale Books was like stepping back in time. She loved its bay windows, the ting of the bell as she walked in, and the smell – a rather masculine smell, a combination of wood and parchment and pipe tobacco and sandalwood and polish that had accumulated over the years.

She hadn't been in for a while, because there hadn't been much time to read over the summer. Autumn and winter were for reading. She remembered seeing in the local paper the owner had died. Nevertheless, the shop was busy. Someone must have taken it over. They'd made a few changes: the displays were a little less haphazard, and it definitely looked less dusty, although the dust had been part of the charm.

Her eyes were immediately drawn to a display at the front of the shop. It was a huge coffee-table book, of photographs by the iconic Riley. It was lavish, beautiful, and at a hundred and thirty pounds, eye wateringly expensive. She picked up the display copy – all the others were shrink-wrapped to protect them – and leafed through the pictures.

An assistant passed by her and smiled.

'Stunning, isn't it?'

Bea sighed. 'It's gorgeous. I love his work.'

'Who doesn't? He's a genius. You should treat yourself.' Then she coloured. 'Sorry – I'm not trying to do a hard sell. Well, I suppose I am. It's a limited edition.'

Bea shook her head. 'I can't afford it.' She smiled. 'It's a lot of jars of organic baby food.' She put her hand on the handle of the pushchair by her side. Maud was gazing up at them as if fascinated by their exchange.

'She's adorable,' said the assistant.

'She's taking up all my money.'

'Oh my goodness. I love the shoes. Teeny little moccasins.'

Bea wasn't going to tell the girl how much they had cost. It was embarrassing.

'Me and Maud are going to choose a book together. You can't start them too young.'

'Absolutely. Get them a book habit. We've got lots of lovely new stock. I'm trying to build up the children's section.'

Bea was curious.

'Is this your shop, then?'

'It was my father's.'

'I heard he'd passed away. I'm so sorry.'

'Thank you.'

'It's great that you've taken it over. I love it in here.'

'Good. Just let me know if there's anything you want. I'm Emilia.'

'I'm Bea.' They exchanged smiles, then Emilia walked away.

Bea looked down at the pile of Rileys.

In a trice, she took the top one off the pile. Then she pushed Maud over to the children's section, and they spent the next ten minutes browsing through any number of board books until they chose just the right one.

'*I Love You To The Moon and Back*,' said Bea. 'It's true, darling Maud. I do.'

She pushed Maud over to the counter.

Maud stared up at Emilia, the board book clutched in her hands.

'Ah – that book's lovely. She'll adore it.'

'If she doesn't eat it first.' Bea smiled. 'Everything goes straight in her mouth at the moment.'

'Is that all?'

'For today. Yes. Thank you.'

Afterwards, Emilia watched Bea go. She was the just kind of customer she needed. Young and vibrant, with a disposable income. What else could she do to attract people like her? Cards and wrapping paper? Women like Bea were always buying cards and wrapping paper, because they had friends galore. She made a note on a pad, and turned to her next customer.

Bea walked briskly up the high street, her heart pounding. She didn't stop until she came to the church, where she swung into the churchyard. She strode on until she reached a bench and sat down. She put her head in her hands momentarily, then looked up. She reached over and pulled up the hood of the pushchair.

There, nestled in the folds, was the copy of Riley's book, still in its shrink-wrap. She picked it up and sat with it in her lap, staring at it.

What the hell was happening to her? What on earth had she become? What was she *doing*?

It had seemed the logical thing to do at the time. She'd wanted the book and she couldn't afford it. It had taken her two seconds to lift one off the pile and slide it into the hood of the pushchair.

A single tear trickled down one cheek. She wanted the book, yes. She wanted to sit at home and leaf through the photographs, studying them, analysing them, wondering at the skill and the talent and the artistry. She could have afforded it if she'd really wanted it. Bill wouldn't have minded if she'd put it on their credit card.

But more than the book, she'd wanted a thrill. She'd wanted to feel alive. She'd loved the adrenalin the feat gave her. It had been the most exciting thing to happen to her in months.

Bea sat back on the bench and looked up at the sky. A few swallows were circling overhead and the breeze rustled the last of the leaves in the trees that lined the path. The church reminded her of her own wedding only three years ago. She remembered the vintage Dior dress she'd had shipped over from the States, pale blue silk taffeta, with its tight bodice and covered buttons and full skirt. She'd been a perfect bride at their perfect wedding.

They had thought they were so clever, she and Bill. Selling up their trendy warehouse flat to start a life in the countryside. They'd agreed they didn't want to bring up their kids in London. Peasebrook had been the answer, with its brilliant commuter service, its cute shops and gorgeous houses. They had felt very pleased with themselves when they bought the gingerbread cottage in one of the back streets, with its tiny walled garden. It was idyllic; the ideal place to start a family. Bill carried on commuting to his ludicrously well-paid job as a digital guru and Bea did up the house and garden. And popped out Maud. Their friends all exclaimed in wonder and envy at how cunning and brave they had been, and came down in their droves to stay in their spare bedroom with its white floorboards and chalky walls and silk curtains and the high bed with mounds and mounds of feather-light bedding.

But now Bea thought she was going mad. She missed work. She had been exhausted when she left. As art director for a women's magazine, she had lived on black coffee and deadlines, working right up to the wire on each issue, dealing with a crazed editor who changed her mind every two minutes and expected her to be psychic. When she left, she never wanted to lift another finger.

Now, she was psychotic with boredom. She adored Maud, of course she did, but once she'd pureed some organic carrots and free-range chicken breasts and frozen them into portion-sized blobs, and hand-washed Maud's little cashmere cardigans in lavender-scented washing powder, and taken her for a walk in the flower-filled meadow down by the riverbank on the outskirts of Peasebrook – what more was there? Apart from cooking a Mongolian fish curry for when Bill cycled back from the train station at seven o'clock at night.

She was living the life she had depicted so many times in the magazine. She thought of all the spreads she'd done outlining bucolic bliss: girls in tea dresses and wellies pegging out washing. Wicker baskets and picnic rugs and muddy vegetables and home-made bloody jam. She had pots of it. Pots and pots and pots.

From the outside, she was living the dream. Inside, she felt bored and empty and meaningless. How on earth had she thought that full-time motherhood was going to be enough for her? She stroked Maud's fat little hand and felt her heart shrivel with the ugliness she was feeling. She was an ungrateful cow. How could this little bundle not be enough?

Maud had fallen asleep, one hand clutching her little towelling blankie with the rabbit in one corner. What would her daughter think, having a kleptomaniac as a mother? Bea knew she'd always been impulsive, but she'd never put her impulsiveness to bad use until now.

What would Bill think if he knew what she'd done? He was under enough pressure, with the travelling and the job. He could barely speak in the evenings when he came home. He just ate and went to bed then got up at six to set off again. He wasn't much fun at the weekend either. For the past two months he'd refused to let them have guests down. He didn't do much. Slept. Watched a bit of telly. Opened his first bottle of beer at midday and drank steadily until he fell asleep again at about nine. If she complained, he snapped at her.

'You're living the dream, remember?'

OK, so it had been she who had orchestrated the massive change. She'd found the house, sold theirs, organised the move. Taken voluntary redundancy so she had a lump sum to live on. Arranged their finances so they could manage the drop in salary. Found ways to make savings so their weekly outgoings dropped by half but without a drop in standards. She'd saved them two hundred pounds a week by stopping them going out to eat or getting takeaways and getting a more economic car and not having a cleaner. Saving money had become her hobby, a point of pride.

She thought now she would do anything to be standing in a crowded train, with a takeaway latte in one hand and her iPhone in the other, brainstorming for a breakfast meeting. She would kill for an impossible brief or a draconian deadline or a crisis. These days, a crisis constituted running out of milk or nappies. Neither of which she ever did, because she had infinite amounts of time on her hands and so was the most efficient housekeeper on the planet.

But was she really so bored she'd resorted to shoplifting?

She walked back through the winding streets and by the time she got home Maud had fallen asleep. She pushed the pushchair into the living room, then sat on the pale grey velvet sofa that exactly matched the one opposite. In between was an antiqued mirrored coffee table that bore nothing but the occasional fingerprint. She spent most of her life polishing them off, and didn't want to think about the day when Maud began to cruise around the furniture.

She put the copy of the Riley in the middle of the table. It was the perfect book to have on display. She admired the black and white graphic on the front cover. She itched to take off the wrapping and look inside, to feast on the images and imagine herself to be one of his models.

Before she had a chance to remove the wrapping, she heard Bill come in the front door. He'd been to the garden centre, to get some posts and some wire for some fruit trees he was planning to espalier in the garden. It was a serious business, espaliering. She wasn't entirely sure what it was . . .

She jumped up and grabbed the book. She slid it under the cushions of the sofa just as Bill came in.

'Hey!' She smiled at him, trying her best not to look like a thieving lunatic. 'How are you? Me and Maud have had a lovely morning.'

'Good.'

'We bought a book. Didn't we, darling?' But Maud was still fast asleep, the book on her lap.

'Great.'

'How about you?'

'I bought a chainsaw.'

'How much was that?'

'Does it matter?'

'No. Of course not.'

'Good. Because we need one. I'm going to hack that old pear tree by the back gate down. It's blocking the light into the kitchen.'

‘Great. We can have a gorgeous pile of logs. Make sure you chop them up evenly, so we can stack them by the fire.’ She held her hands eight inches apart. ‘About this long would be perfect.’

Even as she said it, she knew she sounded like a control freak.

Bill looked at her. ‘Does everything have to be a fucking design statement?’

Bea opened her mouth to reply, but couldn’t think of a good answer. She was puzzled, though. It wasn’t like Bill to be so grumpy. What on earth was eating him?

She had to take the book back. She couldn’t live with herself otherwise. She would confess all to the girl in the book shop. That was the only way to shock herself back to normality.

Eleven

After a busy week, Emilia was looking forward to her first rehearsal that Sunday with the Peasebrook Quartet, although she was nervous too. It had taken hours of practice for her to get just one piece of music fit for human consumption. She knew she would have to get up to speed on dozens of new pieces, and she was terrible at sight-reading: it had always been her weakness. No doubt she would know some of the music, but there would be plenty that was new to her, and she was terrified of letting the side down.

Marlowe had been round earlier in the week, to drop off some sheet music. She had been surprised at how pleased she was to see him – there was something reassuring about his presence. He hadn't stopped, though. He'd been in a hurry to get somewhere else.

'Work your way through this lot. Practise as much as you can. We can iron out everything at the rehearsal, so don't get into a panic. We've got loads of time.'

Emilia tried to be reassured, and went through as much of the music as she could in the evenings. She was pleased no one could hear her as she stumbled through, and when Sunday came she wasn't sure if she'd done the right thing, agreeing. She wasn't nearly as confident in her ability as Marlowe seemed to be.

They were rehearsing in the old church hall at the back of

St Nick's. She walked down with Julius's cello on her back, not sure whether she was relieved to have something completely different from the book shop to focus her energy on, or whether she should be catching up on all the things she didn't get a chance to do when the shop was open. Dave had jumped at the chance to man the shop on Sundays for the interim: she'd left him in sole charge, with instructions to phone if it got too hectic.

They'd been really busy. Autumn seemed to bring with it a hunkering down feeling that drew people back to reading, and the town was filled with people indulging in a weekend break in the countryside. With its Cotswold charm and inviting inns and welcoming shops, Peasebrook wore the colder months well and had become quite a hotspot and Emilia and her team were working hard to raise the shop's profile. Dave had started them a Facebook page and a Twitter account; she'd been talking to several reps about supplementary merchandise; June was starting a monthly book club sponsored by the local wine merchants: for ten pounds you would get a copy of whichever paperback was going to be discussed over two glasses of specially chosen wine.

Of course, the main issue was cash flow. Andrea was still uncovering the extent of the shop's debts, they were waiting for probate, and in the meantime, the bills and the staff still needed to be paid. There was no shortage of ideas for making Nightingale Books the best book shop in the world, but to do that Emilia needed money. And there were plenty of boring things that needed to be done before the exciting things: the computer system badly needed updating; security was non-existent, and the roof was only held on by a wing and a prayer. The autumn winds were gathering strength and Emilia fully expected to find it no longer there one morning, the contents of the attic exposed for all to see.

In the church hall, four chairs were laid out in a semi-circle in front of four music stands. There was much discussion as to the best seating order, but in the end Marlowe dictated that Emilia and he were best at either end, so that she could see him and vice versa.

Any nerves Emilia had were doubled the moment she saw Delphine. Emilia knew the viola player, Petra, from old, but she had never got to know Delphine properly; only by repute from what Julius had said. She was wearing PVC drainpipes, brothel creepers and a frilly white blouse. She had Paris written all over her, with her asymmetric bob and red lips. Emilia felt dowdy in her jeans and hoody with her hair in plaits.

'Do you two know each other?' Marlowe asked, his casual tone not giving anything away.

'Hello,' said Emilia, feeling a nasty burning sensation in the pit of her stomach. 'Thank you so much for playing at the memorial. It meant a lot.'

'We miss your father very much,' said Delphine. 'He was a beautiful player.'

Emilia immediately felt under pressure to be as good as her father, which she knew she wasn't.

She panicked even more when she heard Delphine play. She picked up her violin and played a snippet of Vivaldi's 'Autumn', in honour of the leaves turning to orange outside the window and the fact the sun had had little warmth in it that day.

It was the musical equivalent of a sketch. The bow barely touched the strings, just danced over them, picking out the few notes she wanted to give an approximation of the piece. The notes were pure and perfect and stunning in their simplicity. Delphine was a player at the top of her game.

Was she showing off? Or did she just feel the need to send Emilia a warning shot? A message to her that said you can never be as good as me, as long as you live, as often as you practise.

She finished the piece with a flourish. Petra clapped in delight.

Emilia knew she would look churlish if she didn't join in. Her face ached as she smiled. Delphine gave a tiny self-deprecating shake of her head and a shrug as if to say 'it was nothing'. But Emilia knew she knew how good she was.

And then she sauntered over to Marlowe and slid a hand around his neck, stroking the back of it with her thumb. Marlowe was busy tightening his bow and didn't react, but it was such a familiar gesture, Emilia was left in no doubt: of course they were going out. She could imagine them having sex. French sex. French sex where Delphine was on top with her head thrown back and her eyes half-shut but her lipstick still perfect. Delphine was Juliette Binoche, Béatrice Dalle and Audrey Tautou rolled into one, and a musical prodigy to boot.

That answered that query, then. They were an item. Why did she feel disappointed?

She snapped the locks shut on her cello case and stood up.

She was surprised how unsettled she felt.

Marlowe came over as she took out her cello and pulled out the spike.

'I hope you're not too nervous.'

'No! Well, yes.'

'You'll be fine. We're concentrating on the wedding music for the first half, then we'll start looking at some carols.'

'I should know most of them.' Emilia suddenly felt less daunted. She had spent her school years in the orchestra, after all.

She took her seat and began to tune her cello, pulling the bow across the A string. It sounded discordant and ugly, badly out of tune. It sounded how she felt. Swiftly, she adjusted the pegs until the note rang true.

And then they were off. They were starting with the 'Arrival of the Queen of Sheba', the music Alice Basildon had chosen for her wedding entrance. It was a joyous and upbeat piece of music that Emilia loved, but it was extremely fast and extremely fiddly.

She played atrociously. Her fingers felt stiff and unyielding. Her mind couldn't concentrate. She missed the dynamics. She lost her place. She forgot what key signature they were in and played several wrong notes. And because there were only four of them playing, she couldn't hide behind the others. It made the piece sound dreadful.

Eventually Marlowe stopped.

'Shall we go back to bar twenty-four?' he asked. He didn't look at her or say anything else, which made it worse.

Red with humiliation, Emilia took in a deep breath and studied the sheet music again. Petra gave her an encouraging smile and she felt as if she had one ally, at least. Marlowe raised his eyebrows and gave the signal to start again. She concentrated with all her might, but it was a huge effort. Nothing came naturally. She was playing like a robot, programmed to follow the black marks on the page, not feeling it with her heart or in her soul.

All the time, she was keenly aware of Delphine taking note of every tiny mistake she made. She wanted to throw down her cello and tell her to bugger off. She had never felt so threatened, and it was a horrible feeling.

At last, thank goodness, they got to the end.

'Well done, everybody,' was all Marlowe said.

Emilia kept her head low. She felt as if she had let everyone down. Her eyes felt peppery with unshed tears, but she wasn't going to let them out. Not with Delphine gloating in the corner. There was no point in apologising or drawing attention to herself. They all knew. She would just have to do better next time.

'Let's try the Pachelbel,' Marlowe said, and they shuffled through their sheet music until they found the right piece and put it on their respective stands. Emilia felt relieved. She knew this piece well, and could play it blindfold; she could make up for her earlier debacle and prove herself to Delphine.

Afterwards, Marlowe gave her a nod and a smile that said she had redeemed herself. Just.

'Are you coming to the Cardamom Pod?' he asked. 'It's where we always go after Sunday rehearsals.'

Emilia wasn't sure if she could face it. Having to be polite to Delphine, and feeling self-conscious about her lacklustre performance.

'I've got paperwork,' she lied. 'Mounds of it. The accountant will shoot me if I don't get it in to her tomorrow.'

There was a flurry of protest but Emilia didn't miss the flash of triumph in Delphine's eye. And suddenly she wondered why she should be made to feel bad when she had done her best, and been thrown in at the deep end.

'But why not?' she said. 'I've got to eat, after all.'

She lifted up her cello and hoisted it onto her back with a bright smile.

'Excellent,' said Marlowe.

The Cardamom Pod was housed in one of Peasebrook's oldest buildings, with wonky floors and low ceilings, but it felt funky and modern, with the walls painted a hot dusty pink and the beams whitewashed. It smelled exotic: of warm spices, and Emilia swooned as her mouth began to water, realising that she had been existing on sandwiches and muffins from The Icing on the Cake. She was too tired to cook properly for herself. They ordered bottles of Indian lager and dunked poppadoms into the Cardamom Pod's home-made mango chutney while they chose their food.

'Your father always ordered for us,' said Marlowe. 'He made

us be adventurous. And he always had the hottest dish he could stand.'

'He loved Indian food,' said Emilia, gazing at the menu.

'I think we should propose a toast.' Marlowe raised his glass. 'To welcome you to the Peasebrook Quartet. I know how proud Julius would be.'

Even though she'd played abysmally, thought Emilia, but she didn't say it, because it was ungracious.

'I hope I can live up to him,' she said, raising her glass too. 'I don't think I made a very good start.'

'Two hours' practice a day, remember.' Marlowe gave her a playful stern stare. 'I'll be on to you.'

'Marlowe is terribly strict,' murmured Delphine, ladling as much innuendo into the statement as she could.

Inwardly, Emilia rolled her eyes – she'd got the message – but smiled as brightly as she could as she raised her glass and chinked it against the others'.

Twelve

On Monday morning, when Bill had safely gone off to work and before she could think twice, Bea stuffed Maud into her pushchair and walked into Peasebrook, marching up the high street until she reached the bridge by Nightingale Books. The sign outside was swinging gently in the autumn breeze. Through the bulging bay window, she could see Emilia talking to a customer.

A sign on the door, written in beautiful copperplate writing, said: *Open Monday Till Saturday 10ish until the last customer goes.* Bea smiled, pushed open the door with her bum, dragging the pushchair inside, then waited until the shop was empty. The great thing about a book shop was nobody thought it was odd if you lingered for ages. That was what you were supposed to do after all. So she hovered between the cookery and the art section, all the while keeping an eye on the other customers, until the last one drifted out of the door and there was her opportunity.

She walked up to the till before she could change her mind, and laid the book on the counter.

'I need to bring this back to you.'

Emilia looked up and recognised her.

'Oh! You bought *To the Moon and Back.*' She frowned. 'I didn't realise you'd bought a Riley.'

Bea looked down at the floor.

'I didn't.' She paused. 'I nicked it.'

Emilia looked from the book to Bea and back.

'Nicked it?'

Bea nodded. She took in a deep breath.

'I don't know why. I had a really weird moment. I don't know what came over me. It's not even as if I couldn't afford it. Not really. Not if I'd really wanted it.' She looked at Emilia, bewildered. 'I'm so, so sorry. I had to tell you. To stop myself ever doing anything like that again.'

'I don't know what to say.' Emilia managed an uncertain laugh. 'Except I probably wouldn't have noticed. You could have got away with it.'

'But I didn't want to get away with it. I had to bring it back. To scare myself. I sort of wonder if I might be going mad. It's such a stupid thing to do.' She gave Emilia a smile, half rueful, half scared. 'If you want to have me arrested, then so be it. I deserve it.'

'Of course I won't. You brought it back. That's not the behaviour of a repeat offender.'

'It's the behaviour of someone who needs help. Don't you think?'

'I don't know.'

'Thank you for being so understanding.' Bea thought she might cry. 'I just don't feel like myself any more. Shit. I'm sorry. I'm going to cry. No, I'm not.'

She gave a snort and a gulp, a half laugh, half sob, then pulled herself together.

'Are you OK?' Emilia was intrigued, but concerned.

Bea gripped the handles of the pushchair. She was struggling to speak.

'I thought I was. But maybe I'm not. It's been tough. This whole... motherhood thing. This whole... not having a job thing. This whole moving to the countryside to live the dream.' She was getting more worked up. 'This whole . . . not having anything to do all day thing. Except, you know, mash up carrots and change nappies.' She looked down at Maud in her pushchair. Maud beamed up at her. 'Not that I don't utterly adore Maud. Of course I do.'

'I can't imagine what it's like,' said Emilia. 'I suppose one day I'll find out.'

'It's lovely. But it's . . .' Bea took in a gulp of air. 'I'm not allowed to say it.'

'Boring?' offered Emilia.

'Yes! And of course, it's the most important job in the world blah blah blah and I should be grateful, because I've got friends – more than one – who've been trying for ages and had no luck. But—' She stared at Emilia. She shook her head in disbelief. 'Oh my God. I didn't come in here to dump on you. I'm sorry. I don't know what's the matter with me. I don't really know anyone in this town. And you look . . . nice. Like you might get it.'

Emilia didn't know what to say. 'Thank you. I think.' She put her hands on the book. 'I'll put this back on the pile and we won't say anything more about it.'

'Who nicks stuff from a book shop? That is just so wrong.'

Emilia pointed a warning finger at her. 'We're not saying anything more about it. Remember?'

Bea stood up straight and nodded obediently. 'Thank you. For being so understanding. How's it all going, anyway?'

'I'm panicking a bit, to be honest.'

'Why? I'd have thought this would be the least stressful job in the world.' Bea looked around the shop. 'I'd love to spend every day here.'

'Yeah, but it's losing money hand over fist.'

'What with people nicking stuff and all. That can't help.'

The two girls laughed.

'So what did you used to do? Before the little one?' asked Emilia.

'I was an art director. For *Hearth* magazine?'

'Oh wow. I love *Hearth*. It's how I want my life to be.'

'That's exactly why they sell so many copies.'

Studying Bea, Emilia thought she looked just like the poster girl for *Hearth*. Beautiful and on trend with all the latest accessories and the perfect baby. And she must be smart. *Hearth* was one of the bestselling women's lifestyle magazines, dictating what any modern woman with even a hint of style should be putting on her wall or on her plate or in her plant pots, leading the zeitgeist in interior design and food and gardening. But clearly something was not right.

Bea shrugged her shoulders. 'Anyway, I've brought the book back and I promise I won't darken your doors again.'

'Don't be silly.' Emilia felt drawn to Bea and her self-deprecating honesty. 'And actually, you might be able to help me.'

'Help you?'

Emilia grinned. 'Yes. It could be your punishment. You can give me some advice.'

'Advice on what?'

'I need to turn this place round. Make it appeal to a wider customer base. But I haven't a clue where to start. Oh, and the kicker is – I don't really have any money to do it. Maybe you could give me some ideas?'

Bea put one hand on her hip. She grinned.

'And in return you won't have me banged up?'

'Something like that.'

Bea looked around her thoughtful. 'I love it in here. The shop's got great atmosphere. It's really warm and welcoming. But it is kind of...'

She screwed up her face.

'Dickensian? Out of the ark?' offered Emilia.

'Not out of the ark. I like that it's old-fashioned. But you could make more of it. Keep the spirit, but open it up a bit. Lighten it. Create some little sets, maybe – you know, dress it up? And that mezzanine?' She pointed upwards. 'That is totally wasted on boring old history and maps. Does anyone ever really go up there?'

Emilia looked up. 'Sometimes. My father used to. He keeps his special editions locked in a glass case. But you're right. It's wasted space, really.'

'Maud goes to nursery two mornings. What if I come back and measure up. Take some photos. Then draw you out some ideas.' She frowned. 'What is your budget, exactly?'

Emilia made a face. 'Um – I don't really have one. But I suppose it will be an investment. I can use my credit card.'

Bea put her hands over her ears. 'Don't let me hear the word credit card. Don't worry – I'm used to creating magic out of muck. The great thing is you have lovely architectural features. Like a woman with good bone structure. You can't go too far wrong.' She smiled. 'I know all the tricks. And I've got great contacts. I can get you all sorts of things at trade prices. Lighting.' She looked up at the ceiling. The red velvet lampshades were dusty and she could definitely see cobwebs. 'And paint.' She looked at the floor, at the old red carpet, almost worn through in places. 'And carpets.'

Emilia looked amazed. Bea seemed to have blossomed and flourished right in front of her eyes.

Bea stopped mid flow.

'Sorry. I don't mean to be rude.'

'You're not! It's good to have an objective eye. I've lived with this shop for so long I don't notice that it's a bit old and tired.'

'We won't throw away the spirit of the place. That's vital. The ambience in here is what makes it special. But look – the old fireplace, for example. You should be using that as a feature. It would be wonderful opened up, with a squashy armchair next to it so people could read.'

Emilia stared at the fireplace, which had been bricked up.

'If you get cold feet, and start thinking what on earth am I doing asking that crazy girl to help me, just say. I won't be offended. Or surprised.'

'No. Weirdly, I feel as if this could really work.'

'Window displays,' said Bea with a sigh, looking over at the windows on either side of the door. 'Those windows are just waiting for stories to be told! Can you imagine? Valentine's Day, filled with love stories? Or ghost stories, at Halloween? As for Christmas . . .'

Bea clapped her hands in excitement.

Emilia thought Bea was possibly a little bit mad. But she didn't care. Bea's enthusiasm had lifted the fug of the past few weeks and given her life. She had felt weighed down since her meeting with Andrea, not sure what to address first. It was exciting to hear someone brimming with enthusiasm. For the first time since her father had died, she felt a glimmer of hope.

She told June about her encounter with Bea later that afternoon.

'I feel as if things are falling into place. I've got a vision of what the shop could be like. I know I mustn't get carried away because I can't afford to wave a magic wand and have it how I want it, but at least I don't feel so overwhelmed.'

'I think once you start making changes, things *will* fall into place,' agreed June. 'In the meantime, what do you think about this?'

Emilia looked at the press release June handed her.

There were months of them, piled up under the counter. Endless missives from publicists wanting their book to be given pride of place. Julius never read them, because he wanted to make up his own mind about which books to give preference. He had a brilliant instinct for what would sell well, and he hated gimmicks and hype.

Emilia knew, however, that if she was going to increase Nightingale Books' profit by any significant margin that she had to raise her game. She needed publicity and a raise in profile as much as the authors and publishers of the books she was selling. So why not use them?

Two blue eyes were staring at her from the middle of the blurb. Mick Gillespie. Even a photocopy of him at seventy years old still had it. His expression made you feel as if you were the centre of his universe. Emilia wondered what it was like to be under his gaze in real life.

He was doing a pre-Christmas book tour to promote his no-holds-barred autobiography, which promised any number of secrets and scandals and behind-the-scenes indiscretion. He would give a talk, answer questions, sign books. Not that he needed to do anything, Emilia thought. He just needed to breathe.

Mick Gillespie was the perfect person to kick off her new campaign. No one was immune to his charms. Men and women young and old would be intrigued. She imagined the shop bursting at the seams, the queue snaking out of the door. He was a legend. An icon. As cool as Steve McQueen and James Dean and Richard Burton all rolled into one. Handsome and devil-may-care and charismatic.

'June – that is a genius idea.'

'I knew him once,' admitted June, with a twinkle in her eye.

'No way!'

'Yeah. I was an extra on one of his films. For my sins.'

'An extra? I didn't know you were an extra.'

'Not for long. I was no good at it.'

'But you met Mick Gillespie? It must have been in his heyday.'

June nodded. 'Yes . . .'

'What was he like?'

'Absolutely out of this world. Unforgettable. Magical.'

'Do you think you can pull strings?'

June laughed. 'No. Absolutely definitely not. There's no way he'd remember me. I played a barmaid. If I'd been an *actual* barmaid he might have paid me more attention.'

Mick Gillespie's love for the drink was legendary.

'Well. Nothing ventured,' said Emilia. 'This would bring everybody to the shop. We'd be in the papers and everything.'

She picked up the phone to his publicist. He was probably fully committed already. No book shop in the country was going to pass up this opportunity.

Luck was on her side. Peasebrook would fit neatly in between Mick's current commitments.

'It'll be a chance for him to have a little rest. We've given him the next day off, so where better to spend it than in the Cotswolds?' the publicist said.

Emilia grinned to herself as she hung up the phone.

'Nightingale Books is added to the tour. Mick Gillespie is coming here, to Peasebrook.'

'Goodness!' June looked rather taken aback.

'I think we should get Thomasina to do the food,' Emilia went on. 'An Irish theme. She gave me a card the other day in case I needed any catering. What do you think?'

June was away with the fairies.

'Stop daydreaming, would you?' Emilia teased. 'What drinks should we serve?'

'I'd keep him well away from the drink if I were you,' said June darkly.

'But he must be getting on a bit.' Emilia looked at his picture. 'And they wouldn't let him out on tour if he was trouble.'

'Careful who you're calling old,' teased June. 'He's not much older than I am.'

'Well, we all know you don't look your age.' Emilia gave June a hug. She was so grateful for the older woman's advice and help. She almost felt like a maternal presence, something Emilia had never had, or, to be honest, felt the need for. But with her father gone, June's presence was comforting, and she thought perhaps she didn't appreciate her enough.

She was only too aware how important the people in this town had become to her in such a short space of time. Without their support, she'd have thrown in the towel weeks ago.

'Mick Gillespie,' she sighed, looking at the press release again.

By four thirty in the afternoon, there was just one man in the shop. It was getting dark outside and he was hovering, looking uncertain. This wasn't unusual. Emilia found people were either totally at home in a book shop, or felt a little out of place. He had a dog with him, a shaggy lurcher who looked as awkward and out of place as his owner.

Dogs were a good icebreaker.

'Hi.' She walked over in a friendly but unobtrusive manner, holding a book in one hand so she looked as if she was on her way to put it somewhere rather than accosting him. 'Look at you. You're a lovely boy, aren't you?'

'Thanks,' joked the man, and Emilia laughed, bending down to rough up the dog's ears.

'What's his name?'

'Wolfie.'

'Hey, Wolfie.' She looked up at the bloke. 'Were you looking for something in particular, or are you just browsing?'

He grinned at her and gave a little shrug of his shoulders. She could tell he was on unfamiliar territory. People unused to book shops had an awkwardness about them. An apologetic awkwardness.

'It's a bit . . .' He trailed off as she searched for the word. 'Embarrassing.'

'Oh.' She tried to sound reassuring. 'I'm sure it's not. I'll help if I can.'

She watched him move his weight from one foot to the other. He was cute, she thought. Faded jeans and a white T-shirt with a soft red plaid shirt undone over the top. His hair was dark and scruffy and he had a six o'clock shadow, but both of these things were by design rather than neglect: she could smell baby shampoo and something else more manly.

'Don't tell me – your girlfriend's sent you in for *Fifty Shades of Grey*,' she grinned. On impulse, because her mind had suddenly gone that way.

He looked startled. 'God, no.'

'Sorry. Only you wouldn't believe how many women send their boyfriends in for it. Or how many men think they might spice things up a bit.'

'No. It's even more embarrassing than that.' He scratched his head and raised his eyebrows, looking sheepish. 'The thing is, my little boy asked me the other day what my favourite book was. It was for his homework. And I realised – I've never read one. I've never read a book.'

He looked at the floor. It was as if he was waiting for a punishment.

'Never?'

He shook his head. 'No. Books and me just don't get on. The few times I've opened one I just glaze over.'

He made a glazed-over face and Emilia laughed. Then stopped.

'Sorry. I'm not laughing *at* you.'

'No, I know. It's OK. Anyway, I've decided. I'm a really bad example to him. I want my son to get on and do really well. And I don't want to die, never having read a book. So I want to start reading with him. So I can encourage him. But I don't know where to start. There're bloody millions of them. How do you start to choose?'

He looked round at all the shelves, baffled.

'Well. I can sort you out with something, I'm sure,' said Emilia. 'How old is he, for a start? And what sort of thing do you think he might like?'

'He's five, nearly six. And I don't really know what he'd like. Something short, preferably.' He laughed, self-conscious. 'And easy. I mean, I can read, obviously. I'm not that thick.'

'Not reading doesn't make you thick.'

'No. But his mum's going on at me for not getting involved with his homework.' He looked sheepish. 'She likes any chance to have a go. I'm not with her any more.'

'Oh,' said Emilia. 'I'm sorry.'

'Don't be. It's a good thing. Mostly.' He ruffled his hair, looking awkward. 'But I just want to show her I'm not as rubbish as she seems to think I am.'

'Well, let me see what I can come up with. Give me a couple of minutes.'

Emilia walked slowly up and down the children's bookshelves, turning over possibilities in her mind. Every now and then she would stop, pluck out a book, study it, then put it back. She wasn't sure she had ever met anyone who had never read a book before. Which made the choice even more difficult. She was determined not to put him and his son off for life. She had to hook them in. And she didn't want to patronise him. He might not be a reader, but he clearly had a lively mind. She mustn't judge.

'What's his name? Your son?'

'Finn.' The bloke smiled proudly.

'Ah,' said Emilia. 'That makes the task a whole lot easier.'

She picked out a book, and walked back over to her new customer, who looked at her with an eager curiosity.

She laid it on the counter in front of him.

'This is one of my absolute favourites of all time. *Finn Family Moomintroll.*'

'Yeah?' He picked the book up and eyed it warily.

'I think you'll both like it. It's a bit mad, but it's cool.' She paused. 'It's a bit quirky. It's about this family of Moomintrolls who live in a valley, and all their crazy friends.'

'Moomintrolls?'

'They're kind of big, white creatures who hibernate in the winter.'

He turned the book over to read the back, not saying anything.

'Honestly, it's really cute. I'll give you your money back if you don't like it.'

'Really?'

'As long as you don't spill your tea on it.'

'I promise.'

She slid the book into a blue paper bag with Nightingale Books emblazoned on it. He gave her a tenner and she gave him his change.

'I'll let you know how I get on.' He lifted the bag with a smile. 'Cheers.'

Emilia watched him go. She wondered if she would ever see him again. She thought she'd probably flirted with him a little bit. It was wrong, really, to flirt with customers, but she didn't care. She'd had a tough time lately. At least this proved she was still alive. And it took away the sting of Delphine's hostility the evening before, and her proprietorial attitude towards Marlowe – as if Emilia had been a threat. Which she absolutely wasn't.

As the door shut behind her newest customer, she felt a tiny thrill, and hoped he'd read the book and fall in love with reading. That was the whole point about Nightingale Books. It cast a spell over its customers by introducing them to the magic. And how wonderful, for her to open up a whole new world—

She realised she was being utterly ridiculous. She was romanticising. This wasn't some Hollywood movie where she unwittingly changed someone's life. Get real, Emilia, she told herself. He's had a bit of a row with his ex and he's trying to prove himself. He probably won't even open the bloody book. And he definitely won't come back.

Jackson walked along the road with the book tucked under his arm. That had been easier than he thought. He was a good actor. At school, acting was about the only thing he'd been good at, but because he'd been so naughty they hadn't let him have the lead roles in the annual play. The plum parts always went to the swots. Which was one of the reasons Jackson had hated school so much. It wasn't fair, how it was run. You couldn't be good at everything. And why were you punished for not being clever?

Actually, going into the book shop hadn't been as daunting as he thought. Emilia had been really helpful, and hadn't laughed at his desire to read to his son, or his admission that he'd never read a book. She'd been really sweet and hadn't made him feel like an idiot at all. In fact, he was positively looking forward to reading it. Moomintrolls.

He didn't want to think about the real reason for going in there. The fact that he was supposed to be charming the pants off Emilia Nightingale in order to get her to sell up. Although he thought it was going to be easy. She'd definitely flirted with him. It was impossible not to flirt with Jackson, unless you'd been officially pronounced dead. Even men flirted with him. Straight men. It never got him anywhere, though.

But he had to keep Ian Mendip happy. For the time being anyway. Else he'd be out of a job.

He knocked on the door. Finn answered and barrelled into him.

'Dad! It's not your day, is it?'

Jackson usually had Finn on a Sunday, but he didn't see why he couldn't see him every day if he wanted to.

Finn knelt down and started hugging Wolfie.

Mia appeared, looking wary.

He held up the book.

'I thought I'd come and read to Finn.'

'Read?' She looked very dubious.

'Yeah. It's important. Reading to your kids.'

'It is. Yes. You don't have to tell me that.'

She watched him as he came in. He flopped down on the sofa. He remembered them going to choose it, from the big out-of-town retail park. Five years' interest-free credit. That was another thing he was still paying off. So he might as well get some use out of it.

'Come here, buddy.' Finn was still small enough to sit on his lap. 'I got this crazy book. *Finn Family Moomintroll.*'

Wolfie muscled his way in too. Jackson trapped him between his legs so he didn't jump up on the sofa. He suspected Mia wouldn't approve.

He cracked open the spine and began to read.

He was astonished to find that both he and Finn were soon under the spell of the Moomins and their funny little world. He read two chapters. Three.

'Shall we stop there? Carry on tomorrow?'

'No,' said Finn. 'I want to know what happens.'

Mia was standing in the doorway, watching them. She almost had a smile on her face. Almost. To Jackson's surprise, she came over and sat on the sofa next to him. She reached out for the book and had a look at the cover.

'Looks to me like the Moomins have BMI issues,' she said.

Jackson looked at her. If anyone had BMI issues, it was Mia. She'd lost even more weight. There was nothing of her. But he didn't mention it.

He pulled Finn closer in to him and carried on reading.

While she was cooking a sage and butternut squash risotto, Bea outlined the afternoon's events to Bill, omitting the bit about taking back a stolen book, obviously. Just telling him she was going to do some plans for Nightingale Books.

Bill frowned. 'What's the point of that?'

'I owe her a favour.'

'What favour?'

Bea didn't have a clue what to tell him. She could hardly tell him the truth. She wished she'd never started the conversation. She concentrated on pouring the stock onto the rice while she thought of a suitable reply.

'Maud had a meltdown in her shop. She was really kind to her.'

'That's not like Maud.'

Bea felt awful, blaming her gorgeous daughter who rarely had tantrums.

'She was a bit tired and hungry. Emilia gave her a biscuit.'

'A set of plans in return for a biscuit?'

Bea frowned at him. 'Look, I want to do it. OK? It's nice to use my brain.'

She felt unsettled. It wasn't like Bill to be so ungenerous.

Did he feel left out? She had read somewhere – not in *Hearth*, because in *Hearth* life wasn't allowed to be anything less than perfect – that men could get jealous of new babies, and resent the attention their partners lavished on the newborns. But if anything, Bill was the one who lavished attention on Maud. He spoiled her far more than Bea did.

Maybe he was just tired.

'Shall I see if I can get a babysitter for tomorrow?' she asked. 'We could try one of the new restaurants in Peasebrook? It would be nice to have a night out.'

Bill poked at something on his iPad. 'Nah. Let's stay in. I don't want a hangover midweek.'

They could never go out for dinner without demolishing a bottle of wine each. For some reason they were never as profligate at home. Bea supposed it was because if they started drinking like that in their own kitchen they would be heading for rehab in a month.

Unless guests came, of course. Then the bottle count was shameless. But they hadn't had so many people to stay lately.

Maybe Bill was lacking stimulating company. Guests were hard work but it was always fun, and now Maud wasn't getting up quite so horrifically early, it would be easier.

'Shall we ask the Morrisons down for the weekend?' she asked. 'Or Sue and Tony? We've been a bit unsociable lately.'

Bill gave a sigh. 'It's non-stop washing up and sheet changing.'

'Not really. Everyone gives a hand.' And he never did the laundry. It was Bea who stripped the beds, washed the linen and sprayed it with lavender water before ironing.

He didn't answer.

Bea frowned.

Maybe he was bored. Maybe he was missing their London life? And the London her? Maybe stay-at-home-in-Peasebrook Bea was too dull for him? She was back into her jeans and was carrying hardly any baby weight, but she knew they didn't have sex as often as they used. And certainly never those up-against-the-wall sessions they used to have when they first met when the need for each other overcame them. They were both exhibitionists. Both admitted the thrill of possibly being seen or caught turned them on.

But somehow, what seemed OK in a London alley didn't seem appropriate in conservative Peasebrook. There would be consequences to being caught. A city was anonymous. Here in a small provincial town, wanton behaviour would be frowned upon. She could imagine the gossip already.

Still, Bea was never one to resist a challenge. When they went upstairs to bed, she rummaged in her underwear drawer and took out her best Coco de Mer satin bra and knickers, pulled her Louboutins out of the cupboard, and slipped into the bathroom to get changed. She put on red lipstick, backcombed her hair slightly, and slid into her femme fatale combo.

She sashayed into the bedroom and stood in the doorway, hands on her hips, with a wicked smile.

'Oi!' she said. Bill was lying under the covers, eyes closed.

'Oi!' she said, louder.

She thought she saw his eyelids flicker. She frowned. She walked over to the bed, picked up his hand and put it between her legs, letting his fingers feel the warmth of the silk.

He rolled over, mumbling, and pulled his hand away.

Her mouth dropped open. Never, in all the time she had known him, had Bill turned down an opportunity. She sat down on the bed, looking down at the bright red shoes with the pencil-thin heels and the spaghetti-thin ankle straps, thinking how many times he'd watched her in them, eyes laughing as she walked towards him.

She didn't know whether to be cross or hurt or puzzled.

Thirteen

June had taken the press release about Mick Gillespie home. She poured herself a glass of cool Viognier and sat at the kitchen table to look at it.

His thick hair was now white and cropped close to his head. Those infamous slate blue eyes had no doubt been hand-tinted to enhance that hypnotic gaze. His face was carefully airbrushed to emphasise his bone structure, with just a few judicious laughter lines left, because it would be silly to pretend he was wrinkle-free at his age – whatever that was exactly, but older than her, certainly. He'd kept his exact age shrouded in mystery for so long, but now, it seemed, his venerable years were a useful marketing tool rather than something to be hidden. An opportunity to monetise his dotage.

His autobiography had been much heralded in the press. There would be countless television and radio appearances, for despite his advancing years, Mick (or Michael, as everyone now called him) was good airtime. He was guaranteed to make an outrageous remark or drop a piece of juicy gossip. His lawyers were always on standby, but he was clever. Hints and innuendoes hadn't landed him in court yet, largely because what he claimed was grounded in truth. The lilting accent had long gone, replaced by a RADA/Hollywood hybrid delivered with mellifluous perfection and just the merest hint of Kerry.

His voice was famous: from a whisper to a mighty roar, it was instantly recognisable.

His book promised a searing exposé of his entire career, complete with every dalliance and indiscretion he'd ever had. The lawyers had been through it with a fine-tooth comb and it was said there were many women waiting in trepidation for its release. It was destined to fly off the shelves, for not only were its contents shocking but it was remarkably well written. Witty and observant and colourful. The rumour was he hadn't employed a ghostwriter, but had been responsible for every single word himself.

June didn't doubt it. He'd always had the gift of the gab. She imagined him in his Hampstead conservatory – the go-to resting ground for luvvies – scrawling out his bon mots while a discreet assistant brought him coffee, then wine, then brandy later in the day.

June reflected that if he wrote as well as he talked, if he painted pictures as pretty and convincing with his written as his spoken words, then he was a gifted writer indeed.

She put a hand to her heart to feel how fast it was beating. After all this time, he was coming to Peasebrook. To Nightingale Books.

Maybe she shouldn't have suggested it to Emilia. Nightingale Books was the place June felt happiest in the world. She'd had no hesitation about stepping in to help Julius when he started deteriorating, for she worshipped him, too. He had filled a void in her life. Not romantically at all, but intellectually. And socially. They'd often enjoyed a drink out or supper together or gone to concerts. He was her absolute dearest friend at a difficult time. Retirement had been tougher than she thought. She was a hugely successful businesswoman, and to go from schmoozing and wheeling and dealing to doing almost nothing had been a massive shock. And moving to the cottage that had been her weekend retreat had been strange. It took a long time for it to feel like a permanent home. She still sometimes felt as if she should be packing up on a Sunday night ready to drive back to London.

She loved her cottage, though. The wall-to-wall shelves, groaning with the tomes that had seen her through two failed marriages and several dodgy affairs. She read voraciously, and the cottage was perfect for that, whether tucked up in front of a log fire or sitting in the garden with a glass of wine. She scanned the bestseller lists, flagged up reviews in the newspapers, and every week she would pop into Nightingale Books for the latest biography or prize-winning novel.

She'd seen Mick Gillespie's book previewed in the *Sunday Times*. She simultaneously longed to and dreaded reading it.

She'd tried to forget him. Time had betrayed her. It hadn't been a great healer at all. It had made no difference. She had tried a million different distractions. Other men. Drink. Drugs, once or twice (it had been the sixties, after all). Charity work. Australia. Then, eventually, a kind of release. Two husbands. And motherhood. That had helped her heal. But her boys were off and gone, though they would be back eventually when they'd found wives and had children. The cottage would come into its own then.

The memories were still there, vivid. It had started as a dream come true: a silly competition, to become the 'legs' of an exciting new brand of tights – a necessity as hemlines grew shorter and shorter. Little June Agnew had won and convinced herself she was going to be propelled into a lucrative modelling career, hurled from oblivion in Twickenham to a giddy life of glamour. Through it she had got an agent, Milton, (who appeared from nowhere, but was extremely kind and helpful) who had changed her name from June to Juno and told her she was going to be a star.

With her white-blonde hair and huge eyes and skinny, endless legs, Juno was the queen of mini skirts and kinky boots and white plastic macs, all sugar-pink lipstick and spidery false lashes. There was money (to her it seemed a fortune, but now she knew that other people had been creaming it off and just giving her the bare minimum), a Chelsea flat-share, parties, cameras, late nights – and then a screen test. Everyone had gone into ecstasies. She was, it seemed, a natural. And she had to admit it came easy to her. She memorised the lines they gave her, and pretended. It seemed that was how easy acting was. She could sense Milton's excitement and the stakes getting higher. She was told to watch her weight and her behaviour, and had to have her hair done every morning before she left the flat.

Milton told her to be patient. The big jobs would come. But she had to do the small ones first. He got her a job on a sweepingly lush romantic film set on the west coast of Ireland, about a young girl who gets pregnant by the local aristocrat and wreaks her revenge. The script was by an acclaimed playwright and the director was renowned for savagely beautiful productions. Mick Gillespie was the star. Juno was to play the barmaid in the local pub. She had two lines.

Juno had devoured the script and loved it. She dreamed about the actress playing the heroine getting pneumonia, and them casting Juno, because they'd spotted her talent. The actress remained robustly healthy throughout. But Mick Gillespie noticed her. He noticed her all right.

In Ireland, she'd never known rain like it. It was there all the time. Yet it was soft. It was like having your skin kissed endlessly.

'Does it ever stop?' she asked him and he laughed.

'Not in my lifetime.'

And the smell. She loved the smell of the burning peat that

sharpened the damp. And the colours, smudgy and muted, everything in soft focus, as if you'd forgotten your glasses.

He lent her his cream Aran sweater. It swamped her, but in it she felt safe and loved and special. She wore it to the pub with jeans, her hair tousled and not a scrap of make-up, and they sat by the fire with glasses of Guinness and she thought she had never been happier. She wanted time to stop.

And then, on the last day, her dream was ripped apart. She had been so sure of *them* that it came as a huge shock. She had assumed they would carry on. There had been no indication this was temporary.

He was standing behind her on the cliff, his arms wrapped around her. She fitted just under his chin. The wind was buffeting at them, but he was strong and sure, so she didn't fear falling. Everything was grey: the clouds, the sky, the rocks. As grey as Donegal tweed, apart from the white-tipped waves, which were as skittish and playful as overfed horses, chasing each other into shore, kicking up their tails.

'Well,' said Mick. 'It's been fun, all right.'

'It has,' she replied, thinking he meant the shoot.

'Ah well.' His voice was tinged with regret; a fifth-glass-of-Guinness melancholy though he hadn't had his first yet.

'We can always come back another time.' She put her hands over his. 'Mrs Malone would always make us welcome, I'm sure.'

Mrs Malone was the landlady of the guest house they'd been billeted in.

She felt him tense as she leant further into him. Every muscle in his body.

'Darling,' he said, and she felt her heart plummet. 'There won't be another time. This is it.'

She whirled round to face him.

'What?'

He had a strange smile on his face. 'You must understand. You know the rules. Didn't anyone tell you, when you signed up for the film?'

'Tell me what?' She was confused.

'This is just a . . .' He searched for the words. He found one, but he could sense she wouldn't like it. 'You know.'

'A you know?'

He shrugged. 'Fling?'

She stepped back. He reached out to pull her back. They were very near the cliff edge.

'Fling.' She could barely say the word.

'You knew that!' His eyes were screwed up in consternation.

She shook her head.

'What did you think this was?'

She could hardly breathe. She took in gulps of air to quell her panic. She clutched her middle. It felt as if a surgeon had gone in with a knife and was cutting out her vital organs. No anaesthetic. The pain burned in her gullet.

'Darlin', darlin', darlin' . . .' He put a concerned hand on her shoulder. 'Come on, now.'

She flung his hand away. 'Get off.'

'There's no need for this. We've one last night. Let's make the most of it.'

She ran. She ran and ran and ran, through the rain, down the cliff, down to the road. They had one more scene to shoot but she didn't care. The whole film could go to hell.

She stumbled along the road. The mist was closing in, filling her lungs with its viscosity.

She pulled at his sweater as she ran, tugging it over her head, hurling it into the fuchsia bushes, until she was just in the long-sleeved vest she'd worn to stop it scratching. She'd left everything behind. Her purse. Nearly all her clothes.

She stopped at the crossroads, a crooked signpost giving her a choice.

A car drew up. It was the make-up girl.

'Get in, sweetheart.' Juno just hugged herself tighter. 'Come on! You're miles from anywhere and you'll catch your death. I'll take you back to my place.'

The girl made her retrieve the sweater from the bushes, then went to fetch Juno's things from her digs. She put Juno to sleep on her sofa with a spare blanket. Juno didn't sleep, but got up early to catch a bus to the airport where she got the first flight back to London so she didn't have to travel with the rest of them. She hid in her flat for days, until Milton came to dig her out. He'd got the whole sorry story from someone else on the shoot. She was mortified, humiliated and swore she would never leave the flat again.

She was gaunt and had lost her sparkle. She couldn't get the chill out of her bones from getting soaked when she ran away and she feared she would never feel warm again. Her fingers had chilblains, but the pain of them was nothing compared to the empty gnawing inside her.

She'd been living off the money from *The Silver Moon*. She'd been frugal but now there was nothing left. For a moment, panic overruled pain. But actually, she decided, she didn't care. She would starve to death in her flat. At least then the horrible feeling would go.

'Do you want my advice?' asked Milton. 'Go and do a secretarial course. Everyone needs a good typist. Even me. Actually, especially me. Go and learn typing and shorthand and I'll give you a job.'

She stared at him. She supposed he was being kind, but did he know what he was suggesting? One moment she was on a trajectory to stardom and had found love. Now she had come crashing down and her agent wanted her to be his typist?

She had no fight left in her to tell him what she thought. She should be screaming at him to get her back in the loop, to get her some auditions. But she could see her reflection in the mirror on the wall. Gone was the luminous bombshell with the glowing skin and the eyes filled with promise. In her place was a bag of bones, with lacklustre hair and a blank gaze. Who would employ her looking like this?

'And for heaven's sake,' added Milton. 'Eat something. In fact, come for lunch with me.'

He took her to a tiny Italian on the corner and filled her up with pasta and bread and creamy pudding.

She felt a little stronger when she finished. Starving was a miserable business. So miserable that she did as Milton suggested and signed up for a secretarial course. She was guaranteed employment at the end of six weeks, as long as she attended every lesson and practised every night. And she went back to being plain June Agnew.

She'd done all right for herself. She had gone back to work for Milton. She'd become his right-hand girl, and then realised that there were many Miltons who needed a right hand in the office to organise their lives, so she left him to set up her own agency, providing top-notch administrative staff and the agency had grown and grown. She'd retired three years ago, handing the reins over to two of her sons. She had plenty of money, plenty of friends, and was as happy as anyone had the right to be.

She had unfinished business though.

She looked back down at the press release and it hadn't changed. She could remember those eyes burning into her as if it were yesterday. She hadn't really entertained the thought that she might ever see him again. Of course, she might have passed him on a street in London, or spied him across a crowded restaurant one day. But he'd fallen right into her lap. She wouldn't sleep between then and now.

For heaven's sake, she told herself. You're not a skinny little wannabe actress any more, and he's an old man. Get over yourself.

Fourteen

It had taken Andrea a few weeks to plough through all the paperwork and get a clearer picture of the kind of shape Nightingale Books was in financially. Several more worms had crawled out of the can.

Emilia had unearthed a pile of pro-forma invoices that didn't seem to have been paid. They were from some of their main suppliers. She wouldn't be able to order any more books until she'd paid them.

Then a credit card bill had arrived with the morning post. She opened it and was horrified by the balance. There were no purchases for that month, of course, but neither had any minimum payments been made, because Emilia hadn't been aware of the card's existence. It hadn't been in Julius's wallet.

She searched through the piles of paperwork on the desk, and found two copies of previous bills in unopened envelopes. The withdrawals were all cash. The interest was compounding due to the lack of payments.

She phoned Andrea, who told her to bring the bills round straight away.

'That must have been what he'd been using to pay the wages,' Andrea sighed. 'This is one of those cards with six months nought per cent finance. He must have taken it out to cover his cash flow. But of course now the interest is going to kick in big time. I'll phone the company and put them in the picture. And I'll have to pass it on to your solicitor for the probate.'

'It's nearly four thousand pounds.'

Andrea sighed. 'It's easily done. He's not the first and he won't be the last.'

Emilia felt disconsolate. She was just getting her head around the existing debts and feeling she could manage.

'The debts are just getting bigger and bigger.'

'We can consolidate them.' Andrea tried to sound reassuring. 'Don't worry – you're sitting on a goldmine. You can take out a loan if you need to.'

'I suppose so. I'm just not used to such big sums of money.'

'I wish all my clients felt like that. Honestly, this is nothing in the grand scheme of things.'

'Easy for you to say.'

'I wouldn't say it if I didn't mean it.'

Andrea took Emilia off to the bank in the high street where Nightingale Books had had its account since the day Julius arrived in Peasebrook. There, they negotiated a generous overdraft facility with the bank manager.

'Now you don't have to worry about how to pay the wages.'

Emilia shuddered. 'I've never been in this kind of debt. I don't even go overdrawn usually.'

'It's good debt. It's debt you're investing in the business. It's not Louboutin debt.'

Emilia looked down at her battered old sneakers. 'No,' she said ruefully. She eyed Andrea's shoes – high and shiny and undeniably expensive.

Andrea grinned. 'I've earned them. It's my one indulgence. And there is some good news. Look – your takings are up, week on week this month. You must be doing something right. Not that your dad did anything wrong,' she added hastily. 'But it's obvious his eye wasn't on the ball.'

Emilia looked at the last couple of weeks' spreadsheets. Something *was* working. Dave had turned into a social media guru, tweeting book reviews and special offers, and they'd seen an upturn. They had opened the last few Sundays, and had done rather well. But the in still didn't cover the out.

'But the shop isn't making enough to cover its outgoings now, let alone a monthly payment if I take out a loan.'

'But you need to do that to grow the business. That's how it works.'

Emilia put her hand to her head. 'I understand it all in theory – of course I do. But it's making my head spin. It's the decisions; the *commitment*. The responsibility! Maybe I should just walk away.'

'Are you mad? Don't give up after all this.' Andrea checked herself. 'Sorry. I shouldn't try and influence you.'

Emilia looked at her.

'When I first came in, you said I shouldn't be sentimental.'

'I know.' Andrea gave a rueful shrug. 'But I was walking along the high street the other day. I went past the shop. I saw you in there and you looked as if you belonged there.' She laughed. 'Listen to me! I'm supposed to be Miss Ruthless and Pragmatic. Now *I'm* being all sentimental!'

Emilia sighed. 'I've just booked Mick Gillespie to come and do a book signing.'

Andrea's eyes gleamed behind her glasses. 'Mick Gillespie? Wow!'

'If I sell a hundred copies of his book, it still won't pay the electricity bill.'

'I know it's a big decision for you. It's down to you, Emilia. Whether you want to make Nightingale Books your life. Like your father.'

'I don't know yet. In my heart, of course I do. But in my head . . .'

Andrea gave her a kind smile. 'We can play for time. Let me see what I can do with the figures. I can find ways of offsetting some of the debt.'

'Bloody money,' said Emilia.

'Yes. Well. It makes the world go round. Don't worry. Nightingale Books isn't on the scrap heap yet.'

Emilia walked back along the high street, her hands in her pockets. Just when she thought the shop was on the up, reality kicked in. And it was all new to her. She'd never really got involved in the behind-the-scenes machinations, and now she was cross. She should have paid more attention, but it all just seemed to tick over without her needing to know any of it.

She'd foolishly thought running a book shop would be easy, and that she knew everything. But of course there was more to it than finding someone the perfect read for their upcoming cruise, or recommending a christening gift, or tracking down a book when someone said, rather vaguely, 'Its got a blue cover...'

Andrea had done her best to keep her spirits up, but Emilia felt that keeping the shop open was becoming less and less viable: something she was just doing because she didn't want to let her father down.

She passed The Icing on the Cake, its windows crammed with sugared doughnuts oozing wine-dark jam and shiny chocolate cakes and golden custard tarts. She went in and bought a sausage roll – she was more of a savoury than a sweet person – and devoured the melting pastry and herby sausage meat in three bites.

To cheer herself up, she called Bea with the news about Mick Gillespie. 'You'll never guess who I've got coming to the shop.'

Bea squealed when she heard the news. 'Oh my God – he's my favourite actor of all time. That Aran jumper he wears in *The Silver Moon* – I bought Bill one like it.'

'Do you think people will come?'
'Of course! And we'll dress the shop.'
'Not leprechauns and shamrocks?'
Bea laughed. 'No. I'll think of something clever.' She gasped. 'Do you think we can take him out for dinner afterwards?'
'I'm booking him a room at the Peasebrook Arms.'
'You'll have to give me his room number.'
'Bea – he's an old man!'
'I know. I'm only kidding. But that's great. You'll have them queuing round the block. We'll make it a night to remember.'
Emilia hung up, smiling to herself. Suddenly all the problems of the past few weeks began to recede. She felt a little shoot of hope. Maybe she *could* turn the shop round, with a bit of help and a bit of imagination?

Sarah managed to find a rare parking space on the high street in Peasebrook. She was en route to the hospital for her daily visit but there was something she really needed to do. She locked her car and took a deep breath. She wasn't sure if she was ready for what she was about to do, but if she waited until she was ready she would never go.

She could feel him as soon as she walked into Nightingale Books. The very essence of Julius. The shop *was* him. She looked around, expecting to see him bent over a table of books, looking up to meet her gaze, smiling at her over his spectacles.

The memory, the longing and the sadness were overwhelming. No one had ever made her feel like Julius. That meeting of the mind and the soul. And the body . . . She chastised herself. That wasn't why she was here – to wallow in her memories of what would never be again.

Emilia was hanging up the phone as she walked over to the counter.

'Emilia? It's Sarah. Sarah Basildon.' She wasn't sure Emilia would recognise her, necessarily. Sarah was modest. She never assumed people knew who she was, even though they usually did.

'Sarah. How lovely to see you. Hello.'

'How are you?'

'Oh . . . you know. It's been tough but I'm getting there.'

'You must miss your father dreadfully.'

'Oh God yes.' Then she remembered. Marlowe had told them about Alice at the last rehearsal. A car crash. She'd been taken to hospital. 'But how's Alice? I heard about the accident. I'm so sorry.'

'Well,' said Sarah. 'The great thing is she will be all right. Her leg was very badly injured. But she's in very good hands. We're hoping she'll be back on her feet for the wedding. Literally! Otherwise she'll be going up the aisle on crutches.' Sarah tried to laugh. It was obvious she was being brave.

'Would you give her my love?' Emilia didn't know Alice well, but she liked her. They'd both been at Peasebrook Infants. Alice was a few years below her, but Emilia remembered her in the playground, with her flaxen hair and duffel coat. Emilia had gone on to the high school, and Alice went off to boarding school somewhere, so they'd drifted apart, but Emilia was looking forward to playing at her wedding. It was bound to be a fairy tale.

'She's why I'm here, actually. I wanted a copy of Alice's favourite book – I can't find it anywhere at home. But I thought it would be nice for her to have something to read.'

'Of course. What is it?'

Sarah gave a smile. '*Riders*. Jilly Cooper. Do you have it in stock?'

'Of course! A book shop's not a book shop without *Riders*. Especially round here.' Emilia walked over to the fiction shelves. She could see a range of fat paperbacks in the C section. The

comfort of Jilly Cooper. She'd read them all herself: it w
always a celebration when a new Jilly came out. 'Here we are

'That's wonderful – she'll love that. I remember when she first read it. I didn't get a word out of her for about a week.'

Sarah handed over a ten-pound note. As Emilia wrapped the book in a bag, she hesitated, as if she wanted to say something. Eventually, she cleared her throat.

'Emilia, I wondered if you would come and have tea with me? There's something I'd love to talk to you about. In confidence. Something your father and I had been discussing.'

'Oh!' Emilia wondered what it could be. Her father hadn't ever mentioned talking to Sarah Basildon about anything. Well, not specifically. The Basildons were great customers. They were very good at supporting local businesses in general, and they always bought a lot of books, especially at Christmas. They were very popular in the area. They didn't think they were better than everyone else because they lived at the Big House. 'Of course. When would you like me to come?'

'What about Thursday? About three? That gives me time to nip to the hospital in the morning – I like to go and see her every day.'

Emilia had a quick look at the calendar and the staff rota. There'd be one person in the shop, which was fine at the moment.

'Of course. That's perfect.'

Emilia watched Sarah go, intrigued. It would be good to get out of the shop and go to Peasebrook Manor. She'd had enough of uncovering nasty bills today. After this morning's meeting, she actually felt a bit cross with her father. It was no way to run a business, leaving accounts undealt with. But she was starting to realise Julius hadn't really seen Nightingale Books as a business, more a way of life.

The question was whether it was to be a way of life for her well.

Sarah left Nightingale Books with a sense of relief and headed off to the hospital. She had been putting off going in there because of the memories, but she couldn't spend the rest of her life avoiding the book shop. And she wanted to see how Emilia was. She felt she owed it to Julius, to keep an eye on her. After all, Emilia was on her own, with no mother.

Sarah remembered the day Julius had told her about Rebecca, and the terrible start he'd had to fatherhood.

'It was an awful shock,' he admitted. 'But I was very young. I suppose at the time, I thought Rebecca was the love of my life. Things happened very quickly: her deciding to stay in England, then getting pregnant, so we hadn't really had time to fall *out* of love. I don't know how long we would have lasted in the real world, a young couple with the pressure of a baby. It's very easy to romanticise it.'

'You must have been very lonely, after she died.'

Julius gave her a cheeky grin. 'Oh, don't worry. There's nothing women find more attractive than a single man in charge of a baby. I coped.'

Sarah had pretended to be outraged. 'And there was me thinking I was the first person to melt your frozen heart.'

He looked at her seriously. 'You're the first person I've really cared about.'

She remembered the woozy sensation of realising how much she meant to him. Though despite his declaration she knew she would only ever come second to Emilia, and rightly so. Sarah had a strong maternal instinct. It was an awkward situation, but she wanted to make it clear to Emilia that she was there if she needed her. That if she ever wanted to talk about her father, or just to come up to the house for supper because she wanted get out, then Sarah's door was wide open.

It was the least she could do for her lover.

It was delicate, though. She could tell by the way Emilia greeted her – polite but warm, with definitely no hint of knowing in her eyes – that she had no inkling of their relationship. And she couldn't just say 'By the way, your father and I were long-term lovers, so please do consider me your surrogate mum...'

She thought she had found the ideal way for them to start a conversation and possibly develop a relationship. She smiled when she thought of her brainwave: it really was a brilliant idea. She'd spent a lot of time in the car lately, driving backwards and forwards to the hospital, and car journeys were the perfect catalyst for light-bulb moments. And here she was again, driving out onto the Oxford road. She looked at the book on the passenger seat. Goodness knows where the original copy had gone – she'd given it to Alice for her fourteenth birthday – but it might cheer her up.

'That is the best present ever,' Alice told her as she took it out of the bag. 'Thank you. But what I really want you to do is bring me my laptop.'

'No way,' Sarah said firmly. 'You need to rest, Alice. You've got enough to deal with just getting better. Everything's under control. Your dad's taking charge and being really helpful.'

She didn't add 'for once'. Ralph really had stepped up to the plate. Usually no one was quite sure where he was or what he was up to, and unless he was given a really specific task he did his own thing, but he had been magnificent.

Alice giggled. 'I bet he's driving everyone mad. But honestly, Mum – the thing is I just lie here and worry. If I've got my laptop I can keep up to speed on everything. Otherwise Christmas is going to be a nightmare. It's all in the planning.'

Darling, we've done it often enough. The girls in the office ave all your lists and timetables—'

'But it's the small things. And there were lots of new things I wanted to do this year—'

'It's out of the question.' Sarah cut her off. 'And if things aren't perfect this year, it doesn't matter. Anyway, we need you better for the wedding. That's your big day.'

Alice gave a dismissive wave of her hand. 'The wedding will organise itself. I'm not worried about that.'

'But I want you to enjoy it.'

Alice looked stubborn. 'I won't enjoy it if I'm worried about work, will I?'

Sarah laughed. 'Look – I'll get one of the girls from the office to come in and talk everything through with you. Then you can see how well they are managing.'

'Are you saying I'm replaceable?' Alice looked indignant.

'No. I'm saying you need to look after yourself otherwise you'll end up in a worse state.'

The thing with Alice was that she never stopped. And now she'd been forced to, she didn't like it.

'Who's organising the flyers to hand out at the farmers' market? Who's doing our tweets? Who's ordering the presents for the Father Christmas visits? Who's talked to the reindeer man about the reindeer?'

'It's all under control,' repeated Sarah, who had no idea of the answer to any of Alice's questions. But she wasn't going to let her know that. All that really mattered was that Alice got better. If no one tweeted for a few weeks, or the reindeer didn't turn up, it wasn't the end of the world.

After visiting Alice, Sarah drove back home, observing how the first of the leaves were now leaving the trees. Of course Peasebrook Manor was glorious in summer, an abundance of colour and greenery, but she rather liked being able to see the structure underneath, the bare branches, the absence of colour, the golden stone of the walls and balustrades and terraces dulling to a more subdued grey. The starkness certainly suited her mood, as she watched a flock of starlings scatter themselves across the sky.

She got out of the car. She could see Dillon moving some of the lead planters on the terrace. She'd been avoiding him rather since Alice's accident, because she wasn't sure what to think about what Hugh had told them about the events leading up to it. She didn't want to believe that Dillon could have been instrumental in the accident, yet she could hardly ask him for his side of the story. So it was easier not to think about it. There was too much going on in her head already.

But she was fond of Dillon. It wasn't fair of her to give him the cold shoulder. He'd been devastated to hear about Alice, but was that because he felt guilty? Did he know he was responsible for Hugh's fast driving?

She walked along the terrace to the French windows that led into the morning room. A light autumn breeze caressed her. It lifted her heart just a little. To the right and left of her the velvety lawns of Peasebrook had just had their last cut before the winter and she breathed in the grassy scent. Clusters of great oak trees lined the horizon. The grey ribbon of the drive stretched out into the distance: she could just see the gates.

Dillon looked up as she approached. He stood up, his hands smothered in rich peat. He was planting the bulbs for her favourite tulips: dark purple, almost black.

'How is she today?' he asked.

'She's not too bad,' Sarah told him.

'Will you tell her I said hello? Next time you go in.'

'Of course.'

'When will she be back home?'

'It depends on her leg. She's just waiting for one more operation. We're hoping not too long. But at the moment she's best off in the hospital.'

Dillon looked away for a moment. He looked troubled. As if he was about to say something.

'Is there something the matter, Dillon?' Sarah wondered if he wanted to confess. She would prefer everything to be out in the open.

'No. No, it's fine. I was just wondering – would – would it be all right if I went to see her?'

Sarah thought for a moment. If what Hugh had said was true, maybe Alice wouldn't want to see him. On the other hand, Dillon and Alice had always been friends. Who was she to stop him seeing her?

Alice's mother, that's who. It was her duty to make sure her daughter wasn't put into any more discomfort than she already was.

'I think perhaps not, at the moment, if you don't mind.'

She turned and stepped into the morning room. She felt awful. Dillon had looked crestfallen. But she couldn't deal with what Hugh had told her at the moment, because there would be too many consequences. She couldn't manage without Dillon, therefore she didn't want to investigate any further. But in case it was true, she needed to keep him away from Alice. For the time being, anyway.

Dillon was furious with himself. Why was he such a coward? Why couldn't he just come out with it and tell Sarah what had happened in the White Horse? It wasn't as if they weren't close. Or as close as they could be. Dillon didn't fool himself that Sarah thought of him as an equal. Of course she didn't.

He'd talked to Brian about the Hugh thing, in the pub.

'I don't understand why he didn't get done. You saw how much they'd all been drinking, and he was partying with them.'

Brian chuckled. 'You are a bit green sometimes, Dillon.'

'What do you mean?'

Brian tapped his nose.

'What does that mean?'

'He's a little bit fond of the old Bolivian marching powder, isn't he?'

Dillon still looked puzzled.

'Didn't you see how many times he nipped off to the toilet?'

'For a slash?'

'No, idiot. For a line of cocaine.'

Dillon blinked. 'Cocaine? Bloody hell.' He thought about it. 'So he *wasn't* drunk?'

'No. Just high as a kite.'

'How come the police didn't notice?'

'He'll have charmed them, won't he?'

'You mean they turned a blind eye?'

Brian shrugged. 'Just gave him the benefit of the doubt when he passed the breathalyser. They wouldn't suspect him, would they? He's marrying a Basildon.'

'So the bastard got away with it.'

'Yep. And it's too late to grass him up now.'

'Do you think Alice knows what he gets up to?'

Brian shrugged. 'Probably not. She's a nice girl. He wouldn't want to blot his copybook with her.'

'How do you know, anyway? That he takes cocaine?'

Brian scoffed. 'You ask Pogo. That's where all Hugh's money goes – in Pogo's pocket. Pogo supplies him and all his mates.'

Pogo was the local drug dealer who skulked about in the dodgier pubs in Peasebrook and thought he was a bit of a gangster, with his dreadlocks and gold front tooth. Dillon had been at school with him and thought he was an idiot. He wasn't going to lower himself to ask Pogo for corroborative evidence to incriminate Hugh. Pogo would say anything if he thought it would save his own sorry arse.

'Why haven't you told me this before?'

'I thought you knew.'

Dillon shook his head. He felt shocked. He hadn't thought much of Hugh in the first place, but this was even worse. But what could he do?

If he told Sarah that Hugh had been off his head on cocaine the night of the accident, Hugh would deny it. And no one would believe Dillon over Hugh, because Hugh had passed the breathalyser test. They'd just think Dillon was trying to cause trouble. They wouldn't want to think anything bad of Hugh, because he was the saviour of Peasebrook Manor. The one with the deep pockets. And one of them.

Yet if he said nothing, Alice was going to end up marrying him – a manipulative, amoral coke-head.

He kicked a clod of earth into a flowerbed. It was frustrating, being the lowest of the low. When it came down to it, he was just a nobody.

He walked back to the garden room. He felt angry with Sarah, even though she had done nothing wrong. But he was hurt she didn't want him to go and visit Alice. It wasn't as if she was whiter than white. What would Ralph say, if he knew the truth about her and Julius Nightingale? Not that Dillon would ever say anything, not in a million years. But that made it worse, not better. And Ralph himself was no role model. Dillon had worked out what had been going on years ago. Which was why he was so cross with himself for not seeing through Hugh.

He clenched his teeth. What was the point in behaving with loyalty to people, when they showed *you* none? He pulled off his wax jacket and put the kettle on. Was he the only person in the world who wasn't a bloody hypocrite? Well, him and

Alice of course. If anyone was the innocent party in all of this, it was Alice.

Dillon sat and drank his tea, and as he drank, he came to a decision. He'd go to the hospital and see Alice himself. He didn't need Sarah's permission. If Alice didn't want to see him, she could tell him herself. He swilled out his cup and picked up his jacket. There was no time like the present.

Dillon had been to A&E often enough. As a gardener, it was an occupational hazard and tetanus injections and stitches were par for the course. But he'd never been onto one of the wards. The hospital was a maze, of arrows to different floors and places with different colour codes and letters, of lifts that went to different sections.

Eventually he found his way to the right area. He pushed open the double doors and asked for Alice at the nurse's station. They pointed him towards a private room off the main ward.

He knocked gently and heard her voice. As he peeped round the door his heart leapt as he saw her. She was bundled up in bed, her leg in a cast outside the sheets, her face bandaged up, the one eye he could see still black with bruising.

'Dillon!' There was no hiding her delight.

He came in and held out the Terry's chocolate orange he'd brought her.

'I got you this.'

'My absolute favourite! Let's open it right now.' She shuffled over and patted the bed next to her. 'Come and sit down and tell me everything.'

He sat and started opening the box. He tapped the chocolate orange on the bedside table so it fell into segments, and fed them to her one by one as they talked.

'I'm so bored cooped up in here. I really want to go on a ward, so I've got people to talk to, but Hugh's insisted on a private room. It makes me feel as if people think I think I'm something special.'

'Well, you are,' said Dillon, smiling.

'No, I'm not. And there's so much to do at Peasebrook – Mum refuses to let me know what's going on and tells me not to worry, but I worry more *not* knowing. What *is* going on?'

'Everything's under control, I think. Your mum's doing a lot. And your dad, actually.'

Alice perked up as she had a sudden thought.

'Could you do me a favour?'

'What?'

'Could you bring in my laptop? So I can check up on everything? I've asked Mum but she keeps forgetting. Accidentally on purpose, I think.' Alice put her head to one side and looked at Dillon, eyes bright. 'It's in the estate office. The girls will know where it is. And don't forget the cable.'

'OK,' said Dillon, pleased he could do something for her. 'But should you be worrying about work?'

'I can't not worry. It's impossible.'

'You should try. Or you won't get better.'

'Honestly, you're just like Mum. She's worried I won't get better in time for the wedding. To be honest, I'm starting to wonder if I should just cancel it. But if I do, I won't be able to get married until next year, because Christmas will get in the way.'

'What's wrong with waiting till next year?' Dillon felt a leap of hope. Given another year hideous Hugh might show his true colours.

'No. We've got plans in place. Hugh wants to give up his flat and move into the cottage as soon as possible. We'll forge ahead.' She looked at her leg. 'I've just got one more operation on this and then – then they've got a consultant coming to look at my face . . . They said it could be much worse. I could have lost my eye. So I'm lucky really. Aren't I?'

She smiled at him, and he wanted to scoop her up in his arms because she was so brave, sitting there with her face all battered, thinking she was lucky. He didn't know what to say. Yes, in a way she *was* lucky. He shuddered when he thought about what could have happened. But the whole thing could have been prevented. If it wasn't for the awful man she was about to marry.

He wondered about telling her his suspicions about Hugh on the night of the accident. But Alice was so sweet natured, so trusting, she wouldn't believe a word of it. She would give Hugh the benefit of the doubt. Dillon would just sound spiteful. And of course, he didn't have any proof, except Brian's hypothesis. He had nothing to go on except speculation and gossip.

Alice pointed to a book on the bedside table.

'Read to me for a bit, would you?' she said, changing the subject. 'Mum brought me this in earlier. And I'm getting tired. That's the thing that gets me. I feel all right and then I get exhausted.' She sighed.

'Snuggle down then,' he told her. He picked up the book. *Riders*, by Jilly Cooper. It was huge. He flipped it open.

'I'm not a very good reader,' he warned her.

'It doesn't matter,' she said. 'I almost know it off by heart. I've read it about twenty times.'

'What's the point of hearing it again, then?'

'It's literally the best book in the world.' She managed a smile. 'There are some rude bits, though. Really rude.'

He laughed, and began to read. He felt awkward at first, but he began to get into the story: a bunch of colourful characters vying for hearts and trophies. The room was warm, a bit stuffy, and after a while he could see Alice was falling asleep, so he stopped.

She opened her eyes as soon as he stopped.

'I'm not asleep.'

'Maybe you should go to sleep.' He patted her.

She closed her eyes again. 'That's who you remind me of,' she murmured.

'Who?'

'Jake Lovell. The gypsy boy. Everyone else at school loved Rupert Campbell-Black, but I always like Jake best. You remind me of him.'

'Oh.' Dillon looked down, not sure if this was a compliment.

'It's a good thing. Rupert Campbell-Black was a beast. But Jake was lovely.'

It was as if she was talking about real people. He closed the book and put it back on the bedside table.

'I better go,' he said. 'Visiting time's nearly over.'

'You'll come again, won't you?'

'Of course.'

He wasn't sure whether to kiss her goodbye. She put up her arms.

'Give me a hug. I need a big hug.'

He bent down and hugged her awkwardly.

'You be good,' he replied and walked out of the room.

As he left the hospital, he could feel himself clenching and unclenching his fists. He'd hated seeing her like that, obviously in pain but still so bloody brave. Hugh didn't deserve her. But there was nothing he could do to stop the wedding. Even a smashed-up leg and a smashed-up face wasn't deterring Alice.

Fifteen

The morning room at Peasebrook Manor was the prettiest room Emilia had ever seen. It had primrose yellow walls and pale green silk curtains and two rose velvet sofas in front of a dainty fireplace. Over it was a Victorian oil painting of a girl feeding cabbage leaves to a fat bunny rabbit. The girl, with her rosy cheeks and blonde hair, reminded Emilia of Alice.

Emilia wondered what it was like to live in the Basildons' world. Not that hers was gritty reality – she was only too aware it was rarefied – but this was quintessential country life at its most appealing. This was the room where Sarah took tea or coffee with her guests, and wrote letters and saw to her business. She thought of the back office at the shop and resolved to make it a more pleasant place to work in. Her father had rarely spent time in there; just banished anything he didn't want to look at into its depths. It was cold and damp and dingy. It would have to change.

Sarah came in with a tray bearing tea: a proper china teapot, and dainty cups and saucers and a milk jug and sugar bowl. And a plate of shortbread, thick with caster sugar. She laid it on the table between the sofas.

'Milk?' she asked, and Emilia nodded.

Sarah somehow managed to look dishevelled but devastatingly attractive. She must be in her fifties but looked far younger. She had on jeans and a faded Liberty lawn shirt and pale blue loafers. Her hair was a mixture of honey and grey that looked as if a top London hairdresser had painstakingly streaked it, but was probably the result of Sarah not having been to have her roots done for months. Her hands were red and chapped from gardening, and her nails ragged, but the most enormous diamond glimmered on her ring finger: it was so large it almost couldn't be real, but Sarah wasn't the type to wear costume jewellery. She wore no make-up but a dab of pink lipstick hastily applied in the downstairs loo just before she answered the door. She was the archetypal English rose.

'I've just got back from visiting Alice,' she said as she poured the tea. 'The traffic out of Oxford was awful.'

'How is she?'

Sarah sighed. 'She's in a lot of discomfort, poor thing. And of course all those painkillers make one so fuzzy. But she's making progress.'

She sat down on the sofa opposite Emilia.

'I asked you here because I wanted to talk to you about something your father and I had been discussing for a while.'

Emilia nodded. Sarah clasped her hands. She seemed slightly nervous, not quite meeting Emilia's eye. She fiddled with the diamond ring. Her fingers were so slender it spun round and round.

'We had become quite good friends, your father and I. We spoke – met – often.' She lifted her gaze. 'Ralph is not a great reader and it was good to have a decent conversation with someone about books. Julius was always so brilliant at recommending. He had a feeling for what I wanted to read and I don't think there was one book he suggested that I didn't love. Sometimes he'd make me read things because they were good for me and I always took something away from them. He widened my world . . .'

She drifted off, immersed in her eulogy.

'He was extraordinary,' she finished, and Emilia could see the glitter of tears in her navy blue eyes, as bright as the diamond on her ring.

'I know,' said Emilia.

For a moment, Sarah couldn't speak. Emilia was touched. She could see how difficult Sarah was finding this. She was still astonished by how deep people's feelings for her father ran. They still came up to her in the street or in the shop and told her how much he had meant to them.

'I'd love to do something. To remember him by. He often talked about organising a literary festival. It was a dream of his and I'd suggested that we could do one here, at Peasebrook. We have so many rooms here that could be used. We were starting to think quite seriously about it when he became ill.'

Here, Sarah looked down at the floor. Emilia could see she was struggling.

'He did mention the idea to me, once or twice,' she said. 'There are so many authors and celebrities within striking distance of Peasebrook, and we're not so far from London. It could be a real draw. Especially in a setting like this.'

Sarah had recovered her composure. 'Exactly! We felt we could attract a good calibre of speakers. The thing is, it was his dream, but it was starting to become a real possibility. We're very well set up for putting on events here. And – and I think it would be a shame to let the opportunity slip. I thought about doing the festival in his name.' She swallowed. 'The Nightingale Literary Festival.'

'Oh!' said Emilia. 'That would be a wonderful tribute.'

'I would need your help, though. And the support of the shop. We'd need you to supply the books, of course. And advise on who to ask. I mean, there's masses and masses to think about, but I wanted to see what you thought. Because I couldn't do it without you. It would have to be a team effort.'

Emilia took a piece of shortbread and bit into it. It was a wonderful idea. She could see it all in her mind's eye. Literary lions and lionesses holding forth in the ballroom, the audience hanging on their every word. A glittering programme; the Glastonbury of book festivals. It would be a wonderful boost for the town too – people attending the festival would want accommodation and would go into the pubs and restaurants. And they could get sponsorship from local businesses . . .

But she had to be cautious. She didn't want to get Sarah's hopes up. It was such an enchanting idea, but she couldn't show too much enthusiasm.

'The thing is,' she said, 'I'm not sure what I'm doing with the shop yet. I'm afraid it's not in very good shape financially. It's not making money at the moment: I'm struggling to cover my overheads. It needs a lot spending on it if it's going to even begin to make a profit and I haven't decided yet if that's what I want to do.'

Sarah looked horrified. 'You can't let it close, surely?'

'I don't want to. Of course not. But I can't just keep it going out of sentiment. That would be foolish. And I've got my staff to consider, as well as myself.'

Sarah considered her words. 'I understand.' She sighed. 'Julius never mentioned the shop being in trouble.'

The way she said it gave Emilia the impression they spoke often, and that Sarah was hurt by his omission. She smiled. 'I don't think Dad quite saw that it was. It's all a bit of a muddle. I've only scratched the surface. But he ran it by the seat of his pants, rather.'

'So was he in debt?'

'Nothing awful or to be ashamed of. But there are quite a few outstanding invoices.'

'Gosh.' Sarah looked perturbed. 'He never implied he was in trouble.'

'As I said, I don't think he thought he was. My father's famous line was *I don't do numbers.*'

'Oh dear.' Sarah leaned forward. 'Between you and me, I have rather more experience of getting out of hideous debt than you might imagine. A while ago now we nearly lost Peasebrook. I won't go into it, but it was pretty frightening. So I understand how you feel. And if I can help at all...'

'I have Andrea, my accountant – I was at school with her. She's like a walking calculator in Louboutins. She's been wonderful. But even she can't wave a magic wand. I've got some tough decisions to make. And if I do go ahead, it's going to be hard work. Not that I'm afraid of that, of course...'

'It just goes to show you,' said Sarah, 'that you can think you know someone, but you have no idea.' As she said it, her cheeks flushed pink. She put her face in her hands, and in that moment Emilia recognised that her father and Sarah must have been closer she realised. She wasn't sure how she felt about this realisation. She liked Sarah very much, but there was no getting away from the fact she was very firmly married to Ralph. Should she press Sarah for more detail? Did Sarah *want* her to realise? She thought she perhaps she did. She had more than hinted.

Maybe today wasn't the day. Everything was still a bit raw. They were feeling their way with each other. If they went ahead with the festival, and worked together, maybe the whole story would come out at some point, when they were both ready.

'I think the festival is a wonderful idea,' she said finally. 'And if I do decide to stay open, I think we should do it. As you say, it would be a perfect memorial. My father would be proud.'

Sarah's smile was a bit wobbly. 'He would...'

Emilia put her teacup down. 'I'll let you know as soon as I've decided what I'm doing.'

There was a pause. Sarah was twisting her ring round again. Something unsaid was hanging in the air.

'Emilia – there's something I'd like to share with you. But it's totally confidential. It can't go any further.'

Emilia could see Sarah was struggling with what she was about to say.

'Is it about you and my father?' she asked gently.

There was a spot of colour on each of Sarah's cheeks. 'I loved your father. Very much.'

If she thought about it, she could still feel that love now. A burning heat that went into her very bones; a ball of warmth where her heart sat. They had never known what to do with their love. Acknowledging it in public would have taken them into another realm; a set of circumstances Sarah knew she couldn't manage. Her duty was to her husband, her family and Peasebrook. She couldn't compromise that duty. It wasn't fair on anyone, but most of all it wasn't fair on Julius. He protested that he didn't mind, but Sarah did. She always felt terrible, that he had got the raw end of the deal, and that she was somehow having her cake and eating it.

But if she ever talked about ending it, which she did from time to time when the guilt gnawed at her in the darkness of dawn, he would pull her to him and kiss her. Oh, how they had kissed. Endless kisses that reached deep inside her. Was there anything more momentous, she wondered? To kiss someone so hard you could feel your soul fuse with theirs?

She wasn't proud of her relationship with Julius, for it compromised the two men she loved. For she still loved Ralph in her own way, despite everything he had put her through. Though the two of them lived very separate lives they still had much in common, not least Alice. Never in a million years would she have walked out on what they had.

But she had needed Julius. She knew it was selfish, to carry on, even though he insisted it didn't matter to him. As long as he could have a little bit of her, it didn't matter to him.

She couldn't explain all this to Emilia. Emilia was young. She wouldn't understand the subtleties and compromises and dilemmas that came with later life. And she didn't want to sully Emilia's memory of Julius by making him out to be less than morally upright.

So she chose her words carefully.

'I loved your father, but of course, I'm married, and he was very aware of that. He was a very understanding and considerate man. He respected my situation. But we became very close . . .'

She hoped what she was saying made sense. She wasn't actually lying. She hadn't denied anything as such. It was equivocation, if anything. She didn't need to go into details about the intensity of what they had. The extraordinary passion, even if it had felt pure.

Emilia didn't say anything for a while. When she finally spoke, her voice was gentle.

'I'm glad,' she said. 'I'm glad he had someone as lovely as you. To care about him. To think about when he woke up in the morning.' A tear slid out onto her cheek. 'Sorry. It's just . . . I miss him.'

She rubbed her eye with the heel of her hand. Sarah jumped to her feet. She could never bear to see anyone cry – it might be her duty to keep her emotions in check when it came to herself, but when it came to others, she was open and caring. She sat on the sofa next to Emilia and hugged her.

'I miss him too,' she said. 'Dreadfully.'

'I'm just glad he wasn't lonely.' Emilia's voice wavered. She sounded like a small girl trying desperately not to cry harder.

'I always worried that he was lonely. He was such a wonderful man. He deserved to be loved.'

'Oh, he was loved. Be sure of that.'

Emilia leant into Sarah. It was wonderful to be comforted by someone who had loved her father.

'Nobody knew about us, of course. We could never tell anyone. But I'm taking the risk of telling you because I think you'll understand. And because I want you to know that I'm always here if you need me,' Sarah told her. 'I know Julius would have wanted me to look out for you. And if I can be of support, in any way, just let me know. Even if it's just to talk about him. Or just to come up for tea. Or wine. Or anything. Anything.'

Emilia held Sarah's hands and looked at her. She could see now the depth of the sadness in Sarah's eyes. And she could feel the warmth and kindness that Julius must have been drawn to. And she was grateful to Sarah, for her compassion and honesty. It must have been a painful confession. She felt honoured to be trusted with the secret. She supposed when she had time to think about it, she might be shocked, but she wasn't going to judge. She found it a comfort, that Julius had this woman's devotion. And she knew, from all the books she had ever read, that life was complicated, that love sprang from nowhere sometimes, and that forbidden love wasn't always something to be ashamed of.

Sixteen

A few days later, Bea laid a presentation folder in front of Emilia with a proud smile.

'I tried really hard not to get *too* carried away,' she said.

She had made it into the shape of a book. On the front it read *Nightingale Books*, in silver writing on navy blue. She'd designed a logo – N and B entwined, with a tendril of roses and a tiny nightingale perched amongst them.

'This is the logo – you can use it on all your social media, your bags, the sign outside. A really strong visual that people can recognise and identify with.'

'It's sweet. We could have T-shirts.' Emilia felt a swirl of delight.

'Exactly. This is about creating a brand as much as creating a really immersive shopping experience.'

'OK...' Emilia wasn't used to jargon, but Bea thrived on it.

The first page was a CAD drawing of the shop divided up into sections, using double-sided bookcases. There was a four-sided counter in the centre of the floor space, allowing whoever was serving to see all around the shop.

'I wanted it to feel as if it's got different rooms. Different rooms with different feels,' Bea explained. 'There's so much wasted space, but this gives you twice as much shelf space as well as more room to browse.'

Each section had a page and Bea had created a mood board for each one. The pièce de résistance was the café area on the mezzanine, which also had an area selling cards and wrapping paper and small gifts. There were just three wooden tables, and a marble-topped table with three cake domes.

'Oh!' breathed Emilia. 'Do you think we can do it? It looks absolutely gorgeous. Sort of the-same-but-different.'

'I wanted to keep the spirit of what your dad had here, but move it on a bit. Make it modern but nostalgic. Somewhere people can explore their imaginations: step back into the past if they want, or into another world, or into the future. That's what a book shop should be, after all – a gateway to somewhere else. But books aren't enough – you have to give people a helping hand.'

Emilia leafed through the drawings. Bea really had been clever. She had kept everything that was important, but showed it off to much greater effect. The colours were softer: the walls pale grey, the shelves painted white, which made the shop seem bigger.

'I love it all. I love the lights!'

At the moment, the shop was lit with old-fashioned strip lights, harsh at best. Bea had put in some very cool chandeliers: white twisted glass with red wire threaded through them.

'Well, those are probably very expensive, but it gives you an idea of what could be done.'

Emilia sighed. 'How much do you think it will cost? Because of course, that's the rub. None of this looks cheap.'

Bea made a face. 'Well, you get what you pay for. But some of it can be done with MDF and magic. And we can work with what we've got already. If we rip up the carpet, we can use the floorboards – put a nice chalky paint effect over them. And then painting everything pale colours will give the illusion of more space. And you don't have to do it all at once!'

'But I want to do it all at once,' laughed Emilia. 'And how long do you think it would take? We'd have to close while it was being done.'

'I've done a timetable,' said Bea. 'I reckon two weeks, with all hands on deck. As for price, we'd have to get quotes. It's mostly carpentry; a bit of wiring. Decorating. But of course, as we all know, once you start taking something apart, then you uncover all sorts of horrors.'

'It's a total refurb,' said Emilia, shaking her head. 'There's no point in being half-arsed about it. We'd have to take all the books out and put them somewhere. And I need to put in a new computer system while I'm at it. And security.' She put her face in her hands. 'I'm so excited. But I'm scared. I've got to make the decision and I don't know what to do. It would be so easy to walk away and go back to my old life. Or sell up and start a new one. Either of those would be easier!'

'But not as rewarding?'

Emilia looked around the shop. She imagined everything Bea had outlined brought to life, and how exciting that would be.

She just had to find the courage from somewhere.

And the cash . . .

'I'll get some quotes. There's no point in getting excited until I know what it's going to cost.'

'I've got some good guys who did my house. They're reliable. And fast. And good. They have to be, to work for me.' Bea laughed. 'I'll ask them for a quote.'

'And will you help me do a window display for Mick Gillespie? He's coming at the weekend, remember.'

'Of course!' Bea's eyes sparkled. 'Can I have carte blanche?'

'Carte blanche and a fifty quid budget,' said Emilia. 'And as many copies of his book as you can stuff in the window.'

'It'll be glorious,' promised Bea. 'Maud is at nursery on Thursday afternoon. I'll come and do it then.'

'I can't pay you much.'

'Listen, it's stopping me going mad with boredom. Just give me a signed copy.'

'You're amazing.'

'I know.'

Emilia smiled as her new friend left the shop. Bea made her feel as if things were possible, then put a layer of glitter on the top. She was one of those special people. She was lucky to have her goodwill and her talent, but she wasn't going to be able to rely on her long-term. Bea was way out of her league.

Later that week, Jackson came back to Emilia with his verdict on the Moomins.

'I've decided, I'm going to try and be more like Moominpappa,' said Jackson.

'Well, that's a very good resolution,' said Emilia. 'But you might need to put on a bit of weight.'

'Don't! My ex kept going on about how fat they all were. But at least they're happy. Not making kale smoothies and freaking out if they have an extra raw almond.'

'Is she a bit of a health freak?'

'She's turned into one. She never used to be. She's doing a triathlon and she's obsessed with her heart rate and her body fat and how often she can go training.'

'Sounds awful.'

'I don't mind. It means I get to have Finn more while she goes on endless bike rides. So – what shall I read next?'

'I've just got the perfect book in. I'm trying to build up the children's department and I think you should read this.' She led him over to a display table and held up a picture book. 'I don't know anyone who can't learn something from *The Little Prince*, though you probably need to read it a few times to get the full meaning.' She handed it to him. It was a slender book, with a picture of little blonde boy dressed in blue on the front, standing on a planet. 'It's a funny book,' she went on. 'Funny peculiar. But it explains things. It's my favourite book in the world.'

'I thought the Moomins were?'

'After the Moomins.' She grinned. 'OK. I admit it. I have lots of favourites. That's the trouble with books. You can never choose your favourite. It changes depending on your mood. But I really think you'll like it.'

'I'll give it a try.' He handed over the money. 'Finn's really loving being read to. It's made a big difference to our relationship. I think he just saw me as the one who messed about with him in the skatepark, but we've been having some really good chats.' He looked a bit emotional. 'It's good, after everything that's happened. I don't feel like such a bloody failure...'

'I'm sure you're not a failure,' said Emilia.

Jackson looked embarrassed. 'Sorry. I'm oversharing...'

'Listen, it's part of the job. Everyone comes in here to overshare. I'm part bookseller, part therapist.'

She handed him the book. As he took it, Jackson spotted the poster behind the counter, advertising the evening with Mick Gillespie.

'Mick Gillespie? Is he actually coming here?'

'I know, right? I'm so excited.'

'Have you still got tickets? How much is it?'

'Five pounds – but you get nibbles and a Silver Moon cocktail for that. I've got someone doing special Irish canapés. It's going to be amazing.'

'Mia would love that. She's obsessed with Mick Gillespie. She bought me one of those Aran jumpers for Christmas one year. I looked like an idiot in it.' Jackson shrugged ruefully. 'Can I have two tickets?'

'Of course!' She took two tickets from the drawer.

'She is going to be so made up,' grinned Jackson, pulling out a tenner.

Bea emerged from the window, dressed in a boiler suit, a glue gun in one hand. She smiled at Jackson, and looked at Emilia, enquiry in her eyes.

Emilia had no choice but to introduce them.

'Bea, this is Jackson. Jackson – this is Bea. She's doing a window display for the event.'

The two of them nodded hello at each other.

'If you ever want anything done,' said Jackson. 'I'm quite handy.'

Bea held up her glue gun. 'I'm good. But thanks.'

Jackson turned to go, putting a farewell hand up to Emilia. 'Thanks for everything. See you soon.'

Bea watched him go out of the door. 'I bet he's handy all right. What are you waiting for?'

'Bea!' Emilia feigned shock. 'He's not my type. Although he is cute. But he's totally obsessed with his ex. He's just bought tickets to the Mick Gillespie event for her.'

'She's his *ex*!' said Bea. 'Come on! You need to have some fun. And he needs to get over her. Ask him out.'

'He's a customer! I'm not going to ask him out.'

'Why not? It's not like you're a doctor. You're not breaking some Hippocratic oath. There is nothing that says you can't have a relationship with one of your customers.'

Emilia was suddenly reminded of her father and Sarah. So many questions had been whirling round in her head. How had their affair started? In the book shop? Sarah might tell her one day, she supposed.

In the meantime, she needed to get Bea off her back. Jackson wasn't an option. She could see it in his eyes.

'You've got glue in your hair,' she said, and walked away.

*

Dillon had been in to see Alice every day after work. He'd brought in her laptop and she was jubilant.

'Don't tell my mum,' she warned him. He didn't think it really mattered, her having access to her emails. She had nothing much else to do in the hospital.

'To be honest, it takes my mind off the pain,' she told him.

He was steaming ahead with *Riders*. He was actually starting to enjoy the story and wanted to know what happened next. It was like being in a little bubble, just him and Alice in her private room. The nurse brought them pinky-brown tea in green cups, and he brought in more chocolate.

'I'm going to get so fat,' complained Alice. 'I won't fit into my wedding dress.'

Good, thought Dillon. He wanted Alice to get better, but he'd been hoping and praying that the wedding would be postponed because of her injuries. She seemed determined though. Even though she was in terrible pain, she pushed herself to do her physio.

'I'm walking up that aisle without crutches if it kills me,' she told him.

It exhausted her, though she tried to pretend it didn't. She was lying with her eyes shut as he read. He wasn't sure if she was asleep but it didn't matter. He could always go back and read the chapter again.

He stopped.

She opened her eyes.

'Do you want me to carry on?'

'No.' She sat up. 'I want you to do something for me.'

'Anything, you know that.'

'I'm going to take off the bandage on my face and I want you to look at my scar and tell me how awful it is. I can't look at it myself. But I need to know if it's too bad to get married.'

'OK.'

She picked at the tape holding the gauze in place.

Dillon tried not to show his distress. 'Careful.'

Gently she pulled back the dressing. Underneath was a livid red gash, a v-shaped wound on her cheekbone.

'It should go down and the redness should go and it will fade a bit,' Alice was gabbling. 'But is it really horrific? Is it Frankenstein stuff? Do I look like Herman Munster? All I'm worried about at the moment is not looking awful at the wedding. If it's really bad I'll have to call it off. I want you to be really honest.'

Dillon looked long and hard at the wound. His mind was racing. If he told her it was terrible, then maybe, just maybe, she would postpone the wedding. And in the meantime, he would get a chance to bury Hugh, somehow. Get him to show his true colours so the wedding would be called off for ever and ever. Maybe he could get some coke off Pogo, then offer it to Hugh. Offer him a better deal. He wasn't sure he'd make a very convincing drug dealer, but he thought it would probably suit Hugh to have a supplier on the premises at Peasebrook . . .

No, thought Dillon. He wouldn't be able to pull it off. Hugh would be instantly suspicious.

He couldn't do it to her, though. To him, it wouldn't matter if her whole face were scarred: she was beautiful.

'It's just a bit red and swollen,' he told her.

'Really?' she said. 'I mean, I can have my hair over my face and I'll have a veil . . .'

'Honestly,' said Dillon. 'No one will notice it.'

She sighed. 'You're the only person I can trust to tell me the truth. Everyone else is just lying to make me feel better. And none of them wants the wedding to be cancelled. But I know it doesn't matter to you either way.'

That couldn't be further from the truth, thought Dillon. If anyone wants that wedding stopped, it's me.

'Hugh keeps telling me not to worry and I don't want to go on about it because it just make him feel more guilty about the accident.'

Dillon felt so angry he almost couldn't breathe. The bastard hadn't felt a moment's guilt.

'Are you OK?' asked Alice.

'Fine. It's just a bit stuffy in here.'

'I know. It's awful at night. I can hardly sleep. But I should be out of here soon.'

'That's good news.'

'I'll go mad if I have to stay in here much longer. I'd go mad if it wasn't for your visits. Mum nips in every day, but she and Dad are so busy with Peasebrook and Hugh's working like a lunatic so he can get time off for the wedding and the honeymoon—'

'Please,' he interrupted her. 'I don't want to hear any more about the wedding.'

Alice looked startled.

He reached over and touched her face gently.

'You're beautiful. You do know that?'

She was staring at him. Time stood still for a moment. He stroked her cheek with the back of his fingers.

'You poor little chick.'

He knew he was touching her for longer than was necessary. But she didn't seem to mind. She seemed frozen to the spot.

'Oh Dillon,' she said.

'What?'

Her face scrumpled with confusion. 'You make me feel funny. That's what.'

'Funny.' He smiled. 'I was trying to make you feel better.'

'You do! That's the point – you make me feel as if it doesn't matter how I look.'

'Well, of course it doesn't.'

She bit her lip. 'Thank you . . .'

She leaned forward. She smelt of antiseptic and baby powder and chocolate. Dillon's heart thumped. She was going to kiss him.

Then suddenly they heard Hugh's voice in the corridor, exchanging idle banter with the nurses. Alice pulled back sharply, and Dillon got to his feet, moving away from the bed. Dillon usually left at half six, because Hugh came in at seven and he wanted to be long gone. But today, because of the bandage and the conversation about the scar, he was running late.

The door opened and there was Hugh, in his City suit, his hair slicked back, self-important. He glared at Dillon.

'What the fuck are you doing here?'

'I've been visiting Alice.'

'He's been reading to me.'

'Isn't there gardening to be done?'

'Don't be so rude!' Alice was indignant.

Hugh turned to look at her.

'Jesus Christ,' he said, when he saw her scar.

'Shut up,' said Dillon under his breath.

Hugh looked appalled. 'Look, it's OK. We'll get the best people. There must be something we can do.'

He leaned forward to take a closer look.

Alice looked between Dillon and Hugh. 'Dillon said it wasn't too bad.'

'What is he – blind? He's just told you what he thinks you want to hear. We'll talk to the consultant. We've got time to sort it before the wedding.'

'I think what Alice needs is support,' said Dillon. 'Not a plastic surgeon.'

Hugh stared at him. His eyes were dead, thought Dillon.

'I better be going,' he said.

'You had.'

'You don't have to go,' said Alice. 'Just because Hugh's here.'

'My parking's running out any minute.' Dillon made his way to the door. Hugh followed him and opened it for him.

'I don't want to see you here again,' he said, sotto voce.

'Fine,' said Dillon, thinking *you won't see me, because I'll be gone before you get here.*

'I mean it,' said Hugh.

And it turned out he did, because when Dillon went to see Alice the next day, the nurse at the reception desk stopped him.

'I'm really sorry, it's close relatives only for Miss Basildon.'

'But she's expecting me.'

The nurse looked sympathetic.

'I can't let you through.'

Dillon went to push past her. 'Let's see what Miss Basildon says.'

The nurse put a hand on his arm. 'I'm sorry. If you go any further, I'll have to call security.'

Dillon stopped. He looked at her. 'It's that bastard, isn't it? He's told you not to let me in.'

'I have to obey the wishes of the family.'

'Not the patient?'

The nurse sighed and Dillon knew he couldn't push it.

'Could you tell her I came to see her? Dillon. Could you tell her Dillon came to see her?'

'Of course.'

He turned to leave, knowing full well the message wouldn't be passed on.

Seventeen

On the day of Mick Gillespie's book launch, Thomasina went to the cheesemonger to get some Irish cheese. She stood outside, looking in the window at the display, keeping half an eye on the queue inside until she could be sure that she would be served by Jem. It was the most calculating thing she had ever done.

'I want some Cashel Blue, for some baby tartlets,' she told him. 'And some Gubbeen, so I can make little cheesy choux puffs.'

'Sounds great.' Jem lifted a wheel of Cashel Blue out of the refrigerator and grabbed the end of the cheese wire. 'What else are you doing?'

'Potato cakes with smoked salmon. And Clonakilty Black-pudding with pan-fried apple on skewers. And miniature chocolate and Guinness cakes.'

'Wonderful.' Jem handed her the two cheeses, wrapped in wax paper with the shop's logo printed on it.

There was a silence.

'Twelve pounds seventy,' he said eventually.

She paid him quickly and scurried off. She'd wanted to ask him, because Emilia had given her two tickets. But she didn't have the courage. This was exactly why she didn't push herself forward when it came to men, she thought. She didn't have the guts.

She got back home and started to instruct Lauren on ho to prepare the canapés.

'I'm going to teach you how to make flaky pastry,' she told her. 'It's time-consuming, but it's worth it.'

The two of them spent the afternoon rubbing butter into flour, kneading the dough, rolling it out, cutting up cubes of butter, folding the dough and rolling it out again. The mixture was smooth and soothing beneath Thomasina's fingers and Lauren was a natural pastry maker and had an innate understanding of the process: her results were as neat and professional as Thomasina's. As she looked at the results of their afternoon's work, she felt hugely satisfied.

Thank God for cooking, she thought. Cooking never let her down.

'You look fantastic,' Jackson told Mia, and it was true. She did. She was only in jeans and a silk paisley top, but she looked much healthier than she did in all the fitness gear she wore these days, which just made her look like a shiny stick insect.

She'd been wary when Jackson had flourished the tickets. She had looked at him as if it was some sort of trap. He'd hoped she couldn't resist, especially as he had arranged for his mother to come and babysit for Finn. He was pretty sure that, except for her ridiculous training sessions, Mia hadn't been out for a long time.

'Are you guys going on a date?' asked Finn. He was in his pyjamas, all ready for Cilla to put him to bed.

Jackson didn't know what to reply. Mia put him straight.

'No. We just happen to be going to the same thing. So we're going together.'

'Cool.'

Outside, on the way to the book shop, Jackson turned to her. 'So this isn't a date then?'

Mia made a face. 'No. That would be weird.'

'Oh.' Jackson was a bit stung by her vehemence.

'We're going to a thing together,' Mia reiterated. 'But not *together* together.'

Funny, thought Jackson, I thought I'd bought tickets for something I thought you'd like and invited you out. It was typical of Mia to completely recalibrate the gesture and throw out the original intention. But then, that was partly what he loved about her. Her relentless goalpost moving.

'You'd be annoyed if I buggered off to the pub, though, wouldn't you?'

Mia sighed. 'Go if you want. When has what annoys me stopped you doing anything?'

'I don't want to go to the pub.'

'Then don't!' She looked exasperated.

Jackson kept quiet. They were going round in circles, like they always had done. It was how their relationship worked. They arrived at the book shop. Inside, it was heaving. There were silver moons hanging from the ceiling. And behind a table, a figure with white hair behind a stack of books.

'Mick Gillespie,' breathed Mia. 'Actual Mick Gillespie.'

'He's about ninety-seven!' Honestly, thought Jackson. There was no accounting for women, or pleasing them.

The window of Nightingale Books took June's breath away. She'd seen it in progress, but now it was all lit up from the inside it looked incredible. She pulled her coat around her, standing in the chill air. The window display was crammed with shots from his most famous films. Fifty years of Mick Gillespie playing heroes and villains and sex symbols and icons. He was an icon himself. And amidst them hung silver moons, the symbol from the film that had made his name. *The Silver Moon . . .*

It was almost a shrine.

There were thirty-seven of them in the window. She counted. Thirty-seven Mick Gillespies. And she shivered. He could still do that to her.

Just before she stepped over the threshold, she stood and measured how she felt. It still hurt, even now. That dull tug deep inside her, the one that never left. She imagined it, her feeling: a tangle of scar tissue that would never be allowed to heal.

She was here tonight as a guest, not a member of staff, because she still wasn't technically a member of staff – she just did what she could to help as and when she was needed. She refused to take payment, so Emilia had insisted tonight was for her enjoyment. Mel and Dave were holding the fort, and Thomasina and Lauren were passing round the food and drinks.

They'd sold seventy tickets – the shop wouldn't fit many more – and Mick was sitting behind a wide table, surrounded by copies of his book. Bea had made a veritable throne for him to sit on: a golden high-backed chair that was to be the shop's special signing chair for visiting authors. At the back of the shop, Marlowe was playing Irish tunes on his violin, adding to the atmosphere. It reminded June of the tiny pub in the village they'd filmed in where the locals had often taken over in the evening, entertaining them with their fiddles and whistles and drums.

June took a Silver Moon cocktail: she wasn't sure what was in it, but it tasted delicious and there was a glittery moon perched on the side of each glass. She needed a drink to take the edge off her jitters, although she wasn't quite sure how to identify what she was feeling, or even what she was expecting from the evening. Just to be breathing the same air as him felt momentous.

She picked up a copy of the autobiography and joined the queue for it to be signed. June never usually queued for anything... The shop was buzzing, and she felt pleased. Julius would be so proud of what Emilia had done. She'd rolled up her sleeves and got on with making the book shop work. She was there, behind the till, hands on, smiling and laughing with the customers he had built up over the years, but also the new ones who'd been drawn in by the lure of a legend. June hoped more than anything that things would fall into place and the shop would stay open.

It was her turn. Mick Gillespie looked up at her, his eyes as dazzling as they ever had been, his smile making you feel special... even though you weren't. June knew that well enough. And as she smiled back and handed him her book open at the flyleaf for him to sign, there was no recognition. Not a flicker that he had any memory of her.

'Who will I sign it to?' he asked.

'To June,' she said, waiting for a moment, but there was no reaction. He wrote her name and signed his with a flourish before handing it back to her with another smile. He was so practised. She managed a smile back, although inside she felt fury. How could she still be furious? It was a lifetime ago.

She joined the till to pay.

'Don't be daft,' said Emilia. 'There's no way I'm going to make you pay after everything you've done for me.'

At the back of the shop, Mick Gillespie turned to Marlowe with a glint in his eye.

'Do you know "Whiskey in the Jar"?'

'Of course.'

'Come on, then, boy. Let's show them how it's done.'

And he stood up and as Marlowe struck up the tune on his violin, Mick began to sing. And the delighted crowd gathered round and clapped their hands.

'As I was goin' over the far-famed Kerry mountains...'

June abruptly turned and left the shop. After all, she'd heard him sing that song herself, all those years ago in a tiny pub with a dirt floor and an equally appreciative audience.

June walked the short distance to her cottage. There, in the sky above, was a full moon, as if it had known about the evening and made a special appearance. She got home, slipped off her high-heeled boots and put on the slouchy cashmere bedsocks she used for padding over the flagstones. She threw some logs on the wood-burner, poured a glass of wine and sat with her legs curled up on the sofa in her living room.

She leafed through his book until she reached the section about *The Silver Moon*. It had been his turning point, and was an historic film, so there was a hefty chapter.

There was no mention of her. Not a word about the blonde-haired extra who'd played the barmaid and his affair with her. Not a hint of the passion he had professed to feel at the time. She was insignificant. The scenery was discussed at length, the genius writer, the visionary director – even Mrs Malone, the landlady of the cottage they'd stayed in during the shoot was given a namecheck. But as far as the rest of the world was concerned, she didn't exist and had made no contribution.

She went upstairs. In her sparest spare bedroom she had stored a box in the wardrobe.

She pulled it out. Inside was his Aran sweater and the script from *The Silver Moon*. Beer mats from the pub they drank in. Shells and pressed flowers. She could smell the air if she breathed in deeply enough. She was there, in the drizzle, the scent of damp wool, the taste of his mouth, tinged with whiskey...

And the photographs. Faded and curling now, but here was her evidence. Irrefutable evidence. The two of them, arms around each other, laughing into the camera. You could see the chemistry between them, crackling and fizzing, evident even in yellowing black and white. She remembered the little old man with the donkey and cart looking at the camera in consternation but taking the pictures nonetheless. Not exactly David Bailey, but it had been a memory not a work of art.

And she remembered holding the camera at arm's length, back to front, and the pair of them lying on their backs, smiling, as she took what would now be called a 'selfie', his dark hair tangled up in her platinum blonde.

They had been so beautiful, she thought. There was a purity to the photographs that you never got today. It was the real them, no filter, no fiddling and she'd worn no make-up, yet their beauty shone through nevertheless.

She laid everything out on the bed. It was all there, their story, in the few artefacts. All the proof she needed.

That had been another her. She'd stopped bleaching her hair, going back to her natural brown, and had put on some weight. No one would ever have known she was Juno.

She suddenly felt angry. He had ruined her for anyone else. She had loved her two husbands in a low-key way, and the divorces had been amicable rather than acrimonious. But she'd never felt the same way about anyone as she had Mick Gillespie.

There was a large brown envelope too, that she hadn't opened yet. She lifted it: it was heavy with paper. She opened the flap and pulled out a manuscript: pages and pages typed onto cheap flimsy paper.

In 1967, Michael Gillespie ripped out my heart and dashed it onto the rocks at Coumeenoole Beach. To my amazement, I managed to live without it. And I'm here, living, breathing, and able to tell you the story of what happened when an innocent young girl fell in love with the world's greatest star. It's a fable, really. A warning.

It was her story, of what had happened to her. She remembered writing it, two years after she had come back from Ireland.

She'd sat at her typewriter and written, long into the night, the words tumbling out at a breakneck pace, so fast she couldn't keep up with them.

June smiled as she remembered the sound of a real typewriter. Somehow the gentle tip tap of the computer keyboard didn't have the same satisfaction. She began to read the words, the words of a wounded young girl.

Halfway through, she stopped reading. She found it too sad, the memories. She wasn't that girl any more. She was a part of who she had become, but she didn't need to go back and revisit the pain. She knew now that everyone had heartbreak in their life at some point. What had happened didn't make her special or unusual. It was part of being human. A broken heart was, after all, the source material of a myriad books. Some of those books had become her comfort, and had made her realise she was not alone.

She slid the papers back into the envelope and sealed it back up again.

Mick and Marlowe were in full swing. Mick had produced a bottle of Paddy whiskey and was topping up the audience's cocktail glasses in an expansive 'one for you one for me' gesture, then calling up ballads for Marlowe to play: 'The Irish Rover', 'Molly Malone', 'The Rising of the Moon'... The atmosphere was bordering on riotous.

Eventually Emilia had to call a halt to the proceedings. She could sense Mick getting slightly out of hand, and she wasn't sure about the legality of getting all her customers insensible at this hour of the day. So she gestured discreetly to Marlowe to wind things up, and despite Mick's protests – he would have gone on all night given the chance – the shop gradually emptied, and after much effusive hugging and kissing, Mick headed off to the Peasebrook Arms. Emilia had no doubt he would waste no time making friends in the bar, but she was too exhausted to accompany him herself.

She was cross when Marlowe refused to let her pay him for playing.

'It's the best fun I've had for weeks. Playing the fiddle for Mick Gillespie? I'd have given my right arm for that. I don't want payment.'

'But I wouldn't have asked you if I thought you wouldn't let me pay.' Emilia hated the thought of exploiting anyone's better nature.

'I know. Which is why it's OK.'

'But I won't ask you again.'

'You can pay me next time. But this time: gratis. It was a pleasure. And I did it for your dad.' Marlowe smiled kindly. 'You have his magic, you know. People want to do things for you, like they did him. You're going to be all right.'

'Well, thank you.' Emilia was very grateful. Marlowe had certainly helped make the evening a memorable one. 'People are going to be talking about it for weeks.' She laughed. 'I thought things were going to get out of hand. He's a handful even at his age.'

'He's a legend all right,' said Marlowe in a mock-Kerry accent, buttoning up his coat.

Bea went home after the event feeling slightly high on the buzz. Everyone had raved about her windows; she'd had her photo taken in front of them with her arm linked in Mick Gillespie's, and she felt like her old self. She hadn't felt like Bea since the day she'd left *Hearth*. Mummy Bea was a slightly alien creature she still didn't feel comfortable with.

So she was full of it when she got back home, babbling on to Bill who had got home from work early for once in order to babysit. But he just seemed grumpy and disinterested.

'For heaven's sake,' said Bill. 'Stop wittering on about that bloody shop, will you?'

Bea's mouth dropped open.

'Wittering?' she said. 'I try very hard not to witter, thank you very much.'

'I'm sorry. But it's not as if you're even being paid. And I don't think I can listen to another word.'

'Well, in that case, you can listen to me witter about what Maud ate for lunch. And what shape or consistency her poo is. Because that's what most new mothers talk about. I'm not as lucky as you. I don't have reams of people to talk to about interesting things. So I'm sorry if I seem a bit obsessed, but Nightingale Books is the most exciting thing in my life right now—'

She hadn't realised her voice was getting higher and higher with indignation. Bill put up a hand to stop the flow.

'I'm off to bed. It's nearly midnight. And I have to be up at six. Sorry.'

And he walked out of the room.

Bea was astonished. She crossed her arms. She wasn't going to let Bill get away with this behaviour. She wouldn't tackle him now, but she was going to call Thomasina in the morning. Book them dinner at A Deux, and have it out once and for all, on neutral territory, in private. She was not going to stand here and watch her marriage go down the pan.

Mia and Jackson walked back from Nightingale Books in the lamplight.

Mia had drunk two cocktails and was quite garrulous. Jackson supposed that as she barely ate anything these days they must have gone straight to her head. She was a little unsteady on her feet, and as they reached the edge of the town he took her arm. She didn't seem to mind. She leant on him as they walked up to the house. He thought it felt a bit like the old days, when they'd first got together and had gone out on the town with their mates.

But the minute they got inside the door of the house, Mia went quiet and cold.

'Thanks for a lovely evening,' she said, but it sounded automatic rather than genuine. 'I'm off to bed. Thank you for sitting, Cilla.'

And she was gone.

Jackson was flummoxed. He looked to his mother for an explanation.

'Ten minutes ago she was babbling about what an amazing evening she'd had. Suddenly she's like an ice queen.'

Cilla looked knowing.

'She's scared.'

'Of what? Not me, surely.'

'She feels a fool,' said Cilla. 'She knows she was wrong to kick you out, but she doesn't know what to do about it.'

'Why can't she just say she was wrong?' Jackson was puzzled.

Cilla sighed. 'You don't understand women, do you?'

'No,' said Jackson. 'But if that's what she feels, what am I supposed to do?'

'Woo her back.'

'That's what I thought I was doing.' He shook his head. 'Sometimes I think I didn't get the instruction manual.'

'You'll be all right.'

'How do you know?'

'I just do.'

Jackson hugged his mum. 'Come on,' he said. 'I'll just go up and give Finn a goodnight kiss, then let's get home.'

Ten minutes later he bundled his mum into his jeep, popped Wolfie in the boot and walked round to the driver's door. At the last moment, he looked out and saw Mia peering out of her bedroom window. As soon as she saw him looking, she dropped the curtain and was gone.

In the quiet of the empty shop, Emilia gathered up the last of the cocktail glasses that were scattered around and took them upstairs to wash them and put them back in the box to be taken to the wine merchant.

It had been a wonderful evening. It had lifted her heart. So many people had turned up to see Mick Gillespie, old customers and new. There had been a real buzz in the air.

Of course, Emilia knew that she wouldn't get a star like him to come along to the shop every week. And the novelty would probably wear off. But it had given her a glimpse of what could be done and they had rung more through the till that evening than they did in a week because people had bought other books as well as Mick's. Dave and Mel had worked hard to make the display tables as enticing as possible so people would make impulse purchases, and they had.

Of course, there had been one thing missing. Her father would have loved it. But she was determined not to think like that any more. Julius was gone, and she was clomping about in his shoes, trying them on for size. Sometimes they felt either too small or too big as she stumbled around.

Nights like this, though, made her feel as if his shoes fitted perfectly.

Just before midnight, June heard the wind get up and the rain begin. It was wild; she shut the curtains tight, grateful that she'd had her little cottage double-glazed when she moved in full-time. She went into the kitchen to make a cup of camomile tea, then heard a mighty rapping on the stable door. She froze, wondering who on earth it was at this time. It wasn't as if she was on the way to anywhere. She decided she would ignore it.

Then she heard shouting. An indignant roar that carried through the gale. A roar she would have recognised anywhere.

'For the love of God, would you open the door?'

She marched across, slid back the bolts and turned the lock. She just opened the top half, in case. And there, framed in the doorway, was Mick Gillespie, soaked to the skin.

'Thank Christ for that. Will you let me in?'

'Give me one good reason why I should?' She put her hands on her hips.

'Because it's pissing with rain and I'm soaked through and I'll get pneumonia. I'm an old man.'

She couldn't help smiling. What a bloody fuss. She stood back and he bowled in through the door. She smelled wet wool and him. She took his coat – cashmere and no protection from the rain – and hung it on the Aga.

'They told me at the hotel it was only ten minutes' walk,' he grumbled.

'How did you find me?'

'You don't need to be Sherlock Holmes. And the people in this town aren't very discreet, you know.'

'You recognised me, then?'

'Of course I did,' he said. 'But I didn't know what to say. You didn't say anything so I thought it was best left, maybe. But then I thought: you wouldn't have been there if you hadn't wanted to see me.'

'You're a better actor than I thought. I didn't think you had a clue.'

'I'm trained, remember.' His smile was teasing. Those bloody crinkly eyes . . .

June smiled and handed him a towel to dry his hair, then poured two glasses of red wine. They sat down at the kitchen table, looking at each other.

He looked around in approval. June knew the cottage looked

good. She'd spent a lot of money making it comfortable and stylish, and she had a great eye for art and antiques. She'd perfected the designer farmhouse look: the gleaming pink Aga, the flagstones warmed by underfloor heating, the French kitchen table, the chunky wine glasses stamped with a bee.

'You've done well,' he said.

'I have,' she said, not ashamed to be proud of her achievements.

'I was a shite,' he told her. 'But it was the best thing for you. I'd have led you merry hell and you'd have ended up hating me. Or killing me. I really wasn't a very nice person in those days.'

'And are you now?'

He tipped his head to one side to consider her question.

'I don't think I'm all bad.'

'That's good to hear.'

'You're a nice person, that's for sure. You always were. People like you don't change. Unless they get damaged by people like me. I hope you weren't.'

'Nobody as awful as you, no.'

They grinned at each other.

Mick raised his glass.

'Well, here's to old times' sake. It's very nice to see you.'

'I suppose you were just bored in your hotel room?'

He looked a bit taken aback.

'No. I wanted to see you. I've very fond memories of our time.'

'I wrote a searing exposé,' June told him. 'About how cruelly you treated me.'

'Really?' He made a face. 'It would be the perfect time to publish it. Everyone seems to be obsessed with my past at the moment.'

'Ah, no – it's staying firmly locked away. It was just a therapeutic exercise.'

'Writing's therapy, for sure. I was amazed what I dredged up when I did the book.'

'So you're trying to right wrongs now?'

'Jesus, I haven't enough time left on this earth to do that.'

He roared with laughter. Then stopped and looked at her.

'Just one wrong will do me for now.'

She held his gaze. She wanted to laugh. He was incorrigible, even at this age. He couldn't help himself. She realised that the spell she had been under for so many years was broken. He no longer had a hold over her. How many times had she dreamt of this moment over the years? She couldn't begin to count.

Yet to turn him away would be boring. She couldn't remember the last time she'd been propositioned. She deserved some fun as much as the next person. And he hadn't been a selfish bugger in the bedroom, that much she could remember. She felt her cheeks pinken slightly at the memory as she picked up her glass. She was going to make him work for it.

'What are you suggesting, Mr Gillespie?'

Eighteen

Two weeks later, Thomasina and Lauren were tucked away in the kitchen at A Deux. Lauren was putting the finishing touches to a chicken and pear tagine, chopping almonds and coriander to scatter on the couscous.

'You mark my words – this is a crisis dinner,' Lauren whispered. 'This is the last resort. It's written all over them.'

Thomasina, who was cutting out lavender biscuits to go with the panna cotta, nudged her to be quiet. Discretion was the watchword at A Deux – it was the whole point.

A Deux was booked several nights a week now, and Thomasina had grown in confidence. She and Lauren had become quite a team, catering outside events. She'd had masses of enquiries since doing the canapés at Nightingale Books and it was almost getting to the point when she might have to give up the day job, though she probably never would.

Seeing Lauren blossom and flourish under her tuition had been incredibly rewarding too. That was the joy of teaching: capturing someone, inspiring them, giving them a purpose. Lauren was a different girl. She was focused, conscientious, full of initiative. If Thomasina hadn't seen her potential and tapped into it, she would be excluded from school by now, on a one-way ticket to nowhere.

*

In the dining room, clusters of candles gave a rosy glow to the two guests at the table. Thomasina's cottage was small – just one main room, which you walked straight into from the front door, and where the table was laid. She had bought the best cutlery and china she could afford: knives and forks with mother-of-pearl handles, and pale cream china with an ornate French pattern. The snowy white linen tablecloth and napkins gave an air of formality, but other than that the room had a warmth that wrapped you up, with its dark red walls and the rich Egyptian-style carpet.

Bill sighed, and looked down into his Jerusalem artichoke soup, as if the answer might lie in the swirl of cream on the top.

'I'm sorry. I'm sorry. It's just . . .'

'It's just what?'

'I think I'm going mad.'

He looked up, and Bea saw a bleakness in his eyes that scared her.

'What do you mean?' Bea crumbled up some of Thomasina's walnut bread in her fingers.

'I understand it's been hard for you. Giving up your old life and starting anew. But I'd give anything to be in your position.'

'Oh.'

'I don't think I can carry on.'

'What do you mean?' Bea panicked. 'With what? Do you mean us?'

Oh God. He was asking for a divorce. She'd bored him into wanting a divorce, with her 'wittering'.

'No! Of course not. I mean this way of life.'

Bea took a gulp of wine. Then another. They were walking, so they didn't need to have the driving conversation.

'I hate it. I hate leaving you and Maud. It's bloody exhausting, getting up at stupid o'clock and going to catch the train. By the time I'm back home, I'm too knackered to have a conversation or enjoy my food and the weekends go in a flash. By the time I've had a lie-in to get over the fact I've had hardly any sleep, it's Sunday. And from midday on Sunday my stomach is in a knot, dreading Monday morning.'

'I had no idea you felt like this.'

'I thought it was going to get easier. But I just want a normal life, Bea. I love it here in Peasebrook. I want to be a normal bloke. Join the darts team in the pub. Muck about in the garden. Enjoy my family. Maud looks at me sometimes as if she's someone she thinks she should recognise but isn't quite sure . . .'

He rubbed his face and Bea suddenly saw how terrible he looked. Haggard and red-eyed. She'd put it down to too much red wine.

He looked over at her.

'I don't want to be a high-flyer any more. I don't want to be part of the commuter club, an absentee husband and father.'

Bea fiddled with the knife and fork on either side of her bowl. She had lost her appetite all of a sudden and couldn't finish her soup.

'What do we do about it?' she asked, her voice very small. 'I'm so sorry, I had no idea . . .'

'I don't know, Bea. But I can't carry on. If I'm not careful, I'm going to get sacked. I'm tired and I'm stressed and I'm resentful and I'm making mistakes and being a pain in the arse to work with.'

Bea reached out a hand and put it on top of Bill's.

'I'm sorry,' she said. 'I've been stuck in my own little world, trying to play the perfect wife and mother. And to be honest, I haven't been that happy either. It's as if we've both been forced into a way of life we don't want, in order to sustain this fantasy lifestyle.'

'Exactly,' said Bill. 'I know you're bored. I know you adore

Maud, but I can see you trying to find ways to get through the day.'

'Handwashing cashmere cardigans just isn't doing it for me.' Bea managed a laugh. 'Not even when I get to hang them on the line with fancy artisanal wooden clothes pegs.'

She had a mental image of herself, a veritable layout from *Hearth* magazine. But she wasn't going to be defeated by this. Bea was a strategist. She always had a plan.

'What about if we do a swap?' she said.

Bill raised his eyebrows.

'Swap?'

'I could go back to work. I get people calling me all the time offering me jobs I really, really don't want to turn down. I would love to go back and be a proper grown-up in London. And you could hang out here with Maud.'

'Be a house husband?' Bill frowned. 'I'm not sure about that.'

Bea wrinkled her nose. 'No! You can do some freelance work from home while Maud's at nursery. Though you would have to do a *bit* of house stuff – get food in, bung the washing on every now and again. But it's not hard, Bill. Why do you think I'm so bored? I think you're way better suited to this country life than me. I just don't see myself as a jam-making, WI sort of person. But I think you'd really like the gardening and the log-cutting and the endless trips to the pub.'

'Do you really think it could work?' asked Bill. 'I've got loads of people who want me to do consultancy for them.'

'Yes!'

'You'd have to be the breadwinner. You won't mind the commute?'

'No! I am soooo jealous whenever you head off for that train.'

'Really? You're welcome to it.'

'It will take a bit of time for me to find the right job. But I think it's a great solution. Don't get me wrong. I don't want to move back to London. I think here is perfect, and right for Maud.'

Bill looked as if the weight of the world had been taken off his shoulders.

'I'd love that, Bea. I feel as if life's whizzing past, and I don't have time to enjoy the things I want to enjoy, and any minute now Maud will be sixteen. I want to slow down. I know I'm only just forty, but I don't want to spend the next ten years slogging my guts out. And if it means cutting back on crap that doesn't matter—'

'Like hundred quid candles?'

He caught it. 'Yes!'

'You've got yourself a deal, mister.'

Bea shook hands with her husband over the table.

As Lauren brought out the tagine, Bea sat back in her chair with a sigh of relief. She had been terrified Bill was going to give her some ultimatum. Or tell her he'd found someone else. The thing was, Bea quite liked playing at country mouse but really, she was a town mouse through and through. It would all be here at the weekends, the trugs and the Peter Rabbit carrots and the eggs still covered in chicken shit.

And this time, when they got back home, after the two bottles of ruinously expensive wine they'd drunk to celebrate their decision, Bill was still awake when she came out of the bathroom in her Coco de Mer. Wide awake.

Nineteen

The following Sunday, Emilia gave herself the day off. She had worked flat out for weeks, and Dave was happy to run the shop for the day.

Marlowe had offered to give her a cello lesson, to get her up to speed on the pieces she was unfamiliar with and to practise the Handel. Of all the pieces she had to get that right, as it heralded Alice's entrance.

'It's renowned for being a bitch of a piece for the cello,' he told her, 'but we'll nail it, don't worry.'

It was one of those autumn days that take you by surprise. Although there was a sharpness in the air on waking, warm sunshine and a cloudless sky belied the season. Emilia put on a yellow dress and a pale green cardigan and drove to Marlowe's house, a tiny Victorian lodge on the outskirts of Peasebrook. It was like a cottage out of a fairy tale, all pointy windows with a gabled roof and an arched front door.

Inside, it was chaos. Books and sheet music and empty wine glasses and two smoky grey cats stepping amongst it all. John Coltrane was playing and she could smell fresh coffee. With a pang, she realised it reminded her a little bit of the flat when her father was alive: he was always in the middle of twelve things at once; there was always music; something cooking.

'God, I'm sorry. I meant to tidy up.' Marlowe kissed her. 'Meet Crotchet and Quaver.'

He scooped one of the cats off a chair and patted the seat. 'You sit here. I'll get you a coffee while you set yourself up.'

Emilia got out her cello, and as she looked around the room she spotted evidence of Delphine. A silk Hermès scarf on the sofa; lipstick on a glass; a pair of Chanel ballet flats.

'Delph's in Paris for the weekend – some family knees-up. So we've got all day if you need it.'

OK, thought Emilia. I've got the message. 'Delph'. That was fond familiarity if ever she'd heard it.

After two hours, she was exhausted. Marlowe was a brilliant and patient teacher, and not once did he make her feel inferior. He helped her with her posture and her bow hold. At one point he put his hand on her shoulder. His fingers dug in until he found a muscle.

'You need to relax that muscle. Drop your shoulder.'

Emilia tried desperately to relax, but she found it difficult. The feeling of his hand on her was making her think about things she probably shouldn't. Eventually she managed to untense.

'That's it!' Marlowe was triumphant. 'If you relax that, you'll be able to play for longer, and much better.'

By half twelve, she was exhausted.

'Come on,' said Marlowe. 'Let's walk to the pub and get some lunch.'

They walked to the White Horse and bought hot pork ciabatta rolls with apple sauce and bits of salty crackling, sitting at a table outside next to a patio heater. Emilia didn't want to leave the sunshine, the easy company, the half of cider that was making her sleepy and made her want to slide into bed . . .

'Let's go back through the woods,' suggested Marlowe. 'It's a bit further than the road but we can walk our lunch off.'

The walk through the wood meandered alongside the river. Sunshine and birdsong lifted Emilia's heart: she'd spent far too much time inside recently. She must make the effort to get out and enjoy the countryside around Peasebrook. It was truly glorious, with the trees ablaze with crimson and coral and ochre and the rich smell of dead leaves underfoot.

Eventually they came to a section of the river that was deeper than the rest, the banks widening to form a bowl-shaped pool. The water was crystal clear: Emilia could see the smooth stones at the bottom, covered in moss and there was a willow on the far bank, trailing its branches in the water.

'Fancy a swim, then?' asked Marlowe. 'Doesn't get wilder than this.'

'You have to be joking. Surely it's too cold?'

'Nah. I swim here all the time, even on Christmas Day. It's invigorating.'

'Invigorating?'

Emilia looked doubtful. Yet part of her couldn't resist the challenge.

'Does Delphine swim in this?' She couldn't imagine she did.

'God, no. She's a total chicken.'

That was all the encouragement Emilia needed. She was going to prove to Marlowe she was no wuss. There was only one thing stopping her.

'I haven't got any bathing things,' she said, but she had a feeling that wasn't going to inhibit Marlowe.

'We can go in our underwear,' he said. 'No different to swimming trunks or a bikini.'

Emilia laughed.

'You're on,' she said, and kicked off her shoes and began to unbutton her dress.

Marlowe needed no encouragement. He ripped off his shirt,